THE ADVISORY TEAM

THE ADVISORY TEAM

Colonel Thomas R. Glodek, USA, Ret.

VANTAGE PRESS
New York

This is a work of fiction. However, due to the historical nature of this work, where appropriate, the author endeavors to use the names of actual historical characters in the context of the subject matter.

FIRST EDITION

All rights reserved, including the right of
reproduction in whole or in part in any form.

Copyright © 2007 by Colonel Thomas R. Glodek, USA, Ret.

Published by Vantage Press, Inc.
419 Park Ave. South, New York, NY 10016

Manufactured in the United States of America
ISBN: 978-0-533-15354-1

Library of Congress Catalog Card No.: 2005908509

0 9 8 7 6 5 4 3 2 1

Acknowledgments

I want to recognize several people for their support during the writing of *The Advisory Team*.

Cheryl-Ann Houck for editing, word processing, and encouragement to complete the novel.

Jennifer Houck for creative graphic design.

Lt. Col. Richard F. Pendleton, USA Ret. for support, encouragement and his insights on The Vietnam War after serving two tours in Vietnam and providing very useful maps of Vietnam as reference material.

Margie Schacht, for research on the Internet to obtain data for the novel.

Victor West, Pacific Literary Services, for invaluable manuscript critiques to improve its quality, and editing of the work.

Brigadier General Keith H. Kerr, CSMR, Ret.

THE ADVISORY TEAM

Prologue

Major American wars are remembered by a few respectful words; these are:

The Revolutionary War, "the war for America's independence."

The Civil War, "the war to preserve the Union."

World War I, "the war to end all wars."

World War II, "a great American victory."

The Korean War, "ended in a stalemate."

The Vietnam War, "it is the first war that America lost."

The Vietnam War lasted from 1964 to 1975. It is *the* defining war in American history, not because America won, but because America lost in which 58,214 soldiers were killed. All future wars will be judged by the Vietnam War so there is never another Vietnam—The Vietnam Syndrome.

The primary lesson learned from Vietnam is that no war can be prosecuted successfully without the total support of the American people. A pundit after assessing Vietnam declared there is a new war-fighting strategy for politicians in Washington that sets a higher priority on their own political concerns than providing the necessary military force and resources needed to win a war. In the Vietnam War President Johnson refused to mobilize the military reserves to provide more manpower fearing calling up the reserves would alienate middle America. A larger military force results in more casualities which may then alienate voters back home. Therefore, the use of overwhelming military force is not used so as not to offend voters in the next election.

Second, Vietnam is America's Achilles' heel. America's enemies have learned America is vulnerable to a sustained and protracted war (beyond a guerilla war) or insurgency leading to American casualties until some Americans get fed up and demand an end to the war. It appears that now the generals have to plan for a "quick and clean victory," or a "no win" outcome in future wars fought against radical ideologies who will accept horrendous casualties to achieve a military victory. On December 7, 1941, the Japanese surprise attack on Pearl Harbor galvanized the American public with a common cause to defeat Germany, Italy and Japan in World War II.

In 1959, fifteen U.S. Air Force Advisors were sent to South Vietnam by the Eisenhower administration to train South Vietnam's Air Force how to do maintenance on U.S. World War II aircraft given to South Vietnam. This was the beginning of the U.S. involvement in South Vietnam. By 1962, there were 3,000 U.S. Advisors in the country. In March 1965, the first U.S. combat troops arrived in South Vietnam when U.S. Marines waded ashore south of DaNang. The U.S. government's policy for the American buildup of U.S. forces in South Vietnam was called a graduated response in military strength and bombing North Vietnam. By 1967, U.S. combat forces were stretched to the limit by a defensive posture attempting to contain the infiltration of North Vietnam's troops into South Vietnam, and also defending U.S. military base camps and installations in the country. The American public began to perceive the war as a quagmire. The Johnson administration continued to assert that there was a "light at the end of the tunnel" toward peace in Vietnam. On January 31, 1968, the communists made a surprise attack by 84,000 soldiers in their Tet Offensive with communist soldiers entering the grounds at the U.S. Embassy in Saigon. This attack soon convinced a skeptical American public that information about progress in Vietnam by the Johnson administration was a lie. In 1968, Americans turned against the war, which began five years of protests against Vietnam. On March 29, 1973, under the Nixon administrative policy of Vietnamization, the last U.S. troops left South Vietnam. On April 30, 1975, as communist soldiers riding in Soviet T-60 tanks and trucks entered Saigon and immediately demanded an unconditional surrender by the government of South Vietnam, the surrender ended the long war.

In the years following the end of the war, books were written on Vietnam recounting the experiences of U.S. soldiers who had served in Vietnam. Some books presented an analysis of the war, the prosecution of the war, and how political decisions affected the U.S. military fighting the war. Many of these books pointed out policy problems in the Johnson administration to include the decisions made by Secretary of Defense McNamara with the graduated response prosecuting the war, the draft, whether or not to call up military reserves, and the performance problems by the Army of South Vietnam.

As the late President John F. Kennedy once said, "Success has a thousand fathers but failure is an orphan." The Johnson administration blamed the U.S. military for losing the war. The U.S. military, not to be a scapegoat, blamed the Johnson administration in return for political meddling in Vietnam and not allowing the U.S. military to do its job.

General Tommy Franks, in *American Soldier,* page 441, states; "My concern was prompted in part by America's recent war fighting history. During the Vietnam War, Defense Secretary Robert McNamara and his Whiz Kids had repeatedly picked individual bombing targets and approved battalion-size maneuvers."

On August 5, 2005, there was an article in the *Army Times* entitled "Westmoreland remembered for his role in Vietnam War." In 1976, General Westmoreland wrote a book, *A Soldier Reports,* in which he stated, "America could have won the war in Vietnam if only Johnson and other politicians had gotten out of the way and let the military do its job. He insisted the army of South Vietnam was to blame for defeat."

The *Army Times* article continued stating, "but many disagreed including former Gen. Bruce Palmer, Jr., who had been Westmoreland's deputy and later served as Army Vice-Chief of Staff, called Westmoreland's strategy "the first clear failure in American military history."

General Westmoreland frequently denied that the strategy in Vietnam was an attrition strategy. In *American Soldier,* General Tommy Franks, Commander in Chief, United States Central Command, said, "Vietnam was an attrition strategy." Most military who served in combat in Vietnam, including the author, participated in the search and destroy operations and a body count of dead enemy soldiers which was reported to higher headquarters. The body count of dead enemy soldiers total ended up in Washington, D.C., to measure the success of the war.

Dr. Henry Kissinger, former Secretary of State in the Nixon Administration, said "the Communists could have sustained even higher casualties without affecting their ability to wage war."

Therefore, the proper place to begin the examination of why America lost in Vietnam is to examine the strategies of military attrition and guerilla warfare.

The strategies of military attrition against the enemy, or annihilation resistance (guerilla warfare), were used by the Union, and Confederate armies in the Civil War. The annihilation resistance strategy, or guerilla warfare did not begin during the Vietnam War by North Vietnam against U.S. forces. The strategy of military attrition used by the Union Army in the Civil War led to the Confederate strategy to hold out long enough, particularly during the Wilderness Campaign of 1864, to inflict sufficient punishment which would make the Union Army ineffective, and politically defeat President Lincoln's re-election in November 1864.

James M. McPherson discussed military attrition and annihilation resistance in the book, *The Civil War,* "War and Politics" on page 350.

"Grant and Sherman intended by a series of flanking movements to threaten Confederate communications and force the southern Commanders Lee and Johnson into open-field combat, where superior Union numbers and firepower could be used to greatest advantage. The southern strategy, by contrast, was to block the Union's flanking movements and force northern armies instead to assault defenses entrenched on high grounds or behind rivers, where fortifications and natural obstacles would more than neutralize superior numbers.

"In part, the South's smaller population and resources dictated this strategy, but it resulted also from the contrasting war aims of the two sides. To win the war, Union armies had to conquer and occupy Southern territory, overwhelm or break up Confederate armies, destroy the economic and political infrastructure that supported the war effort, and suppress the

Southern will to resist. But in order to 'win' on their terms, the Confederates, like Americans in the Revolution or North Vietnam in the 1960s, needed only to hold out long enough and inflict sufficient punishment on the enemy to force him to give up his effort to annihilate resistance. This was a strategy of political and psychological attrition—of wearing down the other side's will to continue fighting." In the Vietnam War, protracted guerilla warfare prevailed against misdirected political meddling by the Johnson Administration in U.S. military operations which combined with a flawed military attrition strategy to create an American debacle in Vietnam.

The following were anti-Vietnam War slogans chanted at protests during the Vietnam War.

"Hey, hey, LBJ . . . how many babies did you kill today?"

"Hell, no, we won't go" was an anti-draft Vietnam War Slogan.

"Go to Canada, not Vietnam" was a draft avoidance slogan.

"Make love, not war" was a slogan chanted by "Hippie" war protesters.

"I'm going to Heaven, I served in Hell in Vietnam" appeared on an anti-war protester's sign.

If the War Goes On

"If the war goes on and the children die of hunger and the old men cry for the young that are no more and the women learn how to dance without a partner, who will keep the score?"

"If the war goes on, will we close the doors to heaven?"
      Written by Father John Bell,
      a minister of the Church of Scotland.

September 8, 2006
Collierville, Tennessee

—Colonel Thomas R. Glodek

The map below shows the Ho Chi Minh Trail and communist infiltration routes from North Vietnam into South Vietnam.

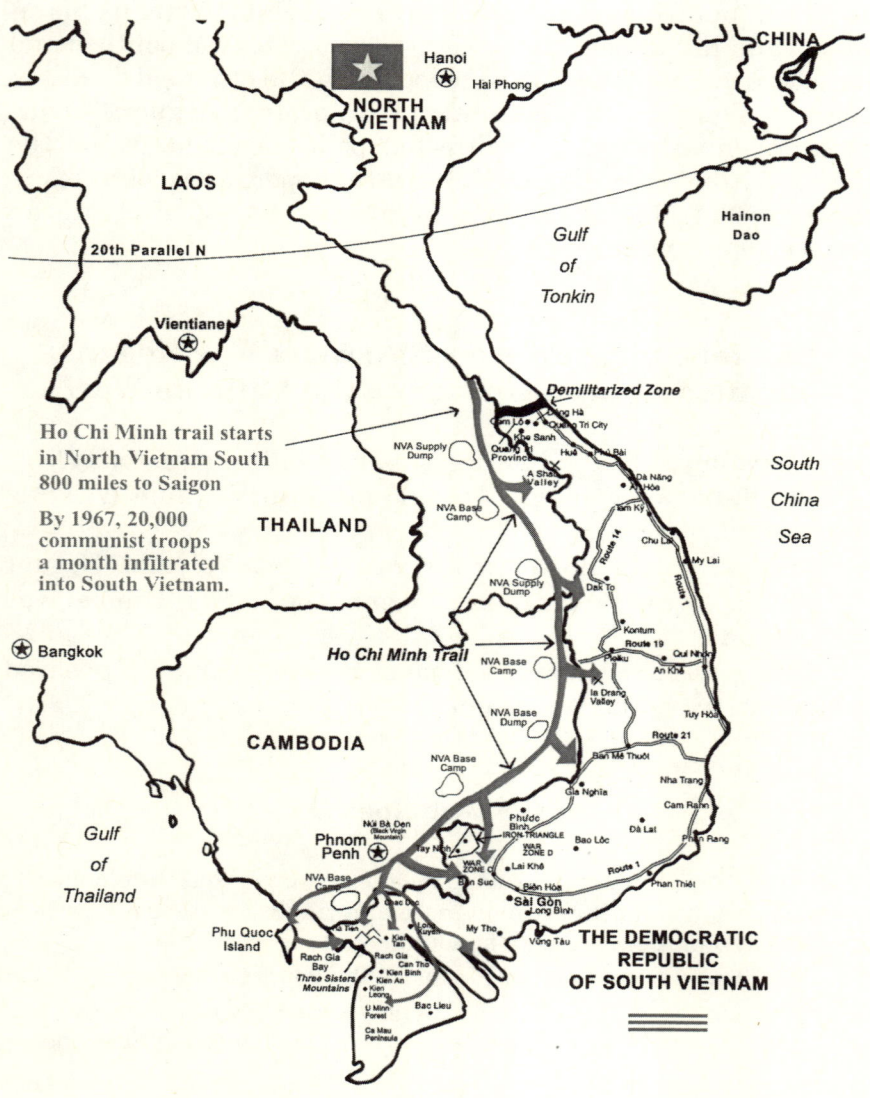

A Tribute to Fallen Friends

The author knew the following men killed in the Vietnam War and one who later succumbed to his injuries from the war:

Lt. Col. Scott F. Sturgis, Infantry, USA Ret.

    Lt. Col. Sturgis and the author were classmates in the Class of 1963 at Gettysburg College. The author was given an eyewitness account of an armor explosion, which Captain Sturgis and the eyewitness, Captain William Blair, now Lt. Col. USA (Ret.) were operating with the 25th Infantry Division in War Zone C inside the Ho Bo Woods and sixty miles northwest of Saigon. Captain Blair and Captain Sturgis were riding in armored personnel carriers in column (APC) when Captain Blair saw a tremendous explosion on the trail ahead of his APC. The APC in which Captain Sturgis was riding had apparently struck a fifty-pound command-detonated land mine, causing the APC to "fly" fifty feet in the air and land on its side. The APC was badly damaged, and Captain Blair didn't think anyone inside the APC was still alive. However, Captain Sturgis was alive, and Captain Blair called in a Huey Medevac helicopter. As they were removing Captain Sturgis from the APC, Lt. Col. Blair said Captain Sturgis looked at him and said, "I guess this is the day I die."
    Captain Sturgis had serious head and internal bodily injuries and was medically evacuated to a nearby field hospital, saving his life. Captain Sturgis went through extensive physical therapy, returned to duty, and completed twenty years of U.S. Army service and he retired in 1983. He wrote an article for the Gettysburg College Alumni magazine, *The Gettysburgian,* explaining his injuries in Vietnam and that he was now disabled;

he encouraged his classmates, "Never give up in life." Lt. Col. Sturgis later succumbed to his injuries from Vietnam.

Captain Joseph Murphy, U.S. Marine Corps.

Captain Murphy and the author were classmates in the Class of 1963 at Gettysburg College. Captain Murphy was the pilot of a U.S. Marine Corps fighter aircraft that went down off the coast of South Vietnam into the South China Sea. His body was never recovered. His final outcome is unknown.

Captain Thomas Hensley, U.S. Air Force.

Captain Hensley was the pilot of a U.S. Air Force F–105 aircraft which was apparently shot down by an enemy surface-to-air missile near the Laotian/South Vietnamese border. His outcome is unknown.

First Lt. Robert C. Keller, U.S. Army.

First Lt. Keller and the author attended Trinity Lutheran Church, and were classmates in the Class of 1959 at Camp Hill High School, Camp Hill, Pennsylvania. First Lt. Keller died in a non-combat related aircraft accident in October, 1966.

PFC James Dennis, MACV Advisor/Radio Operator, Advisory Team 55, Kien Tan District.

PFC Dennis and the author were friends over five months during the times the author was in Kien Tan District. PFC Dennis was on a combat daytime patrol with an Army of South Vietnam (ARVN) infantry company. His company was ambushed near Three Sisters Mountains in Kien Tan District by a North Vietnamese Regular Army regiment of 1,500 soldiers who had infiltrated from Cambodia and occupied the Three Sisters Mountains. A battle took place between the ARVN and NVA, and it was later discovered that the NVA were fresh regiments wearing khaki uniforms and they were armed with AK-47 assault rifles and light and heavy machine guns to attack cities across the Mekong Delta. PFC Dennis was mortally wounded during the battle with a month to serve in Vietnam before returning home.

**The Vietnam Veterans Memorial
Washington, D.C.
Dedicated November 3, 1982**

1

U.S. Representative Ted R. Graham (D-PA) had served ten years in Congress; he was also a Vietnam Veteran.

He leaned back in his desk chair and watched as an electronic board posted votes of U.S. representatives conducting a vote on House Bill 1436. Representative Graham sponsored the bill appropriating fifteen million dollars over three years to fund searching for 2,500 remaining U.S. Prisoners of War or Missing-in-Action POWS/MIAs in Southeast Asia following the end of the Vietnam War in 1973.

A House page delivered a note to the Clerk-of-the-House. The clerk perused the note, rose from his desk, and walked to the center of the House floor. He faced the Speaker of the House, Jim Wright (D-TX), and announced:

"Mr. Speaker, House Bill 1436 passes with 435 yes votes and unanimous consent."

Applause thundered in the House chamber while some representatives shouted, "Who-Ah! Who-Ah!" voicing their approval of the bill.

Speaker Wright rapped his gavel for order. "Mr. Graham, congratulations on your bill. Today the U.S. House of Representatives has shown the commitment of our country to locate the remaining 2,500 POWS and MIAs from Vietnam. We will return them home to be reunited with their families or receive a proper burial on American soil. Although the Vietnam War ended sixteen years ago, it remains our solemn duty to search for the remaining POWs/MIAs until they are properly accounted for." The Speaker rapped his gavel and proclaimed, "The House is adjourned."

U.S. Representatives Jim Cooper (D-NY), Troy Andrews, (D-NJ), and Adam Paxton (D-PA) gathered at Ted Graham's desk and congratulated him on his bill. Jim Cooper spoke to Ted.

"Ted, I'm glad the bill passed with unanimous consent and that Republicans didn't bring up your activities with Vietnam Veterans Against the War in 1970 to raise objections about your sponsoring the bill. The Vietnam Veterans Against the War was a rogue organization with some persons who never served in Vietnam wanting publicity, and was disingenuous."

Ted replied, "I agree, Jim, Vietnam Veterans Against the War went from opposing the war to a radical organization suggesting extreme measures against political people supporting the war."

He continued, "My next project is to write a book to explain why America lost in Vietnam; it will tell what really happened, beyond the fact that Americans did not support the War."

Adam Paxton told the group, "It's seven thirty, and we have reservations at Mack's Steakhouse for dinner at eight, Ted, would you join us?"

Ted looked at them with a feeling of dismay; he wanted to join his colleagues for dinner at Mack's, which had excellent food. "Fellas, I'm honored, however, I am meeting my chief of staff at eight. He is bringing me the unclassified documents for the U.S. Military Readiness hearings I will chair next week. Elaine drove to Carlisle today with our son Mitchell so I could work in my office over the weekend without distractions."

"Are you sure you don't want to relax for one night?" asked Adam.

Ted looked at Adam, "Thanks again, I'll have to take a rain check."

"Okay, Mr. Representative Graham," said Troy Andrews, "just remember your friends ten years from now when you and Elaine reside at 1600 Pennsylvania Avenue, and invite us to the White House for dinner."

"Thank you for your confidence, Troy, I shall remember in ten years to invite you all to the White House to a state dinner if we still hold elected offices," Ted answered jokingly.

A chime sounded, indicating the capitol police would lock the doors to the House chamber in ten minutes.

"Time to go," Jim Cooper motioned to the group.

The representatives walked out of the chamber. Ted stopped

at the elevators to go to the third floor while the other representatives got their overcoats at the cloakroom and left the building. When Ted got to the third floor he walked down the marble hallway to his office numbered 3710. He entered at 8:00; at 8:10 Blain Tedford arrived, they sat down and began their meeting.

Blain took a large looseleaf notebook from his large attaché case and placed it on Ted's desk.

"Ted, this document is tabbed with the Pentagon's reports, readiness reports from major U.S. Commands, line-item cost analysis and point papers from your staff."

"Good work, Blain. I'm staying at the Bedford and working in the office over the weekend. This will be a rigorous hearing. We intend to find out how the one trillion dollars was spent by the Reagan administration and improved military readiness in all services. I'd better not find out that appropriated money was spent on four-hundred-dollar hammers or seven-hundred-dollar toilet seats. If so, my number-twelve-size shoe will be implanted in someone's ass, and people will be fired."

"Okay, boss, I agree, if you need help call me at home; if not, see you for breakfast in the House cafeteria at seven on Monday." Ted and Blain shook hands and Blain left the office.

Ted Graham was editor of the *Law Review* and had received his law degree from Dickinson Law School in 1973. He passed the Pennsylvania bar exam and accepted a position as a prosecutor in the Cumberland County District Attorney's office.

In 1977, Ted was the lead prosecutor in a case involving white-collar savings-and-loan fraud, and when the state won the case, it garnered him publicity for a year in the Harrisburg area. He subsequently received the Democratic Party's nomination. In the November 1978, election he defeated a Republican incumbent for the U.S. House of Representatives. The past ten years he had served on the House Ways and Means, Judiciary, and Armed Forces Committees. In 1988, he was appointed Chairman of the House Armed Forces Sub-Committee on U.S. Military Readiness.

Sunday night he finished his preparation for the hearings. He was looking at the names of persons to testify at the hearing when he saw under the Department of the Army, "Nathan Bedford Stewart," a name from long ago.

His memory went back to Captain Sue Ellen Harris, a beautiful U.S. Army Nurse, with whom he had become infatuated with while at Kelper compound in Saigon. They talked over three days; he had hoped to develop a deeper relationship with her. They communicated for a while; he soon realized that she looked at him as only a friend. He received a "Dear John" letter from her informing him her "beau" was a U.S. Army Captain and a 1963 West Point graduate whom she had known since childhood. Sue Ellen and Nathan Bedford Stewart were eventually married. Ted looked at Lieutenant General Nathan Bedford Stewart's resume.

Education	Year
U.S. Military Academy, West Point, B.S.	1963
Georgetown University School of Foreign Relations, Washington, D.C., M.A.	1975
U.S. Army War College	1980

Recent Assignments	Year
Army Staff, Deputy Chief of Staff, G-3	1988–1989
Commander, V Corps, USAREUR/Seventh Army, Heidelberg, West Germany	1985–1988

Ted thought, *Here is the Army's next Chief of Staff.* He was glad that things had worked out for Sue Ellen.

Ted and Blain had breakfast Monday morning. Ted told Blain he was well prepared and confident for the hearings. Ted's sub-committee staff met at 8:00 in his office and reviewed procedures for the next three days.

They arrived at the House Bryant Room at 8:30 where it was abuzz with House staff members, The *Washington Press* Corps, and *CNN* personnel were testing the television cameras, audio and microphones. Ted saw the Pentagon delegation arrive and noticed a tall, trim and distinguished U.S. Army Lieutenant General with three silver stars on the shoulders of his immaculate uniform, and his nametag, "Stewart." Among the general's decorations were a Silver Star, Bronze Star with "V" device for valor, parachutist's badge, Ranger tab, and Combat Infantryman's badge.

At 9:00 A.M. Ted Graham called the hearings to order with an opening statement. The first witness was called to testify and the hearings began.

Lieutenant General Stewart testified Monday afternoon for two hours on U.S. Army readiness with a commendable presentation.

A headline in the Tuesday *Washington Post* said, "House Sub-Committee Grills Pentagon Brass during Readiness Hearings on the Hill."

The U.S. Military Readiness hearings were adjourned late Wednesday afternoon after three days of intense questions and answers.

Two weeks later Ted and Elaine Graham hosted a private dinner party at the Georgetown Inn. The guests included members of Ted's sub-committee, Jim Cooper, Troy Andrews, Adam Paxton, and their wives. After dinner, Ted rose to speak. He thanked his sub-committee and his fellow representatives for their support on House Bill 1436. He paused and spoke to his guests, "Friends, you are the first to learn that the National Democratic Committee is supporting me to run for the U.S. Senate from Pennsylvania in November." The room sat in silence, and then applauded his announcement.

Ted said, "I'm holding a press conference on Monday to make my formal announcement."

Jim Cooper said, "Teddy, just remember your friends ten years from now when you occupy the White House."

2

It was September 1989, and the beginning of the fall semester at Penn Hill College in Virginia. Warm summerlike days and cool fall nights were turning the leaves on stately old maple, oak, and chestnut trees into a palette of red, orange and gold colors across the pristine campus.

Jefferson Lee Madison, V, was a senior in pre-law with a 3.79 GPA. He was planning to enter the University of Virginia Law School next September.

In 1836, Penn Hill College was founded by Thomas Penn Hill, a physician. He believed that only an educated populace could assure the continuation of a democratic government as written by Thomas Jefferson in the U.S. Declaration of Independence with "the unalienable rights of life, liberty and the pursuit of happiness." The college charter stated the mission of Penn Hill College was to be a private, non-denominational institution of higher learning under the laws of the Commonwealth of Virginia to educate men of good character to serve in the professions of law, medicine, teaching, government service, ministers of the gospel and commerce.

In 1947, Penn Hill College became co-educational with an enrollment of 8,000 students on 2,000 acres and sixty-one buildings on the campus.

The past summer, Jeff, his mother, sister and brother visited his grandparents, retired Senator Jefferson Lee Madison, III and his wife Martha, in Georgetown. Before leaving, his family went to see the Vietnam Veteran's Memorial with its polished black granite panels rising out of the ground to form an apex, and the names of 57,939 persons who died in the Vietnam War etched on its panels. They also saw the bronze statue of three Vietnam Veterans. It had been emotionally chilling for Jeff Madison to witness seeing Americans leaving flowers, American flags, religious symbols and notes along the base of the memorial.

Jeff Madison still did not fully understand the Vietnam War. His father, Captain Jefferson Lee Madison, IV, had served in Vietnam in 1968 to 1969. One of Jeff's fraternity brothers named Malcolm Holly said his father served in Vietnam from 1967 to 1968 and never discussed the war after returning except to say, "Vietnam was a killing field." Another friend's father served with the First Infantry Division and he said, "The Goddamn Washington politicians and peaceniks lost the war, I saw buddies killed for nothing." He was still angry and bitter twenty years later.

The course Jeff Madison selected for the fall semester was a three-credit course entitled, "The Vietnam War in American History," taught by Bernard J. Stone, Ph.D., Professor of History. He had taught at Penn Hill College for twenty-four years and had written books called, *Colonialism and the French Indo-China War; America's Great Victory; Prelude to Pearl Harbor;* and *The Vietnam War in American History,* his most recent book.

Jeff entered the classroom in Grayston Hall and took a seat on the right side of the classroom in the front. He looked at the class and saw the room was full. Dr. Stone had a reputation as a scholar who flunked students who were lazy in course work. The classroom door was closed at 9:00 A.M. when Professor Stone entered. He was in his late fifties, tall and thin with a graying beard and temples. He walked to the lectern, looked at the classroom and said, "Good morning, I've counted forty-one students; I hope all forty-one of you will remain in the course the next twelve weeks." He removed his tweed sport coat and hung it on the back of a chair next to the lectern.

"You will be graded by the following evaluation, two exams worth twenty percent each, a short paper for twenty percent, class participation for ten percent, and a final exam worth thirty percent. Any questions? I expect you to apply yourself, if not, you will be graded accordingly. The semester's course is, 'The Vietnam War in American History.' Let me emphasize at the beginning the Vietnam War was an endeavor to apply American foreign policy in Vietnam since warfare is an extension of foreign policy by another means when diplomacy fails. If the U.S. Government had achieved a political settlement, the Vietnam War would never have occurred. Is that clear? We will analyze, evaluate, and discuss the events and the U.S. policy leading up to the U.S. military involvement in Vietnam. We will evaluate the political, military and U.S. Government situation in South Vietnam, containment and the domino theory."

Professor Stone opened four windows, and pleasant cool morning air filtered into the classroom. He turned to the lectern; "The Vietnam War shook America and changed our country forever."

Jeff and students opened their notebooks and took notes.

"The Vietnam War showed a war cannot be waged to a successful conclusion without the support of the American people. The outcome of any war, whether it involves the United States or another country, is to achieve an advantage to the country, which has a more favorable outcome than when the war began. The outcome of a war must make conditions better than those that existed before the war. The Vietnam War did not end with any advantage for the U.S., or place the U.S. in a more favorable position with North Vietnam than the U.S. had in 1964. The Vietnam War showed there are limits to U.S. Military power, if there is not a combined political and military strategy to win the war.

"General Eisenhower's strategy in Europe during World War II was simple—defeat Nazi Germany, destroy the enemy's ability to wage war by seizing German territory and its war production ability, and destroy Germany's military forces to obtain an unconditional surrender from Nazi Germany.

"The Vietnam War reinforced military lessons taught by the Chinese military philosopher Sun Tsu; he wrote, 'Know your enemy.' If you do not know your enemy, you will win a few battles. If you know nothing about your enemy, you will not win battles and you will be defeated. Most of you in class today are too young to remember Vietnam."

I was four years old, Jeff thought.

"The Vietnam War ended officially for the United States on March 29, 1973. The Nixon administration implemented a program called 'Vietnamization for South Vietnamese' to take over the brunt of the fighting in the war. The U.S. government provided large amounts of military supplies to support the government of South Vietnam and a commitment to bomb again if North Vietnam began to attack in great strength, but in spite of the efforts, after two years the North Vietnamese overran South Vietnam in April 1975. The Nixon administration did not conduct bombing due to Watergate. I'm sure you've seen the pictures showing the chaos of the U.S. Embassy in Saigon as hundreds of South Vietnamese are trying to board U.S. helicopters to get out of South Vietnam on April 29, 1975. On April 30, 1975 the Communists entered Saigon in M-60 tanks and trucks. The NVA commander demanded an unconditional surrender from the government of South Vietnam or a bloodbath would follow, thus ending the Vietnam War.

"I did not support the Vietnam War. I've never served in the military . . . and I didn't believe that the United States could intervene in a country whose government had had no democratic self-government for seventy-one years, or that the U.S. could do better than the French did in the Indo-China War from 1945 to 1954.

"I remember two young men. One was Scott Bennett, the other Charles Johnson. They were average students—probably should have attended Langley Junior College before coming to Penn Hill—they were on the fence on grades for being drafted. Any male student who received a notice of draft eligibility had to register under federal law with his local draft board to obtain a deferment from the draft to attend college. If the student failed to maintain a satisfactory grade point average at Penn Hill, or at any other college, the college had to notify the draft board about his academic situation and the student could lose his deferment status and be drafted into military service.

"Scott and Charles decided to leave Penn Hill; they both enlisted in the U.S. Marine Corps in October, 1966, and went together to boot camp at Camp Lejeune, North Carolina. After boot camp, they were both assigned to the Third Marine Expeditionary Force, Camp Pendleton, California. In February 1967, Scott Bennett was killed in action near the DMZ, and in June 1967, Charles Johnson was killed in action at Hué. I knew Scott

Bennett's family; his parents were devastated. His father told me, 'Bernard, my son died for nothing.' " The entire history class sat in silence.

"In May 1970, there was an anti-war protest on campus, which occurred after the Ohio National Guardsmen shot and killed four Kent State students. About 100 anti-war protesters met downtown and they began marching, shouting and looking for trouble, hoping to challenge the authorities at Penn Hill. As they approached campus, some Penn Hill students joined them. Our President Dewitt Collins took a bullhorn and told them, 'Disperse, and we will talk peacefully.'

"This antagonized them. A sign said, YOU TURN STUDENTS INTO KILLERS FOR UNCLE SAM'S DOLLARS. They began to throw rocks and Dr. Collins took shelter. Windows were broken in Thatcher and Downey Hall and they threw Molotov cocktails and burned two parked cars. One young man hollered," Dr. Stone said, "excuse my language, 'You fucking pencil-neck wimps, no man goes to NAM and comes back alive.' "

The class was mesmerized.

"Virginia state troopers and sheriff's deputies arrived with tear gas and loaded rifles and sprayed tear gas at the protesters. The sheriff said, 'Go home! We will make arrests and prosecute anyone we arrest.' The police wore riot gear with shields; some seventy-five police went into the melee swinging billy clubs and began cracking heads. Thirty-nine protesters were arrested, but none were Penn Hill students. That class showed the anger and frustration over Vietnam. Anti-war demonstrations took place across the breadth and depth of America.

"We held two faculty debates over the war. It was a good way for me to begin my academic career having academic freedom to debate; several professors shunned me for two years over my 'pacifist' position. That is what education is supposed to do, find the truth.

"Okay, back to the business of this course. I will lecture the next three classes. For your next assignment, read the first 100 pages of my book. I expect you to participate. Any questions?" He looked at the class.

A young woman named Susan Cunningham raised her hand.

"Yes, Miss Cunningham, what is it?"

"Dr. Stone, why exactly did you oppose the war, and no bullshit, please, Sir?"

"No bullshit; I did not think the United States acting alone or even with our allies from Australia, New Zealand, South Korea and the Philippines, could do any better than the French did in Vietnam. Why would they? We knew nothing about South Vietnam and I did not think if the French, who ruled Vietnam for seventy-one years, could not win, we sure as Hell couldn't win a war against a Nationalist leader, Ho Chi Minh, and their determination to fight for 100 years. No one took Ho Chi Minh seriously when he said, 'We will fight 100 years.' Any more questions? None?

"At the end of World War II in Europe in May, 1945, Sir Winston Churchill, the wartime Prime Minister of Great Britain, said, 'An iron curtain has descended over Eastern Europe'—referring to communism.

"In 1949, after four years of fighting between Communist forces under Mao Tse-tung and the Chinese Nationalists under President Chiang Kai-shek, mainland China fell to communism. One billion Chinese were now living under communism.

"In June 1950, North Korea attacked South Korea on the Korean peninsula. The Chinese communists invaded South Korea as an ally of North Korea, but the Korean War, or police action, ended with North and South Korea divided at the thirty-eighth parallel in 1953.

"By 1953, the spread of communism was a security concern in the West. Karl Marx and Friedrich Engels wrote in *The Communist Manifesto,* 'Communism would rule the world.'

"In 1947, George Kennan, at the U.S. State Department, enunciated a new theory of containment of the Soviet Union. In 1959, the communist insurgency in Cuba led by Fidel Castro overthrew the weak and corrupt Batista government; communism was now just ninety miles off the U.S. mainland of Florida.

"The containment strategy led to the formation of military alliances for mutual defense against a common enemy in the event of war. Among these defense alliances were the North Atlantic Treaty Organization (NATO), the Southeast Asia Treaty Organization, of which South Vietnam was a member (SEATO), and the Organization of American States (OAS) in South America created during the Kennedy administration. These strategic defense alliances were to protect democratic countries from communism.

"The U.S. government provided assistance by financial aid and military support to Third World countries where unemployment, hunger, poverty and government corruption were prevalent, to prevent communist guerilla forces from exploiting these conditions to foment national wars of liberation. The national wars of liberation were intended to incite the population to rise up against their government and replace it with communism. Particular concern existed about Central and South America, since Fidel Castro's revolution in Cuba was attempting to export communist-inspired revolution into countries by Castro's Lieutenant Che Guevara.

"Financial aid and military assistance were intended to help support weak democratic governments to improve their internal security, intelligence organizations, police, and judicial systems to prosecute communist guerilla insurgents.

"Chairman Mao Tse-tung wrote in *On Guerilla War* that the population in the countryside is an ocean where guerilla fish, swim and live.

"Communist propaganda was designed to get the support of the populace to win the hearts and minds of the people."

Jeff thought to himself . . . *Did the U.S. government fail to do this in Vietnam?*

Professor Stone concluded, "If a democratically elected government cannot eliminate conditions leading to unemployment, poverty and hunger, the country is ripe for a communist-inspired revolution. The communists will exploit adverse conditions to foment national wars of liberation as occurred during the French Revolution, the American Revolution and South Vietnam."

The bell rang. Students got up and left the classroom. While leaving class, a male student yelled, "Yankee, go home!"

Jeff Madison left the classroom and walked down the hallway with Susan Cunningham. "Did Professor Stone answer your question to your satisfaction?" Jeff asked Susan as they reached the entrance door to Grayston Hall.

"Somewhat," answered Susan. "I'm a French major, and I think the professor is a Francophile at heart."

"I'm sure you're right," said Jeff, and stopped on the top step of Grayston Hall. "I'm going to the bookstore to buy *The Vietnam War in American History* and read the assignment. Do you want me to buy you a book and bring it over to you tonight?" asked Jeff.

"Sure," Susan replied. "I'm going to my English lit class right now—how about I take you to lunch at the White Linen next week, would that work to repay you?" The White Linen was a nice restaurant in town.

"It's a deal, I'll bring the book to your dorm, see you tonight."

Jeff began to walk down the sidewalk and Susan walked toward Barkley Hall across campus. Jeff purchased two copies of Professor Stone's textbook and walked across campus to the college library.

Jeff enjoyed studying in Bancroft Library; it was quiet without the noise around his fraternity house. He selected a reading table in the rear of the main reading room and opened an adjacent window. He sat down, removed his textbook from his book pack and began to read *The Vietnam War in American History* by Professor Bernard J. Stone, Ph.D.

The seventeenth-century French poet and fabulist Jean de La Fontaine wrote: "In everything one must consider the end." On March 29, 1973, the end of the Vietnam War came for America in accordance with the Nixon doctrine of Vietnamization when the last U.S. troops left Vietnam. Vietnamization transferred the war fighting to South Vietnam. An agreement had been made between the Nixon administration and South Vietnam's President Nguyen Van Thieu that the U.S. would provide South Vietnam with continued financial aid, military equipment, and strategic bombing support during the war. From 1973 to 1975 the war continued. On April 19, 1975, communist forces were forty miles from Saigon, and on April 21, 1975 President Thieu fled South Vietnam for France. On April 29, 1975, the U.S. began the evacuation of Americans and some South Vietnamese from the roof of the U.S. Embassy in Saigon by helicopter amidst chaos and confusion; hundreds of South Vietnamese tried to push their way through the gate of the U.S. Embassy in Saigon to be evacuated, fearing communist reprisals. Air and ships ultimately evacuated 140,000 South Vietnamese civilians to the U.S. On April 30, 1975, communist forces entered Saigon riding in Soviet T-54 tanks, armored personnel carriers, and trucks carrying communist soldiers. An ARVN Colonel was ordered by the government to negotiate the terms of surrender with the Commander of the communist forces, the Peoples' Army of Vietnam (PAVN) or the North Vietnam Army (NVA). The NVA was the name used during the war by the U.S. Military and the communists' guerilla forces in South Vietnam were called Viet Cong, "VC", or "Charley." Communist "Sappers" were their specially trained soldiers to infiltrate enemy lines and American units' defenses. Sappers found approaches to enemy lines and then used satchels containing dynamite explosives to blow holes into the defensive barriers as their infantry soldiers passed through the openings to assault the enemy position.

The NVA Commander rejected any negotiations with South Vietnam's government (GVN) and demanded an immediate and unconditional surrender saying that a bloodbath would soon follow in Saigon. General Duong Van Minh, the interim president, surrendered Saigon on April 30, 1975, ending the war. Vietnam was reunited in 1976 as the Socialist Republic of Vietnam, with its capital in Hanoi; Saigon was renamed Ho Chi Minh City.

The Vietnam War lasted nine years, from 1964–1973. It was the longest and most unpopular war in U.S. history. No other war in U.S. history divided the U.S. as deeply as Vietnam since the Civil War.

Communist aggression against South Vietnam began following the 1954 Geneva Accords, which had divided Vietnam into two countries along the seventeenth parallel. On July 21, 1954, a cease-fire agreement set up a buffer zone, the withdrawal of French troops from the North and future elections. No elections were held. An agreement between North and South Vietnam opened their borders for 300 days, allowing immigration between the two countries. 100,000 South Vietnamese fled to North Vietnam, and 900,000 North Vietnamese fled to South Vietnam. Among the 900,000 North Vietnamese relocating to South Vietnam were 150,000 well-trained politically indoctrinated North Vietnamese communist political cadre, directed by Ho Chi Minh, to begin the communists' political organization of South Vietnam for their liberation of South Vietnam. By 1956, 400,000 communist political cadre and former Viet Minh, now called Viet Cong, were embedded in South Vietnam. In 1960, the National Front for the Liberation of South Vietnam (NLF) was founded in the Mekong Delta. The NLF was an all-inclusive, monolithic political grassroots organization to establish communist political control of the countryside. The NLF encompassed the entire South Vietnamese population, claiming in its propaganda that all of the South Vietnamese population supported the NLF, which included schoolchildren, teachers, parents, civil servants, farmers, fishermen, laborers, taxi drivers and peasants "opposed" to the GVN. The NLF had its grassroots political organizations in villages, districts, and up to the provincial level which was under the Committee of South Vietnam (COSVN) who had its political control from North Vietnam and Ho Chi Minh's Lao Dong or "Worker's Party."

In 1954 Bao Dai, a prince of the old Hué dynasty, was selected the first president of South Vietnam. He was not suited for political leadership, but preferred to hunt, womanize and spend his summers at a villa on Cote d' Azur in southern France. In 1956, Ngo Dinh Diem, his foreign minister, proclaimed the Republic of Vietnam in 1955 and in a rigged election was elected president to replace Bao Dai.

North Vietnam began its open insurgency against the GVN in the Mekong Delta in 1956. The Viet Cong made daylight military attacks against district towns, assassinated 400 GVN officials, and attacked ARVN military outposts and police stations, capturing huge amounts of small arms, ammunition and communications equipment, and heavy machine guns. By 1959, North Vietnam's war against the GVN had intensified with more control of the population. In 1964, North Vietnam began major troop infiltration into South Vietnam down the Ho Chi Minh Trail through Laos and Cambodia, and the Soviet Union and

Chinese communists also began to provide huge amounts of military aid to North Vietnam. In 1964, the U.S. began bombing North Vietnam below the twentieth parallel.

The U.S. military involvement in South Vietnam began in 1959 when the Eisenhower administration sent fifteen U.S. advisors to Vietnam as aircraft maintenance advisors to South Vietnam's Air Force. By 1962, there were 3,000 U.S. advisors in South Vietnam; by 1966, 385,000 and in April 1969, at the height of U.S. involvement, 543,400 U.S. military personnel were in South Vietnam.

The U.S. did not win a military victory in the Vietnam War. Vietnam veterans returning home were not welcomed with parades honoring their service until years later.

Facts about the Vietnam War show:

- The Vietnam War lasted from August 4,1964 to January 27,1973.
- On March 29, 1973, all U.S. military forces were out of South Vietnam.
- Nineteen was the average age of a U.S. soldier in Vietnam.
- 58,214 Americans died in Vietnam.
- 2,661 Americans were prisoners of war or were unaccounted for in April 1973.
- 3,403,000 Americans served in the Vietnam theater between 1961 and 1973, know as "The Vietnam Era."
- 600,000 communist soldiers died in the war.
- Four million Vietnamese civilians and military on both sides died during the nineteen years of military aggression by North Vietnam against South Vietnam.
- The Vietnam War cost U.S. taxpayers $200 billion dollars or $1.8 billion a month.
- The Vietnam Veteran's Memorial in Washington, D.C., containing the names of 58,253 Americans who died or were missing in action in the Vietnam War, was first dedicated on November 3, 1982.
- The exposure to a chemical defoliant called Agent Orange

was established as a medical condition for Vietnam veterans.
- In 2006, there were 8,295,000 living Vietnam veterans.

On April 17, 1961, President John F. Kennedy had made a decision. Cuban exiles had been trained, armed and directed by the U.S. government to overthrow the regime of Premier Fidel Castro. They were unsuccessful. This military fiasco became known as the "Bay of Pigs," and because of it, Kennedy felt that he had to regain respect from Soviet Premier Khrushchev. President Kennedy decided the best way to gain respect was to stop communism. President Kennedy selected Vietnam as the place to stop communism, and he sent people to Vietnam.

The political and military situation under President Ngo Dinh Diem in South Vietnam in 1961 was tenuous. President Diem was resolutely anti-communist, but his government had used brutal repression to control the country since 1956. Diem was a devout Catholic after converting to Catholicism in France. The two major religions in South Vietnam are Buddhism and Taoism. President Diem was remote, arrogant and appointed his family into key positions in the government and the military. His sister-in-law, Madam Nhu, a fiery woman, represented Diem at meetings with foreign ministers and opposition political groups. Diem did not like U.S. Ambassador Henry Cabot Lodge. By 1963, the Diem government was opposed by Buddhist monks, with intrigue among Saigon's generals, newspapers alleging brutal repression, and a growing communist insurgency gaining political and military strength in the countryside.

The U.S. Military Advisory Group (MAAG) in Saigon and the CIA reported to Washington on November 1, 1963 that something had to be done with Diem or the GVN would collapse within two years. President Diem and his brother-in-law were both assassinated in a coup d'etat and their bodies were found bound inside an M-113 personnel carrier in Cholon, the Chinese enclave of Saigon. They had been shot to death. On November 22, 1963 President John F. Kennedy was assassinated in Dallas.

The political situation in Saigon deteriorated after the assassination of President Diem into an internal Saigon power struggle. From 1963–1965 eight Saigon governments collapsed. In 1965, General Nguyen Cao Ky, Commander of South Vietnam's Air Force, emerged as a compromise leader, whom the U.S. chose to support. General Ky was charismatic, dashing and flamboyant. General Nguyen Van Thieu was selected by South Vietnam's National Assembly as president on October 21, 1967, and General Ky remained as vice president.

In 1965, the CIA did an evaluation of the war in a written report, in which they concluded the war was a stalemate and could not be won. The report was given to President Johnson.

General Douglas MacArthur warned Congress not to get involved in a ground war in Asia after the U.S. experience in the Korean War. He said casualties would be too great to win a ground war against the large Asian population. General MacArthur said the only way to avoid huge military casualties in Vietnam was to drop an atomic bomb on Hanoi. Dropping atomic bombs on Nagasaki and Hiroshima convinced the Japanese High Command to surrender in World War II. It was estimated the U.S. would have suffered one million casualties to invade the Japanese mainland in World War II.

President Nixon rejected the notion of dropping an atomic bomb on Hanoi to end the war as the "Madman Theory." He said dropping an atomic bomb on North Vietnam would stigmatize the U.S. forever in world history.

From 1964 to 1965, the Johnson administration's senior policy advisors did not understand the resolute determination of the communist enemy and Ho Chi Minh's statements saying, "We will endure any necessary hardships to fight and win a war against foreign invaders." North Vietnam was a small country, about half the size of California with a population of twenty-five million and an agrarian society.

North Vietnam had an army of 500,000 men, no Air Force, and almost no Navy to match America's military strength. The Johnson administration badly underestimated North Vietnam's ability to fight and win the war. The Viet Cong were viewed as paramilitary guerillas, dressed in black pajamas, wearing sandals made out of automobile rubber and utilizing only AK-47 assault rifles. North Vietnam and the Viet Cong did not appear to be much of an enemy to defeat in a short war. President Johnson pronounced Vietnam as "Veet-nam", and he called the country of "Veet-nam" "the damn little piss-ant country." He said, "I inherited Kennedy's war in 1963," and Vietnam is "a bitch of a war."

There was a belief in Washington in 1964 that the U.S. could prop up the GVN, train and improve the combat effectiveness of the ARVN, and "win the hearts and minds" of South Vietnam's people by building schools, roads and hospitals and protecting them from the Viet Cong.

The senior policy advisors in the Johnson administration did not understand the revered status of Ho Chi Minh to all Vietnamese. Ho Chi Minh was not a Mandarin, but "one of them." Neither the Johnson administration nor the U.S. Military Command in Saigon/Pentagon realized the depth and breadth of Ho Chi Minh's political influence over South Vietnam's population; nor the political strength of the NLF in the countryside.

In 2002, the U.S. media attempted to obtain information under the Freedom of Information Act and to investigate the Gulf of Tonkin attack on two U.S. destroyers in international waters thirty miles east of North Vietnam on August 2, 1964. The media wanted to determine whether North Vietnam's PT boats actually fired torpedoes and damaged the U.S. destroyer *Maddox,* if the attack did occur, or if it had been fabricated as justification for the U.S. to enter the Vietnam War.

On August 7, 1964, The Gulf of Tonkin Resolution was passed by Congress and the U.S. Senate authorizing the president to take "all necessary measures to win in Vietnam," which allowed for the war's expansion.

The outcome of any war is to provide an advantage to the winner and provide better conditions than existed before the war. The outcome of the Vietnam War never provided any advantage to the U.S.; it did the opposite. It took a decade for Americans to put "Vietnam aside" and to reconcile what happened to the nation, and the lives lost in Vietnam. The famous "credibility gap" developed over whether Americans were told the truth about Vietnam by the Johnson administration reports about the war and the facts of the war. Most Americans supported U.S. sending troops to Vietnam in 1965, and the explanation of a communist threat to American security. The American public supported the war from 1965 to 1967 with a belief the war would be won. By 1967, the "credibility gap" was a huge political obstacle for the Johnson administration, which attempted to reconcile media reports on television and in newspapers, claiming the war could be won, and that the Pacification Program was working in the countryside, which conflicted with the facts in the war. The media questioned why North Vietnam did not want a peaceful settlement if they were losing the war. U.S. troops were being killed 10,000 miles away from home without any clear political purpose, and Vietnam did not appear to be a threat to U.S. national security.

The media in Saigon questioned reports provided by the U.S. Military Information Office in Saigon at nightly 5:00 briefings in Saigon.

The U.S. Military Information Office maximized U.S. success, communist defeats, and *their* heavy casualities. The U.S. military information briefers put a positive "spin" on reports at the expense of the communist enemy in the war.

The media questioned the veracity of U.S. military information briefings asking, "Why do the Viet Cong control the countryside at night, or if progress is being made in the war, why do the communists fight in spite of heavy casualties with no indication they want a peace settlement?" By 1967, 300 U.S. soldiers were being killed a week or 1,200 a month in the war. ABC, CBS and NBC reported their own evaluation of the war and that analysis of the war was subsequently broadcast into Americans' homes on television. The "credibility gap" exploded with Americans believing the war was not being truthfully reported by the Johnson administration and soon eroded American support for the war. The U.S. media in Saigon called the 5:00 military briefings in Saigon, "The Five O'Clock Follies." Americans concluded at the end of 1967 that Vietnam was a quagmire, which fueled anti-Vietnam War demonstrations across America.

The communists' sneak attack over the Tet Lunar New Year ceasefire on January 31, 1968 turned the Vietnam War into a hopeless quagmire. In the Communist Tet Offensive, 84,000 communist soldiers attacked across South Vietnam at 2:00 A.M.

on January 31st, attacking thirty provincial capitals, 100 districts and 400 locations. U.S. Military Police killed eight Viet Cong inside the grounds of the U.S. Embassy in Saigon, while twelve U.S. Army Military Police were killed at the U.S. Embassy during the attack. During Tet, 50,000 communist soldiers, 4,000 ARVN and 2,000 U.S. soldiers were killed and 8,000 communist soldiers captured.

The Tet Offensive was a military disaster for the communists. However, it turned into a political bonanza, which they had not expected. The attack did not lead to an uprising of South Vietnam's people against the GVN. The attack did show the world that the war was not being won if the communists could launch a full-scale attack and breach the U.S. Embassy in Saigon, and "no light was at the end of the tunnel for peace."

1968 was the year the large, organized anti-war protests began across America on college campuses, in cities and Western Europe. On August 26th–29th, anti-war demonstrations turned violent at the 1968 Democratic National Convention in Chicago in which protesters clashed with police. Anti-war protests continued for the remainder of the war and were televised each night. On May 4, 1970 a major tragedy occurred when Ohio National Guardsmen shot and killed four students at Kent State University who were protesting the invasion of Cambodia. Americans had seen enough of the Vietnam War.

In 1973, the end of American involvement in Vietnam brought relief and sorrow.

The Vietnam War as viewed by other world leaders gave a perception that America was no longer a reliable ally. Americans let their elected officials know that Americans would never stand for another "Vietnam War." Communist world leaders viewed America's "Vietnam paralysis" as an opportune time to do mischief in the world against U.S. interests.

Television was the medium that exposed the horror and brutality of Vietnam. At night, reports said:

"300 Americans were killed in Vietnam last week, and 1,400 killed this month. The Johnson administration is optimistic about progress to end the war."

"Search-and-destroy operations were conducted in the Central Highlands to stop communist infiltration. Heavy fighting continues along the Demilitarized Zone in the war."

"Large combat operations were conducted in Operation Junction City in War Zone C, northwest of Saigon, in which eighty-nine NVA were killed, and ten U.S. soldiers also killed. Delegates at the Paris Peace Conference cannot agree whether to sit at a rectangular or round table."

"The U.S. has resumed bombing North Vietnam."

"Communists launched a major sneak attack across South Vietnam with 84,000 soldiers during the Tet Lunar New Year ceasefire."

Many returning Vietnam veterans had problems adjusting to civilian life. Reports taken from Vietnam veterans at hospitals indicated combat veterans having "flashbacks" they described as abnormally vivid—often recurrent recollections of disturbing past events from combat. Veterans described the "flashbacks" as seeing a U.S. soldier or a buddy shot to death; seeing a soldier blown apart stepping on a land mine; seeing a comrade shot in an ambush and bleeding to death; or watching a U.S. *Huey* helicopter shot down, crashing and exploding in the jungle. Vietnam combat veterans were diagnosed with post-traumatic stress syndrome or disorder. The syndrome was attributed to having periods with little or intermittent enemy contact, and then having a sudden, massive and violent attack with intense combat and then the enemy was gone, leaving many casualties. Remaining soldiers wondered, "Am I next?" or "When will I be killed?"

There were no front lines in Vietnam. U.S. soldiers went back time and time again into villages to clear Viet Cong. Front line U.S. combat troops rarely had accurate intelligence about the enemy. The most reliable intelligence was obtained from NVA, VC or Chieu Hois, who defected. The NVA were well-trained, well-led and well-equipped with modern Soviet and Chinese equipment. The NVA and VC planned and organized attacks in secrecy and in great detail, using sandboxes to organize attacks. Communist troops almost always had some plan to escape U.S. firepower. The Viet Cong had hundreds of tunnels constructed during the Indo-China War and World War II in which to hide from U.S. soldiers. Some of the tunnels discovered by U.S. soldiers were two miles long, and they had underground connections into other tunnels with ventilation and outlets far from the entrance to the main tunnel. The communists' tunnels were camouflaged from aerial view and could hold 500 communist soldiers while U.S. troops searched the area. Their tunnels were constructed near U.S. base camps to prepare for attacks on U.S. soldiers.

Communist soldiers moved and fought at night, and feared U.S. firepower. Communist prisoners of war said their own attacks were planned several weeks ahead, and in detail. Elite Viet Cong Sapper Units opened trails up to the perimeter of U.S. military camps and they threw explosive satchels, blowing holes in prepared defense, and Viet Cong then ran quickly to attack the U.S. base camp. Communist commanders blew whistles directing their soldiers during an attack; after an attack, Viet Cong dispersed, regrouped and reunited and lived among the local population and hid from ARVN and U.S. troops. Viet Cong returned to villages after ARVN and U.S. troops departed.

In November and December of 1967 during the communist Tet preparation, communist forces infiltrated into their staging areas. General Vo Nguyen Giap, commander of the NVA, said he had created a diversion by attacking the U.S. Marines at Khe Sanh in October 1967, to divert attention from the Tet infiltration. Viet Cong infiltrated their own arms and ammunition down rivers and canals by boat, appearing to be fisherman, while porters carried their equipment into staging areas where it was hidden. Weapons were stored in cemeteries and hidden inside empty coffins as fake funerals, using elaborate decorations. Viet Cong soldiers infiltrated into Saigon and cities in January; no one suspected that among the thousands of people moving across South Vietnam were communist soldiers preparing to launch a major attack in the early hours on January 31.

It was difficult for U.S. soldiers to know their enemy; a Vietnamese farmer planting rice and a young boy riding a water buffalo might be Viet Cong fighters. They observed U.S. troops, watched their activities and provided this information to the Viet Cong. A Vietnamese girl who smiled and waved at passing U.S. soldiers in the morning might be the same girl who, at night, helped the Viet Cong to dig punji stake pits to wound and maim U.S. soldiers. Viet Cong cut foot-long pieces of wood or bamboo, sharpened the tips to a razor-sharp point and encrusted the point with pig or water buffalo dung. Forty to fifty punji stakes were embedded two feet in a pit covered with leaves or branches so a U.S. soldier would puncture his boot or fall into a pit and puncture his body, causing severe wounds. A puncture wound had to receive immediate medical attention to avoid severe infections.

Some returning Vietnam veterans never recovered from Vietnam. These veterans got divorced, became alcoholics, drug addicts, or homeless and some committed suicide to escape mental demons from "NAM."

The Vietnam War shook American society and reshaped the U.S. military. Congress replaced the inequitable Selective Service Act of 1973 with an all-volunteer U.S. military. A new phrase "The Vietnam Syndrome" became part of America's vocabulary; no future wars would ever become another Vietnam. The U.S. Congress determined any future war would have full support of the American people, a clearly stated reason for the war, the mission of the war, and a stated strategy out of war.

Strong positions developed among Washington's politicians and U.S. military who would not become scapegoats for Vietnam. Former secretary of defense, the late Clark M. Clifford, who served from January 1968 to January 1969 in the Johnson administration, said, "The U.S. military command never presented a suitable military strategy to President Johnson to win the war." The U.S. military command in Saigon/Pentagon maintained that the political meddling of the Johnson administration lost the Vietnam War, and the military fought the war with one hand tied behind its back.

North Vietnam's generals interviewed after the war said they viewed America no differently than the French as an enemy who had to be driven from Vietnamese soil. NVA generals were surprised how much the Americans fought like the French from permanent base camps, deployed large combat operations, and employed ritual artillery barrages before infantry assaults; U.S. harassment and interdiction fire (H&I) did not hinder their operations. The generals said they taught their own soldiers where to hide from U.S. firepower and how to use heavy machine guns to shoot down U.S. helicopters. The helicopter was the tactic the Americans used to defeat them; therefore, they had to defeat the helicopter. North Vietnam saw the anti-Vietnam war demonstrations and knew it was only a matter of time until the Americans went home in defeat. American soldiers fought bravely.

The Vietnam War validated using helicopters for mobility, firepower, and to ferry troops into remote locations. UH-1 Huey helicopters were the real workhorses for U.S. soldiers; the CH47 Chinook helicopter was used to ferry troops and supplies; the Cobra attack helicopter provided tremendous additional firepower with 2.75 rockets and a mini-cannon firing 6,000 rounds a minute. The M–16 rifle became an effective infantry weapon; the M–79 grenade launcher provided more firepower to the infantry squad; and the .81 mortar was accurate to use in the jungle.

A military adage states, "Generals prepare for the last war," meaning what was learned from the last war becomes the planning for the next war. How did the chairman of the joint chiefs of staff and the individual Service chiefs plan to fight a guerilla war in triple-layer canopy jungles, with a six-month monsoon season of impassable rivers, using heavy armor units? The first principle of military war planning is to define the mission, and to structure the force regarding enemy, weather and terrain. Did the military war planners and operational decision makers in the U.S. military command in Saigon/Pentagon believe a combat structure oriented on speed, mobility and firepower with armor units, with mechanized infantry and armored cavalry regiments were appropriate in a guerilla war?

U.S. soldiers fought valiantly and defeated the enemy. After the Battle of the Ia Drang Valley from November fourteenth to the seventeenth, 1965, the U.S. First Air Cavalry Division defeated three NVA regiments, killing 1,000 communist soldiers with a loss of 300 U.S. soldiers. The U.S. military never lost a battle in the war. U.S. soldiers were as tough as the NVA and defeated the enemy. A U.S. Army general said after Ia Drang Valley, it was a great victory, but to fight such future battles would lead to excessive and unacceptable casualties. That general was criticized for his negative attitude rather than showing a "can-do attitude." North Vietnam's generals said the battle of Ia Drang Valley taught them valuable lessons. First, never make a frontal infantry assault against U.S. firepower. Two, don't fight in the daytime. Three, shoot down U.S. helicopters during any attack. Four, get cover from U.S. firepower. Five, move close to U.S. troops and make American artillery or air attacks shoot into their own friendly soldiers, "bullets over buddies."

The U.S. military command Saigon/Pentagon used MACV Special Operations (MAC/SOG) for clandestine intelligence operations in Laos, Cambodia and North Vietnam. Vietnam was an intelligence war. Many Vietnam veterans questioned why special operations units like U.S. Special Forces, U.S. Army Rangers and U.S. Navy SEALS were not deployed to locate NVA/VC positions on extended operations to identify and target them for heavy bombing or invade North Vietnam and destroy its infrastructure. U.S. Special Forces A Teams worked with the Montagnards in the Central Highlands to stop communist infiltration. Some veterans believed MAC/SOG or a special operations joint task force should have infiltrated into North Vietnam, identified strategic targets, and brought more effective bombing over North Vietnam.

Who in the U.S. military command approved using personnel organized, trained and equipped to fight a land war in Central Europe, in Vietnam? Armor units had difficulty operating in thick jungle and monsoon conditions six months out of the year. Did the U.S. Military Command Saigon/Pentagon decide to deploy a military force intact to Vietnam with its tactics, strategy, men, material and equipment, organized to fight a land war in Central Europe and then find neither the tactics nor the strategy fit into the Vietnam War?

Did former Secretary of Defense Robert McNamara, a Kennedy Whiz Kid described as having a computer-like mind, use a "body count" as a measure of success in the war? Did the U.S. military in Saigon/Pentagon believe the attrition strategy with search-and-destroy operations and a body count would win the war? Did the chain of command demand quotas of dead bodies to satisfy commanders up the chain of command for career advancement? Was the body count inaccurate and inflated up and down the chain of command? Did the U.S. Military Command in Saigon/Pentagon believe by killing a generation of North Vietnamese it would make Ho Chi Minh surrender? Former Secretary of State Dr. Henry Kissinger said, "The communists could sustain even higher human casualties, and it still would not hurt their military effort in Vietnam."

Jeff finished reading a chapter. He left Bancroft library and walked to his fraternity house for dinner. He thought to himself, "God, Vietnam must have been a screwed up situation."

3

At 9:00 A.M. on Wednesday, Dr. Stone entered the classroom and walked to the lectern located at the center of the room. He surveyed the class, looked around the room and said, "Very good; we have no quitters, my reputation often precedes my history courses.

"I trust everyone did read the assignment.

"In the last class I lectured on the containment policy, communist counter-insurgency warfare to unseat weak democratic governments, and why I opposed the war in Vietnam.

"Today I shall lecture on American involvement in Vietnam, the opposing military forces in Vietnam, my experience visiting communist Vietnam in 1984, cogent questions which remain from the war, and my five reasons why America lost in Vietnam.

"I reviewed the situation after the French left Vietnam in 1954 and the beginnings of the communist insurgency in South Vietnam in 1956. The period following President Diem's assassination in 1963 led to political instability, which led President Johnson to send U.S. Marine combat troops to Vietnam in March, 1965. This began the American build-up to prop up the GVN and to improve the combat effectiveness of the ARVN and Regional/Popular Forces units called "RF/PF" or "Ruff-Puffs" by U.S. soldiers who had little confidence in their combat effectiveness.

"By 1966, the major U.S. military combat force structure in Vietnam was the U.S. Marines—First Marine Expeditionary Force, U.S. Army First, Fourth, Ninth and Twenty-fifth Infantry Division, First Air Cavalry or Air Mobile, Fifth Mechanized Infantry Brigade, 196th and 199th Infantry Brigade, Eighty-second, 101st Airborne Division, 173rd Airborne Brigade, Eleventh Armored Cavalry Regiment, 225th Aviation Battalion, U.S. Special Forces, Rangers, MACV and Advisors.

"There were U.S. Navy—ships off the coast of South Vietnam, Patrol Boat Riverine (PBR), Patrol Craft Fast (PCF) Swift Boats and Seabees. U.S. Air Force—Tactical Fighter Wings, B-52 bombing from Guam, Thailand and Philippines. HQ of the First Field Force and Second Field Force HQ for command and control of U.S. combat units. HQ I to IV CORPS for command and control of MACV and logistical support. U.S. Army Vietnam provided logistical support. The Saigon Military District protected Saigon."

Professor Stone put a chart in front of the class and commented. "You need to understand the U.S. military structure in Vietnam. The military command in the war originated with President Lyndon B. Johnson as commander in chief, the joint chiefs of staff in the Pentagon; U.S. Pacific Command Headquarters at Camp H.M. Smith, Hawaii; and to General William C. Westmoreland, Commander, Military Assistance Command, Vietnam (COMUSMACV) in Saigon.

"Below General Westmoreland were the joint staff of the Air Force, Navy, and U.S. Marines at Tun Son Nhut Air Force Base in Saigon. Separate from these organizations was the U.S. Military Assistance Command, Vietnam (MACV), which provided U.S. advisors. There was a civilian chain of command under General Westmoreland called Civil Operations and Revolutionary, later Rural, Development Support (CORDS) to administer the Pacification Program. The Agency for International Development (USAID) provided funds and advisors to the Pacification Program.

"The media called the U.S. military headquarters in Saigon 'Pentagon East.' The U.S. government awarded contracts for construction of military headquarters, communication facilities, office buildings, intelligence facilities, swimming pools, post exchanges, officer's and enlisted clubs, movies, bowling alleys and snack bars, giving Saigon a distinctively American flavor. Huge military facilities were built on a deep-water port at Cam Rahn Bay, and other U.S. facilities were built at Nha Trang, My Tho, Can Tho, Pleiku, Vi Thanh and An Thoi on Phu Quoc Island, for the U.S. Navy. The South Vietnamese had their own military headquarters and joint staff in Saigon with one point one million men under arms. Opposed to the GVN and U.S. and allies were North Vietnam and Viet Cong with military support from Russia and communist China. Starting in 1964, Russia provided state-of-the-art military equipment, and new AK-47 rifles in 1967. Rocket-propelled grenades or RPG's were used by the Viet Cong to destroy ARVN tanks, APC's, 82-millimeter mortars, heavy machine guns, and hand grenades. Russian advisors in North Vietnam trained the NVA soldiers how to deploy the air surveillance radar. This training gave the NVA the skills to locate U.S. aircraft and deploy the SA-2 surface-to-air missile batteries and more advanced radar, tracking, heat-seeking missiles fired from the SA-7 surface-to-air missile defense system to shoot down U.S. aircraft over North Vietnam.

"The entire civilian population of North Vietnam was mobilized for the war. Civilians and soldiers in North Vietnam were trained to fire anti-aircraft surface-to-air missiles at U.S. military aircraft. Air raids were conducted. Women and children carried military equipment, food, and medical supplies with bamboo carriers on their backs or on bicycles. 150,000 human ants carried equipment 800 miles down the Ho Chi Minh Trail to supply NVA in Laos and Cambodia. Ninety-nine percent of the soldiers drafted into the NVA who went south to fight in the war never returned home.

"In 1967, the communist military strength in South Vietnam was established at 340,000 soldiers with 85,000 political infrastructure to direct the war. In 1968 there were 125,000 front line communist and 125,000 front line U.S. combat troops facing each other. Four rear area support soldiers were needed to support one front line U.S. combat soldier. The tail was wagging the dog.

"In spite of superior U.S. technology and firepower, human willpower prevailed in the war. The U.S. had superiority in firepower, technology, tanks, airpower, and military hardware, but the U.S. never employed a military strategy, in my opinion, to defeat a determined communist enemy who fought protracted guerilla warfare in the jungles and the rice paddies of the MeKong Delta.

"The U.S. Military Command in Saigon/Pentagon deployed

large-size unit operations patterned after World War II; the NVA or Viet Cong did not adopt a similar strategy. The U.S. employed an attrition strategy of search-and-destroy operations and a body count to measure success for Mr. McNamara to win the war. If the U.S. surrounded NVA or Viet Cong, the NVA adopted a hugging strategy by moving closer to U.S. troops for protection against bombing, air strikes or artillery fire. The Viet Cong avoided the U.S. strategy of cordon and circle the enemy and then destroy them with firepower or bombing. The Viet Cong remained elusive. They fought by ambush tactics, hit and run, booby traps and later fought at times and places of their own choosing to attack U.S. troops returning from patrol, when their guard was down, and conducted violent attacks. They hit U.S. troops with all they had, to maximize U.S. casualties.

"The North Vietnamese generals deployed a two-front strategy. The NVA fought to maul the ARVN so the ARVN would not fight and the U.S. had to assume a greater burden in fighting, leading to higher U.S. casualties. The North Vietnamese strategy was 'bleed the Americans.' No matter how many battles the U.S. forces won, they could not win the war. After the Communist Tet Offensive on January thirty-first, 1968, I submit, the Vietnam War was lost. The U.S. troops could not stop communist infiltration into South Vietnam. U.S. bombing was ineffective to slow the infiltration of 20,000 NVA troops a month into South Vietnam. There were anti-war protests in America, which communist leadership saw and knew it was only a matter of time until Americans left Vietnam and they would win. The French or Americans never broke their 'shadow government' which controlled the South Vietnamese living in the countryside."

Jeff Madison sat and listened to Professor Stone in disbelief. *Did the U.S. government know that in January 1968, the war in Vietnam could not be won, and still persisted in drafting and sending men to Vietnam to fight in a war that was lost?*

Professor Stone concluded, "I have not found any convincing historical or empirical evidence that after January 31, 1968, the war could have been won! The Johnson administration perpetuated the war to *save face* and avoid a defeat. One theory to end the war was to drop an atomic bomb on Hanoi, and to threaten to bomb China if China entered the war. Vietnam was a tragic mistake, a tragedy of biblical proportions. Class dismissed."

It was now the second week of December 1989, and the end of the fall semester. Professor Stone's class on the Vietnam War in American history had thirty-nine of the original students.

Professor Stone entered the classroom, "For most of you, this is good news. Today is next to the last class of the semester. On Friday, you have a three-hour exam. I am pleased with your class participation, questions and attendance the past twelve weeks. Today, I want to conclude my course by summarizing what I see as the role of the Vietnam War in American history.

"President John F. Kennedy chose South Vietnam as the time and place to stop communism as part of the U.S. government containment strategy. The U.S. government wanted to prevent the fall of the government in South Vietnam. There was a domino theory that if one country fell in a region then the next would follow like dominoes in a row. Communists would then format national wars of liberation in neighboring countries that could fall to communism.

"During the Eisenhower administration from 1953–1961, and the Kennedy administration from 1961–1963, there was a perception that U.S. military power was invincible. No one in the world could defeat the United States in a war with our vast natural resources, technology, and the fact that in World War II, the U.S. along with our allies Great Britain and Russia defeated the Axis powers of Nazi Germany, Japan and Italy. America was at its zenith of international power and prestige. No country in the world could challenge U.S. military power.

"Beginning with the earliest estimates from the U.S. Military Assistance Command, Vietnam, the CIA, and the U.S. State Department in Saigon reported a communist insurgency in South Vietnam, under political control of Ho Chi Minh and the communist political leadership in North Vietnam. By 1958, the communists set up what one Army general called a 'shadow government' in South Vietnam. The U.S. government made a decision to expand the U.S. military involvement in Vietnam and to prop up 'our man' in Saigon until the South Vietnamese government was strong enough to exercise political control over the countryside, and the ARVN could fight effectively.

"Each year the U.S. military command in South Vietnam reported that improvements were made or it would take only a few more thousand advisors to assist the ARVN to become combat effective.

"What the U.S. government miscalculated and misunderstood was the political control Ho Chi Minh and the National Liberation Front had established in South Vietnam starting in 1954, and this controlled the people. The U.S. government misjudged the determination and the resolution of Ho Chi Minh to defeat South Vietnam and its U.S. allies in a war, if it took 100 years.

"The U.S. sent U.S. military personnel to fight a war in a country of quicksand. The North Vietnamese were determined to wear down the U.S. Into this muck the U.S. political leaders went, with a leap of faith that American soldiers, tanks, artillery, firepower and technology would certainly defeat a ragtag band of guerillas. In 1965, no one thought a small country like North Vietnam could defeat the United States of America.

"The U.S. Army began to engage the enemy with large-unit operations and decisive battles to destroy the enemy with U.S. firepower. The Viet Cong did not fight that strategy. They fought by avoiding contact until the time and place they selected to fight, and obtain maximum U.S. casualties while denying political control of the countryside to the GVN. U.S. ground troops did not hold terrain and reduce the enemies' operational areas like World War II. Land and villages that the U.S. forces captured one day were back under communist control the next day. The local population shielded, protected, and hid the Viet Cong.

"U.S. military involvement escalated during the war, while the U.S. command pressured the GVN to improve the fighting effectiveness of the ARVN and the Pacification Program. South Vietnam's generals had a different view of the war. They wanted to placate their American counterparts by fighting to avoid casualties. The ARVN required U.S. air support for combat operations, and U.S. helicopter support to ferry ARVN troops into remote areas, increasing the direct U.S. involvement. South

Vietnam's generals did not want to fight at night, and subsequently lost any tactical advantage of surprise against communist forces. The U.S. military command deployed large-scale unit military operations into communist strongholds south of the demilitarized zone to slow communist infiltration, and search-and-destroy operations in War Zone C, War Zone D and the Central Highlands to neutralize regular NVA infiltration. The American strategy deteriorated into a defensive strategy by 1967, due to a lack of manpower.

"South Vietnam generals were more interested in maintaining their military positions of power to maintain their access to financial aid, U.S. aid to build schools, or money to pay, Regional Force/Popular Force Soldiers (RF/PF). Their positions allowed them access to divert money, resources, equipment, and supplies intended for the rural population through rampant graft. Throughout South Vietnam endemic corruption, kickbacks, and misappropriation of construction materials took place, selling stolen U.S. military aid for wartime profits. They bought gold bullion, hotels, businesses and other commercial enterprises like nightclubs with dozens of prostitutes controlled by local tough thugs and civilians, to line their pockets with money.

"South Vietnam's political and military leaders delayed and delayed in the belief that by appeasing their American counterparts, they would leave in six months only to be replaced by 'another American pain in the ass.' The South Vietnamese knew they would remain South Vietnam, and that Americans came and went like birds. Few Americans spoke Vietnamese, which allowed the South Vietnamese to maintain control over Americans, keeping them in the dark about what was being discussed or decided. South Vietnam's generals considered Americans 'stupid cowboys.'

"The U.S. Military Command in Saigon/Pentagon failed to grasp the military strategy of North Vietnam's Commander General Vo Nguyen Giap, and President Ho Chi Minh's combined political-military strategy in South Vietnam.

"Political leadership was the glue that held the National Liberation Front together, and they directed the Viet Cong to attack, harass, ambush, confuse and bleed U.S. military units. The

North Vietnamese main force regiments were trained to attack and maul South Vietnamese ARVN units to make the ARVN quit fighting until the combined NVA and Viet Cong military power was used to directly attack U.S. military units and kill Americans, for the news back in America. The U.S. Military Command Saigon/Pentagon and U.S. military fought with large combat units in battalion size operations with search-and-destroy operations, but the Viet Cong military units did not fight until it was the time and place of their choosing.

"On January 31, 1968, the communists' massive surprise attack over the Vietnamese Tet Lunar New Year destroyed any belief that U.S. military victory would occur in Vietnam.

"In my opinion, the U.S. should have used the Tet Offensive as justification to invade North Vietnam, or begin an immediate withdrawal from Vietnam.

"The credibility issue became a major point of anti-war protests. 'Someone has been lying to the American people for three years about the U.S. winning the war, and Pacification is a big lie.'

"After 1968, the Johnson administration had neither credibility with the American people to justify the war, nor dramatic military success to convince North Vietnam they could not win the war; they were between a rock and a hard place and I submit, by 1968, the Vietnam War was lost, and men sent to Vietnam were cannon fodder.

"As a scholar of history, I believe the Vietnam War is the worst example of inept national political leadership and the military use in American history. Did 58,214 Americans die in Vietnam for 'a big mistake'? Secretary of Defense Clark Clifford thought so. 'This soldier died in the Vietnam War for a big mistake' would be a hideous epitaph on the headstone of a U.S. Vietnam soldier."

"In 1964–1965, the political leadership in the Johnson administration relied upon the advice of civilians called the president's 'Wise Men.' Former Secretary of Defense Robert S. McNamara said, 'It was difficult to know how to conduct the Vietnam War in the beginning, due to the lack of people who spoke Vietnamese, who could read a Vietnamese newspaper, or understand the cultural, political, religious, or ethnic aspects of the population, or knew any leaders personally to act as advisors to Washington on the war.'

"The U.S. Military Command in Saigon/Pentagon shared equally in the military defeat employing a flawed attrition strategy to wear down the enemy.

"The American Civil War offers many cogent points for comparison about military tactics and strategy in the Vietnam War. General Robert E. Lee, commander of the Confederate army, used classic guerilla war tactics after Gettysburg during the Wilderness Campaign in 1864–1865 fighting and outnumbered against a superior Union Army commanded by General Ulysses S. Grant. It was a guerilla war strategy.

"How many U.S. generals had read Mao Tse Tung's book, *On Guerilla War* before going to Vietnam, or were U.S. senior officers more interested in careerism without opposing the failed strategy in Vietnam?"

Professor Stone paused for a moment and leaned against a desk in the classroom. The class was quiet and students waited for the professor to continue.

"I have identified six questions which must be answered about Vietnam, and then I will tell you the five reasons I've concluded that America lost in Vietnam."

Question No. 1

Did the Johnson administration employ a flawed military strategy called graduated response recommended by Secretary of Defense Robert S. McNamara to direct the war so as not to threaten Russia's or communist China's national security?

Question No. 2

Did President Johnson receive flawed advice from his senior policy advisors, with the belief that strategic bombing of North Vietnam, an agrarian country, would break North Vietnam's will to fight? By 1967, North Vietnam had received huge military support from Russia and communist Chinese with new AK-47 assault rifles, ammunition, heavy machine guns, tanks, armored personnel carriers, communication equipment, and Russian advisors trained North Vietnam soldiers to fire SA2 and SA7 surface-to-air missiles. Ho Chi Minh was neither a "puppet," nor "stooge" of the Soviet Union. The Vietnam War was not to expand Russian or Chinese communism into South Vietnam. Ho Chi Minh said, "It is a war to unite Vietnam and to drive all foreigners from Vietnamese soil, if it takes 100 years."

Question No. 3
Were the Washington politicians who never served in the U.S. military, but who supported the war to garner votes really "chicken hawks"?

Question No. 4
Did the National Selective Service Policy for military service in Vietnam create massive numbers of legal "draft dodgers" by exempting married men, college students in good academic standing, and individuals assigned to a U.S. Army Reserve or National Guard Units, from service in Vietnam? Was the Vietnam War fought by men "At the bottom of the barrel"?

Question No. 5
Did the U.S. Army's personnel assignment policy with a twelve-month tour of duty in Vietnam and individual soldier replacements in combat units lead to constant turnover and poor unit cohesion and erode combat experience among officers and non-commissioned officers?

Question No. 6
Did the U.S. Army's personnel policy of assigning officers to six months in a field/combat assignment and six months on staff create turnover and erode experience in U.S. Army units? Did the personnel policy of assigning enlisted soldiers to a twelve-month field/combat assignment create anger among enlisted soldiers toward officers, causing poor morale, drug use and "fragging" in the 1970s when enlisted soldiers rolled hand grenades into officers' tents to kill them?

Professor Stone said, "I have identified five reasons why America lost the Vietnam War. "Write these down."

A student raised his hand with a question.

"Yes, Earl," asked Professor Stone.

"Dr. Stone, where did you get your information about your six questions?"

The professor replied, "Doing research for my book, and conducting extensive interviews of numerous Vietnam Veterans. Let me now discuss five reasons America lost in Vietnam."

Students in the classroom sat prepared to take notes. Barbara Linder raised her hand to ask a question.

"Yes, Barbara, your question?"

"Professor Stone," she asked. "If the Johnson administration had let the military do its job, could we have won the war?"

Professor Stone replied, "Yes, I'm sure but that was not the case."

Professor Stone passed out sheets of paper to the class. "These are the five reasons with explanations. I'll lecture on these reasons and answers."

Reason Number One. The policy of graduated response was a failure. This policy negated either a negotiated settlement or military victory in the war. North Vietnam had no incentive to seek a political settlement from their belief the Americans did not want to fight a war in South Vietnam.

In 1965, order of battle intelligence on the communists' enemy strength in South Vietnam should have revealed there were 400,000 former communist Vietminh in South Vietnam and 150,000 regular North Vietnamese soldiers, for a total of 550,000 communist regular and guerilla war soldiers opposing the government of South Vietnam and reinforcements from the United States. In 1965, the Johnson administration badly underestimated the communist enemy strength in the war. In March, 1965, the U.S. policy of graduated response sent the wrong signals to the government of North Vietnam, its military commander, General Vo Nguyen Giap, the South Union and Communist China that either the government of the United States feared fighting a ground war in Asia, or was reluctant to commit U.S. military forces into South Vietnam. In March 1965, this seeming ambivalence by the U.S. government to assert decisive military forces convinced the South Union and Communist China to provide huge amounts of military arms, equipment, and training to North Vietnam for its war in South Vietnam. The North Vietnamese subsequently concluded America's approach to the war in South Vietnam was a sign with lack of resolve or commitment to fight in the war. With their perception of American weakness, North Vietnam concluded there was no reason for them to seek a negotiated settlement and thereby leave North and South Vietnam divided as two countries. Instead, North Vietnam continued its national liberation war against South Vietnam. America did not have a "big stick." The McNamara policy of graduated response negated either a political settlement or a military victory. The threat to expand U.S. bombing under the graduated response or to provide sufficient U.S. ground forces failed to deter North Vietnam's infiltration of soldiers into South Vietnam in 1967, which created a stalemate in the war.

Reason Number Two. Political meddling in the Johnson administration.

Policy decisions were made by unqualified civilians who had never served in the military, which violated military doctrine necessary to win the war. The Johnson administration claimed the Vietnam War was a "distraction from more important business of the Great Society" and the war drained badly needed revenue to fund Great Society programs of Medicare, Medicaid, Head Start, education, healthcare and the infrastructure. The unqualified civilians who never served in the military overruled the military's recommendations on how to prosecute the war by taking the war to the enemy in North Vietnam, destroying North Vietnam's infrastructure which allowed them to wage war in South Vietnam, and stop their infiltration into South Vietnam. Secretary of Defense McNamara and his Whiz Kids selected bombing targets and objectives for battalion-size military operations during the war. This conflicted with military planning and undercut the normal chain of command used in combat operations. U.S. State Department officials opposed a military attack in Laos and Cambodia and made troop deployment recommendations to Ambassador Lodge bypassing COMUSMACV General Westmoreland.

Most U.S. presidents accepted military recommendations in past wars. In a speech to Congress and the nation, President Franklin D. Roosevelt said, "December seventh, 1941 is a day that will live in infamy." President Roosevelt mobilized the country to support World War II saying, "No matter how long it may take us to overcome this premeditated invasion, the American people, in their righteousness, will win through absolute victory." (Inscribed on the World War II Memorial in Washington, D.C.)

President Roosevelt sought military advice during World War II from his top military leaders, including General George C. Marshall; General Dwight D. Eisenhower; General Douglas MacArthur; Admiral Chester Nimitz; General Henry "Hap" Arnold; and Carl Spaatz, who directed the bombing over Germany in World War II. The top military leadership during Vietnam was replaced when President Johnson personally approved bombing in the war and selected targets to be bombed on a daily basis from the Situation Room in the White House. Micro-management by civilians was the order of the day as orders were directed from the White House to the Pentagon through the U.S. Pacific Command to General William C. Westmoreland in Saigon. Some critics said of this policy of micro-management done by the Johnson White House, "The chain of command in Vietnam went from a captain, a company commander, to the commander-in-chief in the White House."

The military leadership advised President Johnson to enlarge the U.S. combat forces in South Vietnam to stop communist infiltration; bomb the North Vietnam's industrial infrastructure and capacity to wage war; destroy communist sanctuaries in Laos and Cambodia; open a second military front across the demilitarized zone (DMZ) so North Vietnam had to fight on two fronts and thereby reduce their troops into South Vietnam; call up U.S. military reserves and National Guard units to supplement the draft. President Johnson chose not to approve these military recommendations so as not to lose the support of middle America by calling up the reserves or widen the war into World War III. The military draft continued to be used, providing manpower for Vietnam.

No military leaders attended President Johnson's famous "Tuesday" luncheons at the executive dining room in the White House. President Johnson used these "Tuesday" luncheons to meet with his inner circle of confidants and advisors to discuss numerous subjects and to seek a consensus on Vietnam. President Johnson consulted a group of elder statesmen called "wise men" on Vietnam, which included: Dean Acheson, Arthur Goldberg, George Ball, McGeorge Bundy, Henry Cabot Lodge, Abe Fortas, Averill Harriman, Cyrus Vance, Douglas Dillon, John J. McCloy, Robert Murphy, General Maxwell Taylor and two other retired generals, Omar Bradley of World War II, and Matthew Ridgway, the U.S. Commander during the Korean conflict. Unfortunately, many of these "wise men" had never set foot in South Vietnam or could read or speak Vietnamese. President Johnson said, "All the military wants is bombing, bombing, and more bombing."

President Johnson told General Earle Wheeler, Chairman of the Joint Chiefs of Staff, and General Creighton Abrams, who later replaced General William C. Westmoreland as U.S. Commander in Vietnam, "The civilians are cutting our guts out." Secretary of State Dean Rusk told President Johnson, "Mr. President, the nation cannot support a bottomless pit."

Poitical meddling and decisions were made in the Johnson administration by unqualified civilians who never served in the military. This resulted in violation of military doctrine, which lost the war.

Reason Number Three. Credibility Gap/The Pentagon Papers.

The Credibility Gap began at the daily military briefings given at 5:00 P.M. in Saigon covering events over the past twenty-four hours in the war. The U.S. military briefings emphasized U.S. success and enemy failures without regard to the actual facts of the war. U.S. victories were emphasized and enemy losses were magnified, citing enemy casualties and losses in the war. Gradually, these contradictions were questioned about the information being given at U.S. military briefings and the press dubbed them the "5:00 follies" which became an embarrassment to the U.S. Military Command. This began the Credibility Gap with the misinformation about the status of the war and progress which had been told to the American people about Vietnam. The communist TET offensive on January 31, 1968, in which 84,000 communist soldiers attacked thirty provincial capitals across South Vietnam in 100 district locations, onto the grounds of the U.S. Embassy in Saigon, created a credibility "chasm" which made the American public realize the U.S. government had lied to them about "a light at the end of the tunnel" to end the war.

On June 13, 1971, the publication of the classified Pentagon Papers in forty-seven volumes by *The New York Times* revealed information that two previous administrations had lied to the American people about the extensive and ongoing involvement of the U.S. in South Vietnam since the Eisenhower administration. It reported COMUSMACV General Westmoreland predicted the war would be over by 1967, which General Westmoreland denied.

Credibility Gap/The Pentagon Papers showed the American people that these two administrations had lied to them about the U.S. involvement in Vietnam, which turned the American people against the Vietnam War.

<u>Reason Number Four.</u> "Fighting a War with One Hand Tied Behind the Back."

Political control of U.S. military field operations by the Johnson administration in the Vietnam War was the most political control a U.S. president has exercised by civilians in U.S. history. Military field operations decisions were controlled by Secretary of Defense McNamara, and his Whiz Kids approved operations necessary to win the war by not attacking and destroying communist sanctuaries in Laos and Cambodia; not allowing the U.S. Air Force to bomb the industrial infrastructure in North Vietnam that produced war munitions as well as supply dumps; bomb railroad lines that moved arms materials from Hai Phong to Hanoi, and the hydroelectric dams that produced power to run North Vietnam factories. The Rolling Thunder bombing over North Vietnam from 1964 to 1968 was judged to have had little effect in slowing North Vietnam's war production. Air photo reconnaissance showed the bombing damage was quickly repaired. The Arc Light bombing of the Ho Chi Minh Trail from 1965 to 1968 failed to slow or reduce North Vietnam's infiltration of soldiers into South Vietnam.

Without the ability to conduct decisive military operations to destroy Vietnam's war-making capacity, to stop infiltration into South Vietnam, and continuing ineffective air power had the U.S. so restrained in destroying strategic targets necessary to win the war that the U.S. military had to "fight with one hand tied behind the back" thus losing the war.

Reason Number Five. A Failed Military Attrition Strategy.

The U.S. military attrition strategy never convinced North Vietnam it could not win the war even with superior American fire power, air power, helicopters and joint operations with the ARVN. Ho Chi Minh said: "You can kill ten of my soldiers but so long as I kill one of your soldiers is a ratio I will accept. In the end I will win and you will lose." There was never any indication that North Vietnam felt the U.S. could kill so many of its soldiers that those losses would ultimately lead to a military defeat or that their horrendous casualties would weaken their resolve to continue fighting year after year in the war. North Vietnam had a three million population of young men ages fifteen to eighteen who came of age, that were recruited to train and eventually move south to fight in the war. The odds were too overwhelming that North Vietnam would not continue to use their pool of available manpower to fight a protracted guerilla war to counterbalance the attrition strategy of conducting search-and-destroy operations with a body count to measure success.

General Douglas MacArthur had warned the U.S. Congress never to again fight a ground war in Asia against a massive Asian male population. North Vietnam's losses never deterred its determination to fight 100 years if necessary to drive foreigners from Vietnam soil, as they had done for 100 years against

China, Japanese Imperial Army in World War II, France and now the Americans.

The late secretary of defense from 1968 to 1969 in the Johnson administration, Clark Clifford, a prominent Washington, D.C. attorney, was a power broker for five U.S. presidents from President Roosevelt to President Johnson. He stated in his position as secretary of defense that he had interviewed numerous U.S. generals, studied and analyzed military documents and reports on the war, and based upon the evidence he had accumulated about Vietnam, was that the U.S. Military Command Saigon/Pentagon never presented President Johnson with a suitable military strategy to the conditions in South Vietnam to win the war. Secretary Clifford later called the Vietnam War, "just a big mistake."

The failed U.S. military attrition strategy lost the war.

Former Prime Minister of Great Britain, Margaret Thatcher, thanked President Ronald Reagan for the U.S. military presence in South Vietnam saying, "The U.S. military presence in South Vietnam prevented communist expansion into Southeast Asia."

By 1967, the U.S. should have followed the advice of the late Vermont Senator George Aiken which was to "Declare victory and return home."

A U.S. Army colonel and a North Vietnamese colonel were talking at a conference. The American colonel said, "You know, the Americans never lost a battle in the war."

The North Vietnamese colonel thought for a moment and answered, "That may be true, but it is also not relevant."

Or . . . was the Vietnam War a "Star-crossed experience in U.S. History conforming to Murphy's Law stating, "If something can go wrong it will go wrong," which is what happened in the Vietnam War.

The bell rang and Professor Stone said, "Class dismissed."

The following Friday, the class took a three-hour examination. Jeff Madison received an "A" for the course. An "A" from Professor Stone was an event Penn Hill students called home to tell their parents.

4

(Author's Note: White House discussions are paraphrased from information available. President Johnson pronounced Vietnam as Veet-nam.)

Wyatt Wesley Erby was a ten-year veteran with the United States Secret Service. He was the watch commander who supervised twenty Secret Service agents on duty during the graveyard shift from 11:00 P.M. to 7:00 A.M. at the White House, 1600 Pennsylvania Avenue, Washington, D.C. The Washington, D.C. Secret Service office was located on the ninth floor of the US Treasury Building at the corner of Fifteenth and F Streets in Washington. The Secret Service office inside the White House was located in a command center on the first floor of the West Wing facing the south lawn and the presidential helicopter landing pad for Marine Corps One. It was equipped with worldwide radio and teletype communications to all U.S. Embassies, local law enforcement, and the FBI. All the Secret Service agents carried a .38 caliber Smith & Wesson service revolver and each guard post had M-16 rifles and Browning .16-gauge automatic shotguns. Seven agents patrolled the White House grounds on foot, three were located in a guard house on the roof of the White House, five patrolled inside the White House and five agents manned the twenty-four-hour command post. Brad Dexter, a nine-year veteran with the Secret Service, was the assistant watch commander and was a graduate of Ohio State University as a "Buckeye" football fan. At age thirty-two, he was a bachelor, but was engaged to be married in Columbus, Ohio, in June. It had begun to snow the previous afternoon at 3:30 and the snow was now twelve inches deep, which created many additional challenges for the Secret Service. President Johnson did not let inclement weather affect his travel schedule.

On February 8, 1968, at 0400 Brad Dexter concluded a telephone call at his desk. He listened to the telephone call, looked at his wristwatch, and said, "Roger, negative" as he hung up the telephone. He turned to his right in the swivel chair, and spoke to Wesley Erby and Miles Miller, who were standing adjacent to his desk and were also looking out of a fog-covered window in the office.

Brad leaned forward in the swivel chair, retied the shoelace on his right shoe and said, "That was D.C. Metro reporting the city streets are sanded on Pennsylvania Avenue, Massachusetts, Wisconsin, and on the Wilson and Key Bridges. Tell Major Baker to have all Marine security personnel require all persons entering the White House, as soon as people arrive, to open their overcoats for inspection, and have porters vacuum the rugs inside the White House every hour."

"Roger," said Brad.

Brad Dexter and Miles Miller put on knee-high boots and their secret service parkas; Brad took a Browning .16-gauge automatic shotgun from the weapons rack and loaded it with six shotgun shells. Miles opened the office door as a cold blast of wind blew snow into the office.

"Nice night, care to join us?" asked Brad.

"Be back here by 0530, or call if you're delayed," said Wyatt.

"Roger," said Brad.

Brad closed the door and he and Mike walked to a US Army Jeep, which had four-wheel drive and chains, to the patrol of the White House fence perimeter and grounds. Brad Dexter started the Jeep's engine, turned on its heater, and made a radio call to Wyatt.

"We're leaving, it's 0415."

Brad pulled away in the Jeep; Wyatt could hear the crunching snow beneath the tires and he saw the Jeep's lights sweep across the south lawn, reflecting light on the drifting snow outside the White House.

Anti-Vietnam war protestors remained camped in tents across the street from the White House in Lafayette Park. They had been camped there since Thanksgiving. The ACLU obtained permission through a legal petition from a judge, allowing the

U.S. Park Service to permit seventy-five protestors, who were mostly white young men, and some women and children, in Lafayette Park until March 1, 1968.

The protestors had camping equipment, heated tents, and fifty-five-gallon metal drums with fires for heat. People in Washington brought them food, water, blankets, unauthorized liquor, and probably marijuana. The U.S. Park Service had installed ten portable toilets in Lafayette Park; once a week the Washington, D.C. Department of Health and Public Safety checked the protestors' encampment for sanitation, and checked the children. The Washington Metropolitan Police and U.S. Park Service Police maintained twenty-four-hour surveillance on them for drugs or illegal weapons. The protestors were permitted to demonstrate from ten–three each day.

Many of the protestors had had previous encounters with police during anti-war protests in San Francisco and Chicago. Their anti-war protest signs were graphic, "Fuck LBJ and the U.S.A. in Vietnam"; "Go to Canada, Not Vietnam"; "Vietnam is LBJ's Killing Field"; and, "Hell, No, We Won't Go!"

Wyatt Wesley Erby was born in Galveston, Texas on March 10, 1933. He was the youngest son of three children of Lester and Annette Erby. Wyatt was given his nickname "Wyatt Earp" at an early age, partly because his father was a captain in the Galveston Police Department. Wyatt was an average student, but excelled in athletics, playing football, basketball, and baseball at Sam Houston High School in Galveston. He was selected as All-Texas High School football in 1950 in his senior year. At 6'1" and 175 pounds he "hit like a Mack truck when he tackled someone," said his high school football coach Damon Byers.

Wyatt chose to play football for the Longhorns at the University of Texas. He converted to a defensive back and played four years at Texas, making All Big Eight Conference 1954. He was graduated in June, 1954 with a bachelor of science degree in law enforcement and then he joined the U.S. Marine Corps to attend officer candidate school (OCS) at Parris Island, South Carolina. On November 9, 1954, he was commissioned as a Second Lieutenant.

Wyatt's first assignment in the Marines was at Headquarters Battalion, MCB, III Marine Expeditionary Force, Kaneohe Bay, Oahu, Hawaii, from 1954–1956. In November 1956, he was assigned to the Marine Corps security detail at the U.S. Embassy in Istanbul, Turkey. In October 1958, he received an Honorable Discharge from the U.S. Marine Corps and he returned to Galveston, married his college sweetheart Renee Ann Wagner; they had two daughters, Katy and Abigail, and now lived in Falls Church, Virginia.

Wyatt was hired by the Secret Service in November, 1958. His first assignment with the Secret Service was at the Seattle, Washington, field office doing advance security work to protect President Dwight D. Eisenhower, and investigating counterfeiting on the West Coast.

On August 2, 1962, Brian Parson, the Secret Service agent in charge of the Seattle field office, told Wyatt he had been selected for training on the Secret Service Presidential Protection detail for President John F. Kennedy. Wyatt was assigned to the Presidential Protection Detail on Air Force One, for communications, agent-coordination assignments, motorcade security, and reviewing background checks on local hoodlums from local police. In June 1963, he flew on Air Force One with President Kennedy to West Germany. He was on the Secret Service detail at the Kennedy Compound in Hyannis Port, Massachusetts, on three occasions. Wyatt had two cherished pictures taken with President Kennedy and on one picture, the president wrote, "To Wyatt Erby, *Semper Fi,* John F. Kennedy."

Wyatt heard the sound of the Jeep pull up, a few seconds later Brad opened the office door and a blast of cold arctic air blew in behind him.

He reported, "The snow is eleven inches deep and it is nineteen degrees."

Brad had a .16-gauge shotgun in his left hand, and five dead chickens with their feet tied in his right hand.

"Hungry?" asked Brad.

Wyatt looked at the chickens, "Where did you get those birds? I hope you didn't shoot them."

"No, sir," said Brad. "I found them hanging on the perimeter fence along Pennsylvania Avenue; someone's idea of a joke."

Wyatt said, "Take them home and cook them for your fiancée."

"No, thanks," said Brad. "I'll spoil a good meal."

Brad took the five chickens and deposited them into a large rubber container outside the office.

Wyatt reported, "I made the commo checks. The D.C. Metro police say roads have cinders and salt, no major problems. The Fairfax and Arlington County Sheriff's traffic units reported fourteen inches of snow and a four-hour delay into and out of the District. Andrew's Air Force base tower reported Air Force One is de-iced and all runways salted; visibility is 2,000 feet, and winds thirty to forty-five knots out of the Northeast with gusts fifty to sixty knots, emergency travel only. Seven U.S. Air Force jets are patrolling Washington skies."

At 0700, the day shift arrived at the Secret Service Command Center. Wyatt told the Day Watch Command, Bailey Milligan, "No problems last night. The president has a luncheon and strategy session in the Situation Room at 1300. All White House entrances are shoveled and salted."

"Thanks, Wyatt." The day shift went to work.

The White House switchboard operator called the Secret Service Command Center to inform them that the president's 12:00 noon meeting would start in five minutes in the oval office.

Stanford Wallace, Special Assistant to the President for Foreign Policy, admitted six U.S. senators on the Senate Banking and Finance Committee into the Oval Office. The Senators were a joint conference committee of Democrats and Republicans meeting with the president to discuss funding priorities for Fiscal Year 1969 starting October 1, 1968. The meeting started at 12:00 noon and was still in progress at 1:30 P.M. in the oval office.

President Lyndon B. Johnson stood up behind his mahogany desk, looked out the window at the snow on the White House lawn, and then turned to the senators seated in his office.

"I imagine a few folks around here would shit their pants if I told them I wanted to travel today," he said as he laughed. He looked at his vest watch and said, "It's time to adjourn the meeting. Gentlemen, I'm hungry and I'm thirty minutes late for a 1:00 o'clock working lunch; we'll adjourn for today.

"I'll have a conference call with the director of OMB, Secretary of Treasury, Chairman of the House Appropriations Committee and Secretary of Defense; we'll have another meeting in a week or two. In the meantime, Veet-nam is my top priority. The Goddamn Veet-nam War is eating up taxpayers' money, which I want used for the Great Societies in education, Medicare, Medicaid, the infrastructure and unemployment benefits. Veet-nam is costing me two billion dollars a year—it makes me sick."

U.S. Senator Jefferson Lee Madison, III, of Virginia said, "Mr. President, we understand your concern over the budget, and your concern over Vietnam; but, Sir, we must provide the necessary money to the Pentagon, General Westmoreland, and South Vietnam to meet their requirements for Vietnam. There are now 535,000 U.S. military personnel in South Vietnam; General Westmoreland is requesting an additional 206,700 ground combat forces. Mr. President, how many more U.S. troops will be needed, 100,000, 200,000?"

President Johnson looked at Senator Madison, "My God, Jefferson, how do we get the money to pay for the war, must we raise taxes or create a federal deficit leading to higher inflation? And what about the Great Society?

"We've told the American people a light is at the end of the tunnel in Veet-nam, and that the South Vietnamese will assume a greater proportion of fighting the war, and pacification is winning the hearts and the minds of the people. Now we've just seen the communist military Tet Offensive, and that throws a monkey wrench into everything. What a bitch of a war I inherited.

"I will not approve General Westmoreland's request for 206,700 more troops; we're no closer to winning the Goddamn war now then we were in 1965. It's demoralizing."

The president sat down at his desk and poured himself a glass of cold water. He took a swallow and patted his forehead with a handkerchief. He placed his head on the headrest of his leather chair and looked at the ceiling in the Oval Office.

"Our boys have been fighting those communist bastards since 1965; we have almost 30,000 dead, and why? We win battles, but we cannot win the war, why not? We kill the Goddamn

Viet Cong by the thousands, and they still come back for more each year.

"To invade or not to invade North Vietnam is the question, would an invasion bring Russia or China into the war for World War III?

"Those unpatriotic bastards in the media like Harry Smith at ABC, Chet Huntley and David Brinkley at NBC and my main pain in the ass at CBS, Walter Cronkite, berate me nightly. Those sons-of-bitches are killing me. I think they enjoy destroying me. The way they report the war makes me look like I'm a monster, not a president who is trying to end the war with honor.

"Now the media is asking how can we be winning the war if 84,000 communist troops attack across South Vietnam and get into the grounds of the U.S. Embassy in Saigon?

"The U.S. Military Command in Saigon reported seventy percent of South Veet-nam is under GVN control, yet a CBS news crew said, 'They could not drive safely up Highway One from Bien Hoa to Cam Rahn Bay, so how can the GVN be in control?' General Westmoreland tells me we've made significant military progress, and the ARVN are an improved combat force, but in the same breath he requests an additional 206,700 U.S. troops. Nothing makes any sense to me anymore about Veet-nam.

"The communists kill 300 American boys a week, yet I'm told by the U.S. Military Command in Saigon we're making genuine progress."

The president said, "Gentlemen, let's take a ten-minute break."

The president called the White House operator and said, "Locate Stanford Wallace and tell the luncheon guests I am running late." The president hung up the telephone and looked again at the snow outside his window.

"Gentlemen, Veet-nam is going from bad to worse; I'm going to make a decision about seeking re-election in November. I've got to get a handle on Veet-nam; my senior policy advisors and I are meeting this afternoon and tomorrow to achieve a consensus on the war." LBJ took a short telephone call from Ladybird.

"Where were we? Let me say this, we'll get our estimate for

Veet-nam costs to OMB as soon as I can get estimates from Defense and my Veet-nam ambassador. We'll meet next week."

Stanford Wallace received President Johnson's message and told the luncheon guests the president was running late.

Stanford Wallace was a career Foreign Service Officer. He had worked for the U.S. State Department and first met Lyndon B. Johnson (D–TX) as a senator in 1948 when hearings were held over the Berlin airlift to send West Berlin food and supplies. Stanford Wallace graduated from Georgetown University School of Foreign Service. Besides his native English, he spoke French and German fluently. He had served in diplomatic assignments to Paris, Vienna, Bonn, West Germany, Morocco, and Johannesburg, South Africa. President Johnson requested him to join his diplomatic staff at the White House as Counselor to the President. Stanford still had contacts with French and Russian diplomats. Stanford knew Monsieur Francois Jean Gille, who served in the French Embassy in Hanoi from 1947–1954, and he had known Bao Dai and Ngo Dinh Diem from his diplomatic assignment in Hanoi.

Stanford told President Johnson about a discussion he had with Monsieur Gille in 1965 before U.S. combat troops arrived in South Vietnam.

Gille had told him, "Don't make the same mistake as the French and underestimate the dignity, will, and determination of the Vietnamese people. They are an ancient civilization with a common language, culture, and history for 1,000 years. North Vietnam is under the communist leadership of Ho Chi Minh and the People's Army of Vietnam, and they are well-organized, well-trained, and well-led. Don't underestimate their ability to endure hardship."

Gille said, "Westerners do not understand the Oriental mind or their concept of fatalism. What they do and how they think will never make any sense to us. They do not think or act the way we act. We take action—they wait—we wait—they take action. The Oriental's sense of harmony and timing is extremely important; time is inconsequential. Unless the United States wins the war in a year, you will not prevail with North Vietnam. Time is on their side. The South Vietnamese are not like the North Vietnamese. The South Vietnamese peasants don't care about Saigon or the government; the generals act like squabbling children, what one has the other wants. Vietnam could turn into a mistake for the United States in South Vietnam like France; it is a losing cause."

The president knew there would be angst at the luncheon. He knew after five years he had tremendous legislative accomplishments such as passing the Civil Rights Act of 1964 and Great Society legislation, but his legacy could tarnish without success in Vietnam. Nothing was working on the military front in the war. His generals told him the only priority in 1965 was the war; Pacification would occur later. Three years later the war was a stalemate at best, there was the Tet Offensive, and the Pacification Program was a failure. President Johnson took a telephone call and he was visibly more agitated.

"I'll be there in ten Goddamn minutes; Sarah, tell Wallace to get'em a drink."

He hung up the telephone, stood, looked at the senators and said, "The Air Force has been bombing North Vietnam since 1965. We've bombed the piss out of the Ho Chi Minh Trail to stop communist infiltration into South Vietnam. I've been told North Vietnam uses 150,000 porters riding bicycles and carrying every conceivable piece of military equipment and food; like ants creeping down the Ho Chi Minh Trail, to support communist NVA combat divisions in South Vietnam. We have not been able to slow the infiltration; even with their heavy casualties we cannot achieve peace. What am I suppose to do, Senator? Surrender? Surrender like the French after 'Din Bin Phu' in 1954?"

"No way, Sir!"

"I will not be the first president in U.S. history to lose a war. It will be a cold day in hell before that ever happens to Lyndon Baines Johnson!" LBJ said sternly.

President Johnson sat down again in his leather chair behind his desk.

"Mr. President," said Forrest Parker, "may I speak?"

"Speak your mind, Forrest," said the president.

"Thank you, Sir," answered Senator Parker.

"Mr. President, the majority of Americans realize you are

trying to achieve a just and honorable peace in Vietnam. The problem now is the American public does not understand why the United States, as the world's strongest military power, with tremendous technology and firepower, cannot defeat a small, agrarian, and poor country like North Vietnam. We won World War II in four years against far greater enemy forces. Mr. President, the war in 1968 has come down to whether our American technology will prevail, or their will power. It appears human determination will prevail in the end.

"If South Vietnamese government rallied the people of South Vietnam to fight to save their country as the communists are fighting to defeat them, we would win the war in two years. The United States cannot fight a war that ought to be fought by Vietnamese boys. Ho Chi Minh and his National Liberation Front have strong control of the South Vietnamese countryside. The GVN, the U.S. military, and the Pacification Program have not broken that control, and the French could not break it either. Sir, the American people want a victory, or get out of South Vietnam, it's that simple.

"We should invade North Vietnam and destroy it, or drop two atomic bombs on Hanoi. We cannot win this war with their sanctuaries in Laos and Cambodia. The communists in South Vietnam are not the same as when we fought the Japanese in World War II. The Japanese fought with large conventional military forces, at set locations, which the U.S. did attack, or bomb, and we consistently defeated their army. We don't have that kind of situation in South Vietnam. Mr. President, we have three options in my opinion. Attack North Vietnam across the DMZ, destroy their sanctuaries in Laos and Cambodia, or bomb their infrastructure and ability to wage war. That is my opinion, Mr. President." Senator Parker folded his hands on the table.

Stanford Wallace knocked on the door of the Oval Office.

"Yes?" asked President Johnson.

"Sir, it's Stanford Wallace; it's now one-thirty, shall I postpone your luncheon?"

"No, I'll be there shortly," replied the president.

"Gentlemen, it was a good meeting, thank you for sharing

your thoughts," said the president. They shook hands and left the Oval Office.

The president and Stanford Wallace walked to the Executive Dining room. Two Secret Service agents addressed the president outside the dining room.

"Mr. President."

"Howell, how are y'all today?" asked the president.

"Fine, Sir."

"Jenkins, how are you?"

"Fine, Sir."

Stanford Wallace preceded the president into the dining room.

"Gentlemen, the President of the United States." Everyone stood up. President Johnson shook hands with his luncheon guests.

"Let's eat, I'm hungry," said President Johnson. "Who made it to the luncheon in this bad weather?" asked the president.

"Just as you instructed, Mr. President," said Stanford and he looked around the room. "Vice President, Hubert Humphrey, Secretary of State, Dean Rusk, Secretary of Defense, Clark Clifford, National Security Advisor, Walt Rostow, Ambassador Ellsworth Bunker, Chairman of Joint Chief of Staff, General Earle Wheeler, Director of Central Intelligence, Richard Helms and Military Aide-de-camp, Colonel White."

After finishing lunch, the president and his senior policy advisors adjourned into the White House Situation Room, which had secure communications, encryption machines to send classified messages, and secure telephone lines so the President could speak to any world leader or any U.S. military commander in the world. On the walls were world maps marking the locations of U.S. ships, U.S. Air Force aircraft, Navy nuclear submarines, attack submarines, aircraft carriers, and worldwide command centers at NORAD, NATO, PENTAGON, SOUTHCOM, CENTCOM, PACOM, and SHAFE. A red phone was conspicuous for the president to launch nuclear war. The room seemed warm to LBJ, he preferred it to be cooler. He asked Colonel White to turn down the heat.

The president addressed the group: "I called you here today

to discuss Veet-nam. This meeting will last as long as it takes to form a consensus on our position on the war to present to the government of North Veet-nam. I will not accept the proposition that we cannot win in Veet-nam.

"Prior to the North Vietnamese Tet, it looked as if our efforts in Veet-nam had begun to pay off. The Pacification Program was working to win the hearts and minds of the people. The CIA now tells me that the attack on the Marine Base at Khe Sahn was a diversion to get our attention focused on Khe Sahn, like Dien Bien Phu, as North Vietnamese infiltrated military personnel into South Vietnamese to execute the Tet attack."

The president was showing emotional stress on his face.

"Gentlemen, how could the North Vietnamese plan, organize and execute a sneak attack with 84,000 troops, into thirty provincial capitals, and attack the U.S. Embassy in Saigon and no one in South Veet-nam, the U.S. Army Intelligence, the CIA, or the U.S. Joint Staff have a clue about the attack? Jesus Christ Almighty, help me—I do not understand it at all! Where was our intelligence? Where was the Goddamn intelligence? The Tet attack will cause us to lose the war!

"We're supposed to be able to hear a fly fart with the sophisticated electronic intelligence, yet the Goddamn communists organize an attack like World War II and we don't get wind of anything. It is preposterous! If we tried to do the same thing, every Goddamn newspaper in this country would learn about our plan; it would be on CBS with Walter Cronkite the next night, yet the NVA get away with it without anyone in the world knowing about it. I'm now concerned we are on the verge of losing control of the whole kit and caboodle in Veet-nam. I've heard some of your convictions about the war before, and probably already know your positions, but I am determined to see the Veet-nam War brought to an honorable and successful conclusion. I remember that statement by Ho Chi Minh: 'You may kill ten of my soldiers, but as long as I kill one of your soldiers, I will accept that percentage, in the end, I will win the war and you will lose.'

"I won't accept that proposition. I have instructed our field commanders to observe ceasefires, truce periods, and ordered the bombing over Hanoi ceased as an incentive for North

Veet-nam to begin meaningful peace negotiations. What do I get in return? Nothing; they violate ceasefires and attack our troops, kill 2,000 of our boys and blame the GVN and the U.S. We need to kill more of those bastards and show Ho Chi Minh and Vo Nguyen Giap they will not win this war."

LBJ pounded his fist on the table and continued to address the meeting, "We are winning the war on the battlefield and losing the war at home. This is a fact! To North Veet-nam, casualties mean nothing. The Tet attack is a devastating blow to the war and the notion we were winning the war and that the Pacification Program was working. Everything is in disarray. Information from the Headquarters, U.S. Military Command in Saigon, and the U.S. Embassy about the impact of the communists' Tet Lunar Offensive is being evaluated. It was pointed out that near Ben Tre, intelligence reports indicated the Viet Cong were moving into staging areas, and General Weyand and John Paul Vahn pulled back fourteen U.S. infantry battalions to protect Long Binh. The Viet Cong were routed, which probably prevented Saigon from falling. Ho Chi Minh has written and told me no meaningful peace negotiations will take place until all U.S. troops are withdrawn from Veet-namese soil. . . . Therefore, how do we withdraw all U.S. forces and still not have South Veet-nam fall to communism?

"I've tried to do the right thing since 1965. McNamara told me to follow a policy of graduated response so as not to send the wrong signal to Russia or China by threatening their own national security over the Veet-nam War. My concern over Russia or Communist China coming into the war has mitigated my decisions over the war. Westmoreland complains he doesn't have sufficient troops to defend Veet-nam from communist infiltration and also wage offensive operations against the enemy for decisive results.

"To invade or not to invade North Veet-nam remains a dilemma. The Pentagon says we must destroy North Veet-nam's ability to wage war and destroy their infrastructure to make war. A joint invasion of North Veet-nam with South Veet-nam and U.S. air support could be justified after the Tet invasion. President Thieu tells me, to invade North Veet-nam and succeed requires one million South Veet-namese and U.S. troops. South Veet-nam does not have the manpower, military strength or equipment with armor, artillery and airpower to invade North Veet-nam alone.

"America's T.V. networks report that North Veet-nam's leaders see our anti-war protests and they are convinced that time is on their side in the war . . . To win the war. Then I'm questioned about a credibility gap. There is no credibility gap. The military press in Saigon reports the war through the information they receive. I am not running a cover-up from the White House, distorting information about our progress in the war. The American public is entitled to know everything about the war, but I'm not going to tell North Veet-nam, Russia, and China we're losing the war and we'll surrender. Gentleman, take a twenty-minute break," said the president; his face showed frustration and drops of perspiration were on his forehead.

After the break, the president returned to the Situation Room and resumed the meeting. "Let's start with the intelligence estimate from Director of Central Intelligence, Richard Helms. What have you got, Richard?" asked the president.

Richard replied, "Mr. President, the current situation is tenuous. Strong pockets of resistance continue in Hué, Cholon, My Tho, and Pleiku. Saigon is under ARVN and U.S. control; the Tet Offensive now casts negative doubts about the Pacification Program, the Strategic Hamlet Program, and GVN control of the countryside. The latest casualties are fifty thousand communists killed, eight thousand communists captured, four thousand ARVN killed and two thousand U.S. troops killed. Communist military strength is three hundred thousand with some eighty-five thousand communist political infrastructures. Intelligence reports indicate a possible mini-Tet attack in May."

President Johnson asked, "Dick, why can't we get timely intelligence on the Veet-Cong?"

"Mr. President," he replied, "The enemy is extremely secretive, very efficient and doesn't use open communications. They employ couriers to deliver instructions planned in great detail, and when a command is given, the commander does not know the mission until he opens a sealed package with the mission.

Only the very top echelon in North Vietnam knows the big picture. We estimate the communists have 125,000 front-line combat troops against 125,000 U.S. front-line combat troops. It is parity at best. The North Vietnamese Army and the Vietcong are today a more aggressive and stronger enemy than what we faced in 1965. Russian and Chinese military aid has virtually upgraded every aspect of their military posture and air defenses of Hanoi and North Vietnam. North Vietnam and Hanoi now deploy heavy air defenses that have SA-7 surface-to-air heat-seeking missiles to shoot down our F-100, F-105, and Navy F-4 attack aircraft comprising some 1,000 anti-aircraft guns protecting Hanoi. Russia and China have given North Vietnam new T-60 Russian tanks, armored personnel carriers, rocket-propelled grenades, communications equipment, .50-caliber machine guns, .82-mm mortars, thousands of AK-47's, land mines, food, medical supplies, uniforms, and boots. They are as well armed as American soldiers and now pose a formidable enemy for U.S. forces.

"We believe North Vietnam wants to cut South Vietnam in half across the Central Highlands to end the war on their terms. Recent intelligence reveals they are preparing to use ten thousand troops to attack Can Tho, Chau Duc, Vi Thanh, and Rach Gia. At the same time, twenty thousand communist soldiers continue to infiltrate a month down the Ho Chi Minh Trail into South Vietnam as replacements for their decimated battalions. They are able to maintain combat effectiveness and their casualties have not deterred them."

"Thank you, Dick," said the president.

"Hubert," the president said to Vice President Humphrey.

"Mr. President. As you are aware, I have been a staunch supporter of your policies on the Vietnam War. I have spoken publicly many times to support our troops in Vietnam. After three years the war remains unabated, or as many in Washington are now calling the war a quagmire. It is apparent from talking to my former colleagues from both sides of the aisle that we must make an informed but conclusive decision on how to proceed in the war following the communists' recent Tet offensive.

"South Vietnam did not become a political entity until 1954

after the Geneva Conference creating the country. Their governmental apparatus is rife with instability. Their military has a fragile institutional base with some good commanders, but for the most part, weaknesses in the junior officers' and non-commissioned officers' ranks. They have a draft to obtain manpower but exclude sons of either the rich or influential who pay someone else to take their sons' place in the ARVN. The French colonialism hindered the development of their military so the French could maintain control.

"Now, three years after we sent U.S. combat troops to help defend South Vietnam, we've learned firsthand not only the deficiencies in their military, but also that the ARVN has no mature logistical support system, antiquated weapons, small air force and a few ships in their navy.

"Without U.S. support, South Vietnam would have fallen to North Vietnam by 1967. In spite of our troop buildup, huge logistical base, and training their soldiers, these same deficiencies remain. Their military leadership is not aggressive, won't fight at night, and has an enclave mentality. From the U.S. intelligence reports I've read they are politically and militarily corrupt.

"The question remains the same; stay another year, take more U.S. casualties, in hopes that eventually the GVN will be more politically stable and the ARVN can get strong enough to fight their own war. Mr. President, I've concluded it is now wishful thinking that either of these events will occur soon, or in seven to ten more years. The communists send 20,000 fresh troops a month into South Vietnam, which is now stretching U.S. forces to the limit to defend our numerous military bases, and yet conduct continuous offensive operations.

"Sir, the time has come to cut our losses, and to announce a gradual withdrawal of U.S. troops in early 1969. The more time we waste will only increase U.S. casualties and divide the country over the war. Thank you, Mr. President."

"Thank you, Hubert," responded the president.

The persons in the Situation Room sat in silence.

President Johnson spoke: "That was an excellent executive summary of our current position in Vietnam. I've observed that even as our military presence grows in the war, very little if anything has changed in the past three years.

"We get glowing reports from Saigon on how much progress is being made in improving the fighting capacity of the ARVN, RF/PF, Pacification, winning the hearts and minds of the people, but pressed to show where really substantive improvements have been made, making a difference in the lives of the people in the countryside, everything is modified by a caveat, but it is not certain the GVN and ARVN can continue to provide the security to turn the people in the countryside against the Veetcong once U.S. forces are withdrawn from South Veet-nam. In reality, we probably need ten more years, which we do not have, to get the job done."

President Johnson looked at the twenty-four-hour military clock, which read 1725. "Gentlemen," said the president. "It's late, meeting adjourned. It will be tough driving home in this snow tonight, be careful out there. We'll reconvene tomorrow morning at nine A.M. sharp. Tomorrow each one of you will have as much time as you need to convince me to stay with the war and send General Westmoreland another 206,750 more soldiers or to announce in March that I will not seek another term as president; let the next administration figure how to end the war with honor. We will adjourn with a consensus at five P.M. Good day, gentlemen."

The next morning, the meeting resumed in the White House.

"Good morning," said President Johnson. "Let's get started. I asked Lieutenant General Hayden to join us this morning and give us an estimate of the military situation in Veet-nam, communist capabilities, and probable courses of action against the disposition of American and other allies of the South Veet-namese, South Korea, the Philippines and Australia. General Wheeler, Secretary of State Rusk, Ambassador Bunker, and Secretary of Defense Clifford, will follow Lieutenant General Hayden. General Hayden."

"Mr. President, distinguished guests. I am Lieutenant General Robert Hayden, Director of Operations, JCS Staff in the Pentagon. This briefing is top secret, no Foreign Intelligence dissemination, which means it was taken from sensitive communications interception, secret U.S. sources and debriefings of communist prisoners of war."

Lieutenant General Hayden began with classified military maps containing the locations of U.S. and allied military forces in South Vietnam; U.S. Naval warships; USAF tactical fighter and B-52 bomber aircraft. He showed squadrons' top-secret charts with maps of North Vietnam's air defense network, identified strategic targets in the six bombing grids over North Vietnam, military installations, major industrial facilities, and communist infiltration routes down the Ho Chi Minh trail into South Vietnam. He also showed classified maps of the communist political boundaries in South Vietnam, which were different from the political and provincial structure of South Vietnam. He presented overlays on the map of suspected locations of the Committee on South Vietnam (COSVN), which was the communist political cadre with authority from the People's Revolutionary Party (PRP) in North Vietnam to direct the war in South Vietnam.

He showed classified maps indicating locations of NVA main force regiments and disposition of ARVN, airborne, ranger, and marine battalions protecting Saigon, some weaker ARVN units were shown in locations closer to U.S. Army combat units. ARVN Twenty-first Infantry Division and ARVN Ninth Infantry Division are in U.S. Fourth Corps, in the proximity of the U.S. Ninth Infantry Division at Dong Tam. Therefore, it appeared one strategy of the South Vietnamese Joint Staff was to use stronger U.S. military forces to shield the ARVN and to fight the war with superior U.S. firepower. ARVN Generals did not fight, claiming the enemy was too strong, and held back in conducting offensive operations so as to not incur heavy casualties which could get them removed from command. Lieutenant General Hayden said the NVA/VC have the following capabilities:

1. To attack U.S. military units at will.
2. Communist military forces continue receiving military arms and equipment from Russia and Communist China.
3. NVA regiments attack and maul ARVN battalions.

4. Viet Cong attack U.S. military to "Pick them off, one by one" to support their dual strategy in the war.
5. NVA now have Soviet anti-tank weapons, bazookas and .50-caliber machine guns to shoot down U.S. helicopters.
6. The communist soldiers use "hugging techniques" to counter U.S. artillery fire and air strikes by moving their troops close to U.S. forces to make the U.S. "fire bullets over buddies."
7. Vietcong receive support from people living in the countryside with food, hiding places, medical care, re-supply and intelligence on U.S. forces.
8. Information received from interrogations of captured NVA said, Ho Chi Minh told their soldiers, before going south for the Great Tet Uprising that, "We see the burning of American cities and how people in America protest against the war in Vietnam. It is now only a matter of time before the Americans quit and leave Vietnam and we will win the war against foreign imperialism. No sacrifice we now make is too great at this critical time in our national history to once and for all drive all foreigners from Vietnamese soil, time is on our side—we will prevail in this war!"

A lengthy discussion followed Lt. General Hayden's briefing. President Johnson asked questions among his advisors; would a ground attack against North Vietnam after heavy strategic bombing attacks over North Vietnam, and this military escalation bring China or Russia into the war as an ally of North Vietnam? Could the U.S./South Vietnam conduct a joint attack with 200,000 troops and open a second front of the war north of the DMZ? Should the President attempt to obtain approval from Congress for U.S./ARVN to attack Cambodia and Laos and destroy Communists' sanctuaries in both countries?

The President said, "General Hayden, summarize the main points from your briefing."

The President picked up a telephone and said, "Mrs. Wilson,

please come into the Situation Room to take classified notes for me."

Mrs. Wilson knocked on the door. Colonel White showed her to a vacant seat next to President Johnson.

"Mr. President, to summarize, Sir, this is our assessment of strategic airpower in the war: Bombing damage assessments done in the six grids over North Vietnam called Rolling Thunder, from 1965 to 1968, primarily done below the 18th Parallel, have not diminished North Vietnam's ability to wage war. It is air power failure."

President Johnson removed his glasses, lay them on the table, drank a glass of cold water; he said, "Continue"; the president began to rub his eyes.

Lt. General Hayden continued. "Our satellite photographic reconnaissance shows clearly that targets such as railroad lines, industrial sites, bridges, and dams that were bombed have been quickly repaired."

The room sat in silence.

"There have been 141 bombing raids above the DMZ, a loss of 300 aircraft and 1,000 crews. The Rolling Thunder air attacks have lost 900 aircraft and 2,000 crews. North Vietnam has now constructed a sophisticated air-defense network of SA-2 surface-to-air missile sites and their SA-7 radar SAM sites. They have installed 1,000 anti-aircraft batteries around Hanoi. Their air defenses constitute serious challenges to bombing except conducting high-altitude bombing raids using B-52 aircraft. Russia and China continue to bring military support to North Vietnam. Their ships are unloaded at Haiphong Harbor against which we have done only limited bombing to avoid hitting a Russian ship in an act of war. North Vietnam continues to receive huge quantities of modern military equipment from Russia and China such as AK-47 assault rifles, ammunition, .30 caliber machine guns, tactical radios, RPG rockets, land mines, military clothing, and medical supplies. That concludes my briefing, Sir."

"Thank you, General Hayden," said LBJ. "Gentlemen, take a fifteen-minute break."

LBJ left the meeting and he returned saying, "The weather

is getting worse, we'll conclude by 5:00. You'll have reservations and cars to take you to the Hilton."

"General Wheeler, please begin your briefing."

General Earle Wheeler was in his second term as Chairman of the Joint Chiefs of Staff in the Pentagon.

"Mr. President, distinguished guests, I want to present the current U.S. strategy in Vietnam, since General Hayden gave you the current disposition of friendly forces and our current..." On a table next to the president was a white light that began to blink Flash level two; Flash level two was an international incident or war.

President Johnson picked up the telephone, "This is the president." The room sat in silence.

A voice on the telephone line said, "Mr. President, this is Major General Benson calling to speak to the secretary of defense. Your White House operator said he was in a meeting in the Situation Room. Mr. President, please excuse my intrusion, but a few minutes ago at 1435 Zulu, 2135 European time, the Pentagon Operations Center received a top secret-TWX-message from General Kane at NATO Headquarters."

"General, give me the details straight," said President Johnson.

"Sir, at 2125 hours, eight February sixty-eight a pilot named Major Butler reported on the aircraft emergency radio channel that he was being forced to land a C-130 Cargo aircraft by two Soviet MIG-25 near Leipzig, East Germany."

"What the hell? Why?" asked the president.

Major Butler said, "The Russian MIG's fired air-to-air sidewinder missiles across the bow of the C-130 and gave him the international emergency signal to land immediately or they would shoot down the aircraft. Major Butler was escorted to the air base near Leipzig. He and the co-pilot were told upon arrival that the C-130 was flying outside the air corridor and its altitude was below the minimum nine thousand feet, and it was a CIA spy plane photographing East Germany's military installations as an act of war."

"Oh shit," said the president. "Where is the C-130 now?"

Major General Benson responded, "According to the Ops

Center at Wiesbaden, the C-130's flight originated at ROTA, Spain, stopped at Wiesbaden picking up new communications equipment, spare parts, and new radar for delivery into West Berlin. That is all I know, Sir."

"Nothing is classified on that C-130, is it, General Benson?" asked the president.

"No, Sir."

President Johnson cupped the phone, "Clark, take this call."

"Yes, Sir, Mr. President." The secretary of defense took the telephone from the president and General Benson restated the incident to him.

Secretary of Defense asked, "What is the current NATO Threat-Con level?"

General Benson said, "Level two."

"My God," said Secretary Clifford, "Level two?"

"Flash Level one is war, get it down to Level three!" said the president.

"Yes, Sir," said Secretary Clifford.

"Major General Benson, the president has ordered NATO Commander General Kane to lower the THREAT CON to Flash Level three. Do you read me?" asked Secretary Clifford.

"Yes, Sir," said General Benson.

"General Benson, send a TWX message to NATO to General Kane, instruct him to contact General Volokoff in Moscow for an explanation of the incident. Tell General Volokoff that this is serious, and do not allow the East Germans to enter the C-130. Tell him NATO is on War Level three. I will be in my office in two hours. Do not release any details to the press."

"Yes, Sir."

Secretary Clifford asked President Johnson if he wanted to provide further guidance. "Tell Ambassador Dohrr in Bonn to make a diplomatic protest to Moscow, and I shall call Secretary Brezhnev for an explanation about the incident, and not to harm or detain the crew or NATO will take retaliatory measures. I certainly hope this is not another Russian plan to harass NATO. I hope it's only a stunt," said the president. "What does NATO want me to do?"

"Nothing right now, Mr. President. NATO has responded

with ten U.S. fighter aircraft scrambled over West Berlin and NATO is now on a Level three alert."

"My God," said President Johnson, "level one is all-out war."

"Level three will get their attention," said Secretary Clifford. "I instructed Major General Benson to get a full report to me, which I will review as soon as this meeting is over. In the meantime, Ambassador Dohrr in Bonn is making a diplomatic protest to President Heinze of East Germany regarding the incident, and informing him not to seize the C-130 or detain the air crew or NATO will detain any Russian military aircraft in the West German Corridor."

"My God," said the president. "Here we are talking and we get an incident involving NATO and the WARSAW Pact near the brink of war! All right, Clark, tell the Pentagon when they send a message to NATO that I will not comment publicly on this incident to make Americans more hostile to the Veet-nam War, and I consider this to be harassment by Russia against NATO. The East Germans must release the C-130 and the crew immediately. Tell those Goddamn Russians that if this incident is an act of war against the United States, NATO will respond in kind."

"Yes, Sir," said Secretary Clifford.

"All right, gentlemen, it's just another day here on the farm," the president jokingly commented to the group. "Please continue, General Wheeler."

"Thank you, Mr. President."

General Wheeler was a West Point graduate with a thirty-six year military career and in his second two-year term as Chairman of the Joint Chiefs of Staff. It was well known that the U.S. military in Saigon/Pentagon did not like how Secretary of Defense Robert McNamara used systems analysis and numbers to measure progress in the Vietnam War. The numbers he wanted on paper could not win the war. General Wheeler worked to smooth over the numerous dissenting opinions in the Pentagon about Vietnam, and many unqualified civilians making military decisions about the war without having sufficient knowledge of military doctrine. A major complaint from the military was the constant number of ceasefires during peace negotiations and on Vietnamese holidays, which North Vietnam did not honor. Instead, they used the ceasefires to improve their military positions on the battlefield and improve the opportunity for future attacks on U.S. forces.

"Mr. President," said General Wheeler, "I want to re-state the strategy in U.S. military operations in Vietnam remains on three tasks. One is to force Hanoi to cease and desist in the South; two is defeating the Viet Cong in the South; three is deterring China from intervening with a graduated response. We have not attacked the enemy's homeland in North Vietnam except to do bombing of selected targets below the twentieth parallel and then later below the eighteenth parallel over North Vietnam. We have not been permitted to invade and destroy the communists' base camps and sanctuaries in Laos and Cambodia or attack across the DMZ and to open up a second front against North Vietnam across the DMZ.

"Therefore, we are fighting a defensive war to stop communist infiltration into South Vietnam. In 1965, General Westmoreland stated he did not want a defensive posture in the war specifically. He said 'there will not be a static defense posture, no defensive roles, and no enclave strategy.' We now find U.S. forces fighting in the position General Westmoreland did not want to employ. The Joint Chiefs of Staff control him, and the layers of command from Saigon through Camp Smith, Hawaii, to the JCS are slow, cumbersome, and convoluted for quick reaction to either targets of opportunity or to act upon fresh intellegience against the enemy. For example, all bombing raids over North Vietnam must be examined, evaluated and receive approval from the Pentagon, which wastes precious time. We have worked with the South Vietnamese Joint General Staff, President Thieu, and MACV to execute the following: One, to defeat any enemy offensive; Two, provide security of the GVN in Saigon and provincial capitals; Three, restore security to cities and towns.

"General Westmoreland wants 206,750 more U.S. soldiers for an end strength of 731,750 by the end of calendar year 1968. We continue to use air mobility with helicopters to find the enemy, carry U.S. and South Vietnamese troops into battle, gunship support, position artillery, and to supply our troops in remote locations to stop the enemy. To stop enemy infiltration we have done carpet-bombing of enemy base camps, and bombed NVA troop concentrations and supply lines along the Ho Chi Minh Trail. The current search-and-destroy operations began in the belief that combat in Vietnam had moved from the insurgency/guerilla warfare to large-unit operations. Attrition has not led to the end of the conflict.

"We know from the battle at Ia Drang Valley from November fourteenth to November seventeenth, 1965, that U.S. soldiers can defeat the enemy. Four hundred fifty soldiers from the First Battalion of the Seventh U.S. Calvary in the First Air Calvary Division defeated a superior force of three NVA regiments with a force of two thousand North Vietnamese, in which one thousand NVA were killed, and we lost three hundred fine American soldiers. We can defeat the enemy, but political restrictions on what we need to do to win the war prevent the U.S. military from achieving victory." Some of the people at the table reacted to General Wheeler's comments about "political control" of the military affecting the war.

"General Wheeler, speak your mind—this is not the time to be quiet or stifle your opinion on how I direct the war as commander-in-chief," said LBJ. "We now know General Vo Nguyen Giap who commands North Vietnam has said, 'His strategy is a peoples' war.' "

General Wheeler continued the briefing, "Regular combat operations continue by the U.S. First Air Calvary, Fourth Infantry Division, Twenty-fifth Infantry Division, Eleventh Armored Calvary Regiment, 196th Infantry Brigade and the 173rd Airborne Brigade. In War Zone C and D the ARVN Fifth Division found enemy-concealed facilities and command posts, ammunition, supply dumps, hospitals, some connected by tunnels and possibly the COSVN Headquarters some sixty miles Northwest of Saigon. U.S. troops found the same thing in War Zone D located in heavy jungle and rainforest and elephant grass between Ben Cat and Chon Thanh near the Cambodia border.

"Now, about intelligence. We employ interrogations of NVA and Viet Cong prisoners of war, interrogated Chieu Hois, deserters, run combat patrols, use aerial surveillance, Long Range Reconnaissance Patrols (LRRPS), listening devices along infiltration trails, and intelligence from USARV. But the NVA attack the U.S. at the time and place of their choosing in many instances, and our intelligence is stale. The NVA and Viet Cong have the support of the South Vietnamese in the countryside to gain intelligence, feed them, hide them, and set up booby traps, ambushes, and punji pits to maim or kill U.S. soldiers. The ARVN are not aggressive. The South Vietnamese Joint Staff is content to let the U.S. fight the war. John Paul Vann, who fought as a U.S. Army officer and who is now a high-ranking member of the U.S. Pacification Program, told the U.S. Military Command in Saigon that, "If the Goddamn Vietnamese Army would fight we could win the war, so we'll just have to teach them how to fight."

"May I have a few more minutes, Mr. President?" asked General Wheeler.

"General, take all the time you need."

"Thank you, Sir. To summarize, Mr. President . . . The Vietnamese have been fighting since 1941 when the Japanese Imperial Army occupied Vietnam—that is a total of twenty-seven years from the Japanese, the French and now Americans. In Vietnamese families, three generations of men are dead. Some Vietnamese units fight with great valor and distinction, but for the most part, their military leadership is corrupt and incompetent.

"America has the technology to fight and win the war, strong and courageous soldiers, but the war has lost its meaning to the American people and it has become a nightmare of protests. Mr. President, the U.S. needs to tell chairman Mao and the Chinese communists not to intervene in Vietnam or the U.S. will block every opportunity for industrial and technological assistance China may hope to receive from the West in the future. Besides, I do not think China would intervene for North Vietnam since the Vietnamese dispelled the Chinese in the year twelve hundred A.D. after a hundred years of war. The Vietnamese hate the Chinese. They do not want China back in their country; it took a hundred years to drive them out the first time."

President Johnson looked at his vest watch; it was 11:45 A.M. "Let's break until 1:00 P.M. Secretary Rusk, Secretary Clifford and Ambassador Bunker, please join me for lunch," said the president.

The meeting reconvened at 1:00 P.M.

President Johnson thanked General Hayden and General Wheeler for their briefings. The president said he talked to Secretary Rusk, Ambassador Bunker, and Secretary of Defense Clifford about the Pacification Program. He said he recalled a comment President Kennedy made after the Bay of Pigs debacle in May 1961, "That to reverse Nikita Khrushchev's assessment of him as weak, he had to find somewhere to show U.S. resolve: The only place we can do that is in Veet-nam, we have to send more people there."

"President Kennedy's viewpoint has been a leading viewpoint for me and this administration on where to stop the expansion of communism, which I chose to do in Veet-nam in 1965. I continue to believe I made the right decision in 1965 to send U.S. military forces to Veet-nam. I believe then, and still believe now, that the United States must contest any expansion of communism if it threatens U.S. national security interests. If South Veet-nam falls to communism there may not be an immediate domino reaction, but South Veet-nam will become the catalyst to begin instability and military attacks against Laos, Cambodia, and, eventually, against Thailand. When Thailand is threatened the United States will defend Thailand to protect our national security interests for stability in Southeast Asia."

The president paused. "I have concerns to share with this group today. I am greatly perplexed and just plain Goddamn angry at our intelligence failures in Veet-nam. I'm spending $100 million a year on intelligence. I get better information on Veet-nam from reading the *Washington Post, Time,* or *Newsweek.* It has become my belief that the failures to get timely intelligence for commanders in the field may cost us victory in the war.

"How could 84,000 communist soldiers make a sneak attack across South Veet-nam without any CIA and military intelligence agencies and their vast array of intelligence collection apparatus not get one speck of information about the Tet offensive last January? Not a clue, do you hear me?

"I will now be personally getting involved with the CIA, U.S.

military intelligence in all services, our State Department, Agency for International Development and meet with President Thieu to 'fix' this miserable goddamn mess that is hurting us in Veet-nam.

"Let's continue. Secretary Clifford, continue your briefing."

"Thank you, Mr. President. I too share your concerns about the massive intelligence failures in Vietnam. I will do my best to fix the problem at the Pentagon and in Saigon with General Westmoreland in ten days from today when I visit Saigon, the J-2 Major General McChristian, and talk to the CIA Saigon Station chief in person. I will get to the bottom of our intelligence failures in this war. You have my word."

"Since being appointed Secretary of Defense in January of this year, I have been working fourteen hours a day, at age seventy-one, to get a handle on Vietnam. I'm a lawyer, not a general. I have a penchant for evidence. Over the past six weeks I've received eleven briefings on Vietnam at the Pentagon, visited General Westmoreland in Saigon, talked with our allies, read over 500 pages of classified information on Vietnam back to 1962.

"I wanted to have myself as knowledgeable as possible on Vietnam as I would to prepare a court trial.

"I've examined opposing positions about the war after talking to former Secretary of Defense McNamara, Ambassador Lodge, General Taylor, President Thieu, and President Johnson to make sure I would be technically prepared about what I report to this group, Mr. President.

"Mr. President, I recommend today that in the very near future you make a speech from the Oval Office to inform the American people and the world an immediate timetable to begin an orderly withdrawal of U.S. military forces from Vietnam."

Everyone sat in stunned silence upon hearing Secretary Clifford's remark.

President Johnson looked at Secretary Clifford. "Mr. Secretary, did you have a drink at lunch today?"

Light laughter followed the president's remark.

"No, Sir, Mr. President. I've done my homework on Vietnam. I am announcing my position on the war.

"Mr. President, after my doing two months to evaluate the

information provided to me by the generals, talking to political leadership on the hill, getting briefing by General Westmoreland in Saigon, and our own talks, the U.S. military has never presented you with a suitable military strategy to win the war.

"In 1965, Pacification was deemed to be irrelevant and could wait until the enemy was defeated.

"An attrition strategy was employed to apply the Americans' superior firepower, mobility, search-and-destroy operations with a body count to convince North Vietnam's leadership that their casualties would be too great and they would realize they could not win the war fighting the United States. After three years of attrition strategy, we are no closer to winning the war or to having North Vietnam surrender than we were in 1965. It was a serious strategic mistake, in my opinion, to follow Secretary McNamara's policy of graduated response for U.S. military forces into the war. This approach was viewed by North Vietnam, China, and Russia to indicate American weakness or uncertainty about entering into a ground war in Vietnam.

"We never employed an offensive strategy of attacking with numerically superior military force to defeat the enemy. If there was a concern of China or Russia coming into the war due to our threatening their own national security, we had no business going into Vietnam in the first place.

"The opportunity was lost to attack and destroy North Vietnam's infrastructure to wage war. We permitted the enemy too much time to react to our strategy and tactics. In retrospect, I fail to see how the strategy using graduated response to build up our military forces could have prevailed in the war to defeat the communists. We allowed parity to exist the first three years from 1965 to 1968.

"Beginning in 1967, we knew from captured enemy soldiers, North Vietnam began to infiltrate 20,000 new soldiers a month out of North Vietnam down the Ho Chi Minh Trail to fight as combat replacements or to form new NVA battalions. In 1967, we had about 350,000 U.S. military in Vietnam. Out of this force, about 125,000 were frontline U.S. combat soldiers. In seven short months the enemy had infiltrated another 140,000 fresh NVA combat soldiers to oppose our rotating combat base. It is no wonder that the enemy continues to fight with their casualties. U.S. forces were stretched too thin, with some guarding our huge permanent base camps and installations, and the remainder were the combat force facing a relentless enemy. I hear over and over, 'We win victories but cannot hold ground; after we leave, the enemy came right back.' It is a dog chasing its tail—doing combat search-and-destroy operations one day, and returning a month later to do it over again. Mr. President, we never had enough ground combat forces to get the job done!"

He continued, "Mr. President, I have yet to find any generals who approved deploying armor and mechanized infantry regiments to Vietnam given the tactics of the enemy, a six-month monsoon season of swollen impassable rivers, and a thick, triple-layer canopy jungle as terrain. It's incredulous!

"It seems to me such a decision was incompetent, to send U.S. forces organized, equipped, and trained to fight a land war on the rolling hills of Eastern Europe against Soviet armor divisions intact to Vietnam!

"I am a lawyer, not a general. Even I can see that our strategy is not working in this war. Our field and combat operations are too slow. The enemy chooses their terrain, time, and duration of engagements against our military operations in the rice paddies and jungle.

"Don't misunderstand what I'm saying; the concept of air mobility utilizing helicopters to take the fight to the enemy has proven to be highly successful. Our soldiers have never lost a battle and have fought gallantly, bravely and have severely hurt the enemy. The problem today, Mr. President, is whether we escalate the war and destroy the enemy's infrastructure in North Vietnam, destroy their sanctuaries in Laos and Cambodia and add 200,000 U.S. Special Forces, Navy Seals, and Marines to track the enemy day and night, call to do bombing and artillery and destroy them like rats in a barrel of water; we will convince once and for all we cannot tolerate their heinous crimes and show them they will not win this war!"

The table, except the President, stood and applauded to hear what Secretary Clifford told the President. He needed to be told but the generals would not tell him about Vietnam.

He continued, "Mr. President, who in your administration applied the information available on the enemy to formulate a response to their tactics?

"In August, 1967 the CIA and U.S. military in the Pentagon agreed that the enemy strength in South Vietnam was 340,000 soldiers. Previous estimates had been about 200,000 to 600,000. At least there was an agreement, but who neglected to add that by 1967, North Vietnam had begun infiltrating 20,000 soldiers a month to fight in the war? This is not a hypothetical number. Out of the communists' 340,000, some 85,000 are political cadre and infrastructure. They have political control from Hanoi to direct VC military units. Add a 240,000 infiltrated a year to the 255,000; the communists' military combat strength is 495,000 soldiers to defeat. Subtracting 40% casualties in a year still leaves 297,000, and add 240,000 it becomes 537,000 troops. This is why we cannot win this war! The air power is a failure, attrition is a failure, and North Vietnam has no reason to think they cannot win the war."

President Johnson looked weary and very tired.

"Let me close, Mr. President. I have talked with our top generals and asked them, 'How long will the war last under the current conditions?' No one knows!

"I asked the generals if our current military strategy will convince North Vietnam to seek peace—the answer is NO!

"Mr. President, as your Secretary of Defense, it is my duty to tell you today the Vietnam War cannot be won!"

On March 31, 1968, President Lyndon B. Johnson made a televised address to the nation from the Oval Office. He announced that he would neither seek re-election nor a draft movement to be re-elected for president in the presidential election on November 5, 1968.

The Republican nominee, Richard M. Nixon, won the presidency campaign claiming he had a "secret plan" to end the Vietnam War. The "secret plan" was called Vietnamization which was a word coined by Secretary of Defense Melvin Laird, turning the war fighting over to the South Vietnamese and beginning a gradual American withdrawal from Vietnam beginning in June 1969.

5

On February tenth, 1968, it was late afternoon and an unusually warm day in Tucson for the time of year. Arthur Edward Norris and his wife, Janet, their children Sarah, eight, Arthur Jr., seven, and Jennifer, five, and a new Labrador retriever puppy, "Tyler" had recently moved into a new home at 6280 Broken Arrow Drive in Tucson. The home was north of Gates Pass Road in West Tucson, and from the front yard, they had a view of Mount Lemmon.

On February twenty-fourth Arthur would leave Tucson for a two-year assignment with the CIA in South Vietnam. Arthur now spoke English, Spanish, Russian, and decent Vietnamese from attending a twenty-six-week Vietnamese language school at the Defense Language Institute in Monterey, California. In August, he and his family had returned to the United States after living in Munich, West Germany, seven years. Arthur had been a CIA Operative for clandestine intelligence operations against the Soviet Union and the Warsaw Military Pact. It had been a demanding and productive assignment for him so far in his eleven years of employment with the agency. During his assignment, he used his Russian language training to record radio broadcasts into Eastern Europe on Radio Free Europe and Radio Liberty from Munich. He was assigned on temporary duty in West Berlin and had monitored Russian radio broadcasts during the construction of the Berlin Wall in August, 1961.

In September 1962, he went on a temporary duty undercover assignment to Nassau, Bahamas, to monitor Russian naval radio traffic during the Cuban Missile Crisis in September and October of 1962. Arthur had been an Army Field Artillery Officer, and due to his U.S. Army experience, he became a CIA Specialist to evaluate Soviet rocket and artillery forces. He compiled a database of information on Soviet rocket forces, missiles, and the suspected locations of missile sites, which were targeted on NATO and Western Europe. He also established a Soviet rocket and artillery order of battle to evaluate the Soviets' intercontinental ballistic missile capabilities space program and satellites. He concluded from his analysis that the Soviets did not possess rocket boosters strong enough to lift intercontinental missiles with the range to strike the United States during the Cuban Missile Crisis. He concluded that Premier Khrushchev's threat to install missiles in Cuba was to intimidate President Kennedy.

Arthur's analysis had been written in a CIA report to The National Security Council, and concluded that the Russians were taking a huge gamble after the failed Bay of Pigs Invasion by Cuban exiles in April 1961, to put missiles in Cuba. The CIA's report to President Kennedy enabled the president to go "eyeball to eyeball" with Premier Khrushchev and "not blink" and state that any attack on the United States or any other friendly country was the same as an attack on the United States, which would bring United States retaliation against Russia. Russian Premier Khrushchev backed off and withdrew Russian military ships bringing missiles into Cuba, averting World War III.

Arthur's most significant intelligence operation in Europe was working with two other experienced CIA Operatives for the defection of a Czechoslovakian Army Colonel. The colonel despised Russians because of their treatment of the Czechoslovakian people, and for executing Czech intelligence officers who fought against the Nazis in World War II. The colonel called Russians barbarians and traitors who treated Czech military officers like "errand boys." Colonel Emil Danek had spent six months in Moscow attending a Soviet logistics school, and it was during the time with Russian officers he concluded them to be alcoholics, womanizers and brutal to subordinates. The colonel also did not think Warsaw Pact countries would fight with Russia in any war with NATO. Colonel Danek concluded Russia cracked down on Hungary in 1956 for deviation from the Soviet party line and Russia would crack down on Czechoslovakia for the same reason.

After three years of introspection, the colonel decided to defect, with his wife and two children. In April 1966, he was assigned for an inspection in Prague to evaluate Czechoslovakian logistical support for Soviet Armor Divisions. The following June, Danek took leave, with his wife and children, and flew to Bratislava, Czechoslovakia. The following afternoon they all took a daytime boat tour on the Danube River, got off the boat in Vienna with forged Austrian passports, and fled to the U.S. Embassy seeking political asylum. Colonel Danek brought with him in a false-bottomed suitcase documents containing a Top Secret Warsaw Pact mobilization plan for logistics and troop movements for a war with NATO. The document showed Soviet staging areas with arms, ammunitions, food, clothing and medical supplies pre-positioned in Eastern Europe to support advancing Warsaw Pact armies. The plan also showed Russian invasion routes into Western Europe from Czechoslovakia, Hungary, and East Germany for 250,000 Soviet soldiers, tanks, and artillery.

In August 1963 Arthur met Czechslovakian Colonel Danek in Budapest, Hungary, at an air show. In November 1963, they met in Prague, and Zagreb, when the colonel informed Arthur that he planned to defect to the West with his family.

Josef Stupek, the Czechoslovakian CIA Operative, subsequently met the colonel again in Warsaw and the colonel told him, "I am going to defect." It took six months to obtain altered Czechoslovakian passports, and in June of 1966, the colonel defected. The Russians were furious; eleven Czechoslovakian military officers were executed for treason. The Russians posted a 500,000-ruble reward for information leading to the capture of the colonel. The information provided by the colonel set the Russians back five years in the war planning against NATO. The CIA received confirmation that a Russian handbook of instructions written in Czech, Hungarian, and German was also gone, and the Russians could not use their war plan with NATO.

Arthur was confident of his intelligence skills and experience to accomplish his mission in Vietnam. He could handle weapons and he was in excellent physical condition.

His position in Vietnam would be the Office of the Assistant (OSA) Station Chief for the CIA in Rach Gia, Kien Giang province on the west coast of South Vietnam in the Mekong Delta. His mission was in the Phoenix Program to identify Viet Cong political infrastructure in the countryside and root it out using combat operations with a provincial reconnaissance unit (PRU). He was confident with the Vietnamese language and would only require an interpreter for interrogations.

Arthur walked to the garage, picked up a lawn chair, and brought it to the back porch. He sat down to enjoy some peace and quiet. His family had arrived in Tucson after Christmas. He and Janet enrolled their children in school, bought their home and he was now preparing to leave for Vietnam in fourteen days. He looked toward the sky and the late afternoon sunset and saw a hawk circling, he was preparing to make a rapid descent and snare a rodent or rabbit on the desert floor for a meal.

In July 1947, Arthur's family moved from California to Tucson. His father accepted a promotion as Regional Manager for the U.S. Army Corps of Engineers in Tucson. His mother was a social worker in Chicot County. Arthur grew up in a middle-class neighborhood; he had a younger brother, Stephen, and a younger sister, Katherine. While Arthur was growing up in Tucson he and his friends rode bicycles into the desert and went exploring. He learned the desert was barren, hot, dry and dangerous and could defeat anyone if they were not careful. He also learned about the desert's animals, snakes, insects, plants, shrubs, trees, and how to select cactus which contained water.

Arthur sat in the chair on the back porch and watched as the sun descended behind the Comobali Mountain range, and radiated red, orange, yellow, and shades of purple streaks across the sky. In a moment the sun was gone and the Comobali Mountain range was a black silhouette.

Arthur thought about the assignment to Vietnam. He would miss his family, but he had thirty days home leave after six months. He talked to a fellow CIA colleague, Patrick Hamilton at the Vietnamese language school. Patrick served in Vietnam from 1964 to 1965 with the U.S. Army as a Military Attaché in Saigon. Patrick joined the CIA after serving in the Army, and was going on a two-year assignment to II Corps in the Central Highlands. Patrick said Vietnam was exotic, humid and had many diseases. The North Vietnamese were organized, secretive, and had tight control of the population living in the countryside. Patrick said he thought there were about 400,000 communist soldiers in South Vietnam and it required 800,000 U.S. ground combat forces. Patrick thought the best the CIA could do would be to neutralize the Viet Cong's political leadership so the U.S. and ARVN military could destroy the NVA and VC.

Arthur was born in Sacramento, California on January 30, 1933 and grew up in a churchgoing family. In 1931 his father, Edward, was graduated from the University of California, Berkeley with a degree in civil engineering. His mother, Lillian, was graduated from San Jose State in 1932. Arthur graduated ninth in a class of 300 at Cochise High School. He earned a varsity letter in baseball and was not a "bookworm." In June, 1959 he was graduated Cum Laude from the University of Arizona, majoring in economics and mathematics, and was commissioned as a Second Lieutenant in the United States Army Reserve, Field Artillery.

Arthur checked his wristwatch, got up and walked to the back gate to make sure it was locked.

Janet turned on the back porch light, opened the door and called to Arthur, "Aren't you cold?"

He answered, "No, I'm fine."

Arthur thought about his life after he left Tucson fourteen years ago, and how he met Janet. He spent two years in the U.S. Army and one year in South Korea. He went to work for E.F. Hutton & Company in Los Angeles as a stockbroker after the Army. In 1956, he met his future wife, Janet Lindsey Foster, at Hutton. They got married and had three children, a home, money in the bank and his eleven-year career with the CIA. Arthur's parents taught him to, "Think for yourself, and don't follow the herd."

Janet opened the back door, "Arthur, are you sure you're not cold? I don't want you sick when you leave."

"No, Janet, I'm fine," he responded. "I'm comfortable, I was just thinking about the past fourteen years, Europe and all."

Janet laughed, "Watch out world, when a CIA man thinks. We'll eat in ten minutes," and she closed the back door.

It was getting cooler, but was still pleasant outside. Arthur looked up at the stars in the night sky. He recalled a comment written about him under his picture in the 1950 Cochise High School Year Book:

"Arthur Edward Norris."

"Quick hands at second base for the double-play."

"Always reliable."

"Likes math with Mr. Hudson?"

"A Man of Mystery."

"A Man of Mystery." Arthur was his own man. He dated in high school, but did not have a steady girlfriend. Schoolwork and studies came first. He didn't hang at "Spurs" where students went to flirt and listen to the jukebox.

Arthur viewed his father as a pillar of strength. His dad worked as a civil engineer for the State of California during the Great Depression; he brought home a paycheck every two weeks and donated fifty dollars a month to feed unemployed and homeless people in Sacramento. He worked as a civil engineer in Sacramento, Tucson, and in Phoenix for thirty-seven years. He took a position in Tucson after returning from World War II with the Army Corps of Engineers and he was promoted to regional manager when he moved to Phoenix in 1960.

On September 14, 1957, Arthur and Janet were married by Reverend James Young, Rector of the Episcopal Church of the Redeemer in San Diego. They had a wedding reception for sixty-five guests at the Miramar Naval Officers' Club.

Janet was an "Army brat" and the daughter of Colonel Travis Lee Foster, a career Army officer. On June 4, 1941 he was graduated from Texas A and M with his degree in romance languages, in German, and Italian, which he spoke fluently. His first assignment was to Cavalry School, but he soon was transferred into U.S. Army Intelligence as an interpreter and document analyst. In August 1942, he was assigned to Great Britain and the staff of Supreme Allied Commander, General Dwight D. Eisenhower, at Bletchley Park. From 1942 to 1944 he performed cryptography analysis and translated captured German documents; he went to France with the First U.S. Army in August 1944, and at the end of the war he remained in Germany. His family joined him at Garmish/PartenKirchen where he was assigned to a secret de-Nazification program to debrief former German Nazi SS officers for re-entry into West German society. In 1949, he was assigned to the Army Staff College at Fort Leavenworth, Kansas. In 1950, he received orders to Fort Shafter, Hawaii, where his family remained during the Korean War until 1953. Over the next fourteen years he had assignments at the Pentagon; Heidelberg; Verona, Italy; the U.S. Army War College, and Fort Sam Houston.

In May 1957, Janet graduated from San Diego State and went to work for Hutton. She had done extensive traveling, which helped her adjust to Arthur's career in the CIA and family separations.

Janet opened the door and called, "Dinner's ready." Arthur got up, stretched his arms and legs, and went into the house.

He said, "Jennifer, don't put your feet on the chair." They sat down for dinner and held hands while Arthur said grace.

Jennifer asked, "Daddy, why are you going to Van Nuys?"

Janet said, "Where, Jennifer?"

"You know, you and Dad said you were leaving for Van Nuys in two weeks."

Janet laughed, "Excuse me, Arthur, I can't help but laugh. Jennifer, Daddy is going to Vietnam, not Van Nuys, California."

Arthur shook his head and smiled, "Jennifer, I wish it were Van Nuys so I could stay close to you."

Janet said, "Daddy is going to South Vietnam, it's a long way from Tucson." Arthur thought to himself, *It might be better going to Van Nuys than Vietnam.*

After they finished dinner Arthur went into the living room with Arthur junior and Tyler. He turned on the *CBS Evening News* with Walter Cronkite. Mr. Cronkite reported there was heavy fighting in the ancient city of Hué as U.S. Marines and the ARVN fought to recapture the ancient city, with heavy Marine casualties. There was still fighting in Cholon, the ethnic Chinese enclave in Saigon. The U.S. Military Command in Saigon reported on the communists' Tet offensive. On January 31, 1968, over the Vietnamese sacred New Year and during a ceasefire, 84,000 communist soldiers had attacked thirty provincial capitals at 100 locations across South Vietnam. General William C. Westmoreland, U.S. Commander, said the attack on the U.S.

Embassy was a platoon-sized unit and signified nothing. The U.S. Command said the purpose of the communists' attack was to foment a general uprising among the South Vietnamese population. Five Viet Cong were killed as they tried to capture a radio station in Saigon and play pre-recorded propaganda calling for the population "to rise up in rebellion against the puppet government in Saigon and the imperialist American allies." The Saigon government reported the communist attack on the radio station failed and all the traitors were killed. No damage was done to the South Vietnamese Presidential Palace in Saigon. The ARVN had only minimum causalities in Saigon, and ARVN paratrooper units and Rangers units repulsed the communist attack. President Nguyen Van Thieu said the Communists' attack on South Vietnam failed. Their attack was treacherous and cowardly during the Tet Lunar New Year ceasefire, when Vietnamese families celebrate peace, prosperity, and happiness. President Thieu reiterated the Communist North Vietnamese and their "running-dog Viet Cong allies" would not defeat the government of South Vietnam.

Mr. Cronkite said, "Fighting continues in pockets of resistance in My Tho, Tay Ninh." He went on, "The communists' military Tet attack was a military disaster, but it now appears to be a political bonanza as it demonstrates that South Vietnam's Pacification Program, 'To win the hearts and minds of the rural countryside,' has not been successful." He pointed out that Viet Cong soldiers participating in the attack live in South Vietnam's countryside, which now shows questionable progress in Pacification and contradicts the Johnson administration's claim that Pacification was a success.

Arthur turned off the television. Janet came into the living room and sat down on the sofa.

"Nothing you want to watch," she said.

Arthur looked at her. "Something is wrong with either the political direction of the war from Washington or with the U.S. strategy in the war. It's one or the other; U.S. troops win battles, but don't hold ground. A village liberated one day is back under Viet Cong control the next day. I've heard inside the Agency statements to the effect that the U.S. bombing has not been effective to stop infiltration into South Vietnam. We can't find the little bastards to fight unless they ambush or *choose* to fight. How could a force of 84,000 communist soldiers attack South Vietnam in a sneak attack without anyone in the U.S. or South Vietnamese Intelligence learning about the attack? It doesn't make sense."

Janet said, "Let me get the children ready for bed." She came back with two glasses of chilled white wine. She turned on soft stereo music and said, "It will work out, I'm sure."

"I don't know, Janet. It hasn't worked out since 1965, and there are now 300 U.S. soldiers killed each week. I'll see it all soon firsthand."

Janet took his hand. "Arthur, are you sure you want to go to Vietnam for two years, you are thirty-five, with a family."

Arthur looked at her and said, "Yes, my love, I need to go for myself and for the country."

Janet said, "Very well; I do support your decision." She left the room and took a shower; returned, kissed Arthur good night and went to bed.

On February twenty-fourth, Arthur was scheduled to fly on TWA from Tucson to Los Angeles, and then through Honolulu, and Bangkok, Thailand. The CIA would fly him to Saigon on Air America and avoid the crowded military airfields at Bien Hoa and Ton Son Nhut. Arthur would remain in Saigon for one week to acclimatize himself to Vietnam's heat and humidity and to sign for CIA equipment going to the OSA Compound at Rach Gia. He would receive briefings from the CIA, and the U.S. Military Command.

Arthur's compound in Rach Gia was called the Office of the Special Assistant (OSA) for a CIA cover name. Arthur learned the building where he would live and work for the next two years was being renovated by the Pacific Architects and Engineers.

Arthur would have ample financial resources, with logistical and air support from Air America and PRU who were Cambodian Nungs, ex-Viet Cong, and Chieu Hois, who rallied to the South Vietnam government and young men who would fight to protect their families and their ancestral burial grounds and not have to serve in the ARVN. U.S. Army Advisors, U.S. Army Special Forces, and U.S. Navy Seals were assigned for the intelligence and combat military operations with the PRU's.

Arthur received thirty days' home leave after six months, and a salary of $90,000 a year with tax advantages. The Agency provided him a one-million-dollar life insurance policy.

It was neither the money nor the thrill of adventure he wanted; he believed what he was doing was right to help his country and, yes, if he were successful, the assignment would advance his career.

On November 1, 1957, the CIA hired Arthur, and December 1, 1957 was his first day of work at CIA Headquarters in Langley, Virginia. In June, 1957 he contacted the CIA asking them to mail him an employment application. In June, he received a reply, and a letter of introduction, employment information, and an eight-page application. He listed his education, employment, three references, and answered questions regarding his "affiliations with known or suspected communist organizations." The application had to be returned within ten business days.

In July 21, 1957, he received another letter informing him his application had been received. He was instructed to contact the Federal Bureau of Investigation at the Federal Building in Los Angeles for a personal interview and a polygraph examination. Arthur made an appointment, had the interview, took the polygraph examination, and was told he would receive a reply in thirty days. If he were favorably considered for employment, he would be flown to Langley, Virginia, the CIA's headquarters, for a personal examination.

On October 1, 1957, Arthur received a reply for a second interview on October twentieth, 1957. He was told, "Forget everything you've seen or heard about the CIA." During his interview, he was told that intelligence work was difficult, tedious, sometimes dangerous, and if one got into the wrong place at the wrong time, one could be terminated with "extreme prejudice", meaning killed.

Arthur was told to go home, think over his decision, and return a letter and his decision by November 1, 1957. He and Janet flew back to Los Angeles. He mailed the letter accepting employment the next day.

On November 1, 1957, he received a letter saying he had been hired, and to make plans to move to Langley, Virginia, and report to work December 1, 1957.

On July 30, 1956, Arthur began his career at "Hutton." He had served previously in the U.S. Army for two years at Fort Sill, Okalahoma, and one year with the 406th Field Artillery Battalion, Second Infantry Division in South Korea. His mathematical background prepared him to do well in the Field Artillery Officers' Basic Course. He graduated first in his training class of thirty-five Second Lieutenants and won the Commandant's Academic Award for the highest grade point average during field artillery training in target altitude, firing commands, and powder temperature with 105 and 155 howitzers.

Due to his academic performance at the Field Artillery Officer Basic Course, Arthur remained at Fort Sill and taught map reading, fire and operations preparation, powder temperature and firing artillery commands and safety. He next assignment was to South Korea in August 1954, to the 406th Artillery Battalion, commanded by Lieutenant Colonel Harley B. (for "ball buster") Craft, who had nineteen years of service in the Field Artillery and was "sweating" making "Bird" Colonel and a Brigade Command, or be retired.

Lieutenant Norris spent three months as a Forward Observer (FO). He learned to appreciate the infantry and he was promoted to First Lieutenant, Assistant Battery Commander for Alpha Battery, 406th Field Artillery Battalion under Captain Willis R. Stanley. Captain Stanley was a Regular Army Officer from ROTC, and had decided after seven years of service to resign his regular Army commission and get out of the Army. Arthur was the interim Battery Commander. His battalion was involved in joint training with the Republic of South Korea during training exercises, road marches, and live-fire exercises. Arthur spent 148 days in the field in Korea his first year. Only one problem occurred during his tour in his second year in Korea. It was during spring live-fire training, when two 105 howitzers got stuck in soft mud to the gun mounts. Arthur had to bring a

2.5-ton truck and a chain-and-work detail to pull the guns out of the gunk. Lieutenant Colonel "ball buster" got nervous and very anxious, but nothing came of the incident.

Lieutenant Colonel "ball buster" was promoted to full "Bird" Colonel, and recommended Arthur for a Regular Army commission. Arthur thanked Colonel Craft for his recommendation and said he would think about it. In June 1956, he returned to Fort Sill and after career counseling, Arthur was separated from the U.S. Army. On June 30, 1956, he mustered out and received an Army Commendation Medal for exemplary service in the United States Army from June 1954 to June 1956.

Arthur signed out at company headquarters. He got into his 1952 Ford Fairlane and began driving to Bethesda, Maryland, to visit his parents.

On December 7, 1941 and Pearl Harbor, his father was working for the State of California Department of Transportation. Arthur's father and Uncle Harold drove to Sacramento and enlisted in the service. His uncle enlisted in the Navy. He was commissioned as an Ensign and served aboard a Navy Cruiser in the Pacific Theater during World War II.

Arthur's father enlisted in the U.S. Army and was selected for Infantry Officers' Candidate School at Fort Benning, Georgia. The Captain, who commanded the enlistment office, realized he had a degree in civil engineering, and after infantry officers' OCS, recommended a transfer for him into the Army Engineers. His father received a commission as a Second Lieutenant, Infantry. A message came from Washington, transferring him into the U.S. Army Engineers at Fort Belvoir, Virginia. His father was an instructor at the Fort Belvoir from 1942–1943 for bridge, road, airfield construction, and demolition. In August 1944, he was reassigned to Fourth Army, 301st Army Support Command, 179th Engineer Brigade to rebuild German airfields during combat over Germany.

In 1945, he was repairing a bridge over the Rhine River when the Germans fired their famous 88's and some pieces of shrapnel wounded him. He was discharged from the U.S. Army in September 1945, and returned to Sacramento to the same job he had four years before with the state of California. A new Army

Corps of Engineers district opened in Tucson, and with his seniority and military service from World War II, Arthur's dad bid on the position and was selected as the superintendent.

From 1948 to 1950 the Norris family took vacations, visiting Apaches, Navajo, and Sioux reservations. Arthur had sympathy for the American Indians. Arthur's resentment was against the U.S. government for taking the Indians' land, killing their buffalo and for the U.S. Army who hunted Indians and killed them for resisting an invasion of their hunting grounds and ancestral burial grounds.

The money railroad companies "paid" the U.S. government to "buy" Indian land was a sham, paying one dollar for 500 acres. Arthur believed Lieutenant Colonel George Custer and the Seventh U.S. Calvary got what they deserved at the Battle of the Little Big Horn on June 25, 1876.

Arthur made a plan driving from Bethesda to Los Angeles to "try his hand" as a stockbroker for two years, and hopefully meet a woman with "wife potential." In two years he would be twenty-five, and he wanted his career to take shape. If, after two years it was not working, he would take the law school admission test and apply to the University of Southern California, UCLA, Stanford, and the University of Arizona law schools. His other option was to apply to the CIA, FBI, and U.S. Secret Service. Arthur did not want a humdrum life.

He decided to stop and see the Alamo and stop in Dallas to see his sister Katherine, her husband Max, and their children, Jeffrey and Ailene. His last stop would be to see the Grand Canyon.

He arrived in L.A. on Saturday, July fourteenth, and registered at the Ambassador Hotel. He called his parents and told them about his trip. His father was concerned his car would overheat and was glad to hear that Arthur had arrived safely. Arthur bought a *Los Angeles Times,* had dinner and a drink, and went back to his room. L.A. was a big, bustling city, Arthur was not sure he liked L.A. On Sunday he went to see *Rebel Without a Cause* and drove to Malibu for dinner. Seeing the Pacific Ocean made all the difference to him about remaining in Los Angeles.

On Monday, he went to breakfast, drove downtown and

filled out employment applications at Merrill-Lynch, Dean Witter, and E.F. Hutton. He received messages from the three brokerage firms for an interview. E.F. Hutton offered him a job. Hutton gave him a week to find an apartment, "settle in," and prepare for work on Monday, July thirtieth. Arthur went to Apartment Finders to look for an apartment in Westwood. Apartment Finders located an apartment for him in a six-year-old building. The apartment had two bedrooms, two bathrooms, air-conditioning, kitchen, living room, fireplace, and laundry room. It had a swimming pool and parking on the premises. The rent was $280.00 a month, and the apartment was located at 3119 Gayley Avenue, near the UCLA campus. The manager said tenants were young professionals, not college students, with twenty-four-hour security. Arthur rented the last two-bedroom apartment and moved in July twenty-fifth. He bought a bedroom set, color television, easy chair, dishes and silverware.

On Monday he reported to work and met Howard Wells, Hutton's vice-president of personnel, Stewart Rosenthal, Arthur's training supervisor, and several stockbrokers. Arthur's office was located on the fourth floor. He was introduced to Hutton employees, and among them was a very attractive young woman named Elizabeth Cowen, who was frequently fashionably dressed and properly coiffured.

Stewart Rosenthal told Arthur his first task was to pass the Securities' Exchange Commission Series 7 test to obtain a stockbroker's license. Stewart Rosenthal said the next Series 7 exam was Wednesday, October eighth; it was an eight-hour examination and usually about 50 percent passed the test. Arthur would prepare for the examination in August and September while Hutton paid for a Series 7 "cram" course.

Stewart Rosenthal told Arthur, "If you fail the Series 7 exam, you'll retake the exam at your own expense, and work as a broker assistant until you pass the exam." Arthur observed activity in Hutton's trading departments and followed floor trading of common and preferred stock, options, bonds, and U.S. treasury bills, notes and bonds.

Arthur's starting salary was $400 a week, and it would be increased to $500 a week and a 2 percent commission when he passed the Series 7 exam. Howard Wells said an "ordinary" stockbroker should make $45,000 in two years or he is "slacking." Arthur's working hours were 7:00 A.M. to 3:30 P.M.

Arthur began to study for the Series 7 exam and he liked to "smash" standard tests. He studied mornings at Hutton from 9:00 A.M. to 12:00 noon. He had Series 7 manuals, old tests, and a "How to Pass the Series 7 Test" booklet. He spent the first thirty days doing math questions on options, straddles/hedges stop-loss orders, dividends, bond yields, conversion of stock to cash and bond yields at premium and discount. In October, he began to memorize material. On September twenty-sixth he took the first Series 7 practice exam, and passed with a score of 87 percent; 70 percent was passing. He took the "cram" course and passed the Series 7 exam on October eighth with a score of 90 percent. Hutton was amazed; they hired the "golden boy." Arthur received a bonus of $500, a salary of $500 a week, 3 percent commission, a desk with a view of a park, and free parking for one month.

Elizabeth Cowen, a licensed bond trader, heard Arthur passed the Series 7 with a 90 percent score. She came to his desk, placed her right hand with a French manicure on his shoulder and said, "Arthur, it looks like you're cut out for this rat race, let's have a drink after work." What a bomb! Elizabeth Cowen's reputation was that of a loner with no real office friends.

Now that Arthur passed the Series 7 exam, he needed a roommate. He put a note on the bulletin board by the cafeteria, WANTED—ROOMMATE, WESTWOOD, TWO-BEDROOM, TWO-BATH, A/C, KITCHEN, POOL, PARKING PLUS UTILITIES, $200 A MONTH.

Two days later, a man called him about his ad. The man said he had seen the note for a roommate, that he was a new Hutton employee and needed a place to live in L.A. His name was Charles Wentworth Fenton, IV. He had attended Phillips Exeter and just graduated from Yale University. Arthur was impressed. He told Charles to meet him outside the Hutton cafeteria at 11:30 to talk and see if they had similar interests, like cleanliness and compatibility. Arthur wondered whether Charles, or

"Charlie," would require a valet, a housekeeper, or chauffeur in the apartment?

At 11:30, Arthur departed his office, took the elevator to the first floor and walked down the hallway to Hutton's cafeteria. He saw a young man standing near the entrance. Arthur approached him and the young man extended his right hand and said, "Hello, Mr. Norris, I'm Charlie Fenton, the man who called about your apartment." Arthur extended his right hand and they shook hands.

Arthur said, "Pleased to meet you, Charles, I'm Arthur Norris. No need to call me Mr. Norris."

"I'm pleased to meet you, and I prefer to be called 'Charlie,' not Charles. I grew up being called Charles, and I'm not going to be the future king of England, Charlie is fine."

Charlie looked to be about five foot nine inches tall, chubby, and was well-dressed, wearing a gray designer suit, blue oxford shirt, a blue tie, Johnson and Murphy black oxford shoes and a gold signet ring inscribed with CWF on the "pinky" finger of his right hand. He possessed a cherub face, curly black hair, and blue eyes. The softness of his hands indicated he had never done manual labor in his life.

Arthur said, "Shall we eat?"

"Yes," replied Charlie.

Arthur selected a corner table and they sat down to eat.

Arthur asked Charlie, "When did you start at Hutton?"

"October first," replied Charlie.

Charlie continued, "Howard Allen told me I was to take the Series 7 exam on December twelfth. He also told me a recent hire in July, named Arthur Norris, took the Series 7 exam in October and passed it with ninety percent, and; 'We are very proud of him.'"

"Congratulations, Arthur, perhaps you can share with me the secret of your success for passing the test."

Arthur smiled and said, "Just study, study, and study some more."

Charlie said, "That sounds easy enough."

Arthur told Charlie about the apartment, its location, that rent was $280 and about the commute to downtown Los Angeles on Wilshire Boulevard. He said that no pets were permitted. Arthur told Charlie his only request was that the apartment remain clean. He said he did not smoke and lived a "relatively quiet monastic life." Charlie laughed at Arthur's comment of a "monastic life."

It was 12:40; Arthur said, "Do you have any questions about the apartment?"

Charlie replied, "I harbor no vices or bad habits. I also desire a clean apartment, to buy our own food, and clean the refrigerator every Sunday. I want to install a private telephone line in my bedroom and would be willing to tolerate parties every so often with naked women."

Arthur laughed, "Why don't you come and see the apartment Saturday at one. I'll introduce you to Mrs. Downs, and you can co-sign the lease and move in."

"Great," answered Charlie, sounding happy.

They shook hands. Charlie returned to personnel and saw Howard Allen to pick up his Series 7 study material and start the same 7:00 A.M. to 3:30 P.M. routine as Arthur had done. Charlie told Arthur that Hutton gave him off until Monday to get acquainted and settle in.

Arthur said, "See you at one Saturday."

Charlie replied, "One sharp."

On Arthur's way back to his desk on the fourth floor, Elizabeth Cowan was riding on the elevator.

She said, "Arthur, I noticed you having lunch with that young 'Yalie' preppy. Are you a 'Yalie?' "

Arthur looked at Elizabeth and said, "No, Elizabeth, I'm a cowboy from the University of Arizona. What about you, Elizabeth, where did you go to college?"

"Back east at Sarah Lawrence College," she answered. The elevator opened, "Have a good day—remember my invitation, let's have a drink," she said as she departed the elevator.

"Sure," said Arthur.

Arthur got up on Saturday at seven thirty A.M., went for a run around UCLA campus, came back to the apartment and informed Mrs. Downs he had found a roommate. Arthur said, "He is a pedigreed gentleman."

Mrs. Downs said, "That sounds fine to me."

Arthur cleaned and vacuumed the apartment, took a shower and went to the Omelet in Westwood for breakfast. He called his parents and waited for Charlie to arrive at one. At one sharp Arthur heard the front doorbell. He called on the intercom and Charlie answered. Arthur buzzed the front door open and Charlie took the elevator to the second floor, walked to the end of the hall to apartment ten. He knocked on the door and Arthur answered the door.

"Hello, Charlie," said Arthur. "Come in."

"Thank you; it's warm for October."

Charlie was wearing olive slacks, a navy blue golf shirt, black penny loafers, a Rolex wristwatch and his signet ring.

Arthur asked Charlie, "Where are you parked?"

"I parked on the street."

"Street parking has a two-hour limit, if you don't mind, why don't you pull your car into parking spot at number ten."

"Fine, I don't need a parking ticket."

"I'll show you the location." He got up and they left the apartment. Arthur saw Charlie's car, which was a four-door dark blue 1956 Buick Roadmaster. Charlie opened the driver's door and unlocked the passenger's door with an electric button. Charlie lowered the front door windows and turned on the air-conditioner. Arthur got into the Buick and felt its thick leather.

Charlie asked, "Got enough room?"

"Yes." Arthur had never ridden in such an elegant car. Charlie pulled into Sunset Boulevard, drove south on Sunset, and made a left turn into Galey. Arthur told him to stop behind the building, which was "The Columbia," the name of their apartment building.

Arthur said, "There are twelve parking spaces; Mr. and Mrs. Downs use two spaces." Charlie pulled the Buick into the parking space and he barely had enough room to park without it sticking into the alley. They went to see Mrs. Downs.

She told Charlie, "Park in number one." Charlie thanked her. She said, "Just want the tenants to be happy."

Charlie was happy, he re-parked his Buick into number one

and he and Arthur took the elevator to the second floor. The apartment building had ten units.

Mrs. Downs said, "The Columbia has a very good reputation, it is a safe, clean place to live and we intend to keep it that way."

Arthur told Charlie he thought they would be good roommates, but to look at the apartment. They went upstairs. Charlie loved the apartment and moved in that afternoon. He brought two suitcases, a clothing bag, shoes, a small portable television, radio, record player, tennis racket, golf clubs, new suits, three lightweight sport coats, four new shirts, two ties, a raincoat, robe and slippers. Arthur read the *Los Angeles Times* while Charlie unpacked. At 4:30, Charlie had finished unpacking. He returned to the living room, wiped his forehead with his handkerchief and said, "Home at last." He asked Arthur if he could install a telephone in his bedroom.

Arthur replied to him, "Mrs. Downs said that is fine," and then Arthur asked Charlie if he cared for a drink or soda.

"It's not five, so I'll have a soda." They sat down in the living room. Charlie commented about the comfortable sofa.

Arthur said that Mrs. Downs had told him the entire apartment was repainted, redecorated and had new kitchen appliances. The previous tenants had been from Eugene, Oregon. They lived in Los Angeles six months, hated California, and moved back up to Oregon.

"This apartment appears to be in new condition, it's more modern than apartments I've seen in New York." Charlie finished his soda, looked at his wristwatch, and said, "It's almost five thirty, or eight thirty in Connecticut. May I use your telephone to call my parents in Greenwich, Connecticut? I want to give them my address and telephone number."

"Sure," said Arthur. "This is now your L.A. home."

"I'll take a shower, change, and why don't you select your favorite restaurant and I'll pop for dinner."

"Pop?"

" 'Pop' is an old British term used to mean, 'buy' instead of using the bourgeois words 'to buy.' "

"Charlie, that's not necessary."

"After talking to my mother, I'll need to relax."

"All right, it's your dime, Charlie, I'll pick out a restaurant for you to 'Pop.'"

Charlie went into his bedroom and called his parents. Arthur put on a clean shirt and a pair of slacks and returned to the living room. Arthur heard Charlie saying, "Hello, Mother, and Hello, Father." There was silence. Arthur heard Charlie saying, "Mother, please, no. No, you do not need to come to Los Angeles to see where I'm living." Charlie closed his bedroom door. Arthur heard him say, "For God's sake, Mother, I'm twenty-two; I don't need your approval for an apartment." Silence. "Yes, yes, of course my roommate is a gentleman; he is a stockbroker at E.F. Hutton and graduated from the University of Arizona—yes, he'll pay the rent." Another few minutes passed, Charlie said, "I will, love you, good-bye." In a few minutes, Arthur heard the water in the shower.

In a half an hour, Charlie appeared, wearing a blue sport blazer, white shirt, tie, and gray slacks. He looked at Arthur sitting in the lounge chair watching television.

"Charlie, you don't need to dress for dinner in L.A. like you're in Boston—you are the last of a dying breed. No, sir, not in L.A., the land of the 'big easy'; it's casual clothing," and he laughed. "Forget the white shoes, only a joke."

Charlie returned and was wearing an open-neck blue sport shirt, and gray slacks. He asked, "Where are we going for dinner?"

"The Smoke House in Burbank, near the NBC television studios. They have excellent prime rib, steaks, seafood and nice scenery."

"By scenery, I assume you mean the female variety, not shrubbery."

"Correct," said Arthur. He got up, patted Charlie on his shoulder and said, "You got it, roomie—you'll do well in L.A."

They took the elevator to the parking garage, went to Charlie's Buick and Arthur gave directions to Charlie to the 405 Freeway north, and then Highway 134 east to Burbank. They arrived at The Smoke House at 7:05. They did not talk too much while driving to Burbank, as Charlie wanted to concentrate on traffic and not miss the turnoff to Burbank. The maître d' at the Smoke

House showed them to a booth. Charlie ordered a Beefeater's martini extra dry with two olives and Arthur ordered a glass of white wine. They took a sip of their drinks.

Charlie ordered a second martini and became more relaxed. He said, "A fine choice, and nice scenery. I'll take a few days to get organized. Finding you and the apartment is a big relief. Thank you, Arthur, I appreciate you inviting me to be a roommate."

"I'm glad you decided to be my roommate."

"In a month or so, I'll explain my family, and my own situation." He continued, "I inherited $500,000 when I graduated from Yale. I was at Phillips Exeter for three years until I got my grades good enough to be accepted at Yale. My grandfather, Charles Wentworth Fenton, III, graduated Summa Cum Laude from Princeton in 1910 with a degree in chemical engineering." Charlie continued while Arthur listened in fascination. Charlie said, "500,000 dollars" like it was fifty dollars.

"Anyhow," said Charlie, "I am the product of an Eastern Preparatory School and Yale University. I was accepted at Princeton, but I knew my grandfather offered them a large financial gift as his appreciation. After graduation in June, my parents and I went to my late grandfather's attorney, Mr. Montague Higginbuttom in Philadelphia. The attorney said Mr. Fenton provided for his namesake, Charles Wentworth Fenton, IV to receive $500,000 upon graduation from Yale University, and the sum of one point five million dollars at age thirty-five. This is in return to show him my gratitude for being a steadfast student, a loyal grandson, and maintaining the honor of the Fenton name. My mother and father told me to invest my money. Under no circumstances was I ever to divulge my wealth to anyone. On the telephone my mother wanted to meet you and assure herself the apartment was suitable. They did not want me to come to California; Mother wanted me to stay in Boston or Philadelphia and go to Yale Law School or the Wharton School of Finance at the University of Pennsylvania."

The waiter came to the table; they ordered the prime rib, baked potato, salad, and a glass of merlot wine.

"Mother's name is Margaret; she wanted me to live in

Beverly Hills. I told her your apartment was fine, I did not want to live alone in Beverly Hills."

Charlie said, "Arthur, I'm really counting on you as a friend. My goal in life is to become a director in Hollywood; this stockbroker gig is to please my parents.

"You're the only living person, other than my grandfather's attorney Montague Higgenbuttom, and my mother and father, Margaret and Garrett Fenton, that know what I've told you, my younger brother doesn't even know and he is a junior at the University of Pennsylvania."

Charlie got out a handkerchief and patted his eyes. "God rest Grandpa's soul, he was a remarkable man."

Arthur said, "Charlie, you've done exceptionally well, your grandfather must have been very proud of you."

Charlie said, "Arthur, some of this hurts me. My father and his father, my grandfather, had a strained relationship all of their life until my grandfather died of a heart attack in October of 1951. I was a sophomore at Phillips Exeter, my mother called me and told me Grandmother found him dead, seated in a leather chair in the library of their mansion in Philadelphia. I took it very hard. It was a difficult year. My own father was emotionally detached and was not upset by his death. Grandfather was sixty-two."

Charlie drove back to Westwood after dinner. They stopped at a nightclub on Santa Monica Boulevard. When they went into the club and sat down, a young waitress came to the table, looked at Charlie, and said, "Do ya got I.D.?" The cocktail waitress was rude. Instead of asking Charlie if she might see his driver's license, she said, "I need some I.D. to give you a drink."

Charlie kept his cool. He said, "Here is my Connecticut driver's license; I just moved to Los Angeles."

She looked at it and said, "Okay, what do ya want?" Charlie ordered a Scotch and Arthur ordered a beer. The club was crowded and heavy with cigarette smoke; they finished their drinks, left the club and then drove home.

On Saturday, they both went grocery shopping. Charlie bought a telephone and several hanging plants for their apartment.

When Arthur left work Wednesday, Elizabeth Cowan was waiting outside the building. Arthur thought, *Why not ask her to have that drink?* He approached Elizabeth. "Excuse me, Elizabeth, may I buy you a drink at Buckley's?"

Elizabeth said, "I'd love to, Arthur, but I'm on my way right now to meet clients at five thirty. Could we meet at Chasen's on Friday night for drinks and a dutch treat dinner?"

Arthur thought, *That's Halloween night.* He said, "Fine, Chasen's at seven—should I wear a costume?"

Elizabeth said, "No, Arthur, you will look fine—see you at seven on Friday."

Arthur thought to himself—*This woman is unreal.* Chasen's was a watering hole for L.A.'s rich and famous. It was an expensive restaurant, but he thought to himself, *why not?* He didn't see Elizabeth at work Thursday or Friday. He wondered if she would still meet him at Chasen's on Friday. Arthur told Charlie he had a date with Elizabeth Cowen at Chasen's on Friday.

Arthur called Charlie before leaving Hutton. He told him he was leaving for the day at 4:00, and that he had a dinner date with Elizabeth Cowen in Beverly Hills at Chasen's at 7:00. Charlie said, "Are you wearing a Halloween costume to dinner?"

Arthur said, "No costume, but Joe Harrison told me to stop at the bank as you'll need a roll of dough at Chasen's."

Charlie wished Arthur "good luck and good hunting."

As Arthur drove home along Wilshire, he saw children wearing Halloween costumes running along Wilshire Boulevard. It was a cool fall night but not too cold. An October full moon showed across the Pacific. Arthur turned onto Gayley and parked his car in the garage. It was 4:40. He checked the mail and turned on the T.V. to KTLA to hear today's news. He took a shower, then put on a white shirt, tie, gray slacks, black Oxford shoes and a blue blazer. He left the apartment at 6:15 and arrived at Chasen's at 6:55. One of Chasen's valets parked his Chevrolet in an adjacent three-story concrete parking garage. Arthur entered this famous Hollywood restaurant, walking up wide, ornate white concrete steps and pillars. He opened the smoked dark glass double doors into the foyer.

A well-groomed maître d' approached him. He said, "Sir, I'm the maître d'. You must have reservations this evening."

Arthur replied, "Yes, Arthur Norris and Elizabeth Cowan at 7:00."

The maître d' replied, "Here you are," as he checked the reservation book at his maître d' stand.

"I'm sorry, Mr. Norris, but Miss Cowan still has not arrived. I have reserved your table.

"Miss Cowan is a regular; she knows many important people in Beverly Hills. She will be here soon I am sure."

Arthur looked at his wristwatch at 7:15. The maître d' suggested, "Would you like to be seated at your table or have a drink in the bar?"

Arthur said, "I'll wait in the bar."

The maître d' said, "I'll let you know the minute Miss Cowan arrives."

Arthur excused himself. He walked across the back of the dining room and then behind a high etched glass wall made of mahogany wood with brass trim. Arthur noticed several very attractive young women seated with older-looking men, many with Middle Eastern appearances, enjoying dinner. *Must be some Hollywood starlets and studio producers,* thought Arthur. *Right?*

Arthur took a seat at the bar. He looked at the drink menu. Things were not cheap. Domestic beer: $4.50 a bottle. Imported beer: $6.50 a bottle. Varietal wine: $7.50 a glass. Bottle of Varietal wine: $45.00 to $150.00. 1939 French champagne: $750.00.

Elizabeth Cowan had told Arthur Chasen's was her favorite restaurant in L.A. It always served excellent food, had impeccable service, a well-dressed clientele, and at Christmas, wonderful private parties. It had been built in 1943 and became the watering hole for Hollywood's most famous celebrities: Clark Gable, Spencer Tracy, Humphrey Bogart, John Ford, Greer Garson and Bette Davis. It had been destroyed by an electrical fire in 1953. It was completely rebuilt and redecorated into "Old Hollywood" to walk on a plush, deep blue carpeting, taupe color walls, mahogany wood trim, and light blue and gold on the window drapes. It seated one hundred fifty people, had three rooms for private parties, and a section to convert the first floor into a dance floor for shows or reviews by studios.

Arthur took a seat at the bar. He ordered a bottle of Budweiser. He looked around the room. There were autographed pictures of many Hollywood celebrities on the walls.

Arthur thought to himself, *Where in the hell is Elizabeth?* as he was getting impatient. Then his mood changed. A stunning young woman walked into the bar and removed a sable mink coat. She was wearing a one-piece black body stocking and black leather stiletto heels. She had on a black mask with plastic cat's ears, six black lines were drawn across her face simulating a cat's whiskers. She also had black nail polish and black eyeliner. She smiled at Arthur. Before she sat down, she said to him, "Such a good-looking man dining alone on Halloween."

Arthur replied, smiling, "I'm waiting for my date, she's late."

The cat woman walked to sit down and said to Arthur, "Stop by here next Friday. I might ask you to play cat and mouse with me."

Arthur took a sip of his beer. An older man in his late fifties came into the bar. He had blond-gray thinning hair, and etched lines on his tanned face from too much sun. He looked like a faded Hollywood actor. He wore a white lion tamer's outfit, a shirt unbuttoned to show his gray chest hairs, and matching black boots. The lion tamer walked to the cat lady's table, bent down, and kissed her on her left cheek. Arthur heard him tell the cat lady, "Sorry I'm late, doll, the Goddamn Hollywood Freeway was bumper to bumper getting here."

The cat lady replied, "No problem. I just got here myself—thank you for this elegant sable coat. I love it!"

The lion tamer whispered something into her left ear. She smiled, and laughed, and said, "Thanks for getting me the role."

The bartender brought them two flutes of champagne.

The maître d' came into the bar, walked to Arthur, and told him, "Mr. Norris, Miss Cowan is here; I'll show you to your table."

Arthur followed the maître d' to their table. Elizabeth appeared at the table after she stopped to talk briefly with another couple.

Arthur was amazed when he saw Elizabeth. She appeared fresh and elegant. It was the first time that Arthur had ever seen Elizabeth Cowan except in Hutton's office where she always wore business attire. Arthur didn't want to appear to be staring at her, but what he saw was a stunning and beautiful woman. Her dark, almost black hair was parted and fell to her shoulders around her face. Her make-up accentuated her hazel eyes and her dark red lipstick matched her dark red fingernail polish. She wore a long black velvet skirt cut above her left knee, a satin blouse, black suede shoes, with a long pearl necklace, and diamond earrings.

"Oh Arthur," said Elizabeth, "please forgive me for being so late."

Arthur replied, "I'm glad you made it."

The maître d' seated Elizabeth. The maître d' asked, "May I have the waiter bring you a drink before dinner?"

Elizabeth smiled and said, "Arthur, do you care for anything to drink? I would like to relax."

Arthur answered, "A gin and tonic with Beefeater's Gin."

Elizabeth said, "I'll have a glass of Chardonnay wine."

The maître d' commented, "Very good, your drinks will be here in a moment."

The waiter brought them their drinks. Elizabeth offered Arthur a toast. "To our success at Hutton."

Arthur toasted and replied, "I'll drink to that."

They sipped their drinks. Elizabeth asked Arthur, "What do you think of Chasen's?"

Arthur looked at her: Elizabeth was a lovely woman; he replied, "Elegant, very Hollywood."

They sat and talked. Elizabeth asked Arthur what had brought him to Hutton, and about college and his future plans. Had he known Charlie Fenton before Hutton? Did he like L.A.?

Elizabeth ordered a large Pacific shrimp cocktail, Orange Peking duck, braised potatoes, and steamed Oriental vegetables.

Arthur ordered a large Caesar salad, a medium cut of prime rib, whipped potatoes, and fresh green beans.

Elizabeth also ordered a bottle of 1951 French Chardonnay wine costing $175.00.

Elizabeth told Arthur she was 27, and had been born in Reno, Nevada. When she was 10 her family moved to Carson City, Nevada. She had been engaged once but never married. Following graduation from high school, a wealthy uncle who owned two silver mines outside Virginia City sent her back East to Sarah Lawrence College in Bronxville, New York. She had graduated from Sarah Lawrence in 1953 with a degree in English. She got a job with the advertising firm of Sutton and Taylor on Madison Avenue and worked there for two years. She missed her family and moved to Las Vegas. In June 1955 she went to work at the Sands Hotel and Casino in Convention Sales and Public Relations. While at the Sands she met Frank Sinatra, Dean Martin, Sammy Davis, Jr., Elvis Presley, Shirley MacLaine, and Liberace. The long hours were a killer. She got tired of being "hit on" by executives in town without their wives, drinking and schmoozing. She had gotten engaged to a man she met at the Sands who turned out to be a womanizer. She gave him back her diamond ring and told him, "Shove it where the sun doesn't shine."

She concluded saying, "I moved to L.A. and got my securities license and decided to sell bonds at Hutton. Hutton is fine, but I have bigger plans to sell commercial real estate in Hawaii with all the construction that is going on in the Hawaiian Islands."

They both enjoyed their dinner. They finished dinner with an after-dinner drink.

Arthur insisted on paying the bill. He was glad he was paid that day; their bill with the bar, mandatory 8% tip, and dinner was $335.00.

They left Chasen's. Once out front Arthur waited for the valet. Elizabeth told him, "My car is parked a block away off a side street."

Arthur offered to walk her to her car. Elizabeth declined and said, "Thank you, but I'm licensed to carry a piece; it's in my purse, I'll be all right. I've got to pick up a girlfriend staying at my home over the weekend."

Elizabeth gave Arthur another European-type kiss on the cheek. She started down the front steps, turned back to look at Arthur, and said, "Thanks again for the lovely dinner, see you at work on Monday." Arthur stood on the front entrance waiting for a valet to bring his car. It was a pleasant evening.

The cat lady and the lion tamer emerged out of the double front doors. They stood a moment. The lion tamer turned to the cat lady and told her, "I've left my valet ticket in the car; I'll have to tell them at the parking stand." The lion tamer walked down the steps to the stand a short distance up the street. Arthur was once again standing alone with the cat lady.

The cat lady turned to Arthur saying, "Happy Halloween, hope you had a nice dinner; your date is very pretty."

Arthur returned a compliment to her, "Thank you, you look fabulous in your cat Halloween costume."

The cat lady smiled, "Thank you so much; we're going to a private Halloween party in Holmby Hills. My escort is Jack Stone. He was once a famous actor in the '30s and now he is my agent. He landed me a good role in a new film called *Heartbreak* due out next summer. Please do stop by on Friday. I get here around 7—until I get a major role with Paramount. My name is Cindy Alexander—and yours—?"

"Arthur Norris," said Arthur.

"Nice to meet you, Arthur. You're a nice-looking man, are you an attorney?"

"No," Arthur replied, "a stockbroker."

The lion tamer returned. He told Cindy, the cat lady, "They're bringing my car, let's go down to the curb."

They walked down the steps to the curb. The valet brought a black Mercedes Benz 450 SEL. The license plate was "YUNG STAR." The lion tamer drove away. Arthur thought, *Nice to look at, nice to talk to, but not my type. The cat lady is 25; the lion tamer is 55—that's Hollywood, folks.*

It had been ten minutes; two couples stood in line ahead of Arthur. He motioned to the valet to get his keys and he gave the kid twenty dollars and said, "I'll get my car." The valet said, "It's parked in the garage at A-49." Arthur thanked him and began walking to the parking garage. As he approached the parking garage, he saw a stunning woman with white blonde hair wearing a short, tight, black dress. Arthur thought, *She's either a transvestite or a prostitute.* A black Cadillac Sedan Deville pulled out of the parking garage entrance. The car stopped in front of the woman with white blonde hair. The blonde opened her purse, took out a cigarette, and began gesturing to another man driving the Cadillac. The blonde raised her hands near her face and her talking got louder; Arthur stepped back into the shadows of the parking garage.

Another short stocky man got out of the back seat of the Cadillac, and reached inside his coat jacket as if he were going to pull out a gun. Arthur heard the blonde holler to him, "Don't fuck with me, Butch, Manny will kick your ass if I tell him what you've done." The man got back into the Cadillac. A second car pulled out of the garage and stopped. Elizabeth Cowan got out of the white Lincoln Continental.

Arthur knew it was Elizabeth since she was wearing the same clothing she had worn at dinner. Elizabeth walked to the driver of the Cadillac, pointed at him, took the blonde by her hand, and they both got into the back seat of the Lincoln. Elizabeth got out again, walked to the front of the Lincoln, lit a cigarette, and said, "I'll ride with Sherry," and both cars drove away west on La Cienga. Arthur thought, *What is Elizabeth doing? Those men are mobsters.*

Arthur got his car, drove to Wilshire and back to the apartment. *What was Elizabeth doing,* he wondered, *driving home?* He did not tell Charlie what he had seen. When Charlie inquired, "How was your dinner?" Arthur said, "Fine, Elizabeth is a stunning woman and apparently very intelligent. After dinner she said she had to meet someone."

"She had to see someone after dinner at ten o'clock on Halloween?"

"She said her girlfriend from Las Vegas was visiting for the weekend and got lost on the freeway, and wants a raincheck."

On Monday, a sign-up sheet went around to sign up for the Hutton party bus to the annual USC-UCLA football game on November seventeenth at the L.A. Coliseum. Arthur and Charlie signed up to see the game. The annual pre-game cocktail party was held at the L.A. Athletic Club. Arthur looked at the names on the sign-up sheet and saw Janet Foster, personnel, was signed up for two tickets.

Oh crap, he thought, *Janet has a boyfriend.*

He had talked to Janet at a training class on Hutton Benefits the previous week. He really liked her, she was a very attractive young lady with blonde hair, green eyes, about 5'7" and a nice figure. She said, "Hello," when she met Arthur and was all business. She also said, "Hello" in the hallway at work, but that was the extent of their communication.

On Tuesday, Joe Harrison, another stockbroker, joined Arthur and Bill Albright at their table during lunch in the cafeteria. Joe was a pain in the ass. Arthur knew he had seen Elizabeth the past Friday, but had not told Bill about the date. Joe asked immediately for the details. "Did you get laid? Did she give you that b.s. about a rich uncle and going to college back East at Sarah Lawrence? Arthur, you dork, Elizabeth attended Glendale Junior College. She's not someone to play around with. I have no idea how she got a bond trader's license, and I don't intend to ask her. Keep your fly zipped shut if you're thinking of dating Elizabeth."

Arthur told Joe, "I'm not the type of man who takes advantage of a woman."

"Well, you must have done something, she hasn't been to work Monday or Tuesday."

He said, "Really, I didn't know, she's on the second floor and I'm on the fourth."

"Well, I guess if you got her into the sack, you would have talked to her since Friday night."

"Come on, Joe, be a gentleman, not everyone is as tactless as you. I've got to get back to my desk," he said, and he left. Bill followed Arthur and Joe sat alone at the table. On Thursday Arthur received a telephone call from Elizabeth; she apologized again for Friday night and said a jerk stood up her girlfriend and she had to pick her up in Hollywood. *Some story,* thought Arthur.

Elizabeth said Howard Wells fired her and she came to get her last check. "Could we meet at Buckley's for a drink at 4:30?"

He told her no, he couldn't make it; he and Charlie were going to a concert.

Elizabeth told Arthur that she sold her home in Benedict Canyon and was moving to Honolulu in a week to work in real estate for Premier Properties. She told Arthur she had contacts in Las Vegas to buy properties in Hawaii. It was a chance to get in on the ground floor and make big money. She said her company was listed in the Honolulu directory and if he was in Hawaii, to call her. Elizabeth asked, "Could you please come down and say good-bye after I talk to Howard Allen?"

When she got there, Howard said, "Elizabeth, I wish you the best in Hawaii."

"Thank you, Howard, I'm sorry I didn't use better judgment about my excessive absences." Elizabeth saw Arthur and said, "Arthur, I wish we had met at a different time and under different circumstances, please do call me if you're ever in Honolulu. I promise we'll have a better time than on Friday." She kissed Arthur on the cheek and went out the front door. That was the last time Arthur saw Elizabeth Cowan.

On Sunday, Arthur and Charlie went to Sunday brunch at the Breakers in Santa Monica. While they were eating, Charlie asked Arthur if he were going out of town for Thanksgiving.

"My gosh, Thanksgiving is in three weeks, yes, I'm driving to Phoenix to have Thanksgiving with my family for the first time in years. What about you, Charlie?"

"I have a ticket on American Airlines. Howard Allen said I could leave at two o'clock for a three o'clock flight to Boston."

He said he was going to connect in Boston and drive to Greenwich on Thanksgiving Day and arrive at home by noon. Charlie said his parents, brother Thomas, and Grandmother Ester Fenton, his late grandfather's wife, would have Thanksgiving dinner at 4:00 at his parents' home.

"It will be nice for you to see your family."

"Well, yes and no, after we finish brunch, I'll fill you in about myself. I need your confidentiality, and you already know about my inheritance."

Charlie picked up the tab. They walked into a veranda cocktail lounge with a view of the ocean. They sat down in white wicker chairs next to a glass cocktail table. The room looked like a room from *The Great Gatsby* in the 1920s with white furniture, lime-green and navy blue carpet, and white overhead ceiling fans.

Charlie said, "I like this room, it reminds me of our Nantucket summer home." The cocktail waitress took their order. Charlie ordered Crown Royal Scotch, and Arthur a gin and tonic. When she brought them their drinks, Arthur said, "I'll take the tab."

Charlie sipped his Scotch and stared at the blue Pacific Ocean. He spoke, "I have a rich family. Everything started with my late grandfather, Charles Wentworth Fenton, Jr., who was my father's father. He grew up in Reading, Pennsylvania, in a family with five children. My great-grandfather worked as a textile machinist for Wyomissing Industries, near Reading. Grandfather worked in the textile mills during the summer. He was very bright and graduated first in his high school class in Reading. He received an academic scholarship to Princeton University. He was a "Grinder." He rowed on Princeton's crew for over four years and joined the Princeton Tiger Club. He was graduated in 1910 with a degree in Chemical Engineering. He met Chalmers Bufont Parker at Princeton who was also in the Tiger Club."

Charlie took a sip of his drink. Two people sat down in chairs across from them. He continued to explain his family's history. "My grandfather and 'C.B.' Parker, could you imagine going through your life answering to, 'Chalmers, please come here?' So he went by 'C.B.' Grandfather and C.B. worked at Dupont Chemical from 1910 to 1915."

Charlie excused himself and went to the restroom. Arthur thought to himself, *Only in Los Angeles could one meet a young man worth two million dollars and Elizabeth Cowan.* Arthur was perplexed about Elizabeth, everyone said she was so intelligent, but all he saw was a rude and inconsiderate woman.

Charlie came back and sat down. He continued, "From 1910 to 1915 my grandfather and a colleague named Malcomb Ewing, who had a Ph.D. in chemistry from M.I.T., received three U.S. patents in chemistry at DuPont doing chemical polymerization research. DuPont had proprietary company property patents. In the summer of 1915, while on vacation at Bar Harbor, Maine, they all decided to leave Dupont and start their own company. My grandfather said he and Malcomb Ewing were strong in research and C.B. had a head for business and sales. They pooled their financial resources and borrowed $40,000 from a bank in Philadelphia and bought a chemical company called American Chemical Products. In 1915 Heinz Hagenmeyer, of German decent, said, 'The war in Europe is killing my business,' and he wanted to sell out before he lost everything. They negotiated a sale of his entire business for $65,000 and he received an established business located in a two-story, ten-thousand-square-foot brick building with its own offices, inventory, mixing vats, maintenance equipment, cleaning solvents, one hundred fifty-five-gallon filling drums, office equipment, four trucks and a 'company dog' named Heidi.

"From 1915 to 1925, they worked hard. Grandfather and Dr. Ewing obtained seven more U.S. patents in chemistry for polymerization, making better resins to strengthen textile fibers for multiple applications for rope, carpeting, canvas and parachutes, and thermoplastic resins for coatings and piping.

"In 1931, Dr. Ewing obtained a patent to reduce the viscosity of automobile oil, making it more viscous and not so difficult to start an automobile engine. Between 1931 and 1945, the business grew. In 1949, the business was audited; Dr. Ewing said he wanted to retire to West Palm Beach, Florida, in 1950. In 1950, the business had grown and moved to a five-story building at 1629 Market Street in Philadelphia with chemical production facilities located in Philadelphia, Pittsburgh and Baltimore; distribution facilities in Philadelphia, Pittsburgh, Baltimore, New York, Chicago and Detroit. Their company employed 1,200 people, had 125 trucks, twenty-five chemical railroad cars and sales at $290 million.

"Grandfather built a twenty-five-room mansion on Glenwood Avenue in Philadelphia; he owned a winter home in West Palm Beach, Florida, and a lovely summer home on Nantucket Island. The audit in 1949 showed Grandfather, C.B. and Dr. Ewing they had equity of ninety-two million dollars in stock, cash, investments, land and a net worth of thirty-one million dollars each. Dr. Ewing was given a payout of thirty-one point six million dollars and royalties on his patents and a sumptuous retirement party in June of 1950."

Arthur uncrossed his legs and said to Charlie, "This sounds like the American dream, and it is fascinating, but please excuse me, I need to use the men's room."

"Sorry, Arthur, I tend to get long-winded. Yes, it is quite a story, I'll be brief."

Arthur got up, patted Charlie on his right shoulder, and went to the men's room.

More people came into the cocktail lounge. The cocktail waitress checked to see if Charlie and Arthur wanted another drink.

Charlie said, "No, thanks."

Arthur returned to his wicker chair.

"It helps me to go through this, because for many years I never knew the whole story. My mother filled in details, my grandfather gave me details, but my father never told me anything. In August of 1950, C.B. and Grandfather had a serious disagreement. After Dr. Ewing left it wasn't the same; C.B. came and told Grandfather that Malcomb Ewing did the right thing by retiring at age sixty-eight. He said, 'I'm doing the same thing; why not sell the whole business?' Grandfather would hear nothing of selling the business.

"Well, to make a long story short, C.B. told Grandfather this was his notification that he was going to retire in 1951. This hurt my grandfather. After thirty-five years in the chemical business, his two partners were leaving.

"My father never cared for the chemical business. He said chemical fumes and odors gave him headaches and breathing problems.

"I was fifteen, in my sophomore year at Phillips Exeter, and too young to learn the business.

"Grandfather sent my dad to Lawrenceville Academy from 1927 to 1929 to enter Princeton and American Chemical Products. My father, as my grandfather said, wasn't academically talented. Father was not accepted at Princeton or any Ivy League School; he graduated from Rutgers University in 1933 with a degree in sales and marketing. Grandfather paid him a salary of $36,000 a year in 1933, provided an automobile and he worked in sales in the Northeast.

"My father, however, was an excellent athlete. He played football and baseball at Rutgers and wanted to play professional baseball for the Philadelphia Athletics. Mr. Connie Mack, the owner of the Philadelphia Athletics, told my grandfather, 'Your son has a promising career in baseball, give him a chance to play in the big leagues.' My grandfather said, 'He's already in the big leagues; it doesn't have to be playing baseball. I read Babe Ruth makes $100,000 a year with the New York Yankees. I can pay Garrett $125,000 a year and he would not be a grown man playing a boy's sport.'

"That was the conflict between my father and my grandfather. Grandfather chose me as his own project. I was fortunate to have academic ability and did well at Phillips Exeter and Yale. I majored in economics and minored in drama/theater.

"My grandfather and C.B. did not want outsiders coming into top management. In May, 1951, they sold the business to a chemical conglomerate in Frankfurt, West Germany, for three hundred million dollars.

"On October 11, 1951, my grandfather and Ester returned from a thirty-day cruise to Europe, France, Italy, Spain and Russia. Grandmother said Grandfather complained about indigestion and having trouble breathing. They arrived home on the eleventh and at seven P.M. at Glenwood, Charles, the chauffeur, parked the limousine. Grandfather asked their butler, 'Johnson,' to bring him a glass of bourbon and a glass of soda water to the library. Grandmother had gone upstairs to supervise unpacking of their luggage and the gifts for their friends. She came downstairs and called, 'Charles.' Johnson said, 'Madam, Mister Fenton is resting in the library.' She went into the library and found Grandfather seated in a leather chair with his head lying back on the headrest, barely breathing. Grandmother called his doctor and an ambulance. His doctor went in the ambulance with him to the University of Pennsylvania Hospital where he was dead on arrival. Dr. Solomon said Mr. Fenton had a massive heart attack.

"Grandfather was buried in our family crypt in Philadelphia. On October fifteenth, 1951, there was a large funeral. I came to Philadelphia from Exeter, and I never saw so many people. Among those present were the mayor of Philadelphia, U.S. congressmen, U.S. senators, a representative from President Harry S. Truman, members of the Dupont, Kelly, and Wanamaker families of Philadelphia and people from Wyomissing Industries.

"The *Philadelphia Inquirer* reported five hundred people had attended Grandfather's funeral. After his funeral, my grandmother said she would remain in Philadelphia, and wanted to probate grandfather's will and pay the estate taxes. I was given a week off from Exeter to go to Philadelphia where Grandfather's will was read by Mr. Montague Higgenbottom of Ryan, Marks and Higgenbottom, PPL. We were assembled in the law office of Mr. Higgenbottom on the fifteenth floor of the Peabody Building at 1000 Market Street in Philadelphia.

"Seven people were present. Mr. Higgenbotton read part of the will. 'In part, I, Charles Wentworth Fenton, III, hereby bequest the following sum of money:

" 'To my beloved wife, Elizabeth, ten million dollars; to my son, Charles Wentworth Fenton, II, three million dollars; to my daughter, Ophelia, three million dollars; to my grandson and namesake, Charles Wentworth Fenton, IV, the sum of two million dollars with $500,000 upon his graduation from Yale University and one point five million on his thirty-fifth birthday; to Princeton University, five million dollars; and to charities, four million dollars.' "

Charlie sat staring at the ocean.

The cocktail waitress asked if they would like another drink.

Arthur said, "Yes, two more."

The cocktail waitress returned with their drinks.

"Thanks for being a good listener, Arthur. You are the only person to whom I have told the entire story. I needed to get it off my chest." They finished their drinks, and before heading home stopped at a bookstore to pick up a book Charlie had ordered called, *Film in Hollywood from 1900–1950*.

On Monday, they went to work. Arthur and Charlie tried to alternate driving. But it was apparent that Arthur was a morning person and Charlie was a night person. Arthur went to bed at 9:30 P.M., got up at 5:00 A.M. and was at his desk at Hutton by

6:30 A.M. Charlie usually didn't go to bed until 11:00 P.M. and found it difficult to get up at 5:00 A.M., so they decided to drive separate cars. Charlie arrived at work at 7:30 A.M. Arthur wondered what he would do when he obtained his stockbroker's license, as Stewart Rosenthal required all first-year stockbrokers to be at work at 6:30 A.M.

Time passed quickly. Arthur spoke to Janet Foster at Buckley's a week later. Janet said she and her roommate were going to the USC-UCLA cocktail party at the Los Angeles Athletic Club. Arthur was encouraged by the news that she was bringing her roommate, not a boyfriend. Great!

Charlie asked Arthur for help passing the Series 7 exam. Arthur told Charlie, "After Thanksgiving, I'll tutor you like at Exeter."

On November fifteenth, Arthur and Charlie went to the pre-game cocktail party at the Los Angeles Athletic Club. It was decorated with USC's maroon and gold colors and UCLA powder blue and gold. Each school had a band playing pep songs. People arrived hearing USC's victory march, conquest and UCLA's fight song. Each school brought cheerleaders. Arthur and Charlie stood talking to Joe Harrison, Brad Cherry and Steve Dunlap when Howard Wells and Janet Foster joined them.

Howard spoke above the noise, "I went to Fresno State, what is this all about?" He then said, "Steve, you went to USC didn't you?"

Steve said, "Yes, sir, born a Trojan, die a Trojan!"

Janet Foster stood quietly. Arthur asked, "Janet, are you a USC or UCLA alumnus?"

"No, Arthur, San Diego State, I graduated last May, and you?"

"University of Arizona, class of fifty-four."

A waitress came by and offered them wine. Janet, Arthur and Charlie took a glass.

Joe Harrison said to Arthur, "Hey, Norris, who do you have to know to get personal service?"

Arthur said, "I know E.F. Hutton." Arthur asked Charlie to hold his drink while he went for pretzels and returned with finger sandwiches.

Janet took a finger sandwich and said, "Howard Wells told me you passed the Series Seven exam with a ninety percent."

"Yes, that's true, I was a math minor in college and have done well on standardized tests."

Arthur asked, "Janet, do you plan to become a stockbroker?"

"No, it's technical and too confusing to me." Janet asked, "Aren't you and Charles Fenton roommates?"

Arthur was surprised, "Yes. Charlie—he wants to be called Charlie—and I have been roommates since October."

Janet said, "He has quite a background, I've been told. He spent three years at Phillips Exeter Academy and four years at Yale University. That's about $90,000 in education costs." Janet asked, "What does his father do?"

"Charlie only told me he was an investment banker on Wall Street. I don't know any more than that."

Janet's roommate, Jennifer, worked her way through the crowd; Janet introduced her to Arthur. Jennifer said, "Quite a party and large crowd." Jennifer asked Janet, "Are we going to Lawry's for dinner at seven thirty? It's now six twenty-five."

Janet replied, "Do you want to go?"

Jennifer said, "Sure; well, Mr. Series-seven, so glad to meet you."

Arthur said, "It's mutual." Jennifer went to the ladies room.

Arthur asked Janet, "May I call you for dinner?"

She replied, "Sure," and wrote down her home telephone number on a UCLA napkin. She said, "Jennifer and I are going to the game on Saturday and we have plans after the game, call me after Thanksgiving. Have a nice evening." They left.

Arthur saw Charlie weaving and excusing himself through the throngs of people that were singing, "Fight on for USC, fight on to victory." In another part of the room, the crowd chanted "U-C-L-A beat USC!" Charlie reached Arthur and said, "I hope the L.A. fire marshall doesn't show up."

A tall thin young man with bushy reddish brown hair wearing a tweed sport coat, bow tie, white shirt, and brown slacks called out "Fenton, Fenton" to Charlie, who was standing at the bar. Charlie turned around to see who was calling, and to his surprise, standing a few feet behind him was Brian Perkins. He was

Charlie's frosh roommate at Yale. Charlie motioned to Brian to come forward. He introduced Brian to Arthur. Brian was a freshman at the University of Southern California's school of law.

Brian said, "Pleased to meet you, Arthur; Charlie told me you two met at E.F. Hutton." Brian continued and said, "Charlie Fenton is a good man."

Brian turned to Charlie and asked, "Are you flying back to the Boston to see the Yale-Harvard football game on Saturday?"

"No, we've got tickets to see USC play UCLA at the Coliseum."

Brian looked at Charlie and said, "Mr. Fenton, the Yale Eli's are playing the Harvard Crimson for the first official Ivy League football championship on November twenty-fourth, 1956 at Cambridge."

Charlie said, "Really, for the Ivy League championship?"

Brian sipped a cocktail, "Precisely, Mr. Fenton."

"That does make a difference, I'd like to see the game."

Brian added, "We'll see, Hawkins."

Charlie turned to Arthur and said, "Dale Hawkins is Yale's quarterback."

Brian continued, "And the rest of Yale's seniors, Newell, Yabowlinski, Jenkins, Durant and Powell."

Charlie thought for a moment. He turned to Arthur, "I hope you wouldn't mind if I took a rain check for the game?"

"Of course not, Charlie, if I went to Yale I'd want to see the Ivy League football championship game. Don't worry about your ticket, I'll sell it to someone at the game."

"Thanks, Arthur, I'll go back to Cambridge to see Yale defeat Harvard."

Charlie told Brian Perkins, "I'll fly to Boston, and I will call for a ticket and stay at the Marbury."

He turned to Arthur, "I need to call American Airlines to make reservations on the red eye from L.A. to Boston."

"Go ahead, I'm going to the restroom, and I'll be out front."

Arthur told Charlie, "Let's have dinner at the Great American Food Company in Santa Monica."

"Great."

The pep bands began to play another round of fight songs.

A man waved to Brian Perkins and pointed his finger to the front door indicating, "Time to leave."

Brian put his hand on Charlie's shoulder and said, "Good decision, Charles, Go Eli's—see you in Cambridge on Saturday. Nice to meet you, Arthur," shook hands with Charlie and Arthur and he disappeared into the thinning crowd.

Charlie took the American Airlines' Friday night flight from Los Angeles to Boston. He arrived at Logan Airport at 6:40 A.M., picked up his rental car and drove to the Marbury Hotel near Harvard Square. He slept until 11:00 A.M., had coffee and took a cab to Harvard's Veterans Stadium for the 1:00 Yale–Harvard football game. The trees across Harvard's campus—for late November—were about ready for winter. It was a beautiful New England fall day for the final football game of the year. The weather was cold, brisk, and clear with a temperature of 35 degrees. A stiff wind blew from the Charles River. By the end of the game, the temperature might fall below freezing to light fireplaces the first night of the year.

Charlie purchased a ticket and walked to the Yale side of the field. The stadium was almost full and Yale and Harvard bands played music to stir the crowds. As Charlie walked to his seat, he saw fans waving blue-and-white Yale banners and pennant flags. He waved to some old friends and met and shook hands with classmates who had also graduated last May. He heard a man call out, "Hey, Fenton, over here." He squinted up into the Yale section and saw Brian Perkins waving to an empty seat in his row of Bulldog fans. Charlie also saw Nicole Dumont, whom he had dated during his sophomore year. He had heard that Nicole was finishing her second year to become an actress at the Yale School of Drama. Charlie took his seat and watched the football game. At half-time he went to the men's room and bought a hot dog and Coke. He was returning to his seat when Nicole Dumont appeared in the crowd and said, "Hello, Charles Fenton." Charlie had not seen Nicole in almost a year. She wore a long tan suede skirt, black leather boots, waist-length black leather jacket, and a gray muffler around her neck. She looked great with her brown hair cut in a pageboy and her large brown eyes. "Well, hello, Nicole," Charlie replied. "I saw you in the stands but you were gone at half-time. How are you doing?"

They chatted. Nicole updated Charlie saying that in May she would graduate from Yale's Drama School and then she was going to Paris and study acting and to improve her French. She wanted to try to become a European actress. Charlie told her he was in training to become a stockbroker with E.F. Hutton. They got to their aisle in the stadium. Nicole took a notepad from her purse and wrote down her address and telephone number and gave it to Charlie. "Here's my address and phone number. Call me if you get back to New Haven." A roar went up from the crowd as Yale scored a touchdown, leading Harvard 35 to 7.

Charlie told Nicole, "You look like a *Vogue* model—you'll do well."

She looked at Charlie. "Thank you, Charles—I mean Charlie—always the gentleman. Tell your parents I said hello."

Charlie replied, "I'll be in Greenwich again for Thanksgiving."

"How nice, Charlie, just jetting around the country like the idle rich."

"Nicole, that isn't nice," Charlie interjected. "You know I'm not an idle rich person."

Nicole said, "*Au revoir*," and they shook hands. Charlie rejoined his friends. The football game ended and Yale had won its first official Ivy League football championship 42–14 over Harvard.

Charlie and the crowd of happy Yale fans filed out of Veterans Stadium. Charlie looked for Nicole among the crowd, but she was gone. Brian Perkins invited Charlie to a post-game celebration at the Cambridge Inn; Charlie declined. He thanked Brian, and told him he had to catch a 7:45 A.M. flight back to Los Angeles and did not want to fly back with a bad hangover.

When Charlie arrived at the apartment Sunday evening, Arthur was on the telephone talking to Janet Foster. He waved hello to Charlie and signaled a "thumbs up." Charlie waved hello and went into his bedroom, unpacked his suitcase, took a shower and came out and poured himself a bourbon and water.

Arthur said, "Welcome home. I saw Yale defeated Harvard

forty-two to fourteen, so the football game made your trip. USC defeated UCLA ten to seven, and it rained Saturday."

Charlie answered, "It was a good trip, no problems with connections, but it was exhausting flying at night and then going all the next day."

"I have Chinese in the refrigerator."

"I'm a little hungry." He ate an egg roll and some sweet-and-sour pork and fried rice.

Arthur told Charlie he talked to Janet Foster at the football game. They planned to get together after Thanksgiving.

Charlie said, "I can't believe I'm flying back to Boston on Wednesday."

The Thanksgiving holiday went quickly. Charlie took the 1:30 P.M. American Airlines flight to Boston and arrived at 9:30 P.M. He stayed at the Boston Hilton and drove to Greenwich the next morning arriving home at 1:00 P.M.

Arthur was concerned about driving his Ford to Phoenix. He went to the bank, withdrew $4,000, and made a down payment on a new dark blue 1956 Chevrolet Bel Air Sedan and drove it to Phoenix. He had a nice Thanksgiving with eleven members of his family for the first time in four years.

Arthur and Charlie returned to work on Monday. Charlie had a meeting with Stewart Rosenthal, who said he was scheduled to take the Series 7 practice exam the following Thursday, and the real Series 7 exam on December twelfth. Charlie saw Arthur at lunch and told him about his meeting with Stewart Rosenthal. He asked Arthur if he would tutor him to pass the Series 7 exam. Arthur said, "absolutely."

That night, Arthur gave Charlie 500 review cards to memorize, with a question on one side and the answer on the other. The 500 cards covered questions and answers for the test. He told Charlie to study the 500 cards every night. On Sunday, he would show him how to work word problems using seven equations. Arthur told Charlie it took him three weeks to figure out how to "attack" the test and to read the questions, define what they asked and then to look at the question for a combination of addition, subtraction, multiplication, or division. Arthur said no matter if it were a problem on puts/calls options, hedges/straddles, increase/decrease in price of stock, bond prices on the par/premium/discount, it took on an equation.

The following Sunday they worked from 1:00 P.M.—8:00 P.M. on the test. Charlie felt like a pincushion. They did more reviews Monday and Tuesday. Charlie took the Series 7 exam and passed it with a score of 79 percent. He and Arthur were ecstatic. Charlie called Nicole Dumont and told her he passed the Series 7 exam with a 79 percent. He then called his parents and they congratulated him, but were perplexed how Charlie passed the exam since he was not "a mathematical person."

Howard Wells and Stan Rosenthal were both happy. Charlie was congratulated as the new "rookie" on the sales team with a new desk, a view of downtown Los Angeles, and a raise to $600.00 a week, and one month's free parking.

Charlie took Arthur to dinner at Chasen's on Friday to thank him for his help passing the Series 7 examination.

On Saturday, Charlie went Christmas shopping. Arthur and Janet went to the Los Angeles Art Museum to see the French Impressionist exhibit, and then had dinner in West Los Angeles at the Tiki Hut, a Polynesian restaurant with palm trees, and cocktail waitresses and waiters dressed in South Sea Island attire. They enjoyed a dinner with mai tais, marinated steaks, sweet potatoes, tempura shrimp, banana bread and wine. Janet told Arthur that she lived at Fort Shafter, Hawaii, near Honolulu from 1950 to 1953 with her mother and brother while her father was in Korea. She said she went to the American school on the Post; she was an "Army brat" and had lived around the world. Arthur said he grew up in Tucson, was in the Army in Korea, and worked at Hutton and was still considering other options, which were law school or the CIA.

Charlie brought his new lady friend to the apartment to meet Arthur. He was introduced to her at a Yale alumni Christmas party and her name was Brecken Hutchins. Charlie said a fellow Yalie, Steve Hall, a CPA, invited Brecken and a girlfriend to his Christmas party in Beverly Hills. Brecken was quite attractive and a graduate of Santa Monica Junior College and an aspiring actress. Charlie told Arthur he found her fascinating; she was twenty-six and knew her way around Los Angeles. She had gotten small parts in *The Crucible, Our Town, Les Miserables,* and *A Streetcar Named Desire* in her acting career. Arthur got the impression that she was street smart.

The Friday before Christmas, Arthur, Janet, Charlie and Brecken went to Hutton's annual black tie Christmas party at the Beverly Hilton hotel. "Hutton" did not spare any expense for their party. There were heavy hors d'oeuvres, a carved crystal ice "H", open bar from 6:30 to 7:30 P.M., a dinner with prime rib or lobster, potatoes, rice, salad and red or white wine on the table. After dinner, "Santa Claus" passed out prizes, and a comedian told some "blue" jokes all in good fun, and then dancing. Arthur and Charlie wore traditional black-tie formal attire; Janet wore a seasonal conservative red dress; and Brecken wore a stunning tight black gown with a peek-a-boo front, and she looked elegant befitting a Hollywood starlet. Several men complimented Charlie on his date. Charlie got home at 4:30 in the morning. He told Arthur it was an "interesting evening."

Charlie said Brecken knew exactly what she wanted and was auditioning at Warner Brothers for a role in *Someone Came Calling,* and it didn't matter how she got the role, it was "not what you know, but who you blow"; and she said her time had come. She knew she was more talented than her competition, but lost out, and this time she did not intend to lose out.

Charlie and Arthur put up a Christmas tree and decorated the apartment. The following Tuesday, Arthur, Janet, Charlie, and Brecken saw *The Nutcracker*; Charlie and Brecken went for a nightcap in Hollywood.

Arthur drove Janet home, and she said she was leaving for San Diego on Wednesday and would return to L.A. on Tuesday, could they "do something" on New Year's Eve to ring in 1957? Arthur said he would look forward to that. Charlie did not come home until morning and he said, "Brecken will make it in Hollywood."

On December twenty-third, a large carton arrived for Charlie from Greenwich, Connecticut. Charlie brought the carton into the apartment and opened it. It contained ten Christmas presents with expensive Christmas wrapping paper. Arthur saw the wrapped presents on the floor and he asked, "Did Santa Claus arrive?"

"These are from my parents, some are for you."

Arthur looked at the presents. "Presents for me?"

Charlie looked at the address labels. "Four are for you and six for me."

Charlie told Arthur, "This is my parents' appreciation for helping me pass the Series 7 test."

"How thoughtful. I would like to thank them when you call tomorrow."

It was dark outside and someone knocked at the front door. Charlie answered the door; it was Brecken. She wore a red Santa Claus cap with a white ball on the top.

"Merry Christmas, Charlie," she said and gave him a kiss. "I told you I'd drop by on my way up to Ventura and bring you some presents for the man who has everything. Just kidding, my dear," and she gave Charlie another kiss.

Brecken opened a large shopping bag and took out three presents. She gave two presents to Charlie and one to Arthur. Charlie went into his bedroom and returned with two presents for her. Charlie turned on the Christmas tree lights and Christmas music on the radio.

Charlie poured three glasses of eggnog. He gave one to Brecken and one to Arthur and took one. He raised his glass and said, "Merry Christmas and cheers."

Brecken said, "I really need to leave, do you want to open your presents now?" She looked at Charlie.

"Sure, ho, ho, ho." Charlie opened one present from Brecken and it was a movie director's chair from Metro-Goldwyn-Mayer; on the back, it said DIRECTOR. Her card read, "To a future Billy Wilder—Good luck Charlie, Love, Brecken."

Charlie loved it. He gave Brecken a kiss and a hug. Brecken opened one present. It was an expensive gold-link chain necklace and the other present was a beige cashmere sweater and her initials in brown, BMH-Brecken Marilyn Hutchins. "I love it," she said and kissed Charlie.

Brecken's other gift to Charlie was a movie director's megaphone.

Charlie said, "All I need now is a movie."

Arthur replied, "That will come."

Arthur opened his gift from Brecken; it was a University of Arizona paperweight with the college seal. Arthur thanked Brecken. Brecken opened Arthur's gift, which was a set of Crane stationery.

Brecken said, "Wow, it's almost six thirty, I've got to going. Are we still going to the Ambassador Hotel for New Year's Eve?"

Arthur said, "Sure, aren't we, Charlie?"

"Yes, we have the last table of four and it is a 1920's costume theme party with costumes required. There is a five-course dinner, a bottle of champagne per couple and at midnight, noise makers with the gratuity included."

Brecken said, "A 1920's theme, I know who I'm going to dress like, Jean Harlow."

"Jean Harlow in a slinky white silk dress? What about blonde hair?" asked Charlie.

"I have a wig. Why don't you go as Charlie Chaplin?"

"I will; Charlie Chaplin is my favorite actor."

"And what about you, Arthur?" asked Brecken.

"Who else, but Elliott Ness."

Charlie asked, "and Janet?"

"A flapper."

"What a crew," said Arthur.

"Let's take a limousine," said Charlie. "I'll pop."

Brecken said, "It will be fun."

Charlie and Arthur gave Brecken a hug and she said, "Merry Christmas," and she went out the door.

Arthur asked Charlie how much New Year's Eve would cost at the Chateau Hotel.

"Eighty-five dollars a person."

"Why don't we go down to the Breakers for dinner and then call it a night?"

Arthur said, "Fine."

On Christmas morning they opened their presents. Charlie's parents sent Arthur two Brooks Brothers crewneck wool sweaters, a Brooks Brothers white shirt, and a red, blue and yellow striped regimental tie.

Arthur told Charlie, "What a haul."

Charlie said, "Thank you, I took the liberty of looking at your clothing sizes over Thanksgiving."

Charlie received a typewriter, a world globe, black leather dress gloves, three Brooks Brothers dress shirts, three ties, *The Great Gatsby* and *The Stockbrokers' Guide to Success.*

Charlie and Arthur had their Christmas dinner at the Beverly Hilton Hotel.

Janet and Brecken returned to Los Angeles on Saturday. They went to the Chateau, which had been an established hotel since the 1930's for Hollywood celebrities. Many famous Hollywood movie stars from the Golden Years of Hollywood had lodged at the Ambassador. Janet looked fantastic wearing a black sequin 1920's flapper dress, black headband, red beads, and red shoes. Brecken was stunning. She wore a slinky silver Jean Harlow dress with a lowcut back, spaghetti straps, a platinum blonde wig and silver high heel shoes.

Charlie said, "Jean Harlow would be pleased."

Charlie was a hit as "The Little Tramp" when he did his Charlie Chaplin routine. Arthur wore a Navy "G Man" suit, police badge, and a gray Stetson hat with a toy sub-machine gun. It was an enjoyable night. A photographer took their pictures, which Charlie had framed and hung on the wall of his office at Hutton.

It was now 1957.

Hutton made some major announcements at the annual meeting on Monday, January 7, 1957. The president of E.F. Hutton, an executive vice president, and two senior vice presidents flew to Los Angeles from New York for the meeting. They said that Hutton had signed a ten-year lease on their building, and they were going to remodel the offices and reception area, and install a new telephone system, hire ten new stockbrokers, five broker's assistants, and from March to August they were going to conduct a contest. The bottom line was California was a tremendous market and Hutton was going to get its market share. No personal vacations, except for unusual circumstances, would be approved from March to August.

There would be a six-month sales competition. The top prize was $25,000 second $15,000, and third $10,000. All support staff will be assigned to a sales team and will receive $5,000 for being on the winning team along with two extra vacation days in 1957.

The president of Hutton said, "This year we'll separate men from boys. I want to see ten million dollars' growth. You can do it. Over the next five years, Hutton will open new offices in San Diego, San Jose, Santa Barbara, Anaheim, Santa Rosa, and Bakersfield." He said, "Every stockbroker here should make $75,000 to $150,000 a year."

That night at home, Charlie told Arthur he had to make up his mind about Brecken. She told him after Christmas at dinner that he would have a hard time getting a career in Hollywood without acting experience. She said, "You learn to act by acting—not reading a book." Her friends resented his idea of going to USC and becoming a schoolbook director. She said, "You need to get down in the trenches to learn the business."

Charlie said, "This is becoming a point of irritation for me. I'm not going to defend myself, since most of them never went to college or didn't finish college. They call me the poor little rich kid."

Arthur told Charlie, "You're in the real world now."

Charlie said Brecken told him he should enroll in an acting class at the L.A. Actor's School. She was adamant that you cannot fake it in this business, and "It's too cutthroat, even if you have connections. The only thing that matters about success in Hollywood is money, talent and proven success on the silver screen."

Charlie enrolled in a Saturday class in West Hollywood at the L.A. Actor's Guild. Brecken told him, "You've done the right thing. Give it a year, you'll know, and others will know, if you have talent." She said, "You can't direct a two-hour motion picture without knowing dialogue, good from bad acting, lighting, sound, make-up, and costumes. The casting couch only goes so far."

Janet and Arthur began to see each other on a more regular

basis; by February, they had a romantic relationship. They enjoyed playing tennis, riding bicycles, running on the beach, going to movies and out to dinner, and occasionally seeing Charlie and Brecken for a movie in Westwood.

Hutton's offices were remodeled with new carpeting, painting, a modern telephone exchange system, and training for the sales staff in product knowledge, phone calling procedures, closing sales, stock-market product knowledge and maintaining customer relations. It was a grind for Arthur and Charlie.

Charlie said he was going to see it through until next September and start his career in motion pictures.

Arthur knew he did not need to think anymore whether Janet was "wife material." He proposed to her on June thirtieth during dinner in Beverly Hills. She accepted! They flew to San Antonio for Arthur to meet her parents and drove to Phoenix for Janet to meet his family.

On September 14, 1956, Arthur and Janet were married in the Episcopal Church of the Redeemer in San Diego with their reception at the Miramar Naval Officers' Club.

Charlie and Brecken attended their wedding and reception. Brecken wore a pale blue dress, with a décolleté neckline, white gloves, diamond earrings, a strand of pearls and a white wide brim hat. Charlie wore a gray double-breasted Pierre Cardin designer suit, white shirt with French cuffs, silk tie and black shoes. Brecken and Charlie were now ready to "Conquer Hollywood." Charlie told Arthur he had moved into a new apartment in Brentwood and had rented Brecken a studio apartment near his "for appearances." Charlie said, "Her advice was correct—I was not aware of the hard work it takes to make movies."

Charlie said he received a letter from Nicole Dumont asking him to "Visit her soon in Paris."

Charlie thanked Arthur for sharing his apartment as roommates, and told him he had thoroughly enjoyed rooming with him over the past eleven months. He was going to resign from Hutton in August. He and Brecken were going to Europe to travel until next May. In June he would enroll in the L.A. Actors Guild and then start school in September at the USC School of Film. Brecken had become a solid influence for him in getting into the movie business. He had done what his parents wanted him to do by succeeding as a stockbroker at Hutton. Now, he was going to move along with his own life doing what he wanted to do. Brecken had been a positive influence, the same as Arthur had been for the past eleven months, and he loved both of them.

Arthur and Janet flew on United Airlines from Los Angeles to Honolulu for a ten-day honeymoon. Janet's father rented them a suite with an ocean view at the Royal Hawaiian Hotel. Its décor was out of the 1930s. The world-renowned hotel had every ambiance with its high ceilings, thick carpeting, an ocean bar and Hawaiian music in the hotel. The hotel's grounds were full of lush hibiscus, bougainvillea and orchid flowers.

Janet was the tour guide. They arose early each morning, ran on the beach, took a shower and had breakfast in the hotel. They rented a car and drove around Oahu and down the middle of the island to see the great Hawaiian pineapple plantations. Janet took Arthur to the Honolulu farmer's market, Fort Shafter, and showed him where she lived from 1950–1953. They took a sunset dinner cruise with a Polynesian show and walked Waikiki beach at night. They drove to Diamond Head through Kahala and hiked up to the top of Diamond Head and saw the panoramic view at "the top of the world." They went to Pearl Harbor and saw the *U.S.S. Arizona* memorial and the military cemetery of the Pacific, overlooking Honolulu. They were both sad to leave "paradise."

6

Arthur and Janet Norris arrived home from work at 6:20 P.M. on Friday. Arthur went to the mailbox and found an eight-inch-by-eleven-inch U.S. government manila envelope in the mailbox from P.O. Box 7141, Langley, Virginia. Arthur took the mail into the apartment and told Janet there was an envelope for him from Langley. He sat down at the dining room table and opened the envelope. He read an enclosed letter:

Dear Mr. Norris;
    It is our pleasure to inform you that based upon the favorable results of your background investigation, and the recommendation of our hiring committee, we will offer you a position of employment effective December 1, 1957.

It was October fourth. The letter said to follow the enclosed instructions. Get an acceptance of employment form signed and notarized, and make arrangements with Allied Van Lines to pick up their household goods in Westwood on November fifteenth. Arthur was pleased. He stood up, hugged Janet, and gave her a kiss.

"They hired me!" he said excitedly. "Let's go to dinner at Pontevecchio and celebrate." Pontevecchio's was Arthur's favorite Italian restaurant in Santa Monica. Janet brought out two glasses of chilled Sauvignon Blanc wine, cheese and crackers as a snack.

"Congratulations," she said, "a toast to your new career in the CIA."

Arthur called his parents in Phoenix. He told them he was hired by the CIA and would start work on December first. His parents congratulated him, his father asked if he and Janet would stop in Phoenix on their way back to Washington, D.C. Arthur said they had to move, find an apartment and take some time to make the transition from Hutton to the CIA; therefore they would drive straight from Los Angeles to Washington, D.C. Arthur told his parents he and Janet would arrive at Langley on November twentieth, and stay at the Lee motel until they moved into an apartment.

As they were ending their telephone conversation, Arthur's father said with mirth, "Arthur, I guess this will be the last time for several years that your mother and I will call you by your real name and know where you are actually living!"

Arthur laughed and said good-bye. Janet called her parents and told them that the CIA hired Arthur. Her parents congratulated Arthur and wished him good luck.

Arthur called Charlie Fenton and told him the news; they talked for ten minutes. Charlie was attending the University of Southern California's film school and Brecken was auditioning for a role in the film *Picnic*. Charlie and Brecken were fine. Charlie said his relationship with Brecken was also showing promise for marriage as a wife. When Arthur and Charlie finished their conversation, Charlie told Arthur, "Keep in touch, and don't forget to look over your shoulder to see who is walking behind you!"

They had an appointment with Howard Wells for 10:00 A.M. Monday morning. They went to his office and gave him their letters of resignation and thanked him and Hutton for the opportunity of working at Hutton. Howard read their letters. He shut the office door. "I'm sorry you're leaving our company, I realize you are young and there are other opportunities, but I'm disappointed we didn't have the opportunity to see you rise in the company. There will be great opportunities for Hutton employees in the future, as I said in January. Arthur, you are very intelligent and hard working, and have potential to become the senior executive vice president in New York in ten years, with a salary of $500,000 a year. I'm sure you considered these matters in your decision to leave Hutton. In any event, I wish you both the best. If anything changes, and you return to Los Angeles, keep us in mind. I hold no ill will toward either of you."

Howard Wells told them if they cleared their desks and file cabinets they could leave today. They shook hands and Howard said, "Excuse me," and he took another telephone call. Arthur and Janet left his office. They cleaned their desks, said good-bye and went to lunch at the Great American Food Company in Santa Monica, near the ocean.

Arthur and Janet remained at home another week to get organized and plan their move. They made air travel reservations, and reservations at the Outrigger Waikiki in Honolulu for two weeks. When they arrived home there was a large envelope for Arthur from Langley. It contained information and a large map of northern Virginia and Washington, D.C. It was the Langley chamber of commerce with information on rental homes, apartments, banks, hospitals, doctors, dentists, schools, churches and restaurants. The Agency recommended two apartment complexes; one apartment complex was called "The Woodlands," located on Cedar Crest Road off Dolly Madison Highway, and was twelve miles from the CIA. Many personnel stayed there, it was reported clean, well-run and safe. They had two- or three-bedroom apartments with a living room and fireplace, kitchen, breakfast nook, two bathrooms, large closets, air-conditioning, swimming pool and a carport. The rent was $235 to $250 a month. The other apartment, "The Abbington," had luxury apartments and three to four bedrooms, laundry service, maid service, a full-service restaurant, two swimming pools and country club privileges from $400 to $550 a month.

Arthur called Allied Van Lines; he confirmed they would pick up their household goods on November fifteenth. He called Charlie Fenton and made arrangements for them to meet him and Janet at Alice's restaurant for lunch in Westwood on Saturday. They had lunch and caught up. Charlie had lost more weight and felt better, and Brecken was now a blonde. Charlie said he had joined a fitness club in Brentwood and exercised three times a week from 8:00 to 9:00 A.M. He loved USC's film school and had met Steve McQueen, Alan Ladd, and Natalie Wood at an actor's workshop. Brecken said Charlie had talent to succeed as a director. Arthur told Charlie when they were settled at Langley, he would call him and tell him their address and telephone number. They finished lunch, hugged one another, and left the restaurant. Arthur did not see Charlie for the next twelve years.

Arthur and Janet departed Los Angeles and planned to take the southern route to Virginia. After arriving, they moved into The Woodlands apartment.

Allied Van Lines delivered their household goods on November twenty-fourth. They got unpacked and then spent five days sightseeing around Washington, D.C. and Langley while getting to know the area. Janet prepared Thanksgiving dinner for them with all the trimmings. They called Charlie, told him and Brecken that they found an apartment, and gave Charlie their home address and telephone number. On Thanksgiving night, they saw *The African Queen* with Humphrey Bogart and Katharine Hepburn. On Saturday, they went shopping and bought plants and knick-knacks, which Janet said would make the apartment more like home. Arthur went to the Esso service station, bought two new snow tires and had them mounted on the Chevrolet. Saturday night they went to a steak house for dinner. On Sunday, Janet built a fire in the fireplace and Arthur got organized for his first day of work on Monday. They watched television until 10:00, and Janet went to bed. Arthur had nervous energy. He read J.D. Salinger's *Catcher in the Rye* until 11:30, then went to bed and arose at 5:30 A.M., took a shower and got dressed. Janet fixed him breakfast and at 7:10 A.M. he gave her a kiss and a hug, left the apartment and drove to work.

The traffic was light compared to L.A. He arrived at the CIA building at 8:10 A.M., decided to buy a paper, went back to the "First Cup" coffee shop, ordered a cup of coffee, read the *Washington Post* and arrived at the CIA at 8:50 A.M. He locked his car and walked to the front door of a large five-story, concrete, steel-and-glass building. He opened one of double doors at the main entrance and made a visual examination of the lobby, looking down he saw the great seal of the Central Intelligence Agency on the lobby floor. He also saw surrounding marble walls, a large security desk console fifty feet in front of him with a U.S. flag and a flag of the state of Virginia beside the console.

A man in his fifties, wearing a navy blue uniform and a badge rose and said, "Yes, Sir, may I help you?"

Arthur saw the man was also wearing a Smith and Wesson .38-caliber pistol in a holster on his right hip. Arthur walked to the man, held up his security badge and said, "Good morning, Sir, I'm Arthur Norris, a new employee." Arthur stopped at the console, and saw black-and-white television-like pictures revolving on a screen, showing different rooms and hallways of the building on a continuous basis.

The security guard said, "May I see your one-day identification pass?" Arthur handed it to him; the security guard pulled out a black notebook and moved his right index finger down a page until he came to #501017, which was Arthur's security badge number. He looked at Arthur and said, "Are you Arthur Edward Norris?"

"Yes, I am," Arthur replied. He saw a military nameplate setting on the console; it said Raymond L. Walker, USMC (Ret.).

The guard said, "Have a seat, Mr. Norris, someone will be here shortly to escort you inside the building."

"Okay," said Arthur. "Are you retired from the Marine Corps?" The guard looked at him.

"Yes, Sir, twenty-eight years. Were you in the military?" asked the guard.

"Yes," said Arthur. "Two years as an Artillery Officer in the Army with one year in the 402nd artillery battalion, Second Infantry Division in South Korea."

Walker said, "That's good, the Army's okay."

Arthur took a seat and the security guard made a telephone call. Arthur heard him say, "Mr. Norris is at the front desk . . . all right." He hung up the phone and motioned Arthur to come to the console. The guard extended his right hand and said, "Welcome aboard; it's good to have someone ex-military, the Army does a good job after the Marines secure a beachhead." He laughed and said, "Mr. Baker, the assistant personnel director is on his way here to meet you."

"Thank you," said Arthur.

In a few minutes, a slightly built man in his early fifties appeared, wearing horn-rimmed glasses, a maroon polka-dot bow tie, oxford blue button-down shirt, tweed coat, gray slacks, and penny loafers. "Mr. Norris, I'm Preston Baker, Assistant Director of Personnel."

Arthur thought to himself, *He's Princeton, class of '45.*

Baker shook Arthur's hand and said, "We have twelve new hires arriving today, I'm glad you're here so we can get you started in-processing. Please follow me."

They walked to the left of the security console to a metal door. Mr. Baker punched four numbers into the digital keypad on the wall and a door opened, leading down a long hallway. Above the door, a sign read, NO ENTRY WITHOUT PROPER AUTHORIZATION. They walked down the hallway; it was silent, and no names were on metal doors, only numbers. Mr. Baker stopped at the next-to-last door on the right side; punched four numbers into the digital pad and it buzzed open.

He turned to Arthur and said, "This is the office of the Director of Security." Arthur saw ten desks in two rows in a windowless room with steel file cabinets, and iron bars to secure the file cabinets. On each desk was a typewriter. The men wore business suits and the women wore conservative dresses.

Preston walked to a man sitting at a desk, apparently a supervisor, and said, "John, this is Arthur Norris, a new hire."

Preston turned to Arthur and said, "This is John Maxwell, Director of Security." Arthur and John shook hands.

In a moment, a woman brought a file folder to John Maxwell and said, "Here is Mr. Norris' file."

"Thank you." John looked at Arthur and said "You'll be here most of the day, when you finish I'll take you to the fourth-floor personnel office and complete your paperwork."

John Maxwell told Arthur, "Please remove your jewelry, wristwatch, wallet, and car keys and place them into this manila envelope. Go into the first door on the left and provide a urine sample into the plastic bottle and place the bottle on card number one, don't drink any water until you urinate. You may run tap water."

Arthur went into the bathroom, urinated, and the running water helped him fill the bottle. He put the cap on the bottle, placed it on card number one, and left the bathroom.

"Very good," said John Maxwell. "During the remainder of

the morning you will be fingerprinted, photographed, issued your identification card and have a physical examination, chest x-ray and dental examination."

After the physical and dental examinations were finished, Preston Baker told Arthur, "There is now increased emphasis on physical fitness, and new hires will do physical training three times a week for eight months."

Preston took Arthur into a room which had exercise equipment, sit-up benches, treadmills, and weight machines. Arthur was assigned to locker number 10 and was also issued two t-shirts, athletic shorts, and athletic supporters. Preston told him he would be given a physical fitness test. He would perform sit-ups, push-ups, perform physical dexterity tests by touching his toes and stepping on and off a block for two minutes. Arthur completed twenty-two sit-ups, fifteen push-ups, walked a mile on the treadmill in ten minutes, but barely touched his toes. Preston told Arthur that at the end of the eight months that he would have to do sixty sit-ups, thirty push-ups, and run a mile in less than eight minutes. All trainees had to pass the physical fitness test.

Preston Baker said, "We have too many new hires reporting to us overweight and out of shape; the agency is now instituting a more rigorous physical fitness and weight control program worldwide." A medical doctor took Arthur's blood pressure, standing, and exercising heart rate, and pronounced him physically fit for the training. Preston told Arthur to take his time, take a shower, and then they would go to lunch in the cafeteria.

At 12:15 P.M., Preston Baker and Arthur returned to the Director of Security's office. Then they took an elevator to the employees cafeteria on the third floor. The cafeteria was institutional with a gray linoleum floor, metal tables, white tablecloths, and vinyl-covered chairs. Preston and Arthur stood together in the cafeteria serving line and they each ordered a bowl of soup, turkey sandwich and iced tea. Arthur scanned the cafeteria and saw it did not have any windows. There was a single government clock attached to one wall. The employees wore business attire. Most men wore business suits while some wore sweaters with a dress shirt and tie. They had military-style haircuts, no facial hair, and no sideburns. The women wore their hair set, and not below their shoulders in length. The people sat and ate with little conversation at the tables; it was quiet in the cafeteria.

Arthur and Preston ate their lunch and talked. Preston complimented Arthur on his physical fitness. Arthur said he tried to remain physically fit. They talked about the weather that had gotten colder and they both hoped it would snow a little for Christmas. Preston told Arthur he had noted in Arthur's personnel file that he was graduated Cum Laude from the University of Arizona in 1954 and had studied economics and mathematics and also been in the U.S. Army. Preston said the Agency desired its male employees to have prior military service for field paramilitary assignments. Preston told Arthur that he had graduated from Princeton University in 1944, and during World War II had been a Captain in the Army Air Corps Photo Reconnaissance Intelligence stationed at Bolling Air Force Base, Washington, D.C.

They finished lunch. Preston took Arthur to the Director of Personnel and Administration on the third floor. The office had small windows with steel bars and black drapes on the interior sides of the windows. Arthur was shown to a desk. A young woman who looked like a librarian brought Arthur a stack of papers to complete for his personnel file.

She looked at Arthur and said, "Mr. Norris, I'm Miss Whipple, Mr. Baker's personal assistant." They shook hands. "Please sit down, use a number-two pencil, and complete these forms. Do not erase, as it will discolor the carbon paper and smear the page. If you make a mistake, raise your hand and I'll bring you another form. Any questions? Once you're done, you may go home. Please tell Mr. Baker when you leave. He will escort you out of the building."

Arthur picked up a number-two government pencil and filled out the forms. He looked out the window and saw the gray December sky, and then he sat and read the CIA's employee manual which Miss Whipple gave to him. The manual explained everything he needed to know, including the admonition that

"You now represent the most sensitive agency in the U.S. government. Your behavior must be beyond reproach at all times."

Shucks, Arthur thought, *no more booze and broads.*

He filled out paperwork for his W-2 income withholding statement, an application for U.S. government medical, dental, and disability insurance; $100,000 life-insurance coverage; an allotment for the car payment; and fifty dollars deduction per paycheck for a U.S. savings bond. His starting annual salary with a college degree and two years in the U.S. Army was $48,000 per year. That was $42,000 more than he made in the U.S. Army. He completed the forms and returned them to Miss Whipple.

She said, "We are paid every other Friday; your first pay check will be withheld for two weeks after employment, then your checks are paid in personnel or will be mailed to your home or bank." Arthur elected to have his check mailed to the apartment. Arthur finished filling out the paperwork.

Preston Baker came over to the desk and handed him a Field Agent's training program inscribed: *Arthur E. Norris, Class # 58-A.* The manual contained a sanitized training schedule for the next eight months, so families would know the field training program.

Preston told Arthur to read the manual and that the formal training would start on Monday, January 3, 1958. There were sixteen trainees in his class.

Preston said, "The Christmas holiday schedule begins on December twentieth, and continues to the end of the year. There are plenty of activities for your wife."

Preston continued, "Over Christmas, read the sanitized case files, historical accounts of intelligence craft; German operations in World Wars I and II; the Office of Strategic Services (OSS) under Colonel 'Wild' Bill Donovan; British MI-5; FBI files; military intelligence dossiers and the KGB and Soviet Intelligence Services. You and the other trainees will receive briefings in each directorate, and take physical training from three thirty to four thirty on Tuesday and Thursday." Preston Baker checked his wristwatch. It was 4:05.

"Are there any questions?" Preston asked Arthur.

"No," Arthur replied.

Preston continued; "Just to let you know, Arthur, it's not all work. We have a great Christmas party at a location to be announced."

"Great."

"Okay. See you tomorrow at nine A.M. I've made arrangements tomorrow for you to visit staff sections. We will have your class meet Mr. Helms next Monday in his office for ten minutes."

Arthur shook hands with Preston, got his overcoat, and Preston presented Arthur with a new CIA employee badge and permanent identification card. "Don't lose this, please put it where the security guard can see it. Goodnight."

Arthur took the elevator to the first floor, got out his I.D. badge, and showed it to another security guard standing at the console, and said, "Goodnight." The guard nodded, acknowledging that he saw the badge. Arthur went out the front door. He thought, *I have worked for the CIA for one day.* He pulled the collar of his raincoat closer to his neck and walked to the car. He started his car, pulled out of the parking lot, and went out to Dolly Madison Highway. It was 5:05 P.M.; the temperature was twenty-six degrees outside. Arthur glanced at CIA Headquarters as he drove by.

My God, he thought, *all the secrets that place now holds.*

He pulled onto Dolly Madison Highway and drove to Cedar Crest Lane. The traffic was light, compared to Los Angeles. Christmas decorations were being placed in the stores, and when he passed the shopping center, it was well-decorated with Christmas lights. A Santa Claus was standing next to a large red kettle, ringing a bell. Arthur drove in silence until he saw the sign to Woodland Avenue. He turned right, went down Woodland Avenue, pulled into the Woodland apartments, and parked in carport number eight. As he reached in the car for his briefcase, a man wearing a Stetson hat and overcoat approached him. He had gray hair and glasses.

"Good evening, I'm James Smith."

Arthur stepped backward and raised his briefcase to protect himself. The man had appeared out of nowhere. He startled Arthur. Arthur's heart beat rapidly in a flight or fight response. The man stood in front of Arthur and extended his right hand.

"Sorry," he said, "I didn't mean to startle you. I saw you pull your car into the carport and I wanted to introduce myself. I'm James Smith. My wife's name is Eloise, we live in number five."

Arthur wasn't interested in chit-chat, but he extended his hand and said, "Pleased to meet you. I'm Arthur Norris. My wife Janet and I live in apartment number eight."

"Oh, I know where you live," James said. "Eloise and I knew the people who lived in that apartment before you. I believe it was Mr. And Mrs. Stallworth."

Arthur was getting irritated.

"Well, you know, Arthur . . . may I call you Arthur?"

"Yes."

"Well, we never got to know Mr. and Mrs. Stallworth. Betty and Tim Reed in number three said he only said hello a few times in eight months."

Arthur was getting impatient, especially when Mr. Smith called out "eight," "five," and "three" like cellblock numbers.

James Smith continued. "We saw you move into number eight on November twenty-third. We thought you were moving, so Eloise and I didn't come by to say hello. You know, we've heard the CIA has an ad which recommends people to the Woodlands. Can you imagine all of the spies or weird people who might rent here?"

Arthur was ready to tell him to please leave. "Excuse me, Mr. Smith, I've got to get inside; it's been a long day."

"Oh, don't let me hold you up, Arthur, I'm only trying to be friendly. I like to know my neighbors. By the way, Arthur, where do you work?"

Arthur thought for a minute. He said, "I'm in the import-export business in South America. Do you speak Spanish?"

"Oh my, no," Smith said, "just good old English."

"Good night, Mr. Smith," said Arthur.

James Smith said, "Well, that sounds like Mr. Stallworth. He said he was in the international oil business—you know, Saudi Arabia, Venezuela and all those foreign places. Well, I told Eloise, she said, 'Like crap; he works for the CIA, mind your own business.' He and his wife . . . I never learned her name . . . they were not friendly."

Arthur looked at his watch.

"Well, one day I waited, I followed him to work. Do you know where he went? Right to Langley at CIA . . . yes, the CIA. I came home and told Eloise that perhaps he was a Russian spy or assassin. The next week I was coming out of the apartment and three men dressed in dark suits came up to me in my carport and said, 'A comrade said you followed him.' I said I didn't follow anyone. One took out a picture of me in my car on Dolly Madison Highway. He said, 'Do not follow anyone again.' I was going to call the Langley police, but Eloise said, 'No, mind your own goddamn business.' "

Arthur said, "Mr. Smith, I was one of those three men; I'm in the Russian Mafia, good night." Arthur went into the house. Janet opened the front door.

She said, "I saw you talking to that man, who is he?"

"Him? He is our nosey neighbor; he wants the lowdown on everyone. To make a long story short, I told him I was in the Russian Mafia."

"You didn't, Arthur."

"Yes, I did," said Arthur.

Arthur sat down and took off his suit coat and tie. Janet had a fire in the fireplace. She brought Arthur a glass of chilled Sauvignon Blanc wine, a plate of shrimp, shrimp sauce, cheese, and crackers and they sat down.

Janet asked, "What is the man's name? Did he tell you?"

"James Smith, his wife's name is Eloise. Believe me, he's a jerk. He makes his living prying into other people's business. He tried to pry into ours and after listening to his story about following a man to work who lived in apartment eight, he really wanted to know if I worked for the 'The Agency.' I told him I was in the import/export business, but really a Russian."

"Oh, Arthur, you didn't say that, did you?"

"Yes. It's better than telling him to get lost. What's for dinner?"

"I fixed filet of sole, white rice, asparagus, rolls, and raspberry sherbet for dessert."

"That sounds good," he said.

Janet said, "Honey, what is the first thing the CIA asked you to do today?" Arthur took another sip of wine.

"The first thing?"

"Yes."

"You want to know the first thing the world's pre-eminent intelligence agency asked me to do on my first day of work?"

"Yes, dear," said Janet as she walked into the living room. "Did something go wrong?"

"No, it was comical. I did exactly what they told me to do," Arthur said calmly.

"And what was that?"

"I had to pee into a plastic bottle and placed it on card number one. That's right, and I filled it without any trouble."

"The CIA asked you to pee into a bottle? Why?"

Arthur said, "They are checking for drugs or excessive alcohol content in the urine."

Janet shook her head. "Pee into a bottle! Wash your hands, dear, dinner is served."

Things were quiet during the month of December. Arthur did the assigned reading, took physical training two times a week, and did Christmas shopping. Janet decorated the apartment with lights, and it snowed on Christmas Eve.

Arthur reported to work at 8:00 A.M. on Monday, January 3, 1958, eager to begin training and his new career. When Arthur came through the front door and into the lobby, he noticed "Walker" was on duty at the security guard console.

Arthur walked to the security console and said; "Hello, and Happy New Year," and proudly displayed his new identification card.

Walker said, "Happy New Year to you, Mr. Norris. Here's you new security key card to give you access to all offices from the first to the fourth floor. The fifth floor is off limits."

"Thank you, Walker," said Arthur. "Got to go, the first orientation's at 0900 hours," and he laughed, using military time.

Walker gave him a military salute and said "Yes, sir, if I were fifteen years younger, I would be with you in your class, but at fifty-five, I'm over the hill. Go get 'em, Lieutenant."

Arthur took the elevator to the fourth floor to the Director of Personnel and Administration. He used the card key, the door buzzed, and Arthur thought, *Great, I'm off to a good start.* He entered the room full of people. They were talking and sipping coffee out of china cups. Arthur looked around and thought, *This is my training class.* A voice rose above the murmur, and said "Arthur." Arthur looked toward the voice and saw Preston Baker.

"Arthur, put your coat on the coat rack in the hallway and join us."

Arthur waved hello and said, "Okay." Arthur worked his way across the room and Miss Whipple stopped in front of him. She was a primrose in a black dress. She wore a white rosebud pinned on her collar and a string of white pearls.

"Mr. Norris, so glad to see you made it today. Here's your name tag. Please place it on the right pocket of your suit coat and wear it all day until after the reception tonight. You will need it going through the reception line when you meet Mr. Helms; Mr. Lawrence, Deputy Director; Mr. Warren, Chief of Operations; Mr. Buck, Chief of Counterintelligence and you've already met Mr. Maxwell, Chief of Security."

"So good to see you, Arthur," said Preston, "I was on vacation in December and came back today, how is everything?"

"Just fine" said Arthur. "I read the training dossiers, saw several training films, and took the language aptitude test. I still don't know how I did on the test."

Preston said, "Arthur, we are very proud of you and glad we hired you, you scored in the ninety-eighth percentile, which means you're eminently qualified for language training. You will be able to choose from Arabic, Chinese, Russian, or Mandarian Chinese, depending upon your area of preference. You still have plenty of time to decide. Get a cup of coffee and a pastry or donut." Preston returned in a minute with a distinguished-looking gentleman.

"Arthur, I want you to meet retired Major General Bradford Scott Weber. General Weber is the Director of Personnel and Administration."

"Pleased to meet you, sir," said Arthur.

"I'm very pleased to meet you, Arthur, please call me Bradford, my Army hat is on the shelf."

"Yes, sir."

"Arthur, Preston told me you served in the Army in Korea."

"Yes, sir."

General Weber said, "I was the Deputy Chief of Staff for Personnel, Eighth Army in Korea from 1954 to 1956; we were in Korea at the same time; now we're colleagues, it's a small world."

"Yes, sir, it is."

"Well, Arthur, it's almost time for the orientation," Preston said, and walked to the front of the room and clinked a knife on a cup. The room fell silent. "Gentlemen, it is eight forty-five, please finish your coffee and make your way to the first-floor auditorium and be seated by eight fifty-five. The orientation and introductions will last one hour, if you need to use the restroom, use it now."

The new trainees, including Miss Whipple, filed out of the room. Arthur stopped at the men's lavatory and then went to the auditorium. He was seated next to Harold Hunter, 58-A-1 from Pittsburgh, PA. Arthur introduced himself. Another man sat down on his right side, his nametag said Reinhart Bachman, Ph.D. 58-A-1, Amherst, New Hampshire. They shook hands. At exactly 9:00 A.M., the auditorium lights dimmed and five well-dressed men walked into the room and sat down in the first row of seats. They looked like diplomats.

Major General Weber rose from his chair on the platform and said, "Good morning, I'm Bradford Weber, Director of Personnel and Administration. We are very pleased to tell you today that at the beginning of 1958 we have sixteen excellent men who have decided to join our Agency. Let me introduce them to you at this time by alphabetical order. First, Wesley R. Allen, who comes from Palo Alto, California. Please hold your applause." He called Arthur's name. Arthur stood up a moment and looked around the room of about fifty people. He learned later they were Agency staff.

Mr. Helms was introduced and made a welcoming speech. He spoke for thirty minutes about the history of the Agency since 1947, the wonderful people and the mission. He told a funny story and finished. Mr. Helms introduced his senior executive staff, who each spoke for two minutes, and the orientation adjourned.

The remainder of the day the class met in a classroom to introduce themselves, and relate their backgrounds. The training director was Jonathan Goodsell; he gave the trainees an overview of the next eight months, what to expect, what to tell and not tell their family and friends, and told him that physical training would be Monday, Wednesday and Friday from 3:30–4:30. There would be a final physical examination, which everyone had to pass.

He said, "On Friday at six P.M. there will be a cocktail hour with light hors d'oeuvres with the Agency staff, trainees, and wives in the Donovan Room. The dress is business attire and cocktail dresses for wives. Mr. and Mrs. Helms will have a receiving line and attendance is required."

At the end of the first day, each trainee had a desk, telephone, a drawer in a security safe, locker in the physical training room, and a class schedule beginning January 5, 1958, to September 1, 1958. Each student received an unclassified profile of the class.

There were sixteen trainees: ten of the sixteen had prior military service.

> Thirty-two was their average age.
> They all were college graduates.
> Four held master's degrees.
> One held a Ph.D.
> One held an MBA from Harvard University.
> One was an attorney-at-law.
> Two spoke foreign languages.
> One was an FBI Agent.
> There would be no vacations, except for Memorial Day and July Fourth.
> Class would run from 8:30 A.M. to 3:30 P.M., Monday to Friday, with one hour for lunch from 11:30 to 12:30. There would be a three-week field-training exercise near the

end of the course and each trainee would travel out of the country during the training exercise.

The course schedule included:
- Intelligence tradecraft and clandestine collection.
- Report writing.
- Surveillance/counter surveillance techniques.
- Electronics and communications operations procedures.
- The U.S. Government Intelligence Agencies in the FBI, Pentagon and State Department.
- CIA Intelligence Operations.
- Hostile Intelligence Agencies.
- Photography, safes, methods of entry.
- Weapons training/qualification to carry and fire weapons.
- Three-week overseas field training exercise.

Time went by quickly; it was Easter, then Memorial Day. Arthur was doing well and had a 95 percent test average. Janet was also holding her own doing short day trips, sewing class, and keeping the apartment. Arthur left the apartment at 7:30 A.M. and got home at 5:30 Monday through Friday. He went to bed at 10:00 P.M. and arose at 6:30 A.M. By Friday, he was spent. During the week, Janet cooked dinner and on Friday or Saturday nights they went out to dinner. His class had two parties; one party was held at the local restaurant in the party room and the other party was at the home of a classmate in McLean, Virginia. That party was a blow-out, everyone had fun. Arthur had a great class of intelligent men. June and July were devoted to the field training exercise. Each man had to prepare an operations plan and travel into a foreign country for five days, carry out their plan, return to Langley, and then write a detailed after-action report to be evaluated pass/fail. Arthur went to Mexico City to apply his Spanish. It was exhausting; he did training twenty hours a day in Spanish. He got his plan done, but had some technical problems with his communications that caused him to lose his "agent" for the day. He learned in the debriefing, it was all part of the problem showing what can happen in the real world. Arthur graduated third in the training class with a 97.2 percent score out of 100. He received a gold pen-and-pencil desk set at graduation.

After Labor Day weekend, Arthur met with Preston Baker to discuss his career track. Preston told him that the Soviet Union and Eastern Europe NATO were the CIA's two top operational priorities. They would remain the top priority for the next five years. Preston said, "China work" was being done by locals in Taiwan, Singapore, and Hong Kong. Arthur asked about South America. Preston said, "In addition to the threat by Fidel Castro against Cuba, there are concerns over the stability of governments in Chile, Brazil, and Argentina."

He said Arthur's linguistic ability would work in a European assignment. It was possible that if the revolution in Cuba was successful, and Castro came to power in Cuba, he would get help from the Soviet Union. Such an event would raise great concern in the United States. Preston recommended that Arthur take Russian language training. He said Russian was a difficult language to learn to speak without an American accent. Arthur said he wanted to talk to Janet since they were now expecting their first child.

Arthur talked to Janet. She said her preference would be to remain at Langley two more years. Arthur told Preston their decision and Preston said Arthur would go to Russian language school starting October 4, 1958 until October 1, 1959. He would be tested, and assigned as a Soviet Union Area Specialist, which took two years after language school with frequent trips to Europe, and ultimately an assignment to a consulate in Western Europe for five years as a Soviet Area Expert. He would be assigned to the Economic Mission. His real job would be targeted against the Soviet Union and the Warsaw Pact.

Preston said that with Arthur speaking Spanish and Russian, he could go on temporary assignments to South and Central America. Arthur said he would accept Russian language school. Preston told Arthur to have a meeting of the minds that Arthur would remain in Langley in the Soviet Area Specialist Training Program until June, 1960.

Arthur said, "Yes, that's correct."

That night at dinner Arthur told Janet, and she said, "Fine, but don't forget you are going to be a father and that is your first priority."

Arthur had three weeks before beginning Russian language school. Preston sent Arthur and Janet to Bermuda for rest and relaxation for ten days.

On October 4, 1958 Arthur began his Russian language training. His class ran from 9:00 A.M. to 3:00 P.M. Monday to Friday. The language training was held at a U.S. government building near the CIA's Headquarters. There were ten people in the class. The instructor was a native Russian named Sergei Evachenko who received political asylum after World War II. He was from Minsk in the Soviet Union and had served in World War II at the Battle of Stalingrad against the Germans. He wrote publications advocating détente with the West, was sent to prison for four years, and emigrated to the U.S. for political asylum in 1951. He said Russian isn't difficult if one learns how to pronounce the Russian alphabet, without an English pronunciation. He said he would do his best to make training "not painful." Everyone had to study, do exercises, and learn vocabulary. He said he did not want appear impatient, but the course had to be taught in eight months and students then had to pass a proficiency examination at the end of the course. Therefore, he and his students had hard work ahead. He was available from 3:00 to 5:00 Monday and Wednesday. He spoke five minutes in Russian and five minutes in English. He said, "In eight months you will speak, and understand my same little speech in Russian. Let's begin."

Each night, students had to memorize fifty more vocabulary words. Class went from 9:00 A.M. to 3:00 P.M., and then students listened to Russian language tapes until 4:00 P.M. Arthur was tested after six months and was rated "acceptable." Four people had dropped the class.

After fifty-two weeks, the six remaining trainees were given their comprehension examination. Arthur was rated "acceptable," not "fluent." Arthur had to be "fluent" to have a field assignment that required Russian. Preston Baker told Arthur for the next six months he would be in a full-immersion program, speaking Russian full-time, listening and responding to Russian-language tapes and accompanying U.S. State Department personnel speaking Russian at dinners and social events where Russian was spoken in Washington, D.C. Arthur and Janet went to U.S. Diplomatic receptions, he read *Pravda* and listened to taped Russian radio broadcasts. He concluded his training with a two-week period during which all his activities revolved around the Russian culture, including reading *Pravda,* taking a trip to Russia and using a railroad schedule in Russian, eating, sleeping and "dreaming" in Russian. In June 1960, he passed the comprehensive examination and was rated to be fluent in Russian.

On June 10, 1960, Arthur received notification that his next assignment would be to the U.S. Consulate, Munich, West Germany. He had six weeks accumulated vacation during which time he and Janet drove to San Antonio to visit Janet's parents and then to Phoenix to visit Arthur's family so they could see Sarah. Arthur estimated it would take a month to settle in Munich. Arthur was eligible for a three-bedroom apartment located in U.S. Consulate housing, near Schwabing in Munich. Schwabing is the Bohemian area, like Greenwich Village in New York City. They would fly from Dulles International Airport to Frankfurt and then take the train from Frankfurt to Munich. A liaison from the U.S. consulate would meet them and take them to their guest quarters in Munich. They would have ample time to become acquainted with Munich. Arthur's assignment was five years with an extension of two years if operationally necessary.

Arthur, Janet, and Sarah returned from San Antonio and Phoenix on Sunday, May twenty-second. On Monday, Arthur went to the Agency and cleared his personal belongings, reviewed Russian vocabulary, picked up a book on Russian language and said his farewells.

At 2:10 in the afternoon, Arthur was seated at his desk reading, *Guide to Living in Europe* when the telephone rang.

He said, "Hello, Arthur Norris."

It was Janet. She said, "Arthur, something came in the mail today from Charlie Fenton, it's alarming news."

"What type of news?" he asked. "Is Charlie okay?"

"Yes," said Janet, "do you remember Elizabeth Cowan from Hutton in Los Angeles?"

"Yes," said Arthur.

"She was murdered inside a $750,000 ocean-front mansion in Kahala, Hawaii on May seventh!"

"Janet, please calm down."

"Charlie Fenton wrote a note and said Scott Alexander sent it to him from Honolulu. Scott was a former bond underwriter at Hutton and worked with Elizabeth for a year.

"Elizabeth was murdered? How?"

"Arthur, read the article when you get home."

"Okay, see you about six."

What a horrible incident, he thought. Arthur got home at 5:30; they had a dinner of meatloaf, mashed potatoes, beets and a salad. Arthur and Janet did not talk about the newspaper article about Elizabeth Cowan. Arthur washed the dishes while Janet changed Sarah and gave her a bottle. Arthur sat down in his easy boy chair and Janet brought him the envelope containing Charlie's note and the newspaper article about Elizabeth Cowan. He opened the envelope.

THE HONOLULU STAR-BULLETIN

Honolulu, Hawaii, May 8, 1960

After a six-month investigation of a real-estate pyramid scheme, and vice ring to entice investors, the FBI and local law enforcement in Las Vegas, Los Angeles and Honolulu arrested nineteen people during co-ordinated raids on businesses and private homes.

Two persons were also found slain gangland style inside a $750,000 ocean-front estate in Kahala, and believed to be connected to the raid in Honolulu.

FBI and police officials in Las Vegas, Los Angeles, and Honolulu conducted simultaneous raids on offices of the Premier Real Estate Company in Las Vegas, Los Angeles, and Honolulu. Local authorities received complaints from Premier Real Estate business investors with investments from $50,000 to $250,000. They were told they would receive a 20 percent return on their investment, but never received a payment or had their money returned to them. Police said the company used inflated real-estate appraisals on sub-market properties or foreclosures, and had apparently paid bribes to bank officials to "steer" properties to Premier Real Estate to purchase. A typical transaction would involve six investors putting up $35,000 each toward the purchase of a $400,000 property. Premier would then use the investment money for a down payment on a property with an inflated appraisal of $700,000 sell the property, making a profit of $300,000!

They then paid some investors and continued their pyramid scheme. Their records in Las Vegas and Los Angeles indicated Premier Real Estate started in business in 1957. Over the past three years their transactions totaled seventy-five million dollars, and two principals received payments of one million dollars each for four real-estate transactions of $500,000 each. Several persons working with Premier have connections with organized crime according to the Honolulu police.

The two persons identified at 10629 Ocean View Drive in Kahala, Honolulu, were Elizabeth Cowan and Justin Sloan. Police said they worked for Premier Real Estate in Honolulu and lived in the estate. Both victims had been bound with black nylon cords and shot in the back of the head, gangland style. Police found $250,000 cash in a safe in the home, perhaps embezzled money. A note left on the couch said, "Never steal our money."

Arthur said, "Poor, poor Elizabeth, it is a shame, she was well respected at Hutton; she did a good job selling bonds, but was *always* distracted by her personal life. Someone told me she owned a home in Benedict Canyon in the Hollywood Hills. How could she purchase a home on a bond trader's salary? Charlie Fenton told me he looked at homes in the area, and they began at $450,000."

Arthur said, "Elizabeth lived a double life. It caught up with her."

He went to take a shower. He came back into the living room and told Janet the movers from Allied Van Lines would be at the apartment Thursday morning at 8:00 A.M. to pick up household goods, and we're off to Deutschland.

Janet said, "That's fine. I'll have everything sorted and ready to go. I'll take Sarah to Lindsey Barnhardt's while the movers are here."

"That's great."

During the next two days, he closed out their checking and banking accounts, took his car to Baltimore for shipment to Germany and they said good-byes to their friends.

Allied Van Lines arrived at 7:45 on Thursday and picked up the household goods. Arthur, Janet, and Sarah took a Yellow Cab to Dulles International Airport and stayed overnight at the Marriott. On Friday morning, they departed Dulles on Lufthansa flight number 749 and arrived at Frankfurt, Germany, 9:30 P.M. European time. They got their luggage and took a German taxi to the Kupinski Hotel. The next afternoon they took the train at 11:30 and arrived in Munich at 5:30 P.M. As they were leaving the train, a man wearing a gray suit with a green Bavarian hat called, "Herr Norris, Herr Norris." Arthur stopped as the man approached, and told Janet, "Go inside the terminal with Sarah, NOW!!"

Janet took Sarah just as the other man arrived. He said "Herr Norris" in fluent English with a heavy German accent. "I'm Gerhard Brant, your liaison in Munich to Schwabing."

Arthur repeated the "bona fides" to insure it was not a trick. He said "Schwabing is our destination" and the man confirmed the "bona fides" saying, "Yes, Schwabing." These communications were pre-established for when he met his liaison contact in Munich, before Arthur left Langley. They shook hands.

Gerhard Brant asked, "Is your family with you?"

"Yes, my wife took our daughter inside the terminal." Arthur looked into the train terminal and gestured for Janet to come outside to the platform.

Janet opened the terminal door and came out onto the train platform holding Sarah.

"Herr Brant, this is my wife Frau Norris and I am Arthur Norris." They shook hands. Herr Brant motioned to a baggage handler. He told Arthur and Janet to go to Gate twenty-nine in front of the terminal and look for a black Mercedes Benz S-230, which would take them to the hotel, and their luggage would be brought for them.

Arthur, Janet, and Sarah walked through the bustling train terminal. Arthur heard announcements in German, French, and

English going to Vienna, Frankfurt, Dusseldorf, and Manheim. It made Arthur think of Germany in World War II.

They went to a German customs window and a stern-looking man said, "Your documents, please." Arthur showed him their passports to enter Deutschland. The man said, "Very good, next!"

Arthur, Janet, and Sarah walked to Gate twenty-nine and stood on the sidewalk. They were now in Germany. Arthur wanted to purchase a German/English book and begin learning some of the language, but not as thoroughly as Russian. Arthur looked at the cars, trucks, taxi cabs and repeated to himself in Russian what he saw going by on the street in front of him.

It was a warm and sunny day. A black Mercedes Benz S-230 pulled up to the curb in front of them. Herr Brant got out and opened the front door for Janet, but she preferred to sit in the back seat and hold Sarah. Arthur helped Janet and Sarah into the back seat of the car and he got into the front seat. Herr Brant got into the driver's seat, signaled, and pulled out into passing traffic.

Herr Brant asked Arthur if he spoke German.

Arthur said "No," but he spoke Spanish and Russian. Herr Brant smiled and said, "Ruskie-yah, no sprechen Deutsch."

Arthur said, "Nein."

Herr Brant said it was a thirty-minute drive to Schwabing. His instructions were to take them to the U.S. Consulate's guest quarters until their furniture and automobile arrived in a month. He said the guest quarters were very nice.

Arthur looked out the window of the Mercedes at the passing people and traffic. There were German masonry buildings with gray tile roofs, people riding bicycles, a Lowenbrau beer truck passed them, and then a Spatenbrau beer truck, a police car, and then a sign said SCHWABING. Arthur looked at his wristwatch; it was 6:40 P.M.

Arthur asked Janet, "How's Sarah?"

Janet said, "Sleeping—now—up tonight."

Herr Brant pulled into a driveway with high hedges, a security guard appeared and a man wearing a green and gray German policeman's uniform carrying a submachine gun on his right shoulder. There was an iron bar across the driveway that said ACHTUNG—HALT. The guard came to the driver's side of the Mercedes and spoke in German to Herr Brant. The guard then walked over to Arthur's side and said, "Your passport." Arthur showed him the passports for him, Janet and Sarah. The guard looked at the passports and then at them.

The guard walked back to the driver and said to park the car and sign the entry documents and go to the guest quarter number seventeen at the rear of the compound.

Herr Brant drove past five buildings that looked like small German houses; they had flower gardens and curtains. Herr Brant said; "Here are your quarters."

They went into the house; it was lovely. It looked like a home built in the 1950s, with large furniture, area rugs, a kitchen, dining room, living room, four bedrooms, and three huge bathrooms.

Herr Brant said, "I'll drive you to dinner and then out to buy food tomorrow. There are several German restaurants near here, no hamburger stands."

They slept through the night. Sarah awoke and started to cry at 6:30 A.M. She was wet and hungry. Janet made coffee and toast. She got up, went to check on Sarah, and noticed she sounded congested. Janet looked out the window and saw that it was raining. She picked up Sarah, gave her a pill for congestion and the last of the cough medicine, and put her back into her crib. Janet went back into the bedroom and Arthur was awake.

"How did you sleep last night, my dear?"

"Fine, Sarah is coming down with a cold."

"A cold, she was fine last night."

"I just checked her, she is congested. We only have bread, butter, jam and fruit in the refrigerator. Let's get dressed, call Herr Brant and ask him to take us to the U.S. post exchange for breakfast and to buy cough medicine and find out where we can see a U.S. medical doctor."

Arthur sensed Janet's anxiety and got up. "Sarah, will be fine."

Janet said, "I don't want Sarah to get sick."

Arthur got dressed and called Herr Brant at the Consulate; Herr Brant told Arthur there was a U.S. doctor on call and to bring Sarah to the consulate.

Herr Brant said he would stop on the way to their quarters, get some hot eggs, toast, and coffee, and then he would take them to the consulate. Janet would take Sarah to see Dr. Price at the consulate's medical office.

Arthur told Janet and she was relieved.

Herr Brant came to their quarters at 9:30, he brought them a light breakfast. After attending to Sarah, she seemed better. Herr Brant drove them to the U.S. Consulate on Ludwigstrasse near the Haus Der Kunst in Munich.

They arrived at the consulate at 10:15 and went in past the U.S. Marine guard to the consular services. Arthur and Janet met Ledwig Kramer, their consular affairs officer. It was Friday, June 10, 1960. The consulate wasn't overwhelmed with activity.

Herr Brant said, "Ludwig, this is Arthur Norris of the Central Intelligence Agency and his wife, Janet, and their daughter, Sarah."

"Pleased to meet you," said Ludwig in a heavy German accent. "You need to see Dr. Price for your little girl, yes?"

"Yes," said Janet.

Ludwig said, "Dr. Price is not here, but will be here at 10:30. You are welcome to have breakfast in our dining room and sit and wait for the doctor."

Arthur and Janet said that sounded fine. At 10:45 A.M., Dr. Price arrived. Janet took Sarah and they went with Dr. Price into the medical office.

Arthur signed several papers, was shown his office in the economic division at the trade and commerce section, which had a view of a flower garden outside. He had an office with another man and the offices were nice.

Ludwig said, "There are eighty-one people in the consulate, with an unspecified number of agency personnel." Arthur's boss was Seymore Wells; he had served in the Agency in Europe since 1951 and spoke German, Czechoslovakian, and English fluently. Mr. Wells was out of the country and would return on Monday. Arthur said that he needed a three-bedroom apartment and their household goods would arrive in Bremen on June eighteenth; he had been told the household goods would be delivered by June thirtieth. They were staying in consulate guest quarters.

Ludwig turned to Arthur and said in Russian, "Mr. Norris, did you enjoy your trip to West Germany?"

Arthur was startled, he said in English; "Yes, it was a good trip."

Ludwig said, "In Russian, please."

Arthur replied in Russian.

"Very good, speak in Russian."

Janet came back with Dr. Price and Sarah. Dr. Price said, "Your daughter is fine, no complications or congestion, just a bug from so much travel, let her rest over the weekend and she'll be as good as new."

Ludwig spoke in German to Herr Brant and said to take Mr. and Mrs. Norris and their child to Schwabing to look at apartments at 4914 Koeingsburgstrasse—with four bedrooms.

"They'll be here five years and perhaps more. Norris babies will arrive, Arthur looks young and healthy."

Herr Brant took Arthur, Janet, and Sarah to Schwabing to consulate housing. It was lovely, well-trimmed, fine German construction with masonry and slate roofs and two-story apartments with two-car garages. Herr Brant stopped in front of 4914, parked the Mercedes and they went into the apartment. It had high ceilings, a large living room, dining room, kitchen, sunroom, fireplace, four bedrooms, and three bathrooms.

"WOW," said Arthur, "what a place! This is an apartment, what are the houses like?"

"Then you like it?"

Both Janet and Arthur said, "Yes."

"It's your home for the next five years."

Herr Brant said he would activate the telephone, have the apartment cleaned, the windows washed, and it would be ready for them to occupy on July first.

Arthur said, that was fine.

"Have they told you the automobile policy here?"

"Automobile policy?" asked Arthur.

"Yes," said Brant. "You cannot drive an American automobile. On Monday I'll get your car appraised and the consulate will pay you the appraisal, and you can purchase an Audi, Peugeot, Volkswagen, Citroen, Fiat or Volvo to drive, with German license plates. You and Janet will have to take the German driver's test in the next two weeks. Don't go to the American Commissary. I'll go for you, tell me what you want and I'll bring it to you. Finally, as of now your official name with the consulate is Christopher Lowe, you may use your own name at school, but here Arthur E. Norris does not exist. Seymore Wells will brief you on Monday."

Arthur and Janet both were in pleasant shock. Herr Brant drove them back to the consulate quarters. Janet made two lists of what they would need for the first month. One list was for the post exchange and it included items such as baby diapers, lotion, powder, shampoo, and towels. The other lists were for food.

They spent Saturday resting. Sarah slept most of the day. Janet wrote her parents a letter. At 4:30 Saturday afternoon Herr Brant returned. He rang the front doorbell and had eight bags with him. Arthur paid him $157.29 and thanked him. Janet prepared a meatloaf, mashed potatoes, and green beans. They had German chocolate cake for dessert. They listened to music and Arthur began studying the German language book. Sunday they slept in, had breakfast and relaxed. Sunday it rained all day.

Herr Brant picked up Arthur for work on Monday at 8:00 A.M. They were at the U.S. Consulate by 8:40 A.M. It had stopped raining. Arthur was introduced to Seymore Wells, Station Chief; Daniel Allen, Operations Director; Blake Morgan, Chief of the Economic Section; Barry Winstead, Chief of Counter Intelligence; and later in the afternoon to William Schultz, Consul General, and his assistant, Milton White. Arthur spent the entire day reading protocols and memorandums of agreement with the government of West Germany, receiving his security clearance from cable from Langley, doing administrative in processing and getting his office in order. He used the telephone to call Janet and said hello to Sarah; everything worked fine. Arthur selected a German Audi to drive.

The consulate was stately inside and out; Arthur was shown CIA security procedures, how to open doors, safes and how to reach key personnel after hours.

Arthur and Janet received a German vehicle operator's test booklet, he was scheduled to take the driver's test on Wednesday, which he subsequently passed and obtained a German driver's license. He received a briefing on the mission, organization, and communications of the Agency in Europe and what Arthur "had a need to know." Thursday he drove to the consulate quarters in the Audi. The next Friday, Arthur took Janet for the German driver's license exam; she passed the first time.

Arthur's official title was Special Assistant to the Consul General for Economic Trade and Commerce. His real assignment was as a CIA Operative to do covert collection of intelligence information on the Soviet Union Rocket Forces and the Warsaw Pact.

Seymore Wells outlined Arthur's training and operational plan for the next twenty-four months. It took two years for new agents to be effective in covert intelligence operations in West Germany. Arthur was placed under a field supervisor named Josef Stupek who had once been a member of the Czechoslovakian Intelligence Service. He spoke Czech, Russian, German, and English. Arthur's other field supervisor, Gunter Beckman, was a former Wermacht Oberlieutenant. He joined U.S. Intelligence under a reparation program in 1945. Herr Beckman hated Russians after World War II. He spoke German and English. During the first six months, Arthur would travel with Josef Stupek and Gunter Beckman throughout Western Europe attending trade shows, economic meetings and technical exhibits. Arthur also had to learn Eastern Europe's Security Apparatus operating against the CIA, the Soviet KGB, East German Stasi, Polish Counter-intelligence and operational procedures inside the Iron Curtain. During Arthur's first year he would travel to West Berlin, the U.S. Embassy in Moscow, Prague, Budapest, Madrid, London and Warsaw. Arthur had to learn the specific intelligence collection requirements (SCIRS) and the order-of-battle of Soviet rocket forces. This would include the locations, command and control, types of missiles, unit identifications and uniforms worn by Soviet personnel, both officers and enlisted.

In order to travel alone he had to learn Eastern European railroad schedules, airlines schedules, and passport regulations, and to apply security, and counter-surveillance techniques in all of his operational activities.

Arthur realized after a month how much detail there was to learn to take a train from Munich into East Berlin and to follow East German security procedures.

On July first, Herr Brant came into Arthur's office and said, "Your home in Schwabing is ready, and your household goods will be delivered tomorrow. Please meet me at 4914 Koeningburgstrasse, Munich, West Germany 3101/2168. It will take four hours for the movers to bring in your furniture and to clear inspection."

Arthur thought, *German order and efficiency.*

They moved into the apartment. Arthur was told he was going to attend the annual air show in Weimar, East Germany, with Gunter Beckman and they would be leaving Monday. He would be gone three weeks to Weimar, East Germany, Leipzig, and West Berlin for electronics exhibits where Soviets send their military staff to view the latest technology in communications, security, and target acquisition. Arthur was now moving up into what Preston Baker had said was the "tedious and possibly dangerous part of the intelligence business." East Germany had tight internal security measures and they checked every document and passports thoroughly; if any suspicions arose, one was detained for questioning. If you were a spy, you were shot.

Herr Beckman gave Arthur a list of documents for the next three weeks and whom Janet was to contact in an emergency. Arthur would speak in Russian, with Beckman being his backup. Their mission was to observe the Soviet military personnel in Leipzig, note to whom the Soviets spoke and try to see what items were of interest to them, find out where they stayed, get descriptions of them, name and ranks of officers and where they went to relax and have fun. Beckman said all Russian officers frequented brothels and they would go wherever the Russians went, to observe them.

Beckman was an old hand at espionage, but this was real, and if something went wrong, Arthur could be caught or go on trial as a spy and be shot. The games were over.

On Wednesday morning at 7:00, Arthur drove to the consulate, met Beckman and they took the train to Leipzig from Munich. They were gone for three weeks to Weimar, Leipzig, and West Berlin. When Arthur returned home, his laundry was dirty and he was tired, but glad to see Janet and Sarah. He could not tell anyone where he had been or what he had done, whom he had seen or what took place. Arthur wrote a thirty-nine-page after-action report on his trip. Twenty-one SCIRS were answered and the most significant development and intelligence was that Russian officers now wore different rocket force lapel insignias, and showed a great amount of interest in an electronic device that calculated distances for artillery counter-battery fire, which shortened the time for returning fire on an enemy position. The equipment was made in the United States. How did it get into East Germany? Someone was making and manufacturing illegal arms and selling them to Russia! The trip report went to Langley and the FBI in Washington, D.C.

The trip into Eastern Europe was successful and Arthur was glad to be home in Munich. Janet said everything was fine while he was gone. He could see Sarah had grown and was getting bigger. She was pretty with her blue eyes and blonde curly hair and her teeth were beginning to show in her smile.

The following Monday, Arthur and Gunter briefed Seymore Wells. He was interested to learn about the counter-battery-firing device in which the Russians showed great interest. Seymore said he called to the Agency's headquarters and talked to Donald Morrison, the director of technical intelligence. Mr. Morrison said the Agency was aware of a device, but had not yet obtained one to evaluate. Morrison told Wells to send someone to the next technical exhibit, which would be in Belgrade in May 1961, and to purchase two devices. Arthur was to mail one device to the European Trade Association in Munich, a CIA front business. He was given the assignment to go to Belgrade in May with Josef Stupek and buy two counter-battery-fire instruments made in Communist China by a company licensed in Baltimore, Maryland, called World Electronics, Inc. The FBI told the CIA they believed World Electronics was an operation front for the Soviets' Intelligence Service to export foreign-made products from the United States into Eastern Europe. The FBI would investigate World Electronics Inc. to determine if World Electronics Inc. was a front for Soviet espionage in the U.S. The CIA would find out who was buying their products in Eastern Europe.

Arthur thought, *What an amazing coincidence. What is really going on in the world in spy vs. spy?*

When Arthur wasn't on operations assignments, he recorded broadcasts into Eastern Europe on Radio Free Europe and Radio Liberty in Munich. He processed visas for Russian travel and wrote correspondence in Russian to businesses doing import/export into West Germany from Eastern Europe, read a copy of *Pravda* and monitored Russian-language technical bulletins for information on the Soviets' rocket and artillery forces.

Their first year in Munich went quickly. In June 1961, the CIA received concrete information that the Soviet Union was going to have East Germany build a wall dividing East and West Berlin. There was speculation this was a possible diversion for the Warsaw Pact to attack West Germany before NATO could react to defend West Berlin and countries in NATO. Tensions began to build in early July, 1961. Arthur was sent to West Berlin to monitor Soviet communications. Arthur was told not to tell Janet the full story. NATO's intelligence analysts believed that a Berlin Wall would be built from information being received and there would be a flood of people into West Berlin.

The U.S. Army had one brigade of infantry and armor in West Berlin, but not enough forces to stop an onslaught of Soviet tank divisions into Berlin if they made an attack.

In August 1961, the East German border guards began erecting double rows of concertina wire, and it became chaos. People flooded into West Berlin by car, truck and on foot. Some people got entangled in the wire and were caught and returned to East Germany. Some got through and some did not and were shot by East German "VOPOS," or border guards. Some East German border guards defected into West Berlin. Arthur then began to debrief the defectors and was assigned temporary duty to West Berlin for three months. Janet was a patient and dutiful wife. They were expecting their second child.

In October 1961, Seymore Wells told Arthur to take three

weeks' vacation. The Agency's policy was that operatives would not take vacation in West Germany. The CIA flew Arthur, Janet, and Sarah to France for two weeks, and two weeks in Spain.

The next major crisis was the Cuban Missile Crisis in October, 1962. Arthur was sent undercover into the Bahamas to monitor Russian communications on their ships coming into Cuba from the Atlantic Ocean into the Caribbean toward Cuba. The Russians used disguised commercial fishing trawlers with huge antennas to receive their communications from warships in the Atlantic in and out of Cuba. Arthur arrived in the Bahamas in September, 1962. He didn't return to Munich until November, 1962. Arthur and the CIAs technical staff calculated that Soviets did not have a strong enough rocket booster to fire intercontinental missiles from Russia to the United States. These calculations were critical in the CIA's analysis that led the Soviets to withdraw the threat of installing nuclear missiles into Cuba and avoiding nuclear war.

Three more years went by quickly. Arthur Edward Norris, Jr., their second child, was born on December 10, 1962. Arthur and Janet now had a bigger family, with Sarah, age three, and now Arthur Jr., age one.

The major accomplishment for Arthur's work in West Germany was his involvement for the defection of a Czechoslovakian Colonel, Emil Danek, who was the Commanding Officer of a Czechoslovakian military Supply and Transportation district in Bruno, Czechoslovakia.

On August 3, 1966, the U.S. Embassy in Madrid reported to Langley that a man had walked into the U.S. Embassy stating he had valuable information about the assassination of President John F. Kennedy. He claimed he had heard from conversations with his colleagues that the assassination of the American President was a joint conspiracy between Fidel Castro and secret French underground assassins. The U.S. Embassy told him to write them a detailed letter with specific details for evaluation and how to contact him if it were necessary. Walk-in want-to-be spies were common.

On October 2, 1966, a mysterious package arrived at the U.S. Embassy in Madrid. It contained a book in which five pages had been removed and contained what appeared to be new Top Secret Soviet logistics and transportation documents, classified codes to authorize implementation for war plans with NATO. Hand-written instructions within the pages said to meet a contact at the El Prado gallery at the souvenir stand on October 10, 1966 at 10:00 A.M. A man would be standing near Art Booklets wearing a gray sport coat and a black beret to identify himself. He would meet "your representative" and they would take a taxi to a restaurant called El Rey on the Calle De Los Reyes for tea. This person would provide your contact with very interesting "gifts." To communicate with him the U.S. contact had to speak fluent Russian. My position allows me to travel into Western Europe.

Seymore Wells briefed Arthur, Josef Stupek, and Juan Delos Torres about their plan to meet him. Seymore Wells cautioned them it could be a Soviet KGB trap to kidnap an American to exchange for a Soviet spy now held in U.S. custody.

In late September, Arthur, Stupek, and Torres conducted their operational reconnaissance around Madrid, posing as art dealers. They found the contact's location and developed a plan for the meeting.

On October 7th, Arthur, Stupek, and Torres flew from Frankfort to Madrid and they registered at separate hotels. Arthur would make the contact, Stupek would provide counter-surveillance, and Torres was the back-up for communications on a two-way radio with Stupek. Each man wore a concealed .38 detective special, and Torres also carried a .45-caliber U.S. Army pistol and an UZI submachine gun in his large attaché case.

On October 10th at 10:00 A.M. Arthur arrived at the El Prado art stand, and saw a man standing next to Art Books who was wearing a gray sport coat and a black beret. A tour bus arrived at the same time and the area became crowded with tourists. Arthur's heart was pounding; he bought a newspaper, and the man obviously didn't see Arthur in the crowd. Arthur approached him and said, the bona fides, "Are you an art dealer from Lisbon in Russian?"

The man turned and looked at Arthur and said, "Yes, I'm

from Lisbon." Arthur watched his hands closely. Stupek stood behind a marble column ten feet from Arthur. The man said, "I'm Emil Danek from Moravia," as he extended his right hand to shake hands with Arthur.

Arthur said, "I'm Christopher Lowe from Frankfurt." Arthur wondered if he was a Soviet KGB agent.

Danek said, "Let's go sightseeing, follow me in a cab to 1241 Calle De Los Reyes to the El Reyes Restaurante." He walked out the front door, went to the curb, and hailed a cab. Arthur took the next cab. Stupek and Torres took the third cab.

Arthur and Danek sat down at a table by a window.

Danek said in general terms, "I have connections for very expensive presents from the Russians to help free people."

Arthur reached into his trouser pocket, appearing to adjust his seat as he turned on a tape recorder with a wire he was wearing under his dress shirt.

Danek and Arthur talked in Russian for twenty minutes. Danek said, "If the right arrangements are made, my connection shall provide valuable presents in exchange for reimbursement and a new life." He handed Arthur a book on art and told him to read pages fifty to fifty-five very carefully. If Arthur's company wanted to purchase the Russian "present," he was to turn to page fifty and then read from page fifty to fifty-five and follow the instructions; if his company would not comply with the instructions, they could not do business. Danek stood up and left the room, Arthur turned off the tape recorder. He took the book, *Old European Art Treasures.*

Arthur and Stupek took a taxi to Arthur's hotel room to study the book. Torres sat in a chair at the end of the hallway with a radio for counter-surveillance outside their room. Stupek opened the book to page fifty, where the pages were removed and instead there was a Russian letter which said, "A high-level Czech wants to defect."

The person who wants to defect is a Czech patriot who hates Russians for their brutal oppression of Czechoslovakia. It said the Soviet Union's High Command is reorganizing the rear-area support services for the Red Army. Their new plan pre-positions war materials on railroads, highways, and airfields to rapidly reinforce Soviet troops, ammunition, food, medical supplies, clothing, and fuel to combat units. The Soviet plan is Top Secret. Certain railroad lines now have had flatbed railroad cars reconfigured with anti-aircraft surface-to-air missiles to support advancing Soviet troops. There are about 20,000 new missiles on railroad cars. Combat support, transportation, and medical battalions have been assigned to support Soviet combat units. The Soviet Union's war plan presumes a NATO attack on an Eastern Bloc country and to counterattack 180,000 Red Army soldiers in their mechanized infantry, armor and artillery to counter-attack and defeat NATO, and continue their attack to capture Bonn and Paris.

The Soviet Union's Red Army would launch a tremendous counter-attack on NATO, crush American front-lines and continue attacking into West Germany, France and Italy. They would capture Paris and stop the advance. Paris was the objective.

The defector could provide the supply and transportation war plans for Czechoslovakia and Hungary which are now Top Secret Soviet Union and Warsaw Pact's war plans against NATO.

The book had the railroads, Autobahn routes and pre-positioned sites. Arthur finished reading pages fifty to fifty-five. He turned to Josef Stupek and said, "My God, Josef, a goldmine or a trick? What do you think?"

Josef Stupek said, "Arthur, I've been doing this business for twenty-one years since before World War Two, anything is possible. My gut feeling is it must be real—this guy is taking one hell of a chance just meeting you. I advise you to send the book to Langley to be evaluated and wait for their instructions."

Arthur gave the book to Chief of Operations, Daniel Allen, in Munich. They decided to send it to Langley and follow Langley's instructions. Langley instructed Arthur to meet the Czechoslovakian contact as soon as possible. On November 15, 1966, Arthur met Danek at the Mucha museum in Prague; Arthur gave Danek a book, *A Visitors Guide to Prague,* which contained Langley's instructions to Danek. They met in front of the Josef Ladd exhibit at the Mucha museum, exchanged pleasantries, and then had a cup of coffee where Arthur gave Danek another book, *Prague—The City of History and Splendor*. Danek took both books; finished his coffee, left, and boarded a bus to his hotel.

The instructions from Langley in Russian instructed Danek to mail a letter to an address in Budapest, asking if he could travel to Budapest to meet a representative on December 19, 1966 at 1930 hours in the main dining room at the Kempinski Hotel Corvinus. If he could not arrange this meeting, he was to place the book wrapped inside a plastic cover, walk down the south side of the hotel to a telephone booth, stand inside the booth and face the front door of the Kempinski Hotel. He would see a small pine tree planted in a marble pot. He was to lift the pot containing the pine tree, and slide the book beneath the pot. Then go to the phone booth and call Budapest 4-211-4668 at 8:00 the following night. He would be contacted.

The dead drop was checked five times during the next month; the dead drop was empty. Arthur and his colleagues thought either Danek had changed his mind or had been caught by the Soviet KGB.

Four months had passed until March 1967 when a letter arrived from Prague at the European Trade Group's office in Munich. It said their art contact had been sent to a logistics school in Moscow for six months and the new Soviet's reorganization plans were being implemented beginning January, 1968, and their plans were going to be tested in the near future when the Warsaw Pact invaded Czechoslovakia "who was deviating from the Soviet's party line."

Many logistics officers were currently being reassigned for "compartmented" security, and he could go to Russia in March, 1968 for three years!" He would contact them in the future.

In March 1968 a letter from Prague arrived at the European Trade Group. He was going to defect in June after attending a logistics planning conference in Brno, Czechoslovakia. He had ten days leave following the conference with his wife Anna, and their children, Danuta, Janica, and Stephen all located at a villa in the mountains of Bratislava. He would exchange a "very rare book" at the contact. Before the contact he wanted a deposit of two million U.S. dollars into the Bank of Switzerland in Bern. Mail the bank deposit to Herr Schmidt Box 80, Karnova Hotel, Bratislava. It should contain a deposit code, and a telephone number for him to call and verify the money had been deposited. He also wanted $250,000 in West German Deutschmarks deposited in the Suisse Commerce Bank in Vienna. Mail the deposit to Schmidt in the Bratislava. Finally, $50,000 Deutschmarks would be given to him at the meeting at the Hotel Karona with his contact inside the daily newspaper.

Danek's request was approved at Langley. Counter-instructions from Langley were that Danek and his family would reside at a safe house in West Germany for one year. Then they would receive identity papers and West German passports to travel to the United States. After one year, they would be flown out of West Germany to the United States and reside in a safe house for six months. He then could relocate either to South America or the United States. Danek accepted the offer. Danek mailed a holiday letter to the European Trade Group saying, "On April 2, 1967 at 8:00 A.M. I'll meet the young man who speaks such good Russian in the dining room of Hotel Korona in Bratislava. "DO NOT BE LATE!"

On April 1, 1967, Arthur, Stupek, and Torres flew into Prague. Arthur and Stupek then took a train to Bratislava and got a room in the Euro Hotel one block from the Hotel Karona. On April 2nd, Arthur and Stupek met Torres and they walked to Hotel Karona at 8:00 A.M. Arthur looked into the dining room and saw Danek seated at a table near a window, for countersurveillance. Arthur approached Danek, said "Good morning" in Russian.

Danek smiled, stood up, and said, "Have a seat."

Danek looked at Arthur and said, "I may have been followed last night. I arrived on the train from Prague, and two men got off the train and took a cab to this hotel. I haven't seen them this morning, but they could have changed their surveillance teams." He said, "My wife and children are staying with her sister so they are safe. I'm ready, do you have my book?"

Arthur opened an attaché case with a newspaper and the book and handed him the book with the bank deposits and

Deutschmarks. Danek paid the check. "Let me get a taxi," said Danek. They walked from the hotel to the street.

Danek said, "A tour boat leaves this afternoon from the harbor, my family will board the boat at one o'clock, I shall wait until the last moment and board the boat as a civilian to tour the Danube to Vienna. My papers are very authentic work. Thank you. We will get off, take a taxi and go directly to the U.S. Embassy."

A black taxi stopped at the curb.

"Now go; tell your contact to tell the U.S. Embassy in Vienna that I will arrive tonight, do not delay me!" Danek reached inside his coat and he handed Arthur a wrapped object the size of a large college text-book; Danek said, "Goodbye" and got into the taxi. That is the last time Arthur saw Colonel Emil Danek.

Colonel Danek and his family appeared at the U.S. Embassy in Vienna at 6:15 P.M.

Arthur took Colonel Danek's logistics and transportation plan book to Munich, and sent it in an embassy pouch to Langley; Danek's information was an incredible intelligence coup of inestimable value detailing Soviet and Warsaw Pact war plans against NATO and Western Europe. Much of the information Colonel Danek provided was previously unknown to Western intelligence.

Two days later, a large headline in the Munich newspaper said, "High-level Czech Colonel Defects to West."

The Russians were furious. Information was sent throughout Eastern Europe to capture Danek; a one-million-rubles reward was made for him, dead or alive.

The logistics and transportation planning book, which Colonel Danek gave to Arthur, was determined to be authentic after evaluation. It set the Soviet Union back five years in wartime planning and allowed NATO to develop counter war strategies to destroy Soviet and Warsaw Pact supply stocks in Eastern Europe.

Colonel Danek and his family remained in a safe house in West Germany until May, 1969. As Colonel Danek predicted, on August 20, 1968, the Soviet, Polish, East German, Hungarian, and Bulgarian armies invaded Czechoslovakia to restore Czech adherence to Soviet Party line.

Also in May 1969, Colonel Danek and his family were relocated into South America for five years and then they moved to the U.S. with new identities in the Midwest.

Arthur had now served seven years in West Germany and he was due for reassignment. In June he flew to Langley to meet Preston Baker who was now the Director of Personnel and Administration. Preston told Arthur that he, Arthur, had a very strong file, outstanding personnel evaluations and appeared to be moving toward executive management in the future. Preston said if Arthur took a two-year career in the field in paramilitary operations, his career would be greatly enhanced for promotion. Preston Baker elaborated about a program in Vietnam called the Phoenix Program, which would be funded and staffed by the Agency. William Colby established the Phoenix Program in 1967. Its mission was to collect intelligence information on the Viet Cong or communist political infrastructure in the countryside and to root it out with a unit called the Provincial Reconnaissance Unit (PRU's) and thereby neutralize the Viet Cong's political infrastructure. Preston said the Agency was in the process of building an Office of the Assistant or OSA Compounds in South Vietnam for the CIA. This site would be in Rach Gia.

A tour was in a war zone and he could have 30 days of home leave every six months or could meet his wife in Bangkok, Taiwan or Honolulu. If he were successful in this assignment, he would either return to Langley four years as a Director, or receive an assignment to Europe or South America for five years. If he went to Europe, he would serve two years at the U.S. Embassy in Moscow and five years in West Germany; Madrid, Spain; or Geneva.

Preston told Arthur to talk to Janet and let him know his decision. If he didn't go to Vietnam, he would return to Langley as the Director of Soviet Union operations.

Arthur returned to Munich. He talked to Janet about his assignment options.

Janet said she would support him as her mother had supported her father's Army career, but after Vietnam she wanted an assignment to Geneva, Switzerland, for five years so their children could learn to speak French and German.

Arthur said, "It's a deal."

He wired Preston Baker and he accepted an assignment with the Phoenix Program in Vietnam. A month later Arthur received his reassignment orders sending him to twenty-six weeks of Vietnamese language school at the Defense Language Institute of Monterey, California, with housing in the guest quarters at nearby Fort Ord, and the equivalent military rank of Colonel.

Arthur completed his debriefing in Munich, his polygraph examination, inventory of classified information and documents, and his final debriefing. The embassy gave his family an "Auf Wiedersehen" party with wonderful gifts, hugs, and tears.

On June 30, 1967, they flew from Frankfurt to San Francisco on Lufthansa. After June 30, 1967, no one in the U.S. Embassy ever knew that Arthur Edward Norris had lived and worked in Munich, Germany.

They drove down to Monterey and got located in their guest housing. On July 1, 1967 Arthur started Vietnamese language school and completed the course on December 15, 1967. Arthur and Janet decided to move to Tucson, Arizona where Janet and the children would live for two years while Arthur was in Vietnam. Arthur had old friends still living in Tucson with their children the same ages as Sarah, Arthur Jr., and now their third child named Jennifer. Janet wanted to be near Phoenix to visit Arthur's parents.

They arrived in Tucson on December twenty-seventh, got a room in the Tucson Desert Inn, and Arthur contacted a friend in real estate to help them find a home to buy. Janet wanted to buy a Labrador retriever puppy for the children.

Janet opened the back door and saw Arthur standing in the dark in the back yard. She called, "Arthur, come inside, it's cold; it's time to eat dinner."

Arthur replied "Coming, I just want to make sure the children locked the fence gate in the back yard so Tyler doesn't get out."

He hollered back to Janet, "Make sure the children lock the gate every day or Tyler will get out."

"I put a note on the refrigerator door so the children check the fence gate every night."

Arthur entered the house, put his two cold hands on his wife's warm face, and said, "Love you."

"Love you too, but your hands are cold; get washed for dinner, we'll eat in the dining room tonight, okay?"

"Fine."

Janet called the children from the living room to wash their hands and come to the dinner table, "NOW." The three children and Arthur all arrived in the dining room; they sat down at the dinner table, and said grace.

Janet said, "Arthur, please pass the chicken." At that moment the front doorbell rang.

Janet looked at Arthur, "Who could that be ringing the front doorbell?"

"I don't know," he said, and as he got up from the dining room table to answer the front door, it rang again.

"Just a minute, I'm coming," he called, and pulled the drapes aside by the front door window and looked out to the front porch. He turned on the light and saw a middle-aged man standing outside. He was wearing a dark blue jacket with a Western Union patch on his right breast pocket and wearing a blue-and-yellow hat with Western Union written on the front of the hatband. He was holding a yellow-and-white Western Union telegram and a clipboard.

Arthur opened the front door and said, "Yes, may I help you?"

"Is this the Norris residence?"

"Yes."

The man said, "Got a telegram from Washington, D.C. for you." He handed Arthur the telegram. He told Arthur to sign his name on the bottom line and indicate the time of delivery. Arthur looked at his watch. It was 5:30.

"Please put the date and time below your signature, I need it to verify it was delivered today as instructed."

"It's February fifteenth, so it's on time," Arthur said, and he put down the date.

The man said, "Thank you" and Arthur handed the man a five-dollar tip.

"No, Sir, I can't accept that; punctual delivery is part of

Western Union's service." He continued, "Sometimes it's hard to find the right addresses at night in these new subdivisions, since not all the new streets in Tucson are in the map book; but I did find your address in the latest edition of the map book supplement at 6280 Broken Arrow Drive."

He said, "Good night," turned around, and went down the front steps.

Arthur said, "Thank you, good night," shut the front door, and turned off the front-porch light.

Janet called to Arthur, "Who was that, the welcome wagon?" She laughed. "They always show up at your dinnertime."

"No, dear, it's from Langley."

"Langley! Already? We just got here."

"Let me look at it," said Arthur.

"Arthur, your dinner is getting cold, can't it wait until after we eat?"

"No, dear, it was delivered by Western Union—it's important."

Arthur opened the Western Union Gram letter, it read in teletype format:

TO//A.E. Norris//15 February 68.
FM//CIA HQ, Langley, Virginia//
RE//Attendance at URGENT Meeting this Loc;
Report here NLT 0900, 17 Feb 68.
All tvl arrangements have been made for you
Willard Hotel, 18-21 Feb.
TVL//18 Feb Lv: Tucson on American Airlines #241
AR//Wash D.C. Nat'l 5:10, take cab to Willard
22 Feb Lv: Wash D.C. 9:35 a.m. American Airline #449
AR: Tucson, 2:31 p.m.
Reporting date to So. Vietnam is now 28 Feb 68.
Call 1-210-761-1100 if problems exist. Done//

Janet called Arthur, "Good or bad news?"

Arthur answered, "Sounds like something's hit the fan."

He came into the dining room. "I have to leave Sunday morning for an urgent meeting at Langley."

"Great," said Janet.

"Sarah, honey, please heat Daddy's dinner."

"Okay, Dad."

Arthur ate dinner. After dinner, Sarah and Jennifer did the dishes. Arthur Jr. brought Tyler into the living room.

Janet asked Arthur, "What do you think is wrong; why the urgent meeting just before you leave for two years?"

Arthur said, "I don't know."

"It's probably got something to do with the war and new developments, I know Washington was taken by surprise by that Communist Tet Offensive and we had 2,000 U.S. KIA. Something is not going right, maybe they're planning to invade North Vietnam. I had woman's intuition something would come up just before you left."

Arthur called Sam Wilson, a friend who was in the same Vietnamese language school in Monterey, to find out if Sam had heard anything about the meeting. Sam said he called Jerry Armbruster at Langley about the meeting. Jerry told him it was classified information, but the "scuttlebutt" was that Director William Helms, The Deputy Director, Director of Operations, and the U.S. Ambassador Ellsworth Bunker, met with President Johnson to discuss the war in light of the Communists' Tet Offensive. The president was livid over the lack of intelligence knowledge about the attack, which blindsided him. President Johnson told Helms to use all available resources to get timely intelligence in "Veet-nam," as the President called Vietnam, and to "Whip the bastards asses of those goddamn Viet Cong so we can get this war over and get our boys home. There is going to be a big increase on intelligence collection by the Agency in Vietnam."

Arthur told Janet what Sam Wilson had told him. He packed, and on Sunday morning, Janet with the children drove him to the Tucson Airport. Arthur arrived in Washington National Airport at 5:25 P.M. Washington's weather was cold. Arthur took a D.C.-area taxicab to the Willard Hotel and registered in room 1400. He unpacked his suitcase, took a shower and called Janet at 7:00 P.M., which was 5:00 in Tucson. He told Janet his trip was routine and it was eighteen degrees in Washington. He hoped it would not snow. He talked to Sarah, who asked him,

"Where is Washington?" and to his son Arthur, Jr. He told Janet he loved her and he would call her tomorrow.

Arthur went to the dining room, had a drink, and enjoyed a good steak dinner. He went back to the room, watched television, and went to bed at 10:00 P.M.

At 6:45 A.M. the next morning after breakfast, he went to the entrance of the Willard Hotel. At 7:00, a gray U.S. government GSA van pulled up to the front of the Willard. The driver hollered, "The Pentagon and Langley, Virginia."

Two U.S. Navy Captains wearing black Naval uniforms and black raincoats raised their hands and went to the van. A few seconds later, a U.S. Air Force Brigadier General got out of a car parked in front of the Willard Hotel and walked to the van. Arthur and two other men dressed in civilian clothing walked to the van and the military personnel made room for them. The General asked the van driver how long it would take to get to the Pentagon. The van driver said, "About forty-five minutes."

They rode in silence. Arthur was amazed at the stop-and-go traffic. They went down Pennsylvania Avenue to Constitution Avenue, across the Fourteenth Street bridge, and north on Jefferson Davis Highway to the Pentagon. The two Navy Officers talked about returning to the Pentagon after a trip to Subic Bay in the Philippines, and the General said, his ass was dragging; he was returning from a month's travel to Clark Air Force Base in the Philippines, Kadena Air Force Base in Thailand and Tan Son Nhut Saigon in South Vietnam.

The three remaining men introduced themselves on their way to Langley. There was Arthur, James Whitfield from Orlando, Florida and William Trayner who returned from four years in Morocco and three in Athens, Greece. They were on assignments to Vietnam.

"Here we are, gentlemen," the driver said.

The three men thanked him and they walked to the front entrance. Bill Trayner opened one of the double glass-and-metal doors and they all entered the lobby. There were six men seated on benches in the lobby. Arthur, Bill Trayer, and Jim Whitfield went to the security console and introduced themselves to a security guard named Bruce Mathis.

"Hello, gentlemen," the security guard said to them. "May I help you?"

Arthur said, "We are employees," and he showed the security guard his identification.

"We have new security procedures," the guard told them. "Ordinarily, we would let you go directly to the fourth floor, but with all the anti-war protests going on, we now require an escort to each floor. Mr. Baker, Director of Personnel and Administration, will escort all of you to his office at 0900."

At 9:00 A.M., Preston Baker appeared in the lobby. He saw Arthur and said, "Arthur Norris, it's been a long time!"

Arthur got up off the bench, went to Preston Baker and they shook hands.

"You look fit," Preston said to Arthur.

"And so do you, with a little less hair, and what is left is now much grayer," he said, and laughed.

"Gentlemen," said Preston Baker. "Please excuse our formal security procedures, we get a daily threat here, or attempts to vandalize cars in the parking lot, throw paint on the building, or demonstrate against the Vietnam War. We've added thirty new security guards around the clock to prevent what happened over at the Pentagon, where there was a riot recently. The war is causing havoc."

Preston Baker said, "Please follow me to my office."

They took the elevator to the fourth floor, got off, and walked to the office of the director of personnel and administration. Preston Baker pushed four numbers on the digital security pad and the door buzzed open. The group of four men entered the office. Preston Baker closed the door and Miss Whipple came into the room. She saw Arthur and broke into a big smile.

"Mr. Norris, so nice to see you again. I've heard wonderful things about you. I'm now Mr. Baker's assistant." She walked over to Arthur and they shook hands. Arthur looked at her; she was as prim and proper as ever, wearing a navy blue dress with a white collar and a pearl necklace.

"You look well," said Arthur. "Thank you for the compliment, Miss Whipple."

She turned her head slightly and said, "Oh that's quite all

right, Mr. Norris. I always liked you from the first day you came to work eleven years ago."

Preston Baker came out of his office and said, "Gentlemen, thank you all for getting here on such short notice. Please have a seat. I'll go around the room and introduce each one of you. As you are aware, you have all been selected personally to be a Station Chief in South Vietnam. We selected you based upon your own personal qualifications, interview for the position, ability to do well in Vietnamese language school and career potential. You are to be congratulated. I was promoted to the director of personnel and administration in 1965 after Major General Weber took a position in the Pentagon.

"This morning I want to talk for thirty minutes and review personnel files to make sure everything is current, and records are up to date, and brief you on your individual assignments. After reviewing your file, you will go to the special compartmented intelligence facility (SCIF) and read current intelligence from Saigon."

Preston Baker paused for a moment. "What you hear in the next two days is Top Secret.

"Gentlemen, the U.S. position today, February twentieth, 1968, remains tenuous. The director met twice with the President and National Security Council. When Johnson had learned about Tet Offensive he was visibly shaken. General Weyand prevented Saigon from being overrun by moving twenty U.S. infantry battalions to Long Binh."

Preston Baker continued, "After the President received a briefing in the Situation Room, he said, 'Eighty-four thousand Goddamn Viet Cong attacked South Veet-nam and not one person in the U.S. Intelligence Community knows about it! What in the hell are those people doing? Do you mean to tell me with all the intelligence agencies in Saigon, the Joint Staff, ARVN, J-2, MACV, U.S. Embassy, POWS, that not one person got wind of the attack? They tell me they can hear a fly fart, but they can't detect movement of eighty-four thousand VC? Jesus Christ almighty!!'

"The president's office called the director of the CIA and told him to be in his office at 7:00 A.M. February tenth, LBJ told him,

'We are going to turn the screws on those VC bastards: you gentlemen, will turn the screws!'

"The president has now allocated twenty million dollars from discretionary funds into the Phoenix Program. That is why you are here. You will have three briefings in the next two days. The next briefing is from Mr. Colby."

Mr. Colby entered the SCIF and said, "Gentlemen, we all have met—here is your mission statement. Collect political and military intelligence on Viet Cong infrastructure and root it out with PRU Combat Operations.

"These are my guidelines how to organize your program."

- PRU are under command of local province chief.
- Mission: kill or capture Viet Cong political cadre, tax collectors, intelligence agents, administrators, and propagandists.
- VCI travel with Viet Cong units.
- Vietnamese National Police forces and the Police Special Branch have GVN authority to arrest VCI for detention and interrogation.
- CIA arms and trains PSB.

"Provincial and district Intelligence operations centers work with local military, Chieu Hoi and police to collect VCI intelligence.

"Provincial Interrogation Center is the focal point to hold VCI for processing, interrogations, 'turn around scouts,' or recruit to join local PRU's.

"The profile of the PRU's is usually:"

1. Cambodia Nungs, ex-Viet Cong, and local recruits.
2. Armed with M-16 rifles, M-60 machine guns, .81-mm Mortars, 4.2 Mortars, M-79 grenade launchers, and .50-caliber machine guns.
3. 150-175 active soldiers—3–4 companies.
4. Tiger-striped camouflage uniforms, and U.S. boots.
5. PRU-25 tactical radios in each company.
6. Medical supplies, construction material, concertina

wire, floodlights, chickens, pigs, blankets, mosquito nets, rice, straw, gasoline, sleeping bags and flashlights.
7. Private $125/month U.S. dollars
   Sgt. $175/month
   Lt. $200/month
   Capt. $300/month
   Major $400/month
8. PRUs live in their compounds with families and animals.

   Wednesday the briefings were done. Thursday, Arthur returned to Tucson. He was overwhelmed by what he had learned, but he could not discuss anything with Janet.
   Arthur arrived in Tucson on American Airlines flight #449. Janet, the children and Tyler met him at the airport. Arthur had decided to get started and not to delay the inevitable flight to South Vietnam.
   They had an enjoyable week. On March 1, 1968, Arthur said good-bye, hugged his wife, Sarah, Arthur, Jr., and Jennifer, and said, "I love you all so much, I shall miss you." He took a taxi to the Tucson airport, which flew to San Francisco, then he took a flight on TWA to Bangkok. The CIA met him and flew him to Saigon. On March 9, 1968, the CIA flew him on an Air American C-47 into Rach Gia Airstrip. The U.S. Army Province Senior Advisor met Arthur, and drove him to the U.S. Team OSA House in Rach Gia where he would live for the next two years. Lt. Col. Berry said, "When you are settled, call my office. I'll give you a briefing of what is fact and what is bullshit."
   Arthur took his gear, got out of the Jeep, and said, "Thanks, Colonel, I'll call you tomorrow." He walked past two guards, opened the door, and went into his new home.

7

June 1, 1968, U.S. Army Captain Ted R. Graham checked out of the Open Arms Bed and Breakfast off Union Square in San Francisco. He stepped into a waiting yellow taxi and told the driver "Oakland Army Base."

He looked out the cab's window as the driver drove across the Oakland Bay Bridge at the sight of sailboats tacking with the wind on the Oakland Bay and thought, *I'm going to war.* The cab stopped in front of building 47 and Ted paid the cab driver his fare.

The driver told him as he helped remove Ted's luggage, "Keep you head down and your ammo dry—that's what I did in Korea."

Ted entered a building in which U.S. military personnel walked in all directions as if it were Grand Central in New York City. They were young soldiers. Ted went to a kiosk and asked a civilian, "Where is room one?"

The woman pointed down a hall, "Straight ahead and you'll see a sign, ALL VIETNAM BOUND PERSONNEL REPORT HERE. Ted went into the World War II-type room and got in the line PERSONNEL WITH ORDERS. Army Sergeant Jones said, "Orders, Sir." Ted handed the Sergeant a copy of his orders. Sergeant Jones traced a roster of names and without looking up said, "Captain Graham, Theodore R." He looked up at Ted, "Correct, Sir?"

"Yes, Sergeant," said Ted.

"Sir, I'll need two copies of your orders; go to room four, you will be manifested on the bus to Travis Air Force Base for the flight to Honolulu and Vietnam."

"Thank you, Sergeant." Ted gave him two copies of his orders and went to room four.

Room four had names alphabetically listed and he found the

F-K line. He stood in line for a few minutes and reached the front of the line. A female Adjutant General Captain said, "Captain Ted Graham, Military Assistance Command, Vietnam?"

"Yes, Ma'am," said Ted.

"Here is your bus ticket, keep it with you. Your bus leaves at 1400; there is a dayroom with TV, papers, magazines and telephones. It takes two hours to get to Travis; your bus leaves for Travis at 1800, a five-hour flight to Honolulu, refuel, and an eight-hour flight to Bien Hoa Air Base in Vietnam. Any questions?"

"None," said Ted.

"Good luck," she said.

Ted took his footlocker to the dayroom; it was 1100. Three hours to wait. Ted called his parents collect and said good-bye. He sat down in a chair and looked out the window at Oakland Army Base. A young enlisted couple holding a small boy was sitting in front of him. The man was an Army Sergeant with artillery brass on his lapels. *He must be a battery NCO,* thought Ted. The couple talked and the young wife dabbed her eyes as the young boy put his hand on his dad's face and touched his chin. He heard the Sergeant say to the boy, "Son, you'll be two years old when Daddy gets home." The wife began to cry. Ted sat in silence. The couple and their son got up and went to the cafeteria. It was 1200. Ted read the *Time Magazine* and started to read *The Grapes of Wrath.* Before he knew it, it was 1345 and an announcement came over the public address system, "All U.S. Army Personnel to Travis Air Force Base report to transportation gate seven." Ted picked up his footlocker, walked to gate seven, and waited in line.

A Sergeant said, "Go to the bus, put your footlocker at the loading door and it will be loaded for you and transferred directly to World Airways, Flight 1149. You can retrieve it at Bien Hoa."

Great, thought Ted.

The soldiers boarded a Greyhound bus, and took all the seats. The bus driver drove to Travis, they got off the bus, and the bus driver said to them, "Good luck and God bless you." They filed out and walked into the terminal. Ted took a seat with other

U.S. Army personnel waiting in the terminal. He began to read *The Grapes of Wrath.*

At 1745 the public address system announced: "Attention in the terminal, all U.S. military personnel on World Airways Flight number 1149 for Honolulu to Bien Hoa, South Vietnam, prepare to board the aircraft at gate three."

Ted got up and walked to gate three; he saw a red-and-white civilian aircraft on the tarmac with WORLD AIRWAYS written on the side. Men stood in line to board. A young Army Private stood near Ted and began to cry. Ted saw him and said, "Private, it's okay." The young private looked at Ted with fear in his eyes.

Another announcement came again over the public address, "Final call for all U.S. military personnel on World Airways Flight 1149 to Honolulu and Bien Hoa, South Vietnam, at gate three."

The Private fidgeted with his overseas cap. He looked at Ted and said, "I don't want to go to Vietnam and get killed."

Ted saw the line move forward toward the gate.

Ted looked at the Private's powder-blue fourage cord and his insignia displaying the crossed fifles of the infantry.

"We'd better go," Ted said to the Private. "Private, you'll do fine, you've been well-trained and you'll have excellent NCOs in Vietnam."

With that, the Private bolted out of the line, ran full stride toward the front doors of the terminal and out an open door. A soldier behind Ted said, "Let the chicken-shit go, we don't want his type." Ted looked at the soldier; he did not say another word.

As the line moved toward the aircraft another soldier asked Ted, "Sir, what will happen to that Private when the Army gets a hold of him?"

"I don't know," said Ted. "They'll calm him down, he has to serve, I guess, he was drafted. If he won't serve, he'll probably be given a general court martial for desertion, go to prison, and receive a Dishonorable Discharge from the Army."

"Too bad," said the soldier.

The entire group entered the World Airways aircraft. A flight attendant gave safety instructions and they took off for Honolulu. During the flight, a flight attendant walked down the aisle and Ted asked her how many troops were on board Flight 1149.

She said, "One hundred ninety-seven."

The flight arrived at Honolulu at 7:00 P.M. Honolulu time. Ted walked to the promenade deck at the airport while the aircraft was being refueled. He saw Diamond Head in the distance, hotels on Waikiki Beach and felt the balmy ocean breeze blow against his face. Ted had never been to Hawaii.

The aircraft was refueled and took off. The pilot said it was an eight-hour flight to Bien Hoa, with two meals, snacks, and a movie. Ted ate, watched a movie, and fell asleep. He woke up at 0600. The pilot said, "We'll land at Bien Hoa Air Force Base in thirty minutes."

As the World Airways aircraft approached Bien Hoa, Ted looked out his window and saw hundreds of bomb craters on the hills. The pilot spoke over the public address system and said he would keep the aircraft's engine's running in the event of a mortar or rocket attack on Bien Hoa. The pilot said, "If you have to remain on board, I will taxi, and take off immediately."

The World Airways aircraft rolled to a stop. The flight attendant opened the front cabin door and announced, "All personnel, deplane in an orderly manner." She said, "If you drop something, let it go, it will be brought to you in the terminal."

The personnel deplaned in an orderly manner and soon felt the humid hot air in South Vietnam. Not a second was wasted. Ted looked back at the World Airways aircraft, and refueling trucks were refueling the aircraft for an immediate return flight to Honolulu.

Once the personnel were assembled inside the terminal, U.S. Army Staff Sergeant Evans met the group. He told them to go to the rear of the terminal and board the waiting green buses. Ted thought to himself as he walked through the Bien Hoa Terminal, *I'm in South Vietnam after reading and hearing about Vietnam for five years.*

All personnel boarded two waiting Army buses. An Army M.P. holding an M-16 rifle got on the bus, stood in the doorway, and counted personnel on the bus. The driver was Vietnamese. The M.P. took out a notebook, wrote down the time and the number of personnel on the bus, and said, "At ease. There are forty-six U.S. military personnel on this bus."

The M.P. continued, "It takes two hours to get to Saigon and Kelper Compound. Don't stick your arms out of the window, smoke or chew tobacco. Any questions?" There were no questions. The M.P. leaned toward the bus driver and said, "Dee-Dee Mow" which was the G.I.'s slang in Vietnamese for "Let's go." The bus driver pulled the bus away from the terminal, drove one-half mile on an asphalt road, passed a sandbag bunker, turned left and got on a two-way street past a blue sign saying SAIGON.

The bus windows were covered with heavy-gauge metal wire. Ted wondered how anyone could put their arms out the bus windows.

The bus continued at thirty-five to forty miles an hour down Old French Highway Four. Ted saw heavy, thick green jungle foliage and a clear blue sky. He looked around the bus; some personnel were sleeping, other stared blankly out the window, and some looked straight ahead. The bus passed small wood houses with thatch roofs and a constant flow of mopeds, motorbikes, and motorcycles, Citroens, trucks, South Vietnamese military trucks and Jeeps went by the bus. Ted saw a building that looked like a school with a South Vietnamese tri-color red striped flag flying on the rooftop; a young Vietnamese woman was directing children. The bus continued down Highway Four and passed a rural area of rice paddies with young boys riding water buffalos pulling a plow and a man behind the plow. The bus passed gravesites with mounds of dirt above the ground and a small structure holding incense at the head of the grave.

Ted looked at his watch at 11:00. A soldier sitting next to Ted said, "Where are you assigned, Captain?"

Ted had dozed off for a few minutes and was startled. "Me?" he asked as he looked at a young First Lieutenant who was wearing armor insignia. Ted thought a moment. "I've got orders to MACV, Fourth Corps; no unit assignment."

Ted looked at the Lieutenant's nametag; it was Long. He asked, "What are your orders?"

Lieutenant Long answered, "I'm going to the Eleventh Armored Cavalry Regiment. I had a two-year tour in Germany as an Armor Platoon Leader with the Third Armor Division; a lot of Lieutenants and Captains got orders to Vietnam last March. We thought it was because of casualties from the Tet Offensive in January, but our Battalion Commander was in Vietnam from 1966 to 1967 and said it was just a normal rotation. We'll see," said the Lieutenant.

"Where's home?" Ted asked the Lieutenant.

The Lieutenant answered, "Atlanta, Georgia."

"Atlanta," said Ted, "I've driven around it on Interstate 95 to Florida, but never visited Atlanta, I've been told it's the next major metropolitan area of the South."

Lieutenant Long answered, "It's growing; I was born and raised in Atlanta and went to the University of Georgia. Atlanta is a big city."

"When did you graduate from Georgia?" asked Ted.

"1965," said the Lieutenant. "I'm serving four years, getting out, and going into real estate."

The M.P. stood up, "We're entering Saigon."

The bus driver turned right and drove the bus south on Tran Do and traffic in Saigon was chaotic. Endless rows of cars inched along bumper-to-bumper, with South Vietnamese Army vehicles, Jeeps, motorcycles, and one of the motorscooters had a lovely South Vietnamese woman perched on the back seat holding onto the driver with her arms. At intersections, there were high sandbagged bunkers with concertina wire and South Vietnam paratroopers wearing sunglasses and steel helmets holding M-16 rifles at the bunkers. The bus continued along Tran Do. In the distance appeared a large pale green concrete building. The driver drove beyond the building, which had U.S. Army Jeeps, and U.S. Army Military Police, and U.S. military personnel standing outside in front. The building was in good condition. It had two-story windows facing Tran Do, an orange tile roof, a concrete-and-tile fence about ten feet high, with a guard tower located at each corner. The bus driver turned left at an intersection and pulled the bus and parked it between two yellow cones in front of Kelper Compound.

The M.P. on the bus said, "We are at Kelper Compound"; the

MP opened the door and said, "Take up your foot lockers into the building and wait for me."

In front of the building was a large sign, U.S. ARMY PERSONNEL AND PROCESSING CENTER, SAIGON. Under the sign was a smaller sign, which read: WELCOME COLONEL HUNTER E. DAVIS, INFANTRY, COMMANDING.

The group got out of the bus, located their footlockers, and carried them up wide front stairs and placed them along stucco columns of the front entrance and down the left side toward the back of the building. Beside the building courtyard was a barbecue pit and picnic tables. A ten-foot-high concrete wall formed the perimeter of the courtyard. There were large old shade trees and a large concrete hole in the center of the courtyard, and a cracked concrete sidewalk to a former bathhouse and swimming pool. About 500 feet from the courtyard was a two-story stucco structure in good condition which appeared to be a former French hotel. The old sidewalks criss-crossed the courtyard between the buildings.

Along the veranda of Kelper were white painted signs with black letters: COMPOUND CLASS ROOM, S-1, S-2, S-3, S-4, ADJUTANT, COMMANDER, AND COMMAND SERGEANT MAJOR. Ted looked at the Kelper Compound and thought, *This must have been either a French military compound or a resort in Saigon for French military officers.* There was a sign in the front of the building pointing to the interior hallway that said, INCOMING PERSONNEL and LOCKER STORAGE.

The M.P. from the bus came to the group standing on the front porch and said, "Follow me." They followed the M.P. into the building. Soon he felt the cool air from the air-conditioning in the building. The M.P. said, "Set your footlockers along the wall." Another M.P. came out of the S-2 room. He stood by the footlockers. Ted looked at his watch; it was 12:00. The M.P. from the bus said, "Get out your orders and green I.D. card, and form a line in front of the S-1 office, they will in-process you and tell you what to do." He said, "Good luck on your tour, this is my last weekend. On Tuesday I go back to the world on the same flight you came in on today."

"I hate this fucking place."

Ted asked an M.P., "What is this compound?"

The M.P. said, "I've been told it was a former French officers' resort and hotel; the U.S. Army Engineers refurbished it in 1967; that's all I know. The officers and BOQ have billeting; that building over yonder is Clara Barton Hall. The name of the quarters is Arnold Hall named for PFC Arnold Hall, U.S. Army, killed in 1964." The M.P. saluted and said, "Have a good tour" and went down the front steps back to the bus with his M-16 rifle.

A group of soldiers were waiting in front of the entrance to Kelper Compound got onto the bus for Tan Son Nhut Air Force Base.

A line had formed along the right side of the hallway; Ted entered the S-1 office. It had seven desks with administrative personnel; metal cabinets, typewriters, a copy machine, and U.S. Army personnel seated at the desks. One desk had a sign: OFFICERS and another sign said, ENLISTED. Ted waited in the line for the desk: OFFICERS. First Lieutenant Marks looked at him, and Ted took a seat at his desk.

The Lieutenant asked Ted, "Sir, two copies of your orders, please, Sir." Ted handed the Lieutenant two copies of his orders. The Lieutenant read his orders. "Fine, you'll get your team assignment tomorrow." May I also see your shot record, Sir?" asked the Lieutenant.

Ted got his wallet and produced his current shot record. The Lieutenant looked at a chart and the shot records and said, "All current." The Lieutenant said, "Do you have any immediate family needs such as sickness, terminal illness or personal matters that need immediate attention?"

"No," said Ted.

"Okay, Sir, the next activity is the in-country orientation in the assembly hall at 1300."

"Next."

Ted stood up, the Lieutenant saluted and Ted went back out to the hallway. Ted walked to the front of the building, found a latrine, and a Coke machine; he had not eaten since 0600. He bought a Coke, pretzels, and went to the adjutant's office to find out where to eat and billeting. He knocked on the door. Captain Bryant said, "Yes, Captain Graham, may I help you?"

Ted introduced himself. He told Captain Bryant that he had just arrived in country and wondered where to eat and be billeted. The Captain said, "U.S. Navy Seabees are in the process of building a cafeteria in Clara Barton Hall, but it's not finished. A cafeteria is two blocks away and it opens at 1600 hours. Breakfast is served from 0600 to 0800, and lunch from 1100 to 1300." The Captain said, "All male personnel are billeted in Arnold Hall at Kelper Compound."

Ted asked, "What is Clara Barton Hall?"

The Captain replied, "It's billeting for female officers, mostly Army and Navy nurses."

Captain Bryant said, "The administrative matters will be covered during the in-country briefing in the assembly hall at 1300." The captain asked to be excused. "See you at the in-country briefing." Ted looked at his watch. It was 1245.

Ted thought, *Might as well go inside, find a seat and sit down.*

He walked into the assembly hall down the center aisle between neatly lined metal chairs facing the front of the room. Ted took a chair in front of the room. He saw U.S. Army military arrive wearing khaki uniforms, jungle fatigues, jungle hats and jungle boots. There was rattling of the chairs and the murmuring of soldiers as they filed into the assembly hall and got seated. The assembly hall was the size of a basketball court. It had pale green walls and a row of windows with iron bars on each window. On the left side opposite the hallway were two double doors in the front and two double doors in the back. In the rear of the room was a fenced area with heavy wire and a sign DO NOT ENTER. Ted looked back at the wire cage and saw about sixty M-16 rifles secured inside the wire cage.

The assembly hall got full. In front of the room there was a podium, an American flag, and a movie screen. An enlisted man sat down behind Ted. He said to the man next to him, "This place reminds me of my high school at graduation."

As it approached 1300 four U.S. Army nurses entered the assembly hall through the front double doors, turned left and walked to the back of the room. They were wearing jungle fatigues and had their sleeves rolled up. Ted looked at them; one woman was beautiful with chestnut-brown hair about 5'6" or 5'7", and slender. Ted thought, *She must be a Hollywood celebrity visiting the troops dressed in an Army nurse's uniform.* Ted glanced over his right shoulder and watched as the nurses sat down near the back of the room.

Captain Jefferson Lee Madison, IV entered the assembly hall wearing a U.S. Army Special Forces uniform, Green Beret with Infantry insignia, airborne wings, and a Ranger tab on his uniform.

He had been on active duty four years as a Regular Army Officer. Before arriving in Vietnam, he departed his family's 900-acre Stonehill Farm outside Washington, D.C. His father was United States Senator Jefferson Lee Madison, III of Stonehill Farm, Virginia. Jeff graduated from the Virginia Military Institute second in his class in 1964. He married his high-school sweetheart, Jessica Simpson, and now they had two daughters named Ashley and Leanne. His wife was pregnant with a third child due in May of 1969.

Jeff had the potential to be a General Officer. He served one year at Fort Benning, Georgia, after completing Army Ranger training in 1964 on the Ranger Committee. After that tour, he was assigned to the Third Infantry Division's First Brigade, Third Battalion as Company Commander in Schweinfurt, West Germany. After two years in Schweinfurt, West Germany, he went TDY to Fort Bragg and completed Special Forces training. His wife and family remained at Schweinfurt. He was reassigned to the Fifth Special Forces Group at Bad Toltz, Bavaria, West Germany in 1967. Leanne was born at Bad Toltz and Jeff's father told him the Army Chief of Staff said there was a growing need for Special Forces Officers in the Army and it would be a good second career. Jeff took his father's advice. He was twenty-five years old, 6'2"; weighed 170 pounds and was physically fit. He ran three miles every morning; did fifty push-ups, one hundred sit-ups and had "maxed" every Army PT test on Active Duty. He wanted to serve six months in Special Forces in Vietnam, and then be assigned as Company Commander with a U.S. infantry company.

Jeff saw a vacant chair. He walked down the aisle, bent over and asked, "Excuse me Captain, is that chair next to you vacant?"

Ted looked at Jeff and said, "Yes, it is vacant, have a seat."

Ted asked Jeff "where is home?" Jeff answered, "I'm Regular Army, I've been on active duty four years and my family home is twenty miles west of Washington, D.C. at Stonehill Farm, Virginia, perhaps you've heard of my father, Senator Jefferson Madison?" Ted was amazed at what Jeff told him.

"Your father is a United States senator and you're in Vietnam?"

"Might as well be in Vietnam, it all goes toward my thirty years," answered Jeff.

Jeff asked Ted, "Where's your home?"

"Camp Hill, Pennsylvania."

"Camp Hill, isn't that near Gettysburg and the Army War College in Carlisle? My family and I drove through Camp Hill on our way from Gettysburg where we had toured the Gettysburg Battlefield and then up to Carlisle Barracks to the Army War College where Dad made a speech." Jeff continued, "I was a second year cadet at V.M.I.; that summer I got leave and we took a family trip. Pennsylvania is a beautiful state."

Captain Bryant entered the assembly hall, "At ease," he said. The room fell silent.

He introduced himself. "Good afternoon ladies and gentlemen, I'm Captain Howard Bryant, Adjutant for the U.S. Army Personnel and Processing Center, Saigon. Some of you I've met."

Captain Bryant continued, "Can you hear me?"

A voice behind Ted and Jeff mumbled, "Yeah, asshole, but who cares?"

A murmur emanated across the room. "At ease," hollered Captain Bryant. "This is an important orientation. Pay attention!" The air conditioners kicked on and it got cooler.

"Okay," said Captain Bryant. "That's better, we will be here for two hours. Let me say, ladies and gentlemen, we have four U.S. Army nurses in the room, men watch your G.I. language."

"Fucking-A-right, Captain," a voice spoke up in the back.

Ted looked over his shoulder; everyone was staring directly at the front of the room.

Army Staff Sergeant Collier entered the room. He motioned to Captain Bryant, and Captain Bryant stepped to the podium. "It is my privilege to now introduce Colonel Hunter E. Davis, Commanding Officer, U.S. Army Personnel-Processing Center, Saigon. At-ten-hut."

The room snapped sharply to attention.

Colonel Davis walked to the podium.

"Thank you, Captain Bryant. Take your seats," said the Colonel.

The Colonel looked at the room. He turned to Captain Bryant and said, "How many soldiers are here today?"

Captain Bryant replied, "One hundred sixty-one, Sir."

The Colonel looked over the entire room, "How many of you are on your second tour?" he asked.

Fifteen people raised their hands.

The Colonel said, "Fifteen, okay. I thought there would be more, from the size of the group." The Colonel began to speak.

"Welcome to the U.S. Army Personnel-Processing Center, Saigon. I commend all of you who made a decision to serve your country in Vietnam. Many of our fellow Americans don't agree with or support the Vietnam War. Many of you have completed extensive military training preparing you for Vietnam." The Colonel continued, "Whatever MOS you possess, you have been well-trained and you are now prepared to do your job. It doesn't matter if you're an M.P., supply, personnel, infantryman, truck driver, intelligence analyst or a cook, every job is important. Don't let your fellow soldiers down. Do your duty every day!

"This is my second Vietnam tour. This is a nasty, dirty war. It's hard to identify the enemy, V.C. or Charley. He is elusive, relentless and will use any means to destroy our soldiers. Stay alert, stay vigilant, and know your surroundings. Don't get lapse or lazy as time goes by. Enlisted personnel, listen to your NCOs; many have been in Vietnam before.

"Now, on drugs—they are in Vietnam; if I find any soldier using drugs, he or she is toast. I'll have their ass in jail in a New York minute. Listen to me! *Never* take, use, or consume drugs like marijuana, cocaine or heroin. If you're stoned, you cannot fight. Beer is legal off duty.

"Do your duty, and go home in a year; have faith in God, your country and yourself. In forty-two days I leave Vietnam and will retire from the U.S. Army after thirty years of service in World War II, Korea and Vietnam. That's all.

"God bless you and good luck."

Captain Bryant hollered, "A-TEN-HUT."

The room came to attention and Colonel Davis departed from the assembly hall.

"Take a ten-minute break, be back in your seats at 1400," said Captain Bryant.

Ted and Jeff followed the crowd out of the room.

Jeff said, "That Colonel is a piss-cutter, he reminds me of personnel I knew at Fort Benning, the infantry has its own way of life."

Ted said, "I wouldn't know, I'm an Army Intelligence weenie. I went to Infantry Officers Basic Course at Benning. Eight weeks was enough for me."

They both used the latrine and started back to their seats. Ted saw the four Army nurses. Ted and Jeff walked past them and smiled and said "Hi," and continued to walk. The Captain, whose nametag said Harris, smiled; she did not say anything.

"Not too friendly," said Jeff.

"Guess not," said Ted. They went to their seats and sat down.

Captain Bryant took a position in the middle of the front of the room, "At ease," he said.

The assembly hall doors were closed and the air-conditioning made the classroom tolerable.

"Ladies and gentlemen, it is my pleasure to introduce Command Sergeant Major John 'Bull' Horn, known throughout the United States Army as a 'Soldier's soldier.' " He turned to his left and said, "Here is a senior enlisted E-9 who is completing thirty-four years of service in the U.S. Army in July. Command Sergeant Major Horn enlisted in the Army after quitting high school in 1934 during the Great Depression to support his family in North Carolina. He rose from private E-1 to the highest enlisted rank of E-9 in thirty-four years. He saw combat as an infantryman in World War II, was an infantry platoon Sergeant in

Korea, company First Sergeant in his first Vietnam tour in 1965 and he is now in his final tour before retirement in five months. He received a high school diploma and now has two years of college with the University of Maryland's overseas education program. Among his awards and decorations are the Silver Star, Bronze Star, three Purple Hearts, and three times awarded the Combat Infantryman's Badge, Master Paratrooper and Ranger.

"Please stand for Command Sergeant Major John 'Bull' Horn."

The room snapped to attention again.

"Incidentally, before the Command Sergeant Major begins his remarks, his real name is John Horn. The name 'Bull' came during World War II when he fought in company boxing at Fort Benning. When he came into the boxing ring, he 'snorted' to put fear into his opponent, hence John Bull Horn.

"Ladies and gentlemen, Command Sergeant Major John 'Bull' Horn."

"Thank you, Captain Bryant, for your introduction of this old soldier. Please take your seats."

Bull Horn walked to the podium and looked at the people who came into the assembly room to hear him speak. He was fifty years old, wore a 1950s flat top, and had graying brown hair.

"Most of you are younger than I have had years of service in the U.S. Army," he said. He wore standard starched olive-green jungle fatigues, a CIB with two stars meaning three awards, a Master Parachutist Badge and a Ranger Tab.

My God, thought Ted, *this man is bigger than life.*

Command Sergeant Major Bull Horn dabbed his face with an olive drab handkerchief and said, "Don't tell Colonel Davis, but I'm going to remove my blouse," and he placed his fatigue blouse and on a chair.

"That's better."

He was stocky, about five feet nine, had a thick muscular neck, wide shoulders and a weight lifter's arms.

Ted thought; *He could knock out fifty push-ups right here.*

"Okay, let's get started," said Bull Horn. "Yes, what the Captain just said about me being called 'Bull Horn' is true. I've spent thirty-four good years in the U.S. Army, in the infantry. I've enjoyed being a soldier, but now I'm ready to retire. In five months, I'll finish my second tour in Vietnam, go back to North Carolina and work a 500-acre farm with my wife of thirty years and our two sons.

"It has been a good life, I want all of you to go home in twelve months and be proud of your service in this war.

"Let's get down to business. Your job is to survive. How many of you here are assigned to infantry, artillery or armor units?"

Three quarters of the people in the room raised their hands. About 175 or so of 200, the rest were MACV, Headquarters or Headquarters Company.

"What I have to say applies to everyone. Don't think 'this old fart' (excuse me, nurses) 'isn't talking to me.' Here are Bull Horn's ten rules to stay alive in Vietnam:

"One. Stay alert. You are in a war. You're not playing soldier; if you're shot here, you may not get up.

"Two. The VC or 'Charley' hate you, he wants to kill you, but you kill him first. Be prepared for the unexpected, like ambushes, being hit when you're tired, or haven't had contact in weeks. Look out, that's when the VC know your guard is down and will attack.

"Three. Take care of yourself, your gear, and your weapon; take your anti-malaria pill every Monday. Keep your weapon clean, oiled lightly, and take a daily shower; wash off the crap, flies, sweat and grime that cause skin disease.

"Four. Take care of your feet. Wear clean socks. There are diseases in paddy water, mud, gunk, and grime. Don't let it stay between your toes. I've seen some awful rot from GIs who didn't keep their feet clean. I mean open sores, cracked and bleeding toes, and rashes. Use plenty of soap, wash, and dry your feet.

"Five. Maintain light and noise discipline at night. The same old story applies from World War II. Don't let your dog tags rattle, your canteen rattle, or light a cigarette. You could be shot lighting it.

"Six. Don't talk in the open on the radio. Use authorized call signs at all times. Don't give out friendly positions on map coordinates. Charley is listening with voice interception equipment—many VC speak and understand English.

"Seven. Always, I say always, know your unit's field position, and the position of other friendly units if you call in artillery or air strikes.

"Eight. Anticipate the unexpected. Keep your M-16 at the ready position, kneel and get into the prone position to fire your weapon. Hit the ground if you come under fire, don't stand up and look around to be a target. Take cover.

"Nine. Take your R & R. Never do drugs on R & R. You can end up with your ass in prison in some countries. Some nice Oriental ladies you'll meet want you to get drunk or stoned to rob you, don't let them do that to you.

"Ten. Have faith in God. I am a Baptist—my faith has seen me through tough situations and given me strength. If you're not a believer, you may become a believer.

"This is not a rule," Bull Horn said, "but if you have sex with one of these lovely bar girls in Saigon, you may start to burn or drip in ten days. See a medic, don't try to hide it or you may lose it. Get two penicillin shots, it may take more than one." Bull Horn finished.

"Sorry ladies, I don't know what to tell the women. Any questions?"

There were no questions. "That's it," said Bull. "You'll see me around here today and tomorrow, don't hesitate to ask me anything if I can help you. Thank you and good luck."

He waved and left the room.

Captain Bryant said, "At ease! All those personnel whose names I called, see me in the front room." People headed for the double doors.

Jeff Madison turned to Ted and said, "Well, with Sergeant Major Bull Horn's ten points, we now know all we need to know." Ted smiled.

An announcement blared over the public address system, "Attention in the area, attention in the area. All side arms for officers and weapons for all enlisted persons will be, I say again, will be issued tomorrow at 0800 at the arms room along with 100 rounds of ammunition. Don't leave until you get your side arm or weapon."

"Wouldn't think of it," said Jeff.

Ted looked at his watch. It was now 3:45 P.M. June second, 1968.

"Are you hungry?" asked Ted. Jeff responded, "Yes, I've had nothing but Coke and candy all day. Let's eat."

"Sure, but where?"

Ted replied, "I asked an MP and he said there's a small PX and cafeteria two blocks from here."

They reached the double doors and when they were outside, the wall of heat and humidity hit them.

"Wow," said Jeff. "It's hot. I mean, more than a Virginia hot summer." They descended the concrete steps in the front of the building.

"Where is the PX and cafeteria?" Ted asked an MP holding a M-16 standing outside the building. Two sandbag bunkers on each side were at the entrance, and on top of one was mounted a M-60 machine gun.

Ted asked the M.P., "Think you'll ever have to use that M-60?"

"I hope not; if I do, they're too close," he said, and laughed.

The other M.P. said, "Are you new in country, Sir?"

"Yes," said Jeff. "Very new."

"Well," said the M.P. "it's the pits all the way around. I was up country in Two Corps during the Tet Offensive last January and we lost ten M.P.s including the ones at the U.S. Embassy. The VC is sly and tricky. Watch them," he said. "I leave in three weeks for the 'world,' and I'm on guard. Don't want to buy the farm the last week. Yeah, the PX, it closes at 1600; at 1600 buses start running to Tan Son Nhut. Do you want to wait?" he asked.

Ted looked at Jeff. "Wait? No. I'm hungry, and I want to walk around Saigon."

"Okay," said the M.P., "go down Tran Do two blocks, turn left and a block to Phue Vin, go down Phue Vin about half a block and the PX is on the left, you can't miss it."

Ted and Jeff started down the street following the MP's directions to the PX and cafeteria.

They found the cafeteria and entered. It was air-conditioned and had American music playing "No Satisfaction" by the Rolling Stones.

"I love that song," said Jeff.

They went through the serving line. Ted ordered two hamburgers, fries, a Coke, and a piece of pie.

Jeff said, "You must be a growing boy."

Ted responded, "Who knows when we'll get hamburgers in the field."

Jeff smiled; he ordered chicken, coleslaw, french fries, and iced tea. He sat down and Ted saw two of the four nurses from the meeting seated near the middle of the room. He saw the same Captain from the classroom that had caught his attention. She was beautiful; she looked to be twenty-five, dark chestnut hair slightly parted to one side, intense deep blue eyes, fair skin, very lovely cheekbones and straight white teeth.

The other nurse was blonde, blue-eyed, and slightly plump but pretty. Ted said to Jeff, "That dark-haired nurse is a KNOCKOUT. I wonder what brought her to Vietnam?"

"The Army," said Jeff and he continued to eat.

Ted said, "She can take care of me anytime she wants," and started to eat his hamburgers, he paused, "I'm still a bachelor and it doesn't hurt to look."

"Yeah, I'm married, son, and my wife is expecting our third child and all I can do is look."

Ted glanced around the room. Perhaps there were thirty to forty people in the cafeteria, all American military. Many of them had soiled, dirty uniforms, and mud on their boots. Ted saw Vietnam combat patches from MACV, 82nd Airborne, 199th Infantry Brigade, 25th Infantry Brigade, and 1st Air Calvary Division. "Why are those guys here?" asked Jeff.

"I dunno, probably on their way to R & R, I guess, or just on a pass to Saigon for a PX run."

They finished their meal and went to pay the bill. The two nurses finished and paid their bill and started toward the PX door.

Ted said, "I need to make a PX run."

Jeff laughed, "You mean you need to make a check-out-the-nurse run."

They entered the PX and started to look around; Ted saw the nurses.

Jeff whispered to Ted, "Why don't you just saunter on over, introduce yourself and ask her where she is assigned."

"No, way too forward."

Ted and Jeff looked around the PX; Ted bought six bars of soap, two olive-drab towels and a box of Tide soap.

"Probably will need these," he told Jeff.

Jeff bought flashlight batteries, mailing envelopes, writing paper, stamps, and two cans of snuff. Ted saw the snuff, "You actually use that stuff?"

"Sure enough, I'm from the South, and snuff to us is Southern bubblegum, I love to spit," he laughed.

Ted glanced over at the nurses and saw the dark-haired beauty examining an olive drab tee shirt. Ted heard her say, "It looks okay to me." She had removed her fatigue blouse and had a full figure.

"Let's go, lover boy," said Jeff. "We'll follow them home like we're tracking Charley."

Both groups paid at the same time and started back up Phu Vin Street to Kelper Compound. As they walked along the street, the nurses were ten feet in front of Ted and Jeff. Suddenly, the shorter blonde nurse turned, stopped, and said, "Are you gentlemen following us?"

Ted was shaken. "No Ma'am, just walking back to the Kelper Compound."

The blonde nurse laughed. "You two are the first men we've met in Vietnam."

"Really?" said Ted.

By then, they were standing on the sidewalk in a group amidst the commotion, noise, passing Army trucks, and the constant people passing left and right.

Jeff introduced himself to the blonde, "I'm Jeffrey Madison from Virginia." The dark-haired beauty did not say a word; after a few seconds she extended her hand to Ted and said, "I'm Sue Ellen Harris, from Memphis, Tennessee."

The blonde said, "I'm Kathy Moore from Sacramento."

Ted said, "I'm Ted Graham from Camp Hill, Pennsylvania."

They began to walk. "Do you fellas have your assignments?"

"No," said Ted, "but it will be to an Advisory Team in MACV."

"What about you ladies?"

Sue Ellen said, "I'm assigned to the Third Field Hospital here in Saigon. I'm an O.R., I mean, an operating room nurse."

Kathy said, "I'm also an R.N. I've asked for an assignment to a MASH unit in the field. I want to help where I'm needed the most."

"Hum," said Jeff. "MASH, sounds like Alan Alda."

"Not really," said Kathy, "MASH Units are front-line medical units."

Sue Ellen turned to Ted. "Where are you from?"

"Camp Hill, Pennsylvania. I left there in 1965 to go on active duty, went to Fort Benning and Fort Holabird for training and then I was a Counter Intelligence Agent in Spokane, Washington and got orders to Vietnam."

"And you?" said Kathy to Jeff.

"Me, I'm from McLean, Virginia, my father is a U.S. senator from Virginia."

Sue Ellen gasped, "Your father is a U.S. senator and you're in Vietnam?" She sounded incredulous.

Jeff shrugged, "Naturally, I come from a long line of Southern military tradition, you know, the Civil War, World War One, World War Two and now Vietnam, I'm regular Army. I wanted to go to a U.S. unit, but Dad told me the Chief of Staff of the Army told him that the future of the Army in the next twenty years is Special Forces. I graduated from V.M.I. in 1964, went to Airborne, Ranger, Special Forces and had a two-year tour at Wurzburg, Bad Tolez Fifth Special Forces in Bavaria, Germany."

They got to the compound and walked up the steps to the entrance of Kelper Compound.

"It was a pleasure meeting you ladies," said Ted.

"Yes," said Jeff.

Kathy said to Sue Ellen, "We'd better get our room assignment, I want to check my footlocker."

"Okay."

Kathy said, "I've got to use the little girls' room."

As they stood waiting for Kathy, Jeff said, "I'm sweating like a pig and we've only walked ten minutes. This is going to be quite a year." As they entered the old building they felt the cool air-conditioning and noticed a sign posted on the wall stating: ROOM ASSIGNMENTS ARE NOW AVAILABLE.

Kathy returned, and Ted said, "Well folks, why don't we get our room assignments, relax and get ready for tomorrow?"

The nurses said, "We are billeted in a remodeled former French hotel here on the compound, see y'all tomorrow." They departed and waved good-bye.

Ted Graham and Jeff Madison went to the billeting office and met SFC Stewart.

"SFC Stewart, do you have room assignments?"

"Yes, Sir, you're Captain Graham and Captain Madison."

"Okay, let's see, that's unusual, you're both in the same room—got connections?" asked the Sergeant.

"Not really, Sergeant," said Jeff. "Two G.I.s new in country."

"Okay, Captain Graham, here is your key and Captain Madison, your key. We issue two keys, things change and if one of you remains a day, each one has a key."

Jeff asked, "Why don't we have our weapons?"

"Don't worry, Captain, we have plenty of arms if you need 'em, we'll get 'em to you. You're in room 645, the middle of the sixth floor, a room with a view. You can see the fighting in Cholon. There are suicide VC holed up and you can see tracers at night. Have a good night's sleep."

Ted and Jeff went to the storage area and retrieved their footlockers. They reached an elevator and a sign hung on the door: OUT OF ORDER.

"Damn," said Jeff, and looked up the concrete floors to the sixth floor.

"Let's go, it's one way to stay in shape."

They took their footlockers and started up the stairs. It was hot and humid. Ted felt drops of sweat start running down his face. He took his sleeve and wiped his face. They stopped at the fourth floor for a breather.

"I'm glad we're not moving a piano," said Jeff.

They reached the sixth floor. Jeff looked out over the city of Saigon and saw helicopter gun ships firing a line of tracer bullets toward a group of buildings with the familiar orange tile roofs.

Jeff turned to Ted, "What in the hell is going on over there?" He squinted and put his right hand up to shade his eyes.

Just at that point an Army Staff Sergeant carrying an M-16 said, "Welcome to 'Nam,' Sir, there are some suicidal VC sappers still holed up inside some of those buildings from Tet. I think more VC have infiltrated into Saigon for another attack."

"Another attack," asked Ted. "When?"

"Oh, nobody knows except Charley. We get Intel reports; a second attack could be on the way this summer.

"Where do you work, Sergeant?"

"I work in MACV J-2 Intelligence. I just came over to drop off orders and couldn't find Captain Harmon, know him?" he asked.

"No," said Jeff.

The Sergeant continued. "Two days ago a U.S. Army Captain was shot dead between the eyes by a VC sniper in front of the Cholon PX."

"Shot going to the PX?" Jeff stammered.

"Yes, Sir, shot dead. That's why I'm carrying my M-16."

"How far is Cholon from here?" asked Jeff.

"Oh, about two miles," said the Sergeant.

A large cloud of smoke rose from Cholon. Huey gunships withdrew.

The Sergeant said, "Good luck to both of you. I've got six more months to go."

Ted and Jeff walked along the outside concrete walkway to room 645. "Here we are," said Ted and he unlocked the door. "U.S. Army, Hilton Saigon."

"Ye Gods. It's hot, no A/C."

"No A/C? What a mess, shit."

There was a fan on a table.

Inside the room was a metal-frame bunk bed, clean sheets, a pillowcase, and a blanket.

"It reminds me of the YMCA," said Jeff.

Jeff looked at his watch. "It's 1730."

Ted said, "I'm not hungry, but let's take the 1800 bus to Ton Son Nhut and check out the PX."

"Okay, I've got to use the latrine first."

Ted opened his footlocker and packed his Tide, two tee shirts, and soap. *No room for much more,* he thought.

As he closed his footlocker he glanced at the picture of his parents he had packed.

He heard Jeff say, "Plenty of water, I'll take a shower when we get back."

Ted and Jeff left the room, went back down the six flights of steps, and walked outside Kelper Compound. They stood by the M.P.'s guardhouse.

"Is the five thirty bus on schedule?" asked Ted to an M.P.

"Like a train," said the M.P.

At 5:30, an olive-drab bus pulled up in the street. An M.P. holding an M-16 rifle got off the bus. About twenty-five U.S. Military Service personnel followed him. Ted and Jeff noticed this bus had heavy wire screen on the windows and the windows were almost shut except for twelve inches to let in Saigon heat.

The M.P. turned and a line had formed behind Ted and Jeff. "All aboard," the M.P. said to the group and they filed onto the bus. Ted and Jeff took two seats at the front of the bus.

When everyone was aboard, the M.P. told the Vietnamese bus driver, "Let's go, Sam." The bus driver pulled the bus away into the ever-present traffic.

Ted looked out the window at the unfolding sights of cars and people in front of the bus.

He thought, *I wonder how many VC are looking at us.*

The bus continued through the constant flow of traffic until it had gone four miles. A blue sign appeared and "Sam" turned the bus left. A pedicab darted in front of the bus and Sam hit the brakes, lurching the passengers forward. The M.P. almost fell down the front steps, Sam proceeded slowly and said, "Too many people in Saigon from country; never seen bus."

Sam drove the bus to a security gate. Two Air Force Security personnel wearing blue berets and white gloves emerged from a bunker by the gate. One Air Force Security Guard held up his gloved right hand. He walked to the left side of the bus, saw the

M.P., and waved him through the gate, which was lifted by the other Air Force Security to allow the bus to enter Ton Son Nhut.

The bus entered Tan Son Nhut along a main road. Ted and Jeff looked out the windows at the large metal-clad buildings, some with white stucco and orange tile roofs and U. S. military personnel walked along the roads.

Sam stopped the bus at an intersection. Ted and Jeff could see C-130 aircraft taking off and landing while several U.S. Huey helicopters circled in the distant horizon. Sam drove the bus through the intersection.

NO CIVILIAN VEHICLES BEYOND THIS POINT.

Sam turned right and stopped in front of the Ton Son Nhut PX.

Sam parked and turned the motor off.

The M.P. stood in the middle of the aisle and said, "Listen up, it's 1800, set your watches. The last bus back to the Kelper Compound leaves at 1900. Don't be late and don't come running down the road with an armful of packages waving to stop. It won't stop even if it's 1901, that's Colonel Davis' orders, no stragglers."

He opened the door and everyone filed out and began walking smartly in the direction of the PX.

Jeff turned to Ted, "Want to grab a quick bite?"

"Okay, a quick bite."

They went through the double doors of a cafeteria and heard the song "American Pie." It was a large room to accommodate 150 troops. Ted and Jeff walked to the serving line. Today's menu said: ROAST BEEF, POTATOES, VEGETABLES, ROLLS, BUTTER AND DRINK $1.50; FRIED CHICKEN, MASHED POTATOES, VEGETABLE, ROLLS, BUTTER AND DRINK $1.50, SPAGHETTI, ROLLS, BUTTER, SALAD AND DRINK $1.25. Also on the serving line were red beets, green beans, yams, corn, and Jello for twenty-five cents each. At the end of the line were chocolate cake, apple pie, and ice cream for fifty cents.

Jeff ordered spaghetti, yams, and a piece of chocolate cake. Ted ordered the same, green beans. Jeff paid the bill. The cafeteria was full of U.S. military. They took their trays to a table where a U.S. Navy Chief Petty Officer was seated wearing a denim work uniform and black boots.

Ted asked, "Chief, may we join you? I hope you won't hold it against us being we're Army," Ted said.

The Chief stood up and said, "No, Sir, be my guest."

"New in the country?" asked the Chief.

"Yes, Chief."

"I'm Chief Petty Officer Brian Murphy from San Diego; I've been in country nine months, three more to go."

Ted introduced himself and Jeff.

The Chief saw Jeff's green beret. "Special Forces?"

"Yep, four years service toward thirty."

"Good for you," said the Chief.

Ted sat silent.

"Well, let me tell you both, Captains," he said. "After the Tet Offensive, this war is going to be a long war. I'm in logistics at Cam Rahn Bay and they mortared and rocketed our base like hell during Tet, I was scared to death. We took our weapons and defended the perimeter; two men were killed. I'm here on a supply run. Came down three days ago on a LST boat. We get down once a month."

"What will you take back?" asked Jeff.

"Well," said the Chief. "As I said, it's a haul this time, my crew of six will use a forklift and pallet from the main loading dock and we'll pick up staples for 300 men. Nice to meet you, gentleman," he said, and got up and shook Ted and Jeff's hands.

"Good luck," he said.

Ted looked at his watch; it was 1835.

"Do we have time to go to the PX?" asked Ted. "I really don't want anything," he said.

"Sure," said Jeff. "Just a quick run to look at it; I hear you can buy stereo equipment, cameras, TVs, records and even cars to ship back to the States."

They got up, left the cafeteria and went next door to the PX, which was a warehouse. They went through the front door, and it was air-conditioned.

"Wow, what a relief," said Jeff.

They looked around and saw signs, ELECTRONICS,

TELECOMMUNICATIONS, TELEVISIONS, OVERSEAS CAR SALES and racks of clothing, shirts, aloha shirts, a military uniform area, underwear, raincoats, hats, shoes, writing material, refrigerators, fans and air-conditioners.

"My wife would go nuts in here," said Jeff.

"Let's just take a look at their wristwatches," said Ted. "I'm looking for a watch with luminous night numbers that's water resistant, I might need it."

Ted looked at his watch; it was 1840 hours.

"No time, I'll come back."

Jeff said, "Watches are over there," and pointed him toward a display case.

They walked quickly to the case and saw a Vietnamese sales clerk. She smiled. Ted looked down at the display case and saw a black watch, black strap, large dial face with green numbers, "There it is!"

"Ma'am let me have watch number twenty-six."

"Number twenty-six, okay." She went out, got it and gave it to him. "Pay at the door," she said.

They walked quickly to the cash register line. It was 1845. The line seemed to creep slowly, one more customer ahead of him.

"Ye God," said Ted. "They're checking green I.D. cards."

Ted got out his wallet and I.D. card for the cashier to see.

The Vietnamese cashier looked at his watch, she said, "Number twenty-six is twenty dollars, I.D. please."

Ted showed her his I.D., it was 1855. "Want to wrap it?" asked the clerk.

"No, no, got to run now." He gave her twenty-five dollars; she rang up twenty dollars.

"Here is your change," she said, and started to count the dollars.

"No, keep it," said Ted. He took the watch in a bag and ran out the PX door.

The bus motor was running with red back-up lights on. Ted and Jeff ran to the bus just as the M.P. was closing the door.

"Cutting it close, Sir."

210

There were no empty seats. They rode back in late twilight to the Kelper Compound, and arrived at 2000.

The night-lights around Kelper Compound were lighted. They got out of the bus, went up the steps and to the room. Jeff stopped and bought four Cokes and five Hershey bars.

When Jeff reached the room, another Captain was in the room. "Hi, I'm Wally Semchek, Dallas, Texas," he said.

They introduced themselves.

Wally said he had just arrived. He was on his second tour and would be promoted to Major in thirty days. He was assigned as District Advisor in Phu Bin Province, southeast of Saigon. Wally wore an Infantry Branch Insignia, a Combat Infantryman's badge patch and a Parachute badge.

Wally asked Jeff, "Are you assigned to a Special Forces A Team?"

"No, Fourth Corps, MACV in Kien Giang Province, both Ted and I."

"Both? Pull any strings?"

"No strings."

"Well," said Wally, "I knew some SF guys on my first tour in 1966–67, out in the boondocks in the Central Highlands they were attacked, often with casualties."

Ted said, "I'm tired, I'm taking a shower and going to bed."

Jeff turned on the fan and a light on the desk. The front door was open and it was dark outside. Saigon lights shone on the horizon toward Ton Son Nhut, Cholon, and aircraft lights could be seen landing and taking off at Ton Son Nhut. In the distance were sounds like thunder.

"What's that, thunder?" asked Jeff.

"No," said Wally. "That's artillery H & I, harassment and interdiction fire outside Saigon. Probably 105's and 155's firing at VC locations."

"Oh shit," said Jeff, "I just squashed a cockroach." He removed the cockroach from the bottom of his right foot.

Wally sat on the metal frame bed.

"Better shut the door," he said. "Too many mosquitoes; we don't have mosquito nets. I have mosquito repellant, try this."

The small fan whirled, blowing slightly cooler tepid air

around the musty room. Ted took a shower. Jeff wrote a letter to his wife and parents. Wally placed a clean uniform to wear tomorrow on his cot. He sat on the cot to untie his boots and the old cot squeaked with age going back to World War II.

Ted emerged from the shower with an olive-drab towel wrapped around his waist. "Nice, cold water, I feel better, maybe I can sleep tonight." Ted dressed in a clean olive-drab T-shirt, jungle fatigue pants, clean olive/and leather slippers. He placed his new luminous dial wristwatch on his left wrist, put a towel over it and proclaimed, "It works, it's now 2100 hours."

Ted climbed into the upper bunk, lay down, and watched two black spiders crawling across the ceiling. Jeff finished his two letters, sealed them, gave his wife's letter a kiss and placed the letters on top of his footlocker located at the foot of his metal cot. Jeff went into the shower and returned in a few minutes saying, "Thanks Ted, you got all the hot water."

Wally got undressed and went into the shower. He came out in a short while. "All great, just like home; Jeff better get used to cold water over here, it's not back home on Saturday night."

Wally dried off, dressed in his uniform except for the blouse. He got on his cot and wrote notes into a small spiral notepad in the pocket of his blouse.

Jeff asked Wally, "Are you keeping a diary of events?"

"No, Jeff, just thoughts and reminders to myself; it helps to keep me organized. I did it during my first tour here in 1966 to 1967. It's amazing to read it when I got home. Besides, I'm going to write a book on this war someday."

Ted looked at his wristwatch which showed 2135 hours.

Various sounds emanated outside the room and from Kelper Compound. Soft music coming from AFN radio was playing. A dog barked, probably a German shepherd roaming the courtyard. The sound of a two-and-one-half ton Army truck motor starting could be heard out front. A door slammed down the hall.

Ted thought, *Here I am, my first night in Vietnam; what a day.* Ted thought about Sue Ellen across the compound in Clara Barton Hall. *What is she doing tonight?* Jeff told Ted, "Don't be afraid of the boogeyman—I'll protect you."

Wally lay down and his cot squeaked as if saying, "Another

generation of American soldiers to rest." They all fell asleep. It was 2200 hours. Several hours passed and Ted, Jeff and Wally slept soundly.

Out of the dark and silent night several tremendous explosions took place close to the compound. Wally jumped off the cot, turned on the overhead room light. Several more explosions shook the building with thunderous sounds like close summer storm thunder. BOOM-BOOM-BOOM!!!

Jeff jumped out of the bunkbed, pulled on his boots, went to the window and peered outside. The sound of automatic weapons fire began outside the compound. Jeff could hear somebody running and yelling, "Get out front!"

Ted stood behind the door and asked Jeff, "What do you see?"

Jeff yelled, "Nothing!"

Wally told them calmly, "The VC are probably mortaring Saigon or firing rockets into something around here."

The sounds of sirens pierced the blackness of the night and two more loud explosions broke to the east of Kelper Compound.

Jeff told Wally, "They're probably getting ready to make an attack, let's get the hell out of here. We don't have any weapons!"

Wally said, "No, Jeff! If we need to evacuate they will call over the PA system to get to the classroom gun cage. We should remain in our room." He continued, "Right now it is pure confusion out on the street."

Interior lights began to shine in the compound. More heavy automatic weapons fire with the intermittent burst of an M-60 machine gun rattled in the dark.

Ted hollered, "Wally, we'll be trapped in here."

Wally raised his voice and calmly told Ted, "Captain, calm yourself. This is nothing, only some form of VC harassment. They would be hitting the compound with the rounds if this was under attack."

The explosions stopped. Wally said, "Stay here, I'm going outside to check on what's going on." He took a Bowie knife out from under a pocket in his pants. Jeff asked Ted, "Why in the hell are we staying here?" and they went out on the outside walkway.

Suddenly, six or seven white phosphorus flares lit the night sky almost into daylight. Ted and Jeff stood and watched the flares light up the Saigon skyline.

Wally came back. "The MPs out front told me their street patrols in Saigon reported the VC fired ten, 122-millimeter rockets toward the South Vietnamese Presidential Palace, about three kilometers east of Kelper." Wally continued, "The MP sergeant told me everyone's got bad nerves following the Tet attack."

Ted said, "Sir, I still want to find out what went on, maybe I can learn something."

Wally replied, "I told you what went on, but go if you must; there are some trigger-happy GIs out there, so be careful."

Ted walked along the walkway, down the six flights, and went to the front of the compound. He saw seven MPs wearing body armor and steel pot helmets holding M-16 rifles standing behind a sandbag bunker. Another MP was crouched behind an M-60 machine gun while an assistant gunner fed the ammunition belt into the M-60. Two MPs in body armor and steel pots were holding M-16s and one was talking on a PRC-25 radio.

Ted asked a first lieutenant MP: "What's going on out here?"

The MP looked at Ted, saw he was a captain, and answered, "Sir, the VC fired ten 122-millimeter rockets at the presidential compound. A mobile patrol at the presidential compound has reported there is an ARVN battalion surrounding the compound and no enemy troops seen in the area. "That's all."

Ted returned to the room. It was 0330 hours. The alarm went off at 0600.

"Okay, let's get up, rise and shine, today we go to the Advisory Team," said Ted.

Ted, Jeff, and Wally got dressed and by 0700, they were downstairs and on their way to the same cafeteria where they had had lunch yesterday. As they walked, Wally asked Ted, "What did you find out last night?" He continued, "I didn't think it was wise to go down to the compound or near the courtyard until things were under control. I didn't want to be shot by friendly fire! I know from my first tour some of these G.I.'s are trigger happy and will shoot at anything that moves, especially after that Tet attack in January."

Ted said, "The M.P. told me the VC fired 10 122-millimeter

rockets at the Presidential Compound around 0230 this morning. He didn't know the amount of damage, but he said M.P. mounted patrols around the area with M-113's and Jeeps didn't find anything other than the rocket attack. No follow-up ground attack."

Wally said, "The VC must have taken heavy casualties during Tet and they don't have the manpower to waste."

The three arrived at the cafeteria and had breakfast of eggs, bacon, home fries, toast and coffee for $1.25.

"You can't beat the prices," said Jeff. "Anyone want to make a last PX run?"

"No," said Wally and Ted.

As they walked back, mostly in silence, Ted thought about Sue Ellen Harris.

They got to the Kelper Compound and a female Air Force First Lieutenant pointed to a building and told two other Air Force female Sergeants, "That is Clara Barton Hall, it is the billet for U.S. female personnel."

Ted thought, *Sue Ellen was right.* A voice came over the public address system at 0800 hours, "Attention in the area, attention in the area. There are changes in today's schedule. Captain Bryant will list the changes on the bulletin board at the entrance of the classroom."

The announcement continued: "From 0800 to 0900 check out of your room if you are leaving today. All MACV personnel will depart at 1400 hours on buses to Ton Son Nhut. From 0900 to 1100 all MACV personnel pick up your field-gear issue at the supply warehouse behind building number one hundred. From 1100 to 1200 there will be an in-country orientation briefing for MACV personnel. 1200 to 1300 lunch. 1400 all MACV personnel be prepared to load buses to Ton Son Nhut."

Wally said, "Well, this all applies to you guys. I've got some errands to run around here, so long and good luck. Keep your head and ass down," he laughed and walked toward the administration offices.

Jeff said, "You bet, Sir, I'll keep my ass down for sure, don't want the other side shot off."

Ted said, "Damn, where do we store all our gear?"

He approached Captain Bryant. "Captain, excuse me, where do we store our footlockers and field gear?"

Captain Bryant pointed to an area in the back of the large classroom that had portable wire held by the wood posts. "In there. There will be two NCOs here to receive and check it out at 1300."

"Fine," said Ted.

"Jeff, let's go check out and pick up our field-issue equipment."

"Field-issue equipment sounds like an MI weenie. In the infantry we say, go get your 'Fucking' humping gear."

Off they went to the supply room. There was already a line and a sign saying, YOU MUST HAVE ORDERS TO MACV AND ADVISORY TEAM. NO EXCEPTIONS. SIGNED: COLONEL HUNTER, DAVIS, COMMANDING OFFICER. They waited in line twenty minutes.

A black Army Sergeant First Class stood behind the supply counter.

"Name, Sir," he said to Jeff.

"Captain Jeffrey Madison."

"Madison, Madison," said the Sergeant. "Okay, right here."

He handed Jeff a typed list of equipment. "This is your equipment issue, check the gear you receive. If it's all here, sign it and date the card and drop it into the cardboard box at the right of the door." Jeff looked and saw a large wood box that said "S-4."

"Okay."

The Sergeant said, "If you have a problem, go to the next window and ask for Sergeant Williams, he will reconcile your equipment. Your weapon, a .45-caliber pistol, is inside the box in a holster. Put the suspenders, web belt, weapon, canteen, medical packs and ammo packs in the large room and then put everything in the large wire cage. Captain Hardy, S-4 and the supply NCOIC Sergeant Walls will secure the cage until you pick it up. It will be secure."

"Yes, Sergeant," said Jeff.

He received his gear and took inventory of what was inside the large green duffle bag.

1 ea—.45 caliber U.S. Army pistol and holster
1 ea—Steel pot, camouflage cover, and an elastic band
1 ea—Field suspenders
1 ea—Web belt
1 ea—Canteen and cup
1 ea—Medical pack
2 ea—5 boxes .45-caliber ammunition
1 ea—Poncho liner

"Okay," Jeff told Ted, and he signed the receipt, dropped it into the wood box, and walked to the supply cage.

"Next," said Sergeant Brown.

Ted stepped forward and repeated the procedure, found no discrepancies, and signed his receipt and dropped it into the box and walked to the wire cage.

"Next," said Sergeant Brown.

Ted and Jeff assembled their field gear, put cold water from a fountain into their canteens, attached the .45-caliber pistols to the web belts and both helped each other adjust the suspenders.

"Feel okay?" asked Jeff.

"Good," said Ted.

Ted adjusted Jeff's suspenders.

"Okay," said Jeff.

A sign on the wire cage said, DO NOT LOAD WEAPON. KEEP AMMO IN AMMO POUCH UNTIL YOU REACH YOUR DESTINATION.

They re-checked their footlockers and laid their field gear on their lockers.

A black Army Captain Hardy was seated at a desk by the wire cage, "Everything okay?" he asked.

Ted said, "Yes, we're ready to rock n' roll."

Captain Hardy laughed, "This is the place to rock n' roll."

Ted and Jeff went outside of Kelper Compound, which had gotten crowded. Another new group of GIs was arriving and assembling into the building.

"Wait till they get to the elevator," said Jeff.

Ted laughed, "Didn't you see? It's fixed."

"What? I lugged my locker down all six flights of stairs and you took the elevator? I wondered how you got down so fast!"

Ted look at his watch; it was 10:30. He looked toward Clara Barton Hall hoping to see Sue Ellen. She was not in sight.

"Let's have a Coke," said Jeff.

"Fine," said Ted.

They drank a can of Coke and then walked to the front of the large classroom where an Army Major was setting up a viewgraph with colored slides.

"Morning, men," said Major Howard. He was the Adjutant General, and had a MACV Public Affairs plastic tag on his fatigue blouse.

"Here for the in-country briefing on customs and traditions of Vietnam?" asked Major Howard.

"Yes, Sir," said Ted. "We leave this afternoon for Fourth Corps and an Advisory Team in Rach Gia."

"Rach Gia," said the Major. "I know Captain Fontain, the S-1, I hear it's not a bad place, on the coast—good seafood," he continued, "I've got to finish, have a seat."

It was now 1055 and thirty U.S. Army personnel dressed in jungle fatigues, jungle hats and boots were seated facing the movie screen.

At 1100 hours, Major Howard introduced himself. "Today I want to acquaint you with some do's and don'ts regarding working with our Vietnamese allies.

"Remember, it is their country, they are an old country and have always had a free and independent country with one language." Ted's mind drifted as he listened. Jeff stared blankly ahead.

"Okay, any questions?" asked the Major.

One young private stood up and asked the Major, "Sir, if you suspect a Vietnamese of being a Viet Cong, but you can't prove it, what do you do?"

Another private chimed up, "Private, you wait a week and if he doesn't shoot you, you know he's not a VC." The room swelled with laughter.

The Major said, "Private Sellers, simply tell your NCO what you suspect. That's all—adjourned."

The cooks at Kelper Compound had set up a barbeque for lunch, serving hot dogs, baked beans, rolls, potato salad, pickles, and sodas.

Ted smelled the hot dogs and said, "Let's eat."

They got in line, got their food, and sat down on the grass beneath a shade tree. About one hundred U.S. military personnel were also eating lunch. Ted looked at his watch, it was 1320. *Not too much longer until we leave,* he thought. *I hope Sue Ellen happens to come by Kelper Compound before I leave.*

Jeff and Ted finished their lunchs, put the trash into a large trashcan, and Ted said, "Better hit the latrine before leaving, just like going on a trip as a boy."

They returned and sat on a bench beneath a large tamarind tree in the shade. It was 1330. Ted thought, *No luck,* and just then, Sue Ellen Harris appeared from Clara Barton Hall and was walking directly toward Kelper Compound. Ted Graham was elated to see her.

8

April 14, 1957 was Sue Ellen Harris' sixteenth birthday. Her parents had hosted a birthday party for her at their home, located off Highway 51, five miles east of Canton, Mississippi. The Harris home was built on ten acres of land, which Sue Ellen's father Byron L. Harris, M.D., purchased in 1945 and built their home the same year. The people attending her birthday party were her parents, Byron and Amelia Harris, her two brothers, Benjamin, fourteen, and Danny, ten, Uncle Earl and Aunt Darlene, her father's brother and his wife with their four children, Amanda, Christy, Bradley and Luke. Sue Ellen's mother surprised her and invited three of her best cheerleading friends, Mary Lou Harper, Melanie Stakwoski and Marla Hillman. Two neighbors were invited she had known since first grade, Nathan Bedford Stewart, sixteen, and his sister Scarlett O'Hara Stewart, fourteen; they lived on Magnolia Plantation, a 10,000-acre cotton plantation adjacent to the Harris' property.

    Her guests enjoyed a buffet lunch and a white birthday cake with ice cream for dessert. Sue Ellen blew out sixteen candles on the cake and they sang "Happy Birthday." They adjourned to the living room and Sue Ellen opened her gifts. Uncle Earl gave her two "gag" gifts; one gift was her picture shown with a "suspended," stamped in red over her Mississippi driver's license. The other gift was a wall clock with a policeman who popped out the front of the clock with a nightstick when the clock struck 12:00 P.M. Everyone told a short story about Sue Ellen, which added good humor to her party. At 5:00, they gave Sue Ellen a hug, wished her a happy birthday, said good-bye and left the party for home.

    Nathan Bedford Stewart and Sue Ellen went outside on the front porch and sat down on a front porch swing. It was a pleasant warm day and the katydids were chirping. Nathan's sixteenth birthday was on January 21, 1957. He told Sue Ellen his father was upset with him for getting two speeding tickets from the Mississippi Highway Patrol in three months. One ticket was for driving sixty in a fifty-five-mph zone; the other was for driving thirty-five in a twenty-mph zone. Nathan got up off the swing, looked around and turned to Sue Ellen and told her, "I don't like living at home anymore. I work on our plantation every morning starting at six A.M. before going to school and at night after school and after dinner until seven." Nathan played football and baseball at Canton High School. Next fall as a junior, he would play varsity football.

Sue Ellen looked at Nathan, "Please don't get into trouble; you're a nice guy; I don't want to see you hurt, or have your father whup you. We've known each other since first grade. Remember playing hide and seek, going fishing, riding horses and climbing trees? Do your best; do what your father tells you. I get tired of my mother and father bugging me, but they're only trying to be good parents."

Nathan replied, "You're right, but all I do is work and go to school; someday I'll be out of Canton doing what I want to do. I can't wait."

Sue Ellen told Nathan, "I've got to go inside; don't get in trouble, it's not worth it. There are people here that want to see you screw up since your father has money and they're jealous of you and what you've got over them."

"Okay, Sue Ellen, I just get so discouraged sometimes and I don't have anyone to talk to except you."

Sue Ellen squeezed his hand. "Are we going to the Cheerleader's Sock Hop next month?"

"Yes, of course," said Nathan.

She walked down the front yard with him to his truck, she gave him a hug and said, "You'll be alright, and I'm on your side, 'bye."

In August, 1945 the Harris family moved to Canton, Mississippi from New Orleans. Sue Ellen's father was a physician. He and his wife wanted to raise their family in a small-town rural environment. Her father wanted to be close enough to Jackson to commute daily to Jackson Hospital. Sue Ellen's parents met at

Ole Miss and her father graduated in 1933. He went to medical school at Tulane University Medical School and did his residency and internship in internal medicine at the Tulane University Hospital. Her mother graduated from Ole Miss in 1935, and her parents were married in 1939 when her father began to practice medicine in New Orleans in 1939. In February, 1942 her father, as a physician, received a direct commission as a Lieutenant Commander into the U.S. Naval Medical Corps, and remained in New Orleans at the Veterans' Hospital until he was discharged in August, 1945.

The Harrises moved to Canton in August, 1945. Dr. Harris bought ten acres of land and had a Louisiana-style farmhouse built with a horse barn on the property.

The Harris' property was adjacent to land owned by Bucyrus and Hannah Stewart. They had three children named Jefferson Davis Stewart, or "J.D.," Nathan Bedford Stewart, and Scarlett O'Hara Stewart. Bucyrus Stewart was the largest landowner in Madison and Rankin counties. He was a "rainmaker." Besides owning Magnolia Plantation, he owned three gin mills, three warehouses in Memphis and was a partner in a Mississippi Riverboat operation called the *Magnolia Queen,* which ran from Vicksburg to New Orleans.

Bucyrus Stewart had political influence in the state of Mississippi. He had obtained a zoning variance from the state of Mississippi to build a secondary road off Highway 51 onto his land to load flatbed trailer trucks. He also obtained permission to have the railroad extend a railhead spur onto his land for loading railcars. Loading railroad cars on his property saved him money and time in getting his own cotton directly to Memphis.

He entertained state and local elected officials who hunted deer on his property, and every Fourth of July, he hosted a party for one hundred fifty guests from all over the state of Mississippi.

The townspeople in Canton circulated rumors that Bucyrus made his money bootlegging rum and liquor out of Cuba into Louisiana during the Prohibition, and that he had once shot and killed a man in New Orleans in an argument over money. It was also alleged he owned speak-easies on Bourbon Street in New

Orleans, along with the Cajun Hotel, and Bucyrus also owned a car repair business to appear as being a legitimate businessman.

Bucyrus was 6'5" and weighed nearly 300 pounds and he chain-smoked Cuban cigars. In 1932, he came to Canton and purchased 5,000 acres of land in a "foreclosure," according to the story. He restored a run-down antebellum home built in 1830. His wife Hannah was rumored to have been a dancehall girl (or more) in New Orleans. In 1935, he purchased 5,000 more acres of land and he named his land Magnolia Plantation. He later built horse stables and a barn on his property for ten horses. Local people said he "was still fighting the Civil War." He talked about Civil War battles and the "Goddamn Yankees ruining the South!"

In August 1945 the Harris' children met the Stewarts' children, and they grew up together.

"J.D." went to Canton High School; he was also a big boy at 6'4" and 270 pounds and went to Mississippi State University in 1955 to study agriculture. Most people in Canton believed Bucyrus donated $50,000 to Mississippi State, which was the reason J.D. was admitted and played football.

Nathan Bedford Stewart and Sue Ellen were the same age. They were Tom Sawyer and Becky Thatcher growing up, Nathan was a good athlete who began to play football and baseball in the eighth grade. At the end of tenth grade, Nathan looked forward to getting his driver's license, playing Varsity football, and going hunting. He was slender, yet strong, and sinewy. At Canton High School, he played end at 6'2" and 170 pounds and was a good-looking young man. He wanted to go to West Point, but he found it difficult working on the plantation and maintaining good grades in school. He had trouble in reading comprehension.

Sue Ellen had made her plans for her summer vacation. She planned to ride her mare Buttercup, take Ben and Danny swimming at the Canton municipal swimming pool, help her Mother, practice cheerleading, and read four books. She looked forward to the Fourth of July party at the Stewarts. It was a major event. The party began at 1:00 P.M. with swimming, badminton, horseshoes, and sack races. Mr. Stewart's men set up tents, chairs, lanterns, picnic tables and a barbecue pit where their help cooked chicken, barbecued ribs, hamburgers and hot dogs. There were tables with salads, sliced fruit, bread, vegetables, and a separate table with fresh cakes and pies. It was a feast.

After dark, a company from Jackson set up a fireworks display and the party ended at 11:00 P.M. After the party was over, men went into the Stewarts' home and played cards, drank brandy and talked.

Nathan told Sue Ellen, "The living room was thick with cigar smoke, and that's where the deals were cut."

Sue Ellen never imagined the events that would occur over the summer.

Nathan took Sue Ellen to the Cheerleaders' sock hop dance. It was a warm, pleasant May evening. They talked to their friends, danced, and discussed their plans for the summer. When the band took a break, Nathan was sweating.

He said, "Sue Ellen, let's go outside for some cool air." He took Sue Ellen's hand and they went outside the gym. It was a clear night. They heard the sound of crickets chirping and felt the evening breeze gently moving through the trees.

Nathan looked at Sue Ellen, "Sue Ellen, I must tell you something important. I don't want sound like a sissy, but let me tell you, my family is a mess. I've finally realized it.

"You know how I work, but it never suits my father. This morning he got me up at 5:30 A.M. and said, 'Get up lazy boy, you have work to do.'

"It was 5:30 A.M.

"I got up, got dressed and Miss Beulah, our colored maid, made me breakfast. Mom came in the kitchen and said, 'Nathan, your father was drinking last night.'

"Sue Ellen, we have rifles, shotguns and pistols in our house. My father gets angry and mean when he drinks. He has never beat or hit me, but if it gets worse, I'm leaving home. I told Mom; she said, 'Nathan, he is not well-educated, he had to quit school in tenth grade to support his mother, since his father was an alcoholic. Everything he has, he worked for, starting at age fifteen by working on riverboats on the Mississippi River in New Orleans. He feels today's generation has it too easy.'

"I told Mom if he ever beats me or whups me with a belt, I'd kill him.

"Mom said, 'Nathan, never make that statement again to me.'

"I was downcast and dejected and Mr. McMaster called my parents for a meeting with him last week. He told them I am dyslexic. This is a condition which causes me to interchange letters when I'm reading. You read he saw a bear, I will read, he bare a saw. This is why I have had trouble reading in school. I'm not dumb.

"Mr. McMaster told my parents dyslexia could be corrected. I'm going to Emory University in Atlanta for eight weeks to correct the dyslexia."

Sue Ellen said, "Dyslexia—that's a difficult condition; no wonder you read slowly. You poor boy." Sue Ellen gave Nathan a hug.

Nathan continued, "That's not all; my father said if I am to become somebody, I needed more discipline, he's sending me to the Georgia Military Institute this September!"

Sue Ellen gasped, "Why? You haven't done anything wrong. That's ridiculous, Nathan."

"I can't change his mind; Mother said it will make me a Southern gentleman. J.D. told my Father that he wants to play pro-football. He got a letter from the Baltimore Colts inviting him to their rookie camp this fall in Maryland."

"My, oh my," said Sue Ellen. "This is too much. You're going to Emory for eight weeks, then to the Georgia Military Institute, and J.D. is going to try out for professional football! When do you report to the Georgia Military Institute?"

"On August twenty-fourth for orientation, and classes start September tenth."

Sue Ellen shook her head and looked up at the stars in the night sky. "Here we are ready to start eleventh grade, and Nathan Bedford Stewart, whom I've known since the first grade, is going to the Georgia Military Institute, it's the Civil War all over again! When will it end?"

Nathan said, "I'm glad. For one thing, I'll get out of my

house. I told Father I'd go to West Point. My father said, 'I'm from Missouri, son, y'all have to show me.' "

The band resumed playing "Wake up, Little Susie." Sue Ellen looked at her watch; it was 10:15. "Why don't we leave the dance and stop on the way home at the Brown Cow for a shake."

"Fine," said Nathan, "Let's leave."

They said good-bye and walked out to Nathan's truck. Nathan opened the door for her. Sue Ellen looked into the back seat of his truck and she saw a shotgun, a deer rifle, muddy boots, and several duck decoys on the floor.

"What will you do during hunting season at the Georgia Military Institute, Nathan?"

"Play football and study," he said.

They arrived at the Harris home at 11:15 and the house lights were turned on inside.

"Nathan, I'll miss you." Sue Ellen placed her hands on his face and kissed him.

Nathan looked at her, "It'll be okay, and at least I will be away from my weird-assed family."

"You will succeed," said Sue Ellen. "Write me when you can, or call, please."

"I will."

They hugged and exchanged several light kisses. "I've got to go inside."

Sue Ellen said, "I love you, Nathan Bedford Stewart."

"I love you too, Sue Ellen Harris."

She got out of the truck, walked up the lawn, waved to Nathan and went into the house at 11:30 P.M. The policeman on the clock did not come out.

Nathan drove home "down the old dirt road" and he was home at 11:45. He poured himself a glass of milk and went out onto the front porch, sat on the swing with his dog, "Beau," and thought about the next several years until 1:00 A.M. and then went to bed.

His parents took Nathan to Emory University on June thirteenth for eight weeks. He came home one weekend and saw Sue Ellen just to say hello and then he left for the Georgia Military Institute on September fifth.

The next two years Nathan Bedford Stewart applied himself at the Georgia Military Institute. He was determined to show his father his mettle and regain his self-esteem. He played football at Georgia Military Institute, studied, and graduated twenty-seventh in a class of 150 in June, 1959. In March, 1959, a Georgia congressman nominated Nathan to the United States Military Academy at West Point for the class of 1963, he was admitted to West Point. He played football four years at West Point and planned to make the Army his career, and to marry Sue Ellen Harris.

The next shoe dropped for Sue Ellen after the family returned from their vacation at Biloxi, Mississippi in July. Her father told them they would be moving to Memphis, Tennessee, and he wanted to have a family meeting at 10:00 Saturday morning.

Sue Ellen's father arrived home at 10:15. The doctor came into the kitchen wearing his physician's jacket with Byron H. Harris, M.D. inscribed on the front left pocket.

"How is everyone?"

He removed his white jacket, took off his tie, and sat down at the kitchen table.

Amelia said, "Byron, how did it go today?"

"Fine," he said. "Very routine and no new admissions."

"Sue Ellen, please pour me some iced tea."

Sue Ellen got up from the table, went to the refrigerator, and brought her father a glass of cold iced tea. The entire family had a lot of respect for their father. In addition to being a physician, he was a deacon in the Baptist Church, active in the Ole Miss Alumni Association, and a member of the Mississippi Medical Association.

Her father took a sip of cold iced tea. "I asked our family to meet here today to tell you I've accepted a better medical position with Mid-South Internal Medical Group in Memphis, effective September first."

Sue Ellen interrupted, "Daddy, don't make us move."

"Honey," he took her hand, "listen to me. I've practiced medicine as a single practitioner in Canton the past twelve years. I don't want to delve into the medical profession, but believe me it's changing. The days of the single practitioner are fading."

Sue Ellen clamored, "Yes, Daddy, but why can't you join up with other doctors here?"

Her mother said sharply, "Sue Ellen, listen to your father, don't be rude."

They sat at the kitchen table in silence while her father explained what would happen.

"Over the past two years, my colleagues at medical association meetings have all been saying there is more paperwork, more insurance requirements and more laboratory tests needed to diagnose and treat patients, and my medical malpractice premiums have doubled in the past ten years. At our annual association meeting last December in Jackson, I attended a workshop. It has been predicted that in ten years, unless the Mississippi legislature reduces awards for malpractice lawsuits, doctors will leave Mississippi hospitals and our hospitals will close due to skyrocketing insurance costs. Thank God, I've never been sued for medical malpractice.

"But," he continued, "I'm forty-five years old, and I don't like what I see over the next twenty to thirty years. Dr. Desmond Johnson, a good friend of mine who is a fine internist, and Dr. Sydney Blumberg have invited me to join their Medical Group. I will affiliate with the Baptist Memorial Hospital in Memphis and practice in a group with five other doctors. The office is located at 8100 Primacy Parkway. I've accepted their fine offer and I will receive a substantial pay raise with fewer hours a week in the clinic and hospital.

"We will put our home up for sale on Monday with Joan Brooks of Tri-State Realtors. She told me the house should sell in 120 days. I've made a down payment on a beautiful five-bedroom, brick Georgian colonial home in Central Gardens in Memphis on an acre of land. You children will all attend the Shelby Academy, which is a very fine private co-ed school founded in 1901.

"I've thought carefully about this opportunity and driven to Memphis three times to evaluate all aspects, and I am convinced it is the right thing to do for all of us. I know it will make y'all unhappy," he said, "and y'all will miss your friends. Mother and I have discussed that, but in the long run, we'll be better off."

He looked at his wife and children. "In the next two years, Sue Ellen will begin college, which I assume will be Ole Miss, and Ben and Danny want to go to Tulane, which is fine. You will all be more prepared academically at Shelby Academy than in Canton High School. There are better-paid and trained teachers at Shelby Academy. Sue Ellen, you'll be able to see Elvis Presley."

Sue Ellen said, "Daddy, I like Pat Boone or Tab Hunter."

"Any questions?" They sat in silence.

"What will happen to Buttercup?" asked Sue Ellen.

"We'll take her with us and board her in Germantown. Germantown is a horse town near Memphis."

"What about sports?" asked Danny.

"Shelby Academy has many sports programs; you'll compete with other Memphis Schools."

Amelia said, "I've seen our new home at Central Gardens; it is beautiful. You will each have a bedroom."

Sue Ellen asked, "May I have a going-away party?"

"Yes," said her mother.

"Anything else?" asked their father.

"Should I tell all my friends at school on Monday we're moving to Memphis?"

"Fine, Sue Ellen."

Sue Ellen said, "I know ten girls that will be very glad to see me move to try for my cheerleading position."

"Amelia, please make an appointment with Mr. McMaster, the principal, to tell him we are moving and to get the school and health records sent to Shelby Academy."

Amelia replied, "Yes dear, I will call him and make an appointment to meet with him Monday at ten."

"Okay," said their father, "Meeting adjourned. Oh, one more request, please wait until Monday to tell your friends we're moving."

Sue Ellen interjected, "Daddy, when are we moving for sure?"

"As soon as the house is sold."

Sue Ellen shut out the world. She awoke in the morning, cleaned house and read one book after another and finished Charles Dickens' *A Tale of Two Cities*.

Her mother and father got concerned about why the house had not sold. It had been on the market two months without an offer.

The second week in August, Sue Ellen finished housework, fixed herself a cheese and bologna sandwich, a glass of milk, and went to sit on the front porch. There had been a severe thunderstorm and heavy rain the night before. She sat in the chair and thought about Buttercup, and felt guilty for not paying more attention to Buttercup, who needed to be exercised.

She decided to ride Buttercup. She got up, took the glass inside, came out, and skipped down the front steps and walked to the backyard to the storage shed. Sue Ellen remembered the words from Charles Dickens' *A Tale of Two Cities*; "It was the best of times and the worst of times."

She changed into riding pants; put on her riding boots and took out a western saddle, saddle pad, and bridle. She closed the shed door and carried her equipment across the back lawn to the horse barn. She opened the barn doors and saw her beloved Buttercup standing in her stall. Sue Ellen walked down the aisle to the stall where Buttercup was. When she got to the stall, Buttercup threw her head back and whinnied, as if to say, "Where have you been?"

Sue Ellen's father bought Buttercup for her on her twelfth birthday. She had taken riding lessons at Steeple Chase Horse Stables in Jackson and by age fourteen, she was an accomplished equestrian. For the next two years, she rode Buttercup in horse shows and did jumping competitions and won four blue ribbons at the Madison County Fair.

Summer was always a happy time, but this summer was not happy for Sue Ellen. She did not want to move to Memphis.

Sue Ellen said, "Easy, Buttercup, I know I haven't ridden you much." She put on Buttercup's bridle and led her out of the barn into the yard. Buttercup sidestepped abruptly to Sue Ellen's left side.

Sue Ellen said, "Whoa, Buttercup, whoa." Buttercup was edgy.

Buttercup stood still and Sue Ellen placed the saddle pad and a western saddle on Buttercup's strong back and cinched the saddle girth in place. Sue Ellen placed her left foot into the left stirrup and swung up easily onto Buttercup's back and Buttercup bucked slightly, pranced, and sidestepped as Sue Ellen tried to gentle her in front of the barn.

Sue Ellen pulled back the reins, extended her legs in the stirrups, and braced herself to prevent Buttercup from throwing her. She looked at Buttercup's ears, which were back and flat, meaning Buttercup's bucking, which was telling Sue Ellen, "It's been a long time since you put a saddle on me."

Sue Ellen nudged Buttercup with her legs, made a clicking sound and Buttercup began to canter toward the field east of their house. Sue Ellen decided to ride to the old fishing pond, four miles south of their home down a winding dirt trail and small hill to the pond. The field and trees were green and the August sun shone brightly in the azure blue Mississippi sky. Sue Ellen and Buttercup cantered along the trail toward Tomashing Creek and toward the fishing pond. She nudged her into a gallop while watching the trail ahead for snakes, deer, or rabbits that could spook Buttercup and cause her to bolt and run. They went two miles on the trail and came to a small hill, and rode down the hill toward the pond. Buttercup was sweating; Sue Ellen slowed Buttercup to a walk. They went down the hill and stopped under the shade of a large oak tree. Sue Ellen tied Buttercup's reins to a branch on the tree with enough slack for her to eat the lush green grass.

Tomashing Creek filled the pond where she and her brothers, Benjamin and Daniel, had come fishing in past summers. The creek was named for the local Tomash Indians, and the creek was an offshoot of the Mississippi River with good water, but it got low in the summer. The pond was across from the creek, big enough for a rowboat, but not for a powerboat and had catfish, crappies, brim and bass for fishing.

Sue Ellen sat beneath an oak tree, and leaned her back against the tree under its shade and saw how much the calla lilies had grown. She loved Mississippi. She listened to the cicadas sing and watched the water from the Tomashing Creek flow downstream past the pond. She thought, *Mom said this is all part of growing up.*

One thought after another went through her mind; about Nathan Stewart, selling their home; moving to Memphis; Shelby Academy; how she felt and about Ben, Danny, Bobby Allen, and Buttercup.

She pulled out a handful of grass and let it blow away in the breeze. She heard faint noises behind her in the woods. Sue Ellen thought for a second that it was a bear or perhaps a wild boar coming to the pond for water. She stood up; Buttercup was pulling on the reins, with her ears straight up and alert as she looked up the trail, sensing danger. Sue Ellen untied and mounted Buttercup, who began to prance nervously. Sue Ellen thought, *I better get moving back up the trail.*

Suddenly, two men appeared in the woods in a clearing. They wore blue denim uniforms with black numbers inscribed on a white square on their shirts. Sue Ellen saw them, "They're convicts!" She heard bloodhounds barking and baying. Buttercup got fidgety and Sue Ellen strained to keep her under control.

One convict was a thin gray-haired man who pushed away underbrush and hollered, "Jeb, Jeb, looky here, wooooo-weee, Jeb. It's a filly on a horse, let's git her!"

The convicts pushed forward through the thick underbrush toward the dirt trail and were now were thirty feet from the dirt road and 100 feet beyond Sue Ellen and Buttercup. The old convict was thin, had white hair, scruffy whiskers, and wore a faded denim cap. His Adam's apple protruded out of his skinny neck. The second convict was younger, he was about forty, stocky and had a round red pudgy face and was sweating.

Sue Ellen heard the younger convict holler, "Slim, spook the horse; I'll get a stick and holler and make that horse throw her." Sue Ellen heard louder barking and baying of bloodhounds; lawmen were not far away. She steadied Buttercup, and then with a strong sudden squeeze said, "Run Buttercup, run!" Buttercup reared up, dug her back hooves into the ground, and broke into a gallop directly up the trail toward the two convicts as Jeb struggled to get out onto the trail. Jeb pushed Slim aside, and jumped onto the trail holding a large limb; he held the limb in his right hand waving it and hollered, "Git out here, Slim, and help me stop the Goddamn horse!"

Slim stumbled and fell backward in the thick underbrush onto a large yellowjacket nest; he hollered, "Goddamn it, Jeb, I'm getting stung by yellow jackets."

Slim tripped a second time. He tried to swat the bees away to stand up, but his feet got more tangled among the thorns and bristles caught on his pant legs and he fell face down once again into the yellowjackets' nest.

Sue Ellen and Buttercup closed in on Jeb, who was now standing in the middle of the trail, and frantically waving the tree limb at Sue Ellen as she rode Buttercup toward him on the trail.

Sue Ellen was three feet from Jeb, when she jerked Buttercup to the right, galloped past him, and tried to grab Buttercup's reins. Sue Ellen deftly shifted her weight to the right in the saddle, bent her left leg and with full force kicked Jeb squarely in the face with a boot's heel.

Jeb fell, placing both hands on his face. "You son-of-a-bitch, you broke my nose."

Sue Ellen glanced back and she and Buttercup galloped up the trail. Jeb fell to the ground on both knees, holding his face in a pool of blood. Sue Ellen galloped another 100 feet. She saw six bloodhounds yelping down the trail coming toward her. The dogs startled Buttercup, and Sue Ellen struggled to keep Buttercup under control. The Sheriff and six deputies riding in U.S. Army Jeeps saw Sue Ellen. The Sheriff waved to Sue Ellen and hollered, "Come here, young lady!" She waved back and rode to the Jeep.

"Whoa, Buttercup, whoa," she said.

The man driving the Jeep stopped the motor, "I'm Sheriff Hines, who are you, Miss?"

Sue Ellen steadied Buttercup, "I'm Sue Ellen, Sue Ellen Harris; Dr. Harris' daughter." Sue Ellen panting told the Sheriff, "There were two convicts who came out of the woods and tried to get me. I was at the pond when they came out of the woods and tried to stop me."

The Sheriff asked, "Are you alright?"

"Yes," said Sue Ellen.

Sheriff Hines asked Sue Ellen, "Y'all say they're down the dirt trail toward the creek?"

"Yes, Sheriff."

Sheriff Hines told Sue Ellen, "Go home and tell your mother the sheriff and a posse are trailing two convicts. Lock your doors, call my office when you get home and don't come out until I come back to your house. Do you understand?"

"Yes, Sir," she answered.

"Go now," said the Sheriff.

Sue Ellen turned Buttercup around toward home and they galloped up the trail to the front yard; Sue Ellen jumped off Buttercup and tied her reins to the porch railing. She filled a five-gallon bucket of cold water for Buttercup, and removed Buttercup's saddle to cool her off, and then let her drink water and eat grass. She bounded up the front steps to the front door; and the screen door was locked.

She called, "Mom, Mom, it's Sue Ellen; open the front door." She waited and hollered again. "Mother, open the screen door!" Amelia appeared behind the screen door in the living room.

"What's wrong, Sue Ellen, why are you hollering? I was in the kitchen peeling potatoes."

Amelia opened the screen door; Sue Ellen darted into the living room, breathing heavily. "Mom, I rode Buttercup to the fishing pond. I was fixin' to come right back home when two men in blue denim with numbers on their shirts came out of the woods toward me and tried to spook Buttercup. One was called Jeb and he tried to grab Buttercup's reins. I kicked him in the face with my boot. The other convict couldn't get out of the underbrush; he fell down and yelled he was being stung by yellowjackets. It was horrible."

Amelia listened.

"I got to the top of the hill and heard bloodhounds barking and yelping; I started to ride home and saw lawmen coming down the trail in Jeeps. One of the lawmen waved to me; I rode to him and it was Sheriff Hines with three deputies. Sheriff Hines asked me if I was all right, I said 'Yes, Sir.' He told me to go home, lock the doors, stay in the house and to call his office and tell them when I was home."

Amelia thought for a moment. "Call your brothers, they're playing catch in the back yard; tell them to come into the house and then lock the back door."

Amelia went to the telephone, called Sheriff Hines' office, and told them Sue Ellen was home. Sue Ellen called her brothers; they came into the house and Sue Ellen told them what happened.

Amelia called, "Sue Ellen, y'all come into the living room." Amelia opened a gun case and removed a double-barrel shot gun.

"Y'all stay here, and don't come outside. I'm going out on the front porch to watch down the trail. If you see or hear anything, call me and call the Sheriff—the number is on the table by the phone. I know how to use this shotgun." Amelia went out to the front porch, and sat down with the loaded shotgun placed across her lap. Sue Ellen and her brothers went to separate windows and looked toward the dirt trail.

Forty minutes passed. Two Jeeps came up the trail with lawmen sitting in each Jeep. They stopped in front of the house. A blue van came down Highway 51 with its siren sounding and red lights flashing; four lawmen got out of the van and went to the first Jeep. The stocky convict named Jeb got out of the Jeep with his hands cuffed behind him. One lawman in a uniform opened the back door of the blue van and pushed Jeb into the van. Two other lawmen went to the second Jeep with a stretcher and picked up a body covered with a blue blanket, put it on the stretcher and into the blue van. The van pulled away with its siren screaming and red lights flashing.

Sheriff Hines came to the Harris' house; he stopped at the foot of the porch steps, took off his hat, and said, "Ma'am. We got 'em, one is dead. The old man must of had a heart attack, and we found him lying in the bushes near a large yellowjacket nest. He has bee stings all over his neck and arms. He probably died of toxic poisoning from the bee stings, and had a heart attack. Sue Ellen told me what happened on the dirt trail."

Sheriff Hines told Sue Ellen's mother that the convict Jeb said, " 'That crazy girl tried to trample me to death with her horse.' He has a broken nose and four broken teeth. I don't believe him, but Sue Ellen will have to make a statement on the matter. Jeb also said, 'I never saw no girl ride a mare like that girl rode that mare.' Sue Ellen's riding skills saved her life out there today."

Amelia called Sue Ellen to see Sheriff Hines. "You did a fine job today, Sue Ellen," he said. "I'm glad they didn't get you or your horse. Y'all need to make a statement tomorrow about what happened on the trail; it's routine."

"I've got to get the other convict to jail and the dead man back to the coroner's office. Why don't you come in tomorrow at ten?"

Sue Ellen, Amelia, and her father showed up at 10:00 the next morning at Sheriff Hines' office in Canton for Sue Ellen to make a written statement about the incident with the two convicts.

Shelby Academy was a world apart from Canton High School. Shelby Academy had 1,200 white students from seventh to twelfth grade. Students were well-dressed and many of them in eleventh and twelfth grades drove new cars to school. Sue Ellen, Ben, and Danny were introduced as new students at the convocation on the first day of school. When Sue Ellen stood up and was introduced, some boys made "cat calls," to which the Headmaster said, "That is not tolerated."

Classes began at 7:10 A.M. and ended at 2:30 P.M. There were numerous clubs and extracurricular activities. Sue Ellen joined the drama club, Ben made the senior Varsity football team, and Danny played soccer for the first time. There were social activities; dances, homecoming, and a Christmas party. The academic requirements were rigorous. Sue Ellen was required to study biology, physics, math, history, and physical education. One of Sue Ellen's new girlfriends was Ginger Altman; her family lived in Central Gardens. Sue Ellen and Ginger Altman studied together. Sue Ellen went on a few dates to movies, but she did not want to be a social butterfly. In her senior year, she decided to study drama and theater and to apply to Ole Miss. She was selected as a Shelby Academy cheerleader.

Her father told Sue Ellen, "You have to either exercise Buttercup more, or we'll have to sell her." Sue Ellen said she would exercise Buttercup.

Sue Ellen's academic program was again rigorous in her senior year, studying chemistry, French II, English, American literature, world history, geometry, and physical education. Ben was the starting quarterback on the varsity football team, and Danny played soccer. Dr. Harris took Sue Ellen on admissions interviews to Ole Miss, the University of Tennessee at Knoxville, Georgia and Auburn.

In April, 1959 Sue Ellen was accepted at Ole Miss. She wrote and told Nathan Stewart of her acceptance. He wrote her a letter of congratulations and told her he was accepted at West Point.

In May of 1959 Buttercup got sick with an intestinal infection and blood poisoning. The veterinarian treated Buttercup with antibiotics, but they did not help. A week later, the vet arrived and found Buttercup dead in her stall. The vet called Dr. Harris and he told his daughter after school that Buttercup had died. Sue Ellen had owned Buttercup for six years; she was devastated and cried all night. Dr. Harris gave her medication to help her sleep. Buttercup was buried in an animal cemetery in Covington, Tennessee.

In September of 1959, Sue Ellen entered Ole Miss. She pledged Gamma Phi Beta sorority, was elected to the Ole Miss beauty court to do civic service around Oxford, and joined the drama club. Sue Ellen met Bobby Handford in her freshman year; they dated for two years and broke up. Nathan Bedford Stewart was a Plebe at West Point. J.D. Stewart graduated from Mississippi State and made the Baltimore Colts practice squad. J.D. left the Colts to play Canadian football with the Ottawa Roughriders for three years, but the Canadian football season began in August and the pay was not good enough to continue playing professional football. J.D. returned to Magnolia Plantation, but he could not get along with Bucyrus. J.D. took an assistant football coaching position with Mississippi State and in June of 1964 married Lisa Hartman from Starkville, Mississippi. In 1962, Scarlett O'Hara Stewart was graduated from Canton High School and was accepted at Southern Mississippi University.

Sue Ellen had a full academic program at Ole Miss, and decided not to pursue acting. In her junior year, Sue Ellen and her parents drove to West Point and saw Nathan play football against Penn State. Nathan was now 6'4" tall, very handsome, and weighted 215 pounds. After the football game they had dinner at the Thayer Hotel in West Point, New York. Nathan was serious minded. He told them he earned cadet leave next summer and would return home to visit Magnolia Plantation. He liked West Point's challenge of body, mind, and spirit, and he was glad he chose "The Academy."

In January, Sue Ellen and Nathan's senior year arrived. Sue Ellen applied to the University of Tennessee Nursing School at Memphis and was accepted. In May of 1963 she went to West Point and saw Nathan's graduation and the parade and review of the West Point Corps of Cadets in full dress uniform and had never seen anything so impressive in her life. Nathan graduated 117th in his class and selected Infantry as his branch in the Army. He took leave and received orders to paratrooper and ranger school at Fort Benning, Georgia. Before reporting to Fort Benning, Nathan returned home to visit his family. Bucyrus was not in good health, after suffering a heart attack; he lost seventy pounds, and still smoked Cuban cigars and said, "No Goddamn Yankee doctor is going to put me in my grave." Nathan also learned Bucyrus had lied about his age when he enlisted in the U.S. Army in 1943 at age sixteen. He was now seventy-one, not sixty-five. His Mother, Hannah was all right, but she looked older and grayer.

Sue Ellen graduated from the University of Tennessee in Memphis and graduated in June of 1965 as a registered nurse (RN). Nathan Stewart took leave and came to see her graduation. They talked about their lives, love for one another, but they both wanted more time for themselves.

Nathan's next assignment was to Fort Benning, Georgia, to the Seventy-fifth Ranger Regiment and then to the 525th Parachute Infantry Regiment, Eighty-second Airborne Division, Fort

Bragg, North Carolina. In 1965, Nathan went to the Dominican Republic and in June, 1966, received orders to Vietnam with the Eighty-second Airborne Division.

In June, 1965, Sue Ellen attended a career day by the U.S. Department of Defense at the University of Tennessee. She talked to a female Colonel U.S. Army Nurse named Lynn Charles. Colonel Charles told Sue Ellen about nursing opportunities in the U.S. Army. Sue Ellen decided to accept the Army's program and in June of 1965 was given a direct commission as a Captain in the U.S. Army Nurse Corps.

From 1965 to 1966 she was an operating room nurse at Walter Reed Army Hospital in Washington, D.C., followed by a two-year assignment at Tripler Army Hospital in Honolulu, Hawaii. In March, 1967 she wrote Nathan after she received a letter from him telling her that a Huey helicopter in which he was riding had crashed in a "hot LZ" after being struck by Viet Cong ground fire. The pilot and co-pilot were both killed; Nathan said he fired an M-60 machine gun from the gunner's position and the VC tried to storm the helicopter. Two Army Cobra gunships arrived, in the nick of time, opened fire, and drove off the VC.

He was wounded in his right leg below the knee. He was sent to Camp Zama, Japan for an immediate operation to repair his wounded right leg and calf muscle, and then he was recommended for a Silver Star. Nathan said, "Vietnam is a killing war. My battalion lost 289 men killed over eight months." He was being sent to the Walter Reed Army Hospital for another operation on his leg or he might lose his right leg below the knee if his leg didn't get proper blood flow into the damaged area to heal the wound. Nathan said, "I feel like crap at times." He closed saying, "You help my morale."

Sue Ellen worked long hours at Tripler Army Hospital. The hospital received evacuated personnel from Vietnam suffering numerous wounds, injuries, and medical conditions. Some wounds she saw were frightening. She took thirty days' leave and visited Nathan Bedford Stewart at Walter Reed, and then went to Memphis to visit her family. In March 1968, she received orders assigning her to the Third Field Hospital, in Saigon and reporting on June second, 1968.

On June 2, 1968 Captain Sue Ellen Harris arrived at Kelper Compound. She went to the Adjutant for assistance to amend her orders, she had been assigned to U.S. Military Assistance Command, Vietnam, but not to the Third Field Hospital. Someone in Washington apparently did not know the difference. On Monday morning, June 3, she reported to the Third Field Hospital, but the hospital's Adjutant told her they had no assignment orders for her to the hospital, and that the Third Field Hospital needed operating room nurses badly. Colonel Smith, the commanding officer of the hospital, went directly to MACV and requested that Sue Ellen be assigned to the Third Field Hospital. Sue Ellen left Clara Barton Hall and walked across the courtyard to Kelper Compound. Ted Graham had finished eating a hot dog and Coke as he saw Sue Ellen walking across the courtyard.

Ted waved and called, "Sue Ellen."

She looked to see who called her. "Hi, Ted. I need to go to the Adjutant's office to get my orders amended." She saw the barbecue and asked Ted if they were serving lunch.

Ted looked at his watch and answered, "Yeah, grab a hot dog, chips and a soda and please join me."

"Okay," she hollered to Ted.

"Okay, lover boy," said Jeff. "I'll put your gear on the bus. You've got thirty-five minutes. Remember Colonel Davis' words, no stragglers."

"Roger, thirty-five minutes."

Jeff departed for Kelper Compound.

Sue Ellen returned with a hot dog, chips, and a Coke. Ted looked at her; she wore faint pink lipstick and no make-up, and was a truly beautiful woman. Ted thought, *What is going on with her?*

Sue Ellen sat down on the bench next to Ted. "Wasn't that a terrible rocket attack last night? Those explosions were so loud I thought they were attacking Kelper Compound. My roommate and I looked out the window, but couldn't see anything. A siren in the building sounded and we went to the first floor and heard more loud explosions. We waited in the first floor dayroom for ten minutes. Five MPs came into the building and told us that Kelper was not under attack. The MP Captain said the VC fired ten 122-millimeter rockets at the Vietnamese Presidential Compound."

"I know, Sue Ellen, we heard the explosions. I thought the compound was under attack and we didn't have any weapons. I went to the MP's guard post to find out what was going on. The MP's told me rockets had been fired at the Vietnamese Presidential Compound. It was eerie. I went back upstairs. Everyone was out on the balcony and one guy had a Thompson submachine gun. I don't know where he got it, but I was glad he had it. We went back inside to our room. I dozed off at four and got up at six. Jeff Madison and I are flying to Rach Gia today.

"Sue Ellen, I'm so glad I had a chance to meet you, in of all places, Saigon." He continued, "You are a beautiful woman, which you have heard before, it's unusual that you are in Vietnam. I would assume you would be married and living in Atlanta."

"Thank you, Ted, for your nice compliment. Why is it so surprising to find me in Vietnam? I'm an Army nurse."

Ted thought for a moment, "No offense. Frankly, I would have thought that someone like you would be married living in Atlanta or L.A."

"You're kind," said Sue Ellen.

She looked at her watch; it was 1230. "There's not enough time for me to go into all the details, it's a long story. Do you want the synopsis?"

"I was graduated from Ole Miss; you Yankees call it the University of Mississippi, in 1963. I planned to go to New York after graduation and try fashion modeling, and acting to get into television. My parents did not want me to be alone in New York City. My dad told me he would help pay for nursing school." She looked at her watch; "I went to the University of Tennessee Nursing School in Memphis and lived at home. I dated a guy named Bob, and he wanted to get married in June after graduation. I did not want to get married. Bob gave me an ultimatum to get married or forget it, I said no!

"I learned about nursing opportunities from an Army Medical Corp doctor and at UT Nursing School and looked at the opportunity, so I applied for a direct commission as a Captain and signed up for a four-year obligation on active duty.

"I was assigned to Walter Reed Army Hospital in Washington for one year and two years at Tripler Army Hospital in Honolulu and then got my orders to Vietnam, and here I am today."

Ted glanced at his watch, it was 1245; "I've got to catch the bus to Tan Son Nhut. Sue Ellen, may I write you?" he asked.

"Ted, you seem like a nice person. I need time to catch up and get my act together. There have been too many people telling me what to do for the last ten years. I would enjoy hearing from you, but I won't promise anything."

Ted looked at her, "Sue Ellen, I understand."

Jeff hollered, "Let's go, Ted, five minutes."

Ted asked her where to write.

"Captain Sue Ellen Harris, c/o Clara Barton Hall/In-Country, APO 92124."

Ted looked at her and said, "Off to my destiny." He ran to the bus on Tran Do, waved good-bye to Sue Ellen and she waved goodbye.

He got onto the bus, and the MP said, "You're the last passenger, Sir. Let's go," he said to the driver. The bus driver pulled the bus out into traffic towards Tan Son Nhut.

"Everything go okay?" asked Jeff. "Is she going to be a war bride?"

"No, but perhaps a bride, someday," said Ted.

The bus was full, with thirty-five MACV personnel, footlockers, field gear, and M-16 rifles.

They rode in silence to Tan Son Nhut as each man pondered his own thoughts. The driver blew the horn at several Vietnamese boys running into the street in front of the bus.

The French built Tran Do, Ted thought. It was a wide boulevard with large old trees in the middle of the street.

The bus reached an intersection and the bus driver turned right down a street with white stucco buildings. He stopped in front of a building with a sign, Tan Son Nhut Flight Center. The MP opened the door and said, "Okay, men, get your gear, walk directly to the terminal and wait for the Air Force Load Master to tell you what to do."

They filed out with their gear and went inside the huge MAC terminal. U.S. military personnel were standing in long lines and they jeered when they saw the bus and began to snicker as new men arrived. "Look at those rookies—Charlie is waiting for you," one yelled. The group kept on walking until an Air Force Sergeant motioned them to stop.

He said, "Fall into two ranks. Enlisted in front, officers in back. When I call your name, answer here."

"Arnold?"

"Here."

"Bennett?"

"Here."

"Bright?"

"Here."

"Graham?"

"Here."

"Madison?"

"Here."

He continued to Molinski and said, "You will be on the flight to Can Tho and Rach Gia, right?"

Molinski said, "Yes, Sergeant."

"Men, this flight is to My Tho, Vinh Long, Can Tho, Rach Gia and Soc Trang and it departs at 1530." He checked his watch, called out five names and said, "Go to gate three. The rest of you remain here for the flight up country to Nha Trang, Pleiku, Qui Nhon and Da Nang. I'll call you when the flight departs at 1700."

Ted, Jeff, and PFC Molinski walked to gate three. There were twenty personnel for the C-130 flight to Can Tho.

When they reached the gate, Ted turned to PFC Molinski and introduced himself and Jeff. "I'm Captain Ted Graham," he extended his right hand, "and this is Captain Jeffrey Madison."

Molinski snapped to attention and said, "Pleased to meet both of you, Sir." They shook hands.

Ted said, "Relax, we'll get to know each other. Are you assigned to Rach Gia?" Ted asked.

"Yes, Sir, to the OSA Advisory Team."

"OSA Advisory Team, what's that?"

Molinski looked puzzled, "You don't know, Sir?"

"No."

Private Molinski told Ted, "It's the Central Intelligence Agency, the CIA, the name means Office of the Special Assistant."

"What is that?"

"Sir, I was told it is classified information."

"Really?" asked Ted.

He turned to Jeff; "Now I know why Captain Bryant said we would find out about our assignments in Rach Gia."

"CIA, sounds spooky," said Jeff.

Jeff asked Molinski his first name.

"Joseph, but everyone calls me Moe."

"Moe Molinski. Are you Polish?"

"Yes, Sir, from North Chicago, the Polish capital of America."

Ted looked at his watch; it was 1350. "Let's grab a Coke and some chips, who knows when we'll get a chance for another one." They walked to a Coke machine and Ted put in seventy-five cents for three Cokes.

"So, you're from North Chicago?" asked Jeff.

"Yes, Sir, born and raised. I come from a working family. My dad works at Sears and Mom is a housewife. I have two brothers and two sisters at home."

"Did you go to college or get drafted?" asked Ted.

"I quit college last June after two years at the University of Illinois 'Champagne.' I worked and went to college but it was tough, and my grades were so-so. I had a tough time paying my tuition. I tried to work and play football, which I played in high school. I was a tight end, but I wasn't big enough in college." Ted looked at Moe. He looked to be 6' tall and 190 pounds.

"I enlisted in the Army in September of 1967 and went to basic and AIT at Fort Jackson, South Carolina. I went Airborne for Special Forces as a weapons and communications specialist. I went through six months of Special Forces training at Ft. Bragg and got my orders to Vietnam. At Kelper Compound my orders were changed to MACV. I don't know why or what I'll do in Special Forces in MACV."

The Air Force Sergeant approached the men, "Your aircraft is landing. It will be refueled and depart at 1630."

They picked up their footlockers, duffle bags, field gear, and M-16s and waited at the terminal gate. An Air Force refueling truck went to the C-130 and refueled the aircraft. The cargo door of the C-130 swung open and an Air Force Sergeant hollered, "Let's go," and they went to the back of the aircraft.

"My Tho first, then Vinh Long, Can Tho, Rach Gia and Soc Trang in that order."

The soldiers climbed aboard the C-130 which, got seated into a jump seat, and soon the pilot started both aircraft engines. When they were secured, the Sergeant closed the cargo door, and addressed the personnel.

"Welcome aboard," said the crew chief. "I'm Sergeant Billings, keep your seat belts fastened, if you get airsick use the plastic bag under you seat. Any questions? When we land, the pilot will keep the aircraft engines running, get your gear and move off quickly, safely, and clear the aircraft."

The pilot taxied the aircraft down the runway. The occupants looked out the aircraft's windows as the aircraft gained speed and lifted off the runway and gained altitude and then made a hard left turn. The pilot continued turning the aircraft left and then he leveled off. They sat facing one another. The aircraft's engines hummed with a steady drone; Jeff dozed off. Moe looked out the window, and saw white puffy clouds and blue sky.

It seemed to be a few minutes after getting airborne that Sergeant Billings yelled, "We'll land at My Tho in ten minutes."

The aircraft began its descent and from the aircraft's window Ted saw heavy thick jungle foliage, palm trees and rice paddies as the C-130 hit the runway with a "whomp," bounced, and the pilot reversed the engines. The aircraft came to a stop with its engines running. "My Tho," and fifteen soldiers moved quickly off the aircraft. Ted looked out the back of the C-130; and saw a yellow stucco building with another orange tile roof and he thought, *More French architecture.*

Sergeant Billings closed the C-130 cargo door and the aircraft was airborne toward Can Tho.

"Next stop, Can Tho," said Sergeant Billings.

The pilot called Sergeant Billings on the radio. "We'll RON at Can Tho, I want the mechanics to check the left wing landing gear, which is closing too slowly. Tell the passengers I'm going to ground the aircraft in Can Tho. The left wing flap has low hydraulic pressure. I want our mechanics to look at it."

"Yes, Sir," answered Sergeant Billings.

"As you heard, the pilot is going to ground the aircraft in Can Tho and have the hydraulic pressure in the left wing flap checked."

The aircraft rolled to a stop and the pilot, who was Major Jennings, a U.S. Air Force Major, walked to the back of the aircraft as Sergeant Billings opened the cargo door. The four men got off the aircraft and saluted Major Jennings.

"Sorry to inconvenience you, but safety first. I think the aircraft has a leak in the left wing hydraulic line. It can be fixed tomorrow morning. If not, another C-130 will come to Can Tho tomorrow morning at 1100."

Ted asked the Major, "Where do we RON, Sir?"

Major Jennings answered, "MACV HQ has a new compound outside Can Tho."

"Sergeant Billings?"

"Yes, Sir," said Sergeant Billings.

"Check with MACV about transportation for these men to the Old French Compound."

"French Compound?" asked Jeff.

"Yes, Captain," he said. "I've heard that last year the Army opened a new location, since the Fourth Corps HQ is getting to be overcrowded."

"Where is it?" asked Moe.

"Three miles East of Can Tho," said the pilot.

Sergeant Billings returned. "They're sending a Jeep to take them to the compound. Wait here," the Major told them. "I'm going to find out where to park the aircraft. If I don't see you again, good luck."

They saluted Major Jennings and he walked toward a tower at the end of the runway.

A Jeep arrived driven by an Army Corporal. He asked, "Sir, are you the personnel for MACV Compound?"

"Yes, Corporal," said Jeff.

The Corporal said, "Store your gear in back; it will be crowded, but we're not going too far and it will be bumpy." He drove off out of the airfield and then drove down a wide street in Can Tho. Can Tho had civilian traffic, but not like Saigon. They passed ARVN trucks, pedicabs, motor scooters, bicycles and Vietnamese women wearing the traditional Ao Dai with black silk pants and the tight-fitting silk blouse and conic hats and high-heeled shoes.

"What is the old French Compound?" asked Jeff.

"Sir, all I know is that it was a French garrison that was abandoned in 1954. The ARVN took it over; and apparently never use it, since it needed a lot of work, like new plumbing, electricity and new roofs. The U.S. government took possession of it in 1966. The Pacific Architects and Engineers renovated everything, and it took over a year to make it livable. It's nice, and the VC didn't attack it during Tet."

He turned left down an asphalt road, "Hold on," he said. He tried to avoid a large pothole, but ran into it and the Jeep bounced and then they saw a large arch over an entrance to the compound. The gate was closed and on both sides of the entrance were dilapidated guard posts with broken windows.

The Corporal said, "This is the main entrance." A South Vietnamese MP raised the bar gate to the compound. On the right of the compound was a brick wall, twelve feet in height with six-inch iron spikes sticking out of the top of the wall. The area inside the brick fence was the size of a football field with four guard towers. It looked like a prison. In the distance they saw a U.S. Army Huey helicopter approach and heard the "whomp, whomp" of rotor blades. The U.S. Army Huey descended behind the brick wall.

"Why is that Army helicopter landing?" Ted asked the Corporal.

He answered, "Sir, you'll find out, I can't tell you." The three men looked at one another.

The driver drove around a flagpole at the center of the compound and stopped the Jeep in front of a faded white building with a sign that read, U.S. ARMY SUPPORT COMMAND and they went into the building. It had faded black and white tile on the floor, a TV set, and several chairs and AFN music. An Army Sergeant named Collier greeted them.

"Yes, Sir," he said to Ted.

"We need three rooms. We've been held over until tomorrow morning," said Jeff.

Moe looked out the front door.

Sergeant Collier said, "I have three rooms at the other end of the compound, nothing fancy, but they're clean. They have a toilet; use the building next to the mess hall to shower." He pointed to his left.

"The French built things so screwed up, and they have the worst plumbing I've ever seen." Ted and Jeff looked out a window and saw the high brick fence perimeter around the compound.

Moe asked Sergeant Collier, "Was this a French prison?"

"Yes," said the Sergeant. "It was abandoned in 1954."

"Where is the jail?"

"There is no jail, the prisoners stayed in the courtyard and got interrogated and then were flown to French jails in Can Tho or An Toi on Phu Quoc Island, or Saigon. Here are the keys to your rooms."

They took their keys and Ted asked, "What time does the mess hall open?"

"Five o'clock," said Sergeant Collier. "Nothing fancy."

They went outside and U.S. Army personnel were beginning to walk toward the mess hall. It was 1745.

"Better hurry," Jeff said.

They went to their rooms. Each room had a metal cot, towel, sheets, pillowcase, washbasin, and toilet. They met outside and walked to the mess hall and ate spaghetti, salad, rolls, and iced tea. They walked back to their rooms.

Jeff said, "I'm bushed, I'm going to mail postcards, take a shower and turn in."

"Me too," said Ted.

"Same here, I need to write my parents a letter," said Moe.

They went to their rooms. Another U.S. Army Huey helicopter was heard approaching. Ted looked out the window. He saw piles of long green bags. Suddenly, he gasped. He saw jungle boots sticking out of the piles of stacked green bags. *My God,* thought Ted to himself, *those are dead GIs in body bags.* His heart beat rapidly. He thought, *I'd better tell Jeff.* He put on his jungle fatigue pants, T-shirt, and rubber sandals, walked next door, and knocked on Jeff's door.

"Who is it?" asked Jeff.

"Ted."

Jeff opened the door.

"Did you see what's across the compound in the other corner along the wall?"

"What, VC?"

"No, no, look out the window."

They went to the window in Jeff's room and Jeff folded up a faded windowshade and looked out the window, through a rusted window screen full of holes.

"Look, over there," Ted pointed toward the pile of body bags.

"Those are stacks of body bags," Jeff gasped.

"You're right, dead soldiers," said Ted.

The Huey started its rotary blades and circled into the black night sky.

Jeff said, "Body bags from where?"

"This is the Fourth Corps mortuary collection point; this garrison is a mortuary services company."

"My God to glory," whispered Jeff.

They both leaned toward the window. Ted counted the body bags stacked like cordwood. He counted ten across and five high.

"I counted fifty dead GIs."

"Lord, have mercy."

They watched as five U.S. Army personnel arranged the body bags and tied a white card to a boot or toe sticking out of each body bag.

Jeff said, "I feel sick. I wonder how long they've been here?"

Ted thought, *That's what the C-130 is coming for tomorrow, to fly them back to Saigon and then back to the States.*

"My, oh my," said Jeff. They looked out again. It was dark but they could see with the lights in the compound. It was eerie beyond belief.

Ted went back to his room. The next morning they arose at 0600 and went to breakfast.

Moe asked Ted and Jeff, "Did you see what was in the courtyard last night?"

"Yes, we did."

On their way back to their rooms, a U.S. Army Captain approached them. He asked, "Are you the personnel going to Rach Gia?"

"Yes," said Jeff.

"We got a message that your C-130 is fixed and you will depart at 1000, the driver who brought you here will pick you up at 0930. Any questions?"

"Just one. Last night we saw what appeared to be body bags stacked in the corner of the compound, now they are gone, were they body bags?"

The Captain said, "Yes, and do not tell *anyone* what you saw or how many you thought you counted; they were removed by truck this morning at 0300 and taken to an aircraft in Can Tho for a flight to Saigon. We have U.S. media from Washington and reporters snooping around here with cameras. The media are not permitted inside this compound. Do not tell anyone what you saw; if the U.S. Army finds out, you'll be in deep shit! Got it?"

"Yes," they said.

The Captain looked at Moe, "And that means you, too Private."

"Yes, Sir," replied Moe.

Ted asked the Captain, "So those fifty men were KIA from the Fourth Corps?"

"Yes. Do you need a picture?"

"No."

The Captain departed. They went to their rooms and picked up their gear. At 0930, the Corporal arrived and drove them to the C-130 at Can Tho to meet Sergeant Billings.

"Good morning."

They boarded the aircraft, stowed their gear and the pilot had them in the air.

"It's a thirty-minute flight to Rach Gia," said Sergeant Billings. Before they knew it, they heard Major Jennings lower the airplane's landing gear.

Jeff turned to Ted and said, "Well, my friend, our adventure begins today."

The C-130 touched down with a cloud of white smoke as the airplane's tires squealed on hitting the runway when they landed. Major Jennings taxied the C-130 and stopped the aircraft in front of a former French air terminal tower. The building had broken windows, and yellow paint with the familiar orange tile roof.

Jeff said, "It looks like it's been a long time since anyone used the tower."

Sergeant Billings lowered the cargo door; he asked Ted and Jeff, "Is someone going to meet you? It is 1200, we must depart for Vi Thanh."

Ted said, "I don't know, I assume someone will be here."

Sergeant Billings went inside the aircraft and radioed Major Jennings. There was a five-minute wait and Sergeant Billings came back. "Can Tho says to wait an hour and someone will be out to get you from the Advisory Team at Rach Gia."

"One hour?" said Ted.

"Yeah," said Sergeant Billings.

"What if there is a screw-up and no one shows up?"

"I don't know what to do then," said Sergeant Billings. "Pray, I guess," he said. "Major Jennings said someone would be here in an hour."

"Okay," said Jeff. They got their footlockers, field gear, M-16s, and walked from the C-130 to the terminal. It smelled of urine, and soiled toilet paper was strewn across the floor. The wind picked up, black clouds moved across the sky with heavy thunder and lightning in the distance. They saw rice paddies, water buffalo, and thick jungle foliage.

Jeff walked outside the terminal. "Hey, look at this." He pointed to broken plaster at the end of the building. "Look at those bullet holes, probably AK-47."

They looked up and saw part of the corner under the roof was blown away by gunfire. Interior wood frame was visible and there were fifty to sixty large-caliber bullet holes implanted along the wall.

"Must have been during Tet," said Moe.

Ted looked at the bullet holes. "Looks like AK-47 rounds or .30-caliber rounds."

They went inside the building, and the rain began to pour down, while a strong wind blew through the terminal.

There was graffiti on the walls. It read, "My recruiter said I'd see exotic lands, fucked in 'Nam."

Another one said, "Kilroy was here," with World War II character and a head and fingers looking over a wall.

Jeff said, "This guy's a poet, 'Tet-Vet—class of '68.' "

Moe read, "Charley is watching you," with a cat's large black eyes.

"These guys are creative," said Moe. The rain pounded on the tin roof, and it began to leak like a sieve; it had been thirty minutes since the C-130 departed.

Jeff asked Ted, "Suppose no one shows up?"

"We sleep here and start walking down the road to Rach Gia in the morning."

The rain let up and soon the sun came out, creating humidity like steam. Clouds of steam rose on the asphalt runway and insects appeared everywhere. A vehicle was seen coming down the road with lights on, heading toward the airfield. The vehicle stopped.

An Army Sergeant got out, "Captain Graham, Captain Madison and PFC Molinski?" he asked.

"Yes," said Ted.

"Good, I'm Sergeant Darby. Put your gear in the back, and get in."

They opened the back door to a new white Chevrolet suburban and put their gear in back.

Jeff got in the front passenger seat and Ted and Moe got into the back seat.

"Not a bad vehicle," said Jeff. "Looks new."

The driver said, "It's an OSA vehicle, I went to the OSA Compound for a Jeep and they told me to take the suburban. OSA has all the good stuff, MACV gets all the shit."

He turned the vehicle around and started down a two-lane airport road, past heavy jungle foliage growing along the narrow two-lane bumpy asphalt road.

"How far is Rach Gia?" asked Jeff.

"Five miles."

The driver swerved to avoid hitting two Vietnamese boys riding water buffaloes, and huge potholes. "Hit one of those sons-of-bitches and it'll break the axle."

The suburban passed over a wooden bridge guarded by two ARVN soldiers with Browning automatic rifles sitting on sandbags; they waved to the OSA vehicle.

The jungle receded and soon they came to an open area and a town with French accents.

"This is Rach Gia," said Sergeant Darby. "I was told to take you to the OSA Compound."

He went past two small streets and turned right onto a street that ran parallel to a wide canal. Across the river was more heavy thick jungle. Along the street were Chinese signs, Vietnamese shops, stores and small houses.

"Here are the enlisted billets, it's a former French hotel. The enlisted billets in Rach Gia were damaged during Tet. I hope Charlie doesn't decide to shoot into this building from the area on the other side of the canal. It is a shitty, lousy place to house Army personnel."

He stopped the suburban in front of a two-story faded green stucco building. Next to the building was a parking lot where three new U.S. Army Jeeps were parked. An older man wearing a black fatigue uniform and a maroon French paratrooper's beret walked toward the suburban carrying an M-16.

"That's Mr. Choy," said Sergeant Darby. "He fought with the French and now works for the CIA, oh, I mean CORDS. He speaks fluent French, English and Vietnamese and has a thousand war stories."

Mr. Choy waved as he approached the suburban and in a French accent said, "*Bonjour.*" A spider monkey was sitting on a table near Mr. Choy.

Jeff asked, "Is that your monkey?"

"No," said Choy, "I only feed him and put him in his cage at night, but he is a good watch monkey. He screams and hollers if someone strange stops in front. He doesn't like VC." Choy laughed and gave the monkey a banana.

"What is his name?" asked Moe.

"Kick."

"Kick? Kick the monkey who hates VC. That's good," said Moe.

A tall enlisted man appeared at the front door of the faded green building wearing olive drab jungle fatigues.

"Are you the new guys?" he asked, saluting.

"Yes," said Ted.

They walked past heavy sandbag bunkers stacked up the front of the building to the second floor. On the east side of the building was a vacant lot between the OSA Compound and another building fifty feet on the east side. Jeff looked at the open field. "Someplace to do PT?"

"No, Sir, not there, it's mined with claymore mines." He extended his right hand to Jeff and said, "Welcome, Sir, I'm Sergeant Sam Bowman, from Seattle." Sergeant Bowman shook hands with Ted and Moe. "Are you billeted here at OSA?"

"I don't know," said Jeff.

Ted turned to Sergeant Bowman, "We're assigned to the Phoenix Program, does that mean we work for OSA?"

Sergeant Bowman said, "Tell you what," he turned to Mr. Choy. "Park the suburban, bring in your gear and I will find out what's going on."

Sergeant Darby was sitting in the suburban when Mr. Choy said, "Sergeant, please open the door so I can help with your footlockers."

Sergeant Darby walked to the back of the suburban, he reached inside, pulled out the three footlockers and three duffle bags, and put them on the ground. Jeff, Ted, and Moe were standing behind the suburban.

"Thank you, we'll take them," said Jeff.

They picked up their footlockers and carried them past the sandbag bunkers and down a short sidewalk into the building. Sergeant Bowman opened the front door. They placed their footlockers in a small hallway and went back out to the suburban and picked up their duffle bags and weapons, and brought them into the hallway.

Sergeant Darby closed the rear door of the suburban, saluted and said, "Good luck, and see you around MACV."

Ted, Jeff, and Moe went into the building. To Ted it appeared to be either be a rich man's home or a small hotel. He turned to Sergeant Bowman, who was standing behind a counter that ran ten feet along the front hallway.

Ted asked Sergeant Bowman, "What is this place?"

Sam looked around and said, "From what I've been told, it was a former Chinese hotel."

The building was now in very good condition and air conditioners were humming.

Sergeant Bowman said, "According to what I've been told, the Chinese and Vietnamese don't get along. They have separate restaurants, shops, hotels and schools. This was a Chinese hotel built in 1947. Nate Shaw, the OSA Station Chief, got here last March. OSA had the contractors working twenty-four hours a day until it was properly renovated." He continued, "It's nice; the rooms are all air-conditioned, it has running water, toilets that flush and plenty of room. There is one bedroom down here and three upstairs, it's not like the MACV Compound. Two Briggs and Stratton 7,500 watt generators provide power 24/7."

"Where is the MACV Compound?" asked Moe.

"The MACV Compound is three miles east of here. It's very crowded. There are three enlisted to a room and two officers to a room. It was once the French Provincial Military Compound. About fifty Viet Cong attacked the compound during Tet, and it sustained a lot of damage. The VC tried to climb over an iron fence that surrounds the compound but U.S. troops inside the compound returned heavy fire and killed thirty VC. I got here in April; I was told we killed thirty VC without having many U.S. serious casualties. The Tet attack on Rach Gia was mild compared to Can Tho; which got hit hard."

"We saw Can Tho," Jeff said.

"The Rach Gia MACV dining hall was rebuilt and the MACV Headquarters building has also been repaired. Moe asked, Sam, why do we stay here, and not at MACV?"

"I don't know," said Moe. "Probably for OSA operational security. Most people believe this place is CORDS; Mr. Shaw doesn't allow strangers inside the compound. Don't ever mention the CIA. We have PKU security guards supervised by Mr. Jessee Roberts, the Navy Seal. He wears a Glock in a holster with the hammer in a cocked postion and a Sam Bowie knife with a fifteen-inch razor-sharp blade tied to his right leg. He's also a loner. Don't fuck with him or hassle him if he has been drinking. I just call him 'Sir.' "

"What are PRU's?" asked Jeff.

"You don't know about PRU's?"

"No," said Jeff.

"PRU's stands for Provincial Reconnaissance Unit." He stopped. "Let Mr. Shaw tell you, he gets back on Saturday from Saigon."

A call crackled from the Sony radio located among a bank of communications equipment behind the counter. The communications center resembled a police department's dispatch room.

"Homeplate," a voice said over the radio. "Homeplate, this is Buckshot, do you read me? Over."

Sergeant Bowman responded, "Yes, Buckshot."

"We will arrive at your location in four-zero minutes, do you copy?"

"Yes, I copy, Buckshot." He continued, "There are three uniformed Sierra personnel at this location."

"Homeplate, did you say three new uniformed Sierra personnel at your location?"

"That's affirmative, Buckshot, we're waiting for further instructions from you."

"Okay, Homeplate, Archer gave me instructions until he arrives back. Stand by, Homeplate, over and out," said Buckshot.

"Roger and out," said Bowman.

"That was Major, or I guess I should say Mr. Roland, who is the OSA's assistant for PRU operations. He has instructions for you," said Sergeant Bowman.

"Where's the latrine?" asked Jeff.

"Straight down the hall to the right."

"Have a seat in the dining room. Stan, Billy and Jesse will be here shortly," said Sergeant Bowman.

"We have a new refrigerator on the third floor and a bar we built, with soda and beer, help yourself."

Ted and Moe walked into an adjacent room, which had a heavy, durable four-legged dark wood table and six wooden chairs around it. Along one wall was a large wood credenza with four AK-47's; a .45 pistol in a holster, ammunition, two flashlights, flares, and several tiger uniforms laying on it. On top of the dining table were empty beer cans, dirty paper plates, old *Playboy* magazines. In the corner of the room were stacked four AK-47 assault rifles and two German Mauser rifles.

"To whom do those weapons belong?" asked Jeff.

"Those," said Sergeant Bowman, looking at the corner, "belong to Stan Roland and Billy Flynn; they're captured VC weapons."

"What happens to them?" asked Ted.

"They'll be given to the PRU's or local RF/PF."

"Where are the PRU's?" asked Moe.

"The PRU's have their own compound outside town."

"How many PRU's are there?"

Sergeant Bowman thought for a minute, "I don't know, it varies, probably one hundred and fifty. They are tough, fearless fighters and love to kill VC or NVA. They are mercenaries paid by OSA, Stan can tell you about them."

Jeff, Ted, and Moe sat at the table. Moe glanced at an old *Playboy* magazine. The three sat in silence. Ten minutes later, the front door banged open and in came three men wearing maroon berets, Vietnamese striped tiger uniforms, muddy boots, M-16 rifles with bandoliers of ammunition criss-crossed over their shoulders.

Sergeant Bowman said, "Sir, the new guys are in the dining room."

"Great," said Stan. "I've got to take a shit, tell 'em I'll be right back."

Two other men came into the dining room. "Howdy, I'm Billy Flynn, Navy SEAL, and this is Jesse Roberts, also Navy SEAL." They introduced themselves to one another.

Stan came back and Billy said, "This is wild man Stan Roland."

"Wild man my ass, Billy, I just love to kill Cong."

Stan looked at Ted, Jeff and Moe and said, "Welcome to fucking Vietnam, don't try to be a hero. I've seen too many heroes go home in body bags."

Ted thought about what he had seen at the French prison in Can Tho.

Stan said, "Hey, sit down, I'm charged. We just got back from an 'op' with the PRU's last night; we bagged three of those little brown motherfuckers. Billy, you son-of-a-bitch, you nailed one gook in the head and it exploded like a smashed Halloween pumpkin."

Ye gods, thought Ted. *This guy's crazy?*

Stan took his M-16, released the banana clip, activated the chamber reject mechanism, cleared the breach, snapped the trigger while pointing the M-16 at the ceiling and placed the weapon on the table in front of him. He went to a room and returned with six cans of cold beer. "Drink up, guys, it was a good night."

Ted saw into Stan's room which had three metal cots and looked like a U.S. Army–Navy store full of military equipment.

"Okay," said Stan. "Tell me about yourselves."

Ted, Jeff, and Moe gave Stan a brief synopsis of themselves.

"Good, very good," said Stan. "All good men. Me, I'm regular Army, Infantry, Airborne and Ranger from the University of Alabama. We don't wear standard U.S. Army jungle shit around here." He continued, "I'm on a two-year detail to the Agency, the CIA, and forget I said that, to act as an operations advisor for guerrilla tactics and killing the sons-of-bitches the agency wants dead. I've been here fourteen months, been wounded twice and was submitted for a Silver Star for some shit I did during Tet. No big deal," Stan said.

He continued, "I volunteered for this assignment, I want to work for the CIA after I retire in ten years. I've got ten years' service, will make Lieutenant Colonel in six months, and have a wife and two kids back in Tuscaloosa. I graduated from the University of Alabama in 1958 and have had all infantry assignments at Benning, Korea, West Germany and now here in 'Nam.

From here I go to Fort Leavenworth to Command and General Staff College, and then to command an Infantry Battalion.

"Nate Shaw is the OSA Station Chief; you'll meet Nate on Sunday. He's a nice guy and runs a tight ship and a helluva good operation. Y'all will live here. On the second floor is Nate's room, don't ever go in his room, unless he is in there! That is one quick way to get fired. Nate doesn't ever talk about what he does, and don't ask him. Also, call him Nate, not Nat. He'll tell you what he wants you to know. What we do is legal in this kill-or-get-killed war; but we are going to, and the term is 'root out' those little brown gook bastards. Right, Jesse?"

"I want to shower. Jeff, you and Ted take the large room upstairs, Moe, you take that smaller room. We're lucky, we have air conditioning," he said.

"You'll wear civilian clothes until we get you jungle tiger fatigues to wear in the field. You will all go out on combat operations."

Jeff asked, "When do we go into the field?"

Stan said, "Soon. We'll train you, but you'll get your CIB, believe me, Jeff. Forget the glory, you have a long way to go. Y'all go upstairs and unpack, we'll go the MACV mess hall at 1830, it closes at 1900. Remember, civilian clothes; people will know you're new and probably know about your assignment, but they do not know who you work for or your status. They think CIA is OSA or think they know, and your Army uniform is cover."

Stan went in the bedroom and came out in a few minutes with a towel wrapped around him.

Jeff said, "Excuse me, Stan, how long will we be here? I thought I would be in MACV for six months and then Special Forces or go to an American Unit."

"How long?" said Stan. "As long as you stay alive. Worry about the time later. By the way," he said, "tomorrow we'll go out and zero in new M-16's, fire some M-79's and see what you can do, and hunt some pussy if you want," and he laughed.

He went into the shower and began singing "Dixie."

Jeff, Ted, and Moe went upstairs to a second-floor landing, up another flight of stairs to a hallway. At the end of the hall was a sign, PRIVATE—DO NOT ENTER—N. SHAW.

Jeff and Ted found their room, and Moe was in the small room across the hall. The rooms were cool from the air conditioning.

Jeff took a metal cot on the right side of the room and Ted took the other metal cot. The room was very adequate. They took out their personal belongings from their footlockers, put away their personal items, and stored their field gear at the foot of their bed.

Ted said to Jeff, "I'm standing my M-16 here in the corner against the wall."

They finished and went over to Moe's room. He said to Ted and Jeff, "I never thought a PFC in Vietnam would have a private and air-conditioned room."

"You'll earn it," a voice said coming from down the hall, "you guys have a lot to learn, pay attention. We do dangerous and very important work," said Jesse.

"This is my second tour, and so far I've seen four U.S. Navy SEALS buy the farm and go home in a body bag. There is a .50-caliber machine gun on the roof, I will show you how to lock, load and fire it. We're our own security, forget the bullshit about PRU's, they are around here, but don't depend on them. There are only two of them here at a time.

"You'll see me carry a loaded Glock 9mm-pistol like it is attached to my hip. I do it for a reason, anyone fucks with me and I'll plug the bastard between the eyes," said Jesse.

"Glad you're here," he said.

They all walked to the front door. Stan reappeared in the hallway wearing open-toed flops, gray slacks, and a white shirt. He hollered to Billy, "Let's go, I'm hungry." Billy came out with a beer, wearing a tee shirt, Bermuda shorts, and loafers with no socks.

Stan told Ted, Jeff and Moe, "Don't piss off Jesse. He's a killer." He said again, "Jesse is okay, just crazy."

"All right, Flynn, are you going to eat?" asked Stan.

"You drive the suburban, we'll give the new troops the grand tour of Rach Gia by the sea."

"Oh, by the way," said Stan. "We have a small bar located on the third floor. There's beer, soda and liquor which Nate allows as a convenience. Visitors may use it and each month we take up a collection to resupply it. I hired a nice young girl as bartender who is Major Lam's daughter. He's the PRU Commander, so watch your ass, and don't bring any pussy into the OSA house, Nate's orders. Twice a week a Mama-san comes and cleans our place, mops the floor, cleans the latrine, and changes the beds. We chip in to pay her. She does a good job and this place gets dirty. Twice a week we give *Mama-san* money to go to the local market and buy fresh chicken, fish and rice. The rest of the time we eat at the MACV dining hall. It opens at 0700 and closes at 1900.

"Tomorrow you three take your orders to Captain Lane, the S-1; he knows what to do. You'll also meet LTC Berry, the Province Senior Advisor."

They had been listening to Stan and Billy when the suburban pulled into a gravel parking lot in front of a three-story faded yellow building with the standard orange tile roof.

To the left of the building was a wood-frame building with thick wire on the sides, a tin roof, and wood panel along the walls. At one end was a brick wall under the tin roof, cooking stoves, a grill, refrigerator, and coolers. In the front room were thirty tables and chairs. In the back of the building was a separate room and a sign that said, OFFICERS. It had twelve tables and one long rectangular table that said, SENIOR PROVINCE ADVISOR AND STAFF.

They had supper and drove back to the OSA Compound. Jeff, Ted, and Moe went to their rooms, took a shower and went to bed. It had been a long, long day.

9

On Monday, March 4, 1968, Arthur Edward Norris, now known as Nate Shaw from Flagstaff, Arizona, arrived at the U.S. Embassy in Saigon. Lester Shockley, the deputy director of the Phoenix Program, met him at the Air America terminal at Ton Son Nhut Air Base. Nate was billeted at the Blanchard BOQ. The first three days in Saigon, Nate Shaw completed in-processing at the U.S. Embassy, received booster shots for malaria and typhoid at the 1127th U.S. Air Force Dispensary, and briefings from the U.S. Embassy, CIA's Intelligence Staff and the U.S. Joint Staff, J-2. He called Janet two times from the military affiliate radio system (MARS) at the MACV Headquarters, and no one answered the telephone at their home in Tucson. Nate thought, *Perhaps Janet has taken the children and fled, or they are visiting my parents in Phoenix.* He hoped it was the latter.

Saigon's weather remained humid and stifling hot following the end of the six-month monsoon season. Lester drove Nate from Ton Son Nhut to the U.S. Embassy. As they drove Nate remembered reading that Saigon was the "The Pearl of the Orient." Saigon had seen better days from its grandeur of French colonial style tree-lined boulevards, elegant villas, the buildings painted pale green, light yellow, white or gray with either orange or gray tile roofs. Today it was a big, dirty, overcrowded warzone, yet people still tried to live as if the war was only an inconvenience to their lives. Children squatted to defecate in the streets or urinate wearing no underclothing.

Traffic in Saigon was organized chaos; it crawled daily bumper to bumper along the once-elegant boulevards. Ancient traffic lights were now mostly symbolic. Vietnamese young men rode their motorscooters, motorcycles and bicycles dangerously close to moving traffic and weaved in and out of traffic or onto sidewalks to pass vehicles. Saigon's traffic policemen stood on top of four-foot-high concrete islands turning their green and red paddles, blowing whistles, and flailing arms back and forth at traffic, while cursing the drivers. Nate saw French Peugeots, Citroens, Italian Fiats, Japanese Hondas, and an occasional American Ford. As Mr. Chau drove them along Le Loi Boulevard, Lester reminisced to Nate about Saigon and the Orient over his past fourteen years living in Saigon and in South Vietnam.

Nate watched several Vietnamese old men with brown wrinkled skin and strong muscular legs peddling pedicabs to navigate their passengers through the congested Saigon traffic. The old men wore shorts and tee shirts, and were grinning, showing their red toothless gums and fencerow teeth which had now become stained bright red from chewing betel nut, an Oriental stimulant. Nate thought some of them looked to be in their seventies.

Also mixed among Saigon's traffic were ARVN military vehicles, ARVN soldiers riding in two and one-half ton trucks with M-16 rifles, sedans, police cars, and American military jeeps with soldiers. Lester Shockley said he had to attend a previous appointment. He told Nate to meet him in the Embassy in half an hour. He got out of the car near the embassy and entered an office building on Le Loi Boulevard. Mr. Chau drove Nate to the imposing four-story U.S. Embassy Compound. The Great Seal of the United States of America was mounted on the front wall of the four-story building and an eight-foot high stucco wall surrounded the compound perimeter with an American flag flying on a flagpole in the center of the compound.

Nate got out at the embassy's front entrance while Mr. Chau drove the van into the rear entrance of the compound. It was 1430; Nate picked up two of his suitcases, an attaché case, and walked toward the front entrance which was protected with a sandbag bunker. As Nate approached, a U.S. Military Police Sergeant with his nametag showing Douglas, a paratrooper, emerged from the bunker, holding an M-16 rifle. The Sergeant wore green jungle fatigues, a U.S. Army "steel pot" with camouflage cover, and had a black armband with MP in white on his left arm.

Nate saw Sergeant Douglas with an M-16 in his right hand holding the rifle with his right index finger close to the trigger guard.

Nate stopped, put his suitcase and attaché case on the ground, and spoke, "Sergeant Douglas, Mr. Chau just dropped me off; I'm here to meet Lester Shockley; I'm new in country."

There was a pause as a cloud of gnats began buzzing around Nate's sweaty head; he did not want to make an impulsive move as he stood looking at Sergeant Douglas holding the M-16 rifle. Nate remained still as the gnats buzzed around his face and continued to bother him.

The Sergeant said, "Yes, Sir, may I help you?" The soldier placed his right index finger on the M-16's trigger.

"Yes," said Nate, looking frantically for Lester to appear.

The soldier said in an agitated tone of voice, "I'm Sergeant Douglas, 327th Military Police Battalion, do you have business at the U.S. Embassy?"

"Yes, Sergeant, I'm Nate Shaw, a CORDS civilian contractor here to see Lester Shockley, he's expecting me."

A U.S. Military Police Officer came out of the MP bunker.

Sergeant Douglas said, "Lieutenant Banks, this man is Mr. Shaw to see Mr. Shockley in the embassy."

The officer was a First Lieutenant, a paratrooper, wearing a Ranger tab on his left shoulder.

"May I see your I.D., Mr. Shaw?"

Nate wiped his face with his handkerchief. *This is terrible,* he thought to himself.

Sergeant Douglas watched Nate locate his I.D. card in his wallet.

"Here is my I.D," said Nate, giving the I.D. to Lieutenant Banks.

Lieutenant Banks looked at the I.D. and at Nate, "Sergeant Douglas, call Mr. Shockley and tell him Mr. Shaw's now standing at the front MP guard post."

"Yes, Sir," said Sergeant Douglas.

Lieutenant Banks returned Nate's I.D., and said, "Thank

you, Mr. Shaw. We're edgy after Tet. No offense, Sir. Sergeant Douglas and I were on duty here during the Tet attack; it got hairy. If there had been more VC, they would have gotten into the compound and captured the embassy."

A telephone rang inside the guardhouse. "Excuse me," said Lieutenant Banks. Sergeant Douglas and Nate stood at the bunker.

Lieutenant Banks answered the phone, and Nate heard him say, "Roger. Yes, Sir."

Lieutenant Banks returned and told Sergeant Douglas, "Unlock the gate and escort Mr. Shaw into the embassy."

Sergeant Douglas unlocked a heavy steel padlock and opened its hasp connecting two steel chainlinks with chains that were wrapped around two black wrought-iron poles. He pushed the gate open and said, "Let me help you, Sir," and he started to pick up Nate's suitcases.

Nate remembered his prior CIA agency training, "Always carry your own bags so bags are not switched with look-alikes."

"That's fine, Sergeant," Nate said, and picked up his suitcase and attaché case, went inside the gates, and walked across the compound toward the large set of double doors of the main entrance to the U.S. embassy in Saigon.

Sergeant Douglas stopped in the courtyard. He turned to Nate, and pointed his right index finger toward three large brown spots in the grass at the base of the wall forming a perimeter to the compound.

"Mr. Shaw," said Sergeant Douglas, pointing to the three large brown spots. "See them spots over yonder by that wall?"

Nate looked at the spots, "Yes."

"That's where I killed three Viet Cong sons-of-bitches who jumped down right there at six in the morning on January thirty-first, during Tet." Nate stood in silence.

Sergeant Douglas said, "We got attacked by twenty-five VC at sunrise. They threw dynamite satchels over the wall to kill anyone inside and blow a hole in the wall. I was in back at post three when hell broke loose. The VC came over the wall and my buddy Danny Granger got killed, but hollered, 'The fuckers are coming over the back wall.' Danny was the only MP in front at the time. He hollered, 'Get your ass out here fast! I can't hold 'em.' The VC threw another satchel that landed, exploded, and killed Danny. I ran to the front of the embassy and heard the explosion. When I got to the corner, I saw Danny lying dead, blown apart.

"Three VC were on the wall holding satchels with AK-47's slung over their backs. Three of them jumped down on the grass; I knelt down like I was shooting a deer back home in Texas, put my M-16 on automatic and fired a burst at the gooks. The burst hit three of the bastards and they exploded—cut in half. One VC tried to throw his explosive satchel at me—I fired another burst and blew away the son-of-a-bitch's head—I blew it away. Fifteen MPs arrived at the embassy and fought their way inside. Ambassador Bunker shot and killed a VC inside the embassy.

"Thank God we got MP reinforcements to help; we were runnin' low on ammo and had dead and wounded MPs; I didn't get a scratch. We killed eight VC.

"We took the dead bodies of our buddies to a mortuary at Ton Son Nhut and they took them to a mortuary collection at Long Binh. I cleared Danny Granger's stuff, boxed it and mailed it to his home in Salt Lake City, Utah. I got a letter from his family thanking me and asking me to write and tell them what happened to their son which I did. That attack was a son-of-a-bitch of a surprise—on a ceasefire, no less. I hate those slope sons-of-bitches."

Nate stood silent.

"Anyhow, Mr. Shaw, the bodies of the dead VC lay at the wall several hours until a South Vietnamese unit came and collected them in bags and put the bodies in the back of a deuce-and one-half truck and hauled them away. The gardeners washed the sidewalk with heavy Clorox, but the bloodstains stayed on the ground at the wall. The blood soaked into the ground and those spots have been there six weeks as a reminder of what happened; I guess."

Lester Shockley opened the embassy door and hollered, "Nate, don't get a sunburn."

Nate answered, "Sergeant Douglas was telling me what he did during the Tet attack."

Nate said, "Sergeant Douglas, you are a fine soldier, you did your duty and did it well."

"Thank you, Sir, I have seventy-nine days and a bag drag to the 'world' I want to get home to Longview, Texas, alive."

They shook hands and Nate picked up his suitcase and went into the embassy.

"Sergeant Douglas is a fine soldier," Nate told Lester Shockley.

"You bet your ass, Nate—if it weren't for Scott Douglas and others like him, we all could have been killed during Tet."

Nate entered the U.S. Embassy; he felt the cool air-conditioning. Lester took Nate to his office on the first floor and introduced him to Francis Dowling; he was the director of Vietnam's Phoenix Operations and reported to William Colby, who ran Phoenix at the CIA Headquarters.

Lester asked Nate about his flight, connections, and did he see Bangkok?

Nate said the flight was fine, connections were on time, but he did not have time to see Bangkok. He planned to visit Thailand in the next two years.

Lester said he was preparing a briefing on the Phoenix Program at MACV, HQ. The U.S. Military Command was concerned about having MACV advisors assigned to the Phoenix Program to "assassinate Viet Cong political infrastructure."

"What in the hell is the problem with the military, Nate? The Viet Cong political infrastructure controls the National Liberation Front and the Viet Cong; they kill ARVN and U.S. soldiers. An enemy is an enemy, if he wants to kill you.

"The communist infrastructure is embedded with the Viet Cong. Who cares whether we kill the political infrastructure or a VC? It's too pure. We're not going into villages to kill innocent women and children. If we locate a Viet Cong company of a hundred enemy soldiers in a village, we're not going to say, excuse me, gentlemen, political infrastructure step aside before the shooting starts! The Viet Cong have assassinated 4,000 civilian GVN officials in South Vietnam since 1954. What in the hell happens if a Viet Cong tax collector fires an AK-47 or an RPG rocket at an American M-113 personnel carrier and kills ten U.S. troops? Sorry, he's political cadre.

"Our goddamn military is too squeamish about this war. Careerism is their main concern—to get the Vietnam ticket punched—unless the CIA and Phoenix program breaks the NLF's control of the countryside, we'll lose this Goddamn war in three years. I'll bet on that!"

Lester looked at his watch, "I've got to be at MACV at 1300. Finish your business in Saigon; we'll have dinner at the Continental Hotel and you'll see the seamy side of this war. I've scheduled briefings for you at J-2, and from our intelligence staff over the next two days. Mr. Chau will drive you to your BOQ. Your room is at the Blanchard BOQ, number 407 under CORDS. Call me when you get to Rach Gia. Good to meet you, Nate."

They shook hands and Lester went out the front entrance and stepped into an embassy sedan to MAVC.

In the next two days, Nate concluded his in-processing and briefings; the following day he flew to Rach Gia on an Air American DC-3. Lt. Col. Berry, U.S. Army Province Senior Advisor, sent a Jeep to meet him at the airstrip. The driver informed Nate that Lt. Col. Berry wanted Nate to meet him and the South Vietnamese Province Chief, Lt. Col. Tran Vo Minh in his office tomorrow morning.

Nate Shaw arrived at the OSA Compound confirming the line, "The best-made plans of mice and men go astray."

The renovation of the OSA building was not done and it would require two more weeks to get finished. Nate met Lt. Col. Berry and Lt. Col. Minh the next morning and they talked about PRU Operations; Nate had to obtain a Memorandum of Agreement for the PRU, and Lt. Col. Minh was requested to designate land upon which to construct a PRU compound for one hundred fifty PRUs and families.

The PRU Commander, Major Lam, told Lt. Col. Berry, "We're returning to Chau Phu if we don't get our compound very soon."

Nate called Lester Shockley and told him the situation at the OSA Compound, about the meeting with Lt. Col. Berry, Lt. Col. Minh and the PRUs. Lester told Nate he would send a helicopter to bring him to Saigon on temporary duty and meet the South Vietnamese Special Police Branch Officers, who had legal authority to arrest Viet Cong political infrastructure. Lester said the CIA fund and train PSB personnel and 100 U.S. military personnel would be assigned to the Phoenix Program. MACV personnel would have a cover, wear civilian clothing while working with their Vietnamese counterparts and would live in the OSA compound. Nate would have operational control of Phoenix Operations.

Lester told Nate to spend a week in Chau Duc with Buster "Muddy" Waters, who had known Lt. Col. Edward Lansdale in 1954, and was a good friend of John Paul Vahn, perhaps the most well-informed American in Vietnam. Muddy Waters and John Paul Vahn both spoke Vietnamese fluently, had excellent contacts, and a wealth of knowledge about Vietnam. Nate left Saigon and visited My Tho and Chau Duc and came down with a high fever, abdominal pain, and diarrhea in Chau Duc. Muddy Waters medically evacuated Nate to the 1127th U.S. Air Force Dispensary on Ton Son Nhut.

Nate Shaw sat in a leather chair in room nine at the 1127 U.S. Air Force Dispensary and waited for Major Brett Dawson, M.D., U.S. Air Force Flight Surgeon. Nate was physically weak and emotionally drained. He wore a U.S. Air Force medical blue robe, cotton pajamas, and paper sandals.

Doctor Dawson had examined him yesterday during morning rounds and the doctor wanted Nate to remain one more day and continue taking antibiotics for his infection.

Nate wanted to return to work, but Doctor Dawson told him he needed time to recover. Otherwise the infection could recur in the large intestine.

Doctor Dawson knocked on Nate's door.

"Come in," said Nate.

Doctor Dawson opened the door wearing green medical scrubs, a stethoscope around his neck, a blood-pressure device in his right hand, and medical charts in his left hand.

"Good morning, Mr. Shaw," said Doctor Dawson. "How are you feeling?"

Nate sat up in the leather chair, tightened his robe, and said, "Better, Doctor Dawson."

"Good," the doctor responded. "How's the diarrhea?"

"Better—no problem last night."

"Good," said Doctor Dawson. "Did you eat yesterday?"

"Yes," said Nate. "I had chicken, salad, and rolls with iced tea for dinner; Nurse Dailey brought me apples and bananas to eat at 2100."

"Alright, Mr. Shaw, let's take a look."

The doctor took Nate's blood pressure, listened to his chest with the stethoscope, examined his throat, felt his abdomen, and said, "Your vital signs are fine, and your abdomen feels normal. Your lab work showed you had a dysentery infection in your large intestine caused by the ingestion of water contaminated with human feces bacteria."

"My God," said Nate. "Really?"

"Yes," said Doctor Dawson. "It sounds horrible. Dr. Cannon, our public health physician, told me the Vietnamese don't have modern water purification facilities in the countryside, and use tap water treated with formaldehyde as a disinfectant to make ice, and bacteria may contaminate the water. It apparently doesn't bother them. Now, I'm not saying this is a common practice, but if well water is contaminated by an overflow of a nearby canal used to dispose of human waste, then that canal water will contaminate the water they drink. That is what happened to you with the ice.

"You told me last Wednesday that you started having severe diarrhea several hours after drinking a soda with ice out in the field near Chau Duc. Your ice was contaminated and made you sick. As far as I can determine, you developed a bacterial sickness, not a parasitic infection like shigellosis; that is much more serious and is an acute intestinal infection which can lead to dehydration and death with a high fever if untreated.

"I have given you three antibiotics to arrest the infection; you will have to take it easy for several days. You've lost ten pounds; I want you to remain here until 1600, eat solid meals, and take your medication. Dr. Yost will check you at 1600. I am leaving Ton Son Nhut at 1300 for R and R to meet my wife and two children in Honolulu. Any questions?"

"No," said Nate.

"Good luck, Mr. Shaw, it's been nice knowing you. By the way, Mr. Shaw, who do you work for in Vietnam?"

"I work for the Agency for International Development in Public Safety."

"AID huh? You seem more like a CIA man—just my doctor's intuition."

"Good-bye."

Nate and Dr. Dawson shook hands and the doctor departed. Nate took a shower, went to the dining hall, ate a breakfast of scrambled eggs, toast, and coffee, and later wrote a letter to Janet.

He looked at the sweat-filled smelly rumpled clothing he had worn for two weeks, which hung in the closet, dirty clothing in his suitcase and a letter he received from Janet six weeks ago. Nate glanced at last week's *Stars and Stripes* newspaper, sat down in the leather chair, and took the three pills Dr. Dawson gave him.

He opened the window blinds. He saw a courtyard, and another wing of the dispensary, and heard helicopters and aircraft overhead.

Nate was discharged and returned to work. The next morning the U.S. Embassy/Military Liaison Officer named Lt. Colonel Rick Meyers gave Nate a "Cook's" tour of Saigon. He drove Nate to see the Saigon River, and the infamous Chung Dow Prison, built by the French in 1917. He drove near a protected area where South Vietnamese Lt. General Nguyen Ngoc Tri had a compound containing construction material but in reality had captured weapons, AK-47 assault rifles, .50-caliber machine guns, Chinese assault rifles, Mauser rifles, mortars, ammunition, RPG rockets and land mines he planned to sell to Cambodia.

Lt. Col. Meyers told Nate that General Tri's compound is always off-limits "two blocks in all directions." It is guarded twenty-four hours a day by an ARVN paratrooper battalion allegedly protecting Saigon. General Tri is the director of the

South Vietnamese Joint Staff, and is a graduate of the South Vietnamese Dalat Military Academy, Vietnam's West Point. The General is among the inner circle of Generals running South Vietnam's war; the story given to Americans is that General Tri has commanded ARVN Ranger battalions, a paratrooper battalion, the ARVN Fifth Division, and III Corps, and is an excellent soldier. He is married to Madam Le Kim Tri, who is called "the Dragon Lady" and runs a black market in Saigon.

General and Mrs. Tri live in a walled French villa adjacent to the South Vietnamese High Command. Lt. Gen. Tri has an impressive appearance and wears starched tiger-stripe fatigues, a maroon beret, sunglasses, shined combat boots, and carries an ivory swagger stick, with paratrooper wings and a pearl-handled .45-caliber pistol in a white holster.

Lt. Col. Myers said, rumor has it Lt. General Tri might succeed President Thieu as President of South Vietnam. He told Nate, "In reality, we know that Lt. General Tri also has stolen U.S. aid including lumber, fertilizer, concrete, tin, generators, air-conditioners, clothing, rice and roofing materials to sell to rich Chinese or South Vietnamese businessmen to make an obscene profit. General Tri probably has five hundred South Vietnamese paratroopers as his loyal palace guard, and makes payments 'down the line' for loyalty to him."

Lt. Col. Meyers said, "General Tri appears untouchable. His base pay is $3,000 U.S. dollars a month, but he and his wife have a $300,000 walled French villa and rake in $20,000 a month in graft and extortion. Madam Tri is called 'The Dragon Lady,' she is beautiful and deadly. Current speculation is that President Thieu is going to appoint Lt. Gen. Tri Commander of the Fourth Corps, replacing Lt. Gen Nguyen Van Khai who is both incompetent and corrupt."

On March eleventh, Nate was discharged from the 1127th dispensary and at 1600 he flew from Saigon to Rach Gia. Lt. Col Berry sent a driver to meet him. Nate arrived at the OSA Compound and found it was still not finished. He decided, in spite of construction, to start organizing an office and living facilities. On March fourteenth, Sgt. Sam Bowman, the first MACV advisor, arrived at Rach Gia as a radio-teletype communications operator. Things got worse.

In a second meeting with Lt. Col. Berry, Lt. Col. Minh and Lt. Col. Berry wanted to begin PRU combat operations, but the PRU's soldiers still did not have their compound.

Their Commander, Major Lam, told Nate, "We live in an old schoolhouse without water; unless our compound is done by April first, we will return to Chau Phu."

Lt. Col. Minh complained, "I have no money to pay PRUs, and barely enough to pay my own 400 Regional Force/Popular Force (RF/PF) soldiers in Kien Giang Province."

Nate wondered if there were really 400 RF/PF to pay. Did Lt. Minh pay only 300 and keep the extra money? Lt. Col. Berry wanted Lt. Col Minh to control the PRUs, and Nate took an exception, and said, "We fund the PRUs, and I will control PRU operations." Nate informed Lt. Col. Berry and Lt. Col. Minh he learned 110 new PRUs would move from Sa Dec and Go Cong to Rach Gia and arrive on April 10th. That would bring PRU strength to 175.

The next problem was the OSA building; power was not reliable over twenty-four hours to run air-conditioning, the Sony 1,000 mega-watt radio communications center and lighting. Two 1,500-watt generators had to be replaced with three, 2,500-watt generators. There were also problems of toilets that did not flush, low water pressure, and a disgusting number of cockroaches, ants, water bugs, and rats the size of cats. One worker from PA & E had shot a rat with his pistol when the rat was cornered, bared its teeth, and charged him.

Nate documented the renovation problems and sent a report to Lester Shockley about the condition of the OSA Compound.

Nate received a message from Lester Shockley telling him he would go TDY in Saigon until the repairs of the OSA were completed. He and Sgt. Bowman would be flown to Saigon. Sgt. Bowman would work at the U.S. Embassy Communications Center. Lester Shockley closed his message saying, "Don't despair—get a two-by-four and smack the rats until the building is exterminated!" He told Mr. Kim, the PA & E construction manager, to contact him in Saigon when renovations were finished.

On March twenty-first, Nate Shaw and Sam Bowman departed Rach Gia; the next six weeks Nate saw sides of the Vietnam War that he had never seen, nor was ever disclosed in "Vanilla" briefings he received in Washington.

Nate had been in-country one month. He reported to Lester Shockley at the U.S. Embassy and told him about the situation with Lt. Col. Berry, Lt. Col. Minh, and the PRUs. He asked permission from Lester Shockley to go to the MARS facility to call Janet. Lester said, "Of course, check into the Blanchard BOQ. I reserved a room for you as Colonel A. Shaw. Call Janet, then we'll go to dinner at the Continental Hotel like colonial gentlemen."

Arthur drove to MACV, obtained entrance to the MARS facility, and called Janet. He was thrilled when she answered the telephone and he enjoyed talking to her, Sarah, Arthur, Jr., Jennifer, and hearing Tyler barking. They caught up; Janet said she had written four letters mailed to the Advisory Team, APO San Francisco 94101, Rach Gia and three letters were returned stamped "No Name for Delivery." Nate told Janet to write to the U.S. Embassy in Saigon c/o APO San Francisco 94115 and they would be forwarded to him in a mail pouch. They said their "I love you's" and Nate hung up and felt better, his morale was higher after talking to Janet and his children.

He drove back to the U.S. Embassy. It was 7:10 P.M. Lester drove an embassy French Citroen to the Continental Hotel, which was parked by valet parking when they arrived under a large green canopy. The Continental Hotel was a place of intrigue and written about by Graham Greene in *The Quiet American* as a world-famous "watering hole" for spies, counter-spies, and expensive prostitutes. They walked through the lobby of the Continental on a thick burgundy carpet. There were ceiling fans, and a lobby with planted ferns, tropical flowers, and bonsai trees. They walked past the main bar and saw numerous young and beautiful Vietnamese women wearing short tight dresses with spiked heels. Several smiled at Lester and Nate. Lester went to the men's room.

"Let's eat outside and watch the scenery." Nate thought of Charlie Fenton's comment at the Smokehouse in Pasadena ten years ago. The maître d' took them to a table facing Tu Do Street. Before they were comfortable, two very attractive young Vietnamese women approached their table wearing jewelry, mini-skirts, delicate make-up.

One with long, black hair asked Lester, "May we join you?" The other smiled at Nate and ran her long red fingernails up and down his neck, and said, "I am a very good companion" in perfect English. The two women stood and smiled at Lester and Nate. The other girl pressed Lester's shoulder and rubbed his neck. Nate sat in silence.

Lester said, "Thank you, ladies, we are flattered, but not tonight."

One girl said, "You miss good time, G.I. Why not tonight, no money?"

Lester pulled out his leather vest wallet, removed $100.00 and gave each girl $50.00 and said, "No tricky, no money tonight, honey; next time both of you for all night." The girl smiled and kissed Lester's cheek. "Thank you," she said. They walked back to the bar swinging their hips, as one glanced back and waved her bright red fingernails and said, "Next time for sure, G.I—all night" and they both went back into the hotel bar to charm another customer.

Lester said, "My, oh my, temptation, temptation, and more temptation, lordy be."

A waiter approached their table and speaking English with a French accent, said, "Good evening, gentlemen, will you be joining us for dinner tonight?"

The waiter was distinguished-looking with smooth, clear, light-brown skin, straight white teeth, black hair groomed straight back on his head in an Errol Flynn cut, wearing a starched white shirt, black bow tie, white waiter's jacket, black trousers, and black patent leather shoes.

Lester ordered himself a double Beefeater's martini, and for Nate a Beefeater's gin and tonic with two limes. "My treat tonight."

The waiter returned with their drinks and brought them two cups of mixed nuts.

Lester took a sip of his martini and made a Jackie Gleason, "Mumm-good-mumm good."

It was now getting dark and streetlights shone along Tu Do Boulevard. They looked at the people on Tu Do Boulevard. Several Vietnamese National Police in white shirts and dark trousers took positions along Tu Do, with about fifty ARVN military police.

Lester said, "Americans call the Vietnamese National Police 'white mice.' "

He then said, "This is the time of night shit happens in Saigon—VC terrorist attacks. I hope not tonight."

The veranda filled up with people having dinner. Some men wore formal attire or military uniforms, and others were joined by "Companions"; the two pretty young Vietnamese women returned with two older gentlemen. The same one who talked to Lester said as she passed, "Next time, G.I."

Nate told Lester, "I've never seen so many beautiful women. Where do they come from?"

Lester said, "Nate, this is Saigon—these women work for somebody who brought them here to be 'Companions.' Many of them come from the countryside and other cities to work in Saigon. It is all being controlled as a money-making business by Vietnamese in high places—either the GVN or ARVN."

Lester ordered another round of drinks. Lester talked about the war, living in Europe and the waiter brought them menus, and took their orders for dinner. Lester ordered two large fresh shrimp cocktails, cold Chinese noodle salads, the Chateaubriand for two, braised potatoes, with fresh asparagus spears. He ordered a bottle of 1959 French merlot.

When they had finished their dinner, the veranda was full as the orchestra played Glenn Miller's "Tuxedo Junction" in the ballroom. Many of the guests now had companions.

Lester ordered two snifters of cognac after dinner. Nate asked Lester, "How much do these girls charge for sex?"

Lester surveyed the veranda. He replied, "It's the old law of supply and demand. These women are smart and work together." Lester leaned to Nate, "See that older gentleman with our girls? They'll rub his legs, his crotch during dinner and talk sweet. If he accepts, they'll tell him, 'We must go together by the rules.' The price, $300.00 paid to the waiter up-front and they go to the room for one, maybe two hours and they want a tip for $50.00; total $350.00 to $400.00. If the guy is loaded, the hotel will tell them and the price is $500.00. One girl all night is $800.00 cash for whatever is your pleasure. They can make $2,000 to $3,000 a week with one-half to their sponsors. It's all business. No fuss, no muss. Some V.D. is a problem."

Nate was relaxed. He was fascinated by Vietnam and how they could have such an elegant dinner at a world-class hotel in the middle of a war zone. It was surreal; *Any minute,* he thought, *I could wake up in Tucson.*

Lester paid $150.00, which included a tip. He told Nate, "The same meal in a comparable hotel in New York City or Washington would be $275."

A valet brought the French Citroen, and Lester pulled into traffic on Tu Do Boulevard. He turned off the radio, turned up the air-conditioning, and told Nate, "Nate, we need to talk business."

Nate shut the passenger window and looked at people dining at a sidewalk café.

"Nate," Lester began; "we have a high-ranking North Vietnamese named Tran Van Phuc at the Chung Dow prison in Saigon. He was among nineteen NVA soldiers and political cadre captured near My Tho during Tet. We interrogated Phuc without any success. As best we can determine, and from information obtained from other prisoners, he is a high-ranking member of the Lao Dong Communist Party in Hanoi, and a possible friend of Ho Chi Minh and probably a colonel in the NVA. We *must* find out soon, the South Vietnamese PSB want his ass.

"You speak Russian, and we want you to talk to him in Russian. He is permitted to go outside one hour a day."

Nate asked Lester, "What would me talking to him in Russian do to make him cooperate?"

Lester replied, "We know the PSB have listening devices in interrogation rooms—that's why he's silent. He told the PSB he lived in Moscow and his father was a member of the French Cultural Legation in Moscow from 1930 to 1937. He lived in Moscow from age twelve to seventeen, went to school and learned to speak Russian, I'm sure. The French government used his father, Dr. Lam Tuan Phuc, as their example of what the French called progressive education in Vietnam to educate the people. We believe his father was a member of the Lao Dong Communist Party and closely affiliated with Ho Chi Minh and Le Duc Tho. Nate, we have two days or the PSB will throw his ass in prison or shoot him."

Nate asked, "How do I contact him?"

Lester said, "I made arrangements for you to talk to him tomorrow from three to four at Chung Dow Prison. I'll pick you up at two and get you through the red tape at Chung Dow with the Vietnamese. This meeting is SECRET and with plausible denial. Phuc could be a fake with disinformation to embarrass us. I ask you to do your best."

"I will," said Nate.

"The other matter is Top Secret concerning General Nguyen Ngoc Tri and Madam Tri.

"We learned on July first he is taking command of Fourth Corps, on orders from President Thieu. He will command three ARVN divisions, twenty-first, ninth, and seventh with 15,000 troops. His real job is Coup'd etre' protection for President Thieu. One division is always on call to get to Saigon. It doesn't bode well for the Phoenix Program, or Pacification in Fourth Corps.

"Our source on the joint general staff informed us that Tri paid $50,000 U.S. dollars for his assignment to command Fourth Corps. He'll rip off $100,000 a year in shakedowns of his subordinates, diversion of financial aid, materials, and extortion of the Chinese in the Mekong Delta. Our source also told us after Tet, he arrested four prominent Chinese businessmen in Cholon. He claimed they were North Vietnam sympathizers, and jailed them under the South Vietnam's War Security Act. He seized their three hotels claiming they were purchased by 'War profiteering and trading money,' and also took control of a company which exports rice to Taiwan and Japan. Those businesses were worth two million U.S. dollars.

"He assigned his nephew, Colonel Do Duc Long, to command the ARVN Tenth Infantry Brigade in Saigon as a 'Conservator of the properties' to signal other businessmen not to cooperate with the enemy. We know Madam Le Kim Tri owns two shops and three flesh clubs on Trung Le Boulevard, which sell black-market products stolen from warehouses. The products she sells are: hair spray, Tide laundry soap, tampons, pantyhose, sport clothing, under clothing, shoes, toothpaste, tooth brushes, television sets, towels, washcloths, sunglasses, razors and hairdryers. She has cutouts run her sleazy vice dens along Trung Le, which now include a strip joint, massage parlor and 'girl' bar. She 'recruits' her women from the countryside, brings them to Saigon and puts them up in fleabag hotels as prostitutes, informants, and to push drugs, marijuana or opium-laced cigarettes on U.S. troops. She probably has fifty girls working for her at any one time.

"It's a shell game to identify where they operate; two of our undercover agents posing as civilian contractors bought opium-laced cigarettes in the 'Have Fun Club.' The club was closed, and it was reopened a week later called the 'Saigon Princess.'

"We've had enough of the General and Madam Tri.

"Our source on the Joint Vietnamese Staff is paid $10,000 a month which is deposited in gold certificates into the Bank of France. The source says General Tri is going to organize a fake 'VC' attack on the warehouse, and use prisoners to unload the warehouse onto an ocean-going barge, sail up to Cam Rahn Bay and sell the goods. Fertilizer, wood, tin, concrete, nails, saws, wheelbarrows, electrical generators and electrical wiring will be sold to rich Chinese businessmen for a quick profit of $200,000 U.S dollars.

"We plan to greet General Tri at the barge and take him out with a hit squad and perform a coup de grace at the villa on Madam Tri. It is called Operation Scarecrow," continued Lester. "Frank Dowling told me to brief you in person in Saigon. I will employ twenty Cambodian Nungs to do the job."

Lester stopped the Citroen at the Blanchard; he looked at Nate and said, "Nate, this is Vietnam, not Europe—This is a dirty, nasty war, we're dealing with corrupt evil people, who would sell their mother for $10,000. We do what we have to do;

who knows how many American GI's got hooked on dope in Saigon at Madam Tri's shithole clubs. This is not a lawn party in the Hamptons; it is a nasty place where people get killed. See you tomorrow at 1000."

Nate opened the car door, got out of the Citroen, waved good-bye to Lester, and entered the Blanchard BOQ. He showed his I.D. card to an M.P., took an elevator to his room, number 409, took a shower and retired.

The following morning Mr. Chau drove Nate to Ton Son Nhut, the post-exchange, and he bought mosquito spray, a flashlight, batteries, sunglasses, Bayer aspirin, and heavy shoes to replace his hush puppies. He came to the U.S. Embassy at 10:00 A.M.

Lester made the required telephone calls; he told Nate, "General Luong, the ARVN Assistant Deputy Chief for Intelligence, speaks fluent English. The General said, 'The meeting with the traitor Phuc will be conducted on our terms and under our control, or no meeting.' Here are the General's conditions:

"One—A contribution of $15,000 U.S. dollars for the Saigon Children's Fund at the Bank of Canton by 11:00 A.M. He will go to the bank at 1:00 P.M. to pick-up the deposit as I control the Saigon Children's Fund.

"Two—Your CIA man is permitted thirty minutes with the traitor.

"Three—No notes. Do not touch the prisoner or have the prisoner touch the CIA man.

"Four—Sign a form that the prisoner is being treated humanely under the Geneva Convention."

Lester received a call from Francis Dowling regarding General Luong's conditions.

Francis Dowling said, "It's worth the risk, if Nate Shaw can talk to him in Russian, I'm sure he'll open up. Go ahead, deposit the money, and sign the consent form. We need Luong's cooperation."

Lester deposited $15,000 dollars at the Bank of Canton.

Lester and Nate drove to Chung Dow Prison, a former French prison built in 1917 on the Saigon River. The prison was notorious for brutality and summary executions of Viet Minh and Viet Cong, and dumping the bodies into the Saigon River.

Lester parked the Citroen outside Chung Dow; they were met and went through security procedures. A PSB officer escorted them to General Luong's office.

"Thank you for your generous contribution to the Saigon Children's Fund, I will put it to good use."

General Luong said, "Follow him." An aide to General Luong opened a heavy steel door, they walked past cellblocks showing green mold, smelling of urine and vomit, and saw men chained to walls. General Luong did not say a word. It was dark, dank and a horrible dungeon—a human hellhole. Nate saw the famous stone wall where prisoners were summarily executed. General Luong stopped in front of a cell, "Mr. Shockley, here is the traitor. You have thirty minutes."

A guard came, unlocked the cell door and put Phuc's hands into handcuffs and legs into leg irons above his feet.

"The traitor is yours," General Loung told Lester.

General Luong made a comment in Vietnamese to Phuc, which Nate understood.

"You traitor bastard, my preference is to cut off your dick, stuff it down your throat and shoot you; these stupid fucking Americans want to talk to you; talk to the asshole cowboys." Nate heard about General Luong's dislike of Americans.

General Luong and Lester walked back to General Luong's office. Nate Shaw extended his hand toward Colonel Phuc in friendship.

Nate said in Vietnamese, "I am here to help our countries—we must act quickly. Do not fear me."

Colonel Phuc stared at Nate and said, "You imperialist—what can you do to help me? America will lose the war and go home in disgrace."

Nate said in Vietnamese, "What is your name? I am Nate Shaw."

The prisoner said, "Nate Shaw, of CIA" in perfect English.

The prisoner then said, "My name is Tran Van Phuc, North Vietnam 276th Battalion, captured near My Tho by ARVN on February 27, 1968. No more."

Nate said, "Phuc—General Luong will kill you."

Phuc said, "I am not afraid to die for the liberation of our fatherland."

Nate was exasperated.

"Phuc, do you speak Russian?"

Phuc's eyes lit up, "Yes, good."

"Let us walk outside to talk."

Nate rang a bell; General Luong appeared.

"May we go outside for fresh air in the courtyard?"

General Luong glared at Phuc, and said, "You communist bastard, no tricks or I will shoot you here and now," and he placed his right hand on a pistol. Phuc and Nate went out into the courtyard. Nate said in Russian, "What must I do to have you trust me?"

Phuc said in Russian, "Don't lie to me."

Nate said, "How can we contact Hanoi?"

Phuc said, "The war will end when the puppet government in Saigon is defeated and all Americans are gone."

Nate looked at his watch—twenty minutes.

Phuc said in English, "I graduated in 1941 from American University in Washington."

Nate was dumbfounded at hearing Phuc speak perfect English.

"I came home to help fight and drive the Japanese and French and now Americans from Vietnamese soil. Now I fight the Americans."

General Luong hollered, "Fifteen minutes."

Phuc said, "Do this, Mr. Nate. Send this message to Hanoi Peoples Committee, Building 701, Code 290106.

Spring rain brings flowers
Flowers bloom until fall
Fall withers the flowers
Spring returns flowers.

Nate memorized the message.

"Five minutes," said General Luong.

"This message will make action happen—believe me," said Phuc. "I have nothing more to say, return me to my cell."

They returned to Phuc's cell, bid farewell, and Nate repeated the code and message in his mind.

He met Lester and wrote down what Phuc told him. Lester drove to the U.S. Embassy and sent a flash message to CIA Headquarters with the code and message. The U.S. State Department relayed the code and message to Hanoi.

In twenty-four hours Saigon and newspapers around the world said: "Hanoi agrees to talk with U.S."

"In an undisclosed meeting site, a U.S. envoy met with the North Vietnam's Deputy High Command, General Tran Van Phuc, who agreed to renew talks to end the war."

The message Nate Shaw received in code said: "I am alive and well. This man can be trusted. Arrange to meet U.S. in Vientiane, Laos."

"Deputy Commissioner to Ho Chi Minh, Tran Van Phuc."

Nate Shaw could not believe what he read in *The New York Times*.

Tran Van Phuc was released by the GVN and flown to Hanoi after the CIA paid $150,000 to the Bank of Canton for the South Vietnam Refugee Fund, which went to a high-ranking GVN official or ARVN General.

When Nate returned to Rach Gia, the OSA building renovation was finished! The building, he learned, had once been a Chinese hotel now being rented by the CIA, for the "Office of the Special Assistant." The building had six rooms with two large bathrooms on the first floor, and four rooms on the second floor. In front was a canal and on the other side of the land was the thick jungle foliage. It now had air-conditioning, running water, and toilets that flushed. Nate selected a front bedroom on the second floor. The following week, heavy-gauge wire was strung across the front of the building to deflect rocket-grenade fire, and two guard posts surrounded by sandbags were built up the front of the building. Nate's room was now equipped with a Sony 1000 megawatt short-wave radio, and an encryption machine to contact Fourth Corps Headquarters and MACV Headquarters in Saigon.

Buster "Muddy" Waters told Nate in Chau Duc, "The Tet Offensive has now put a shitty face on the war. The Pacification Program once touted to be successful is a failure and the strategic Hamlet Program moving Vietnamese peasants and their families has alienated the people living in the countryside who now support the Viet Cong."

Nate Shaw's chain of command was from Lester Shockley, Deputy Director of Phoenix, to Francis Dowling, the CIA Station Chief in Saigon. Nate Shaw drew a $25,000 monthly operations fund. His mission was:

1. Stand up the Provincial Interrogation Center.
2. Get "in bed" with the PSB Chief, arrest Viet Cong infrastructure and conduct bilateral intelligence collection for information for use on PRU combat operations.
3. Organize, train, and fund the PRUs at a strength of 175 men; finish the PRU's compound.
4. Organize and staff the Provincial Intelligence Operations Coordination Center (PIOCC's) with MACV and District Intelligence Operations Collection Centers (DIOCC's).
5. Stand up the New Life Cadre Program to make presentations in the countryside.
6. Hire a Vietnamese interpreter.
7. May 1, 1968, PRU combat operations will commence.

Nate Shaw received a letter from Lester Shockley. The letter informed Nate that seven MACV personnel were assigned to him and they would report to OSA on June 1, 1968. Four were U.S. Army Officers, two U.S. Navy Seals, and two Special Forces enlisted.

The Province Senior Advisor was the coordination point for U.S. Army operations in Province, and U.S. Army helicopter support. MACV personnel would receive their Officers and Enlisted Efficiency Reports from Nate Shaw, Rater, and the Province Senior Advisor, Endorser. Clearly, U.S. Army personnel were assigned to work for the CIA. MACV personnel would wear civilian clothing when contacting Vietnamese civilian agencies, and wear their tiger uniforms and maroon berets in the field. MACV personnel were to billeted at the OSA compound.

On April 19, 1968, Nate Shaw received an embassy pouch informing him the names of MACV personnel assigned to OSA:

Major Stanley Roland, U.S. Army, Infantry; Captain Theodore R. Graham, U.S. Army, Military Intelligence; Captain Jefferson Lee Madison, IV, U.S. Army, Special Forces; Petty Officer First Class Billy Flynn, U.S. Navy SEAL; Petty Officer First Class Jesse Roberts, U.S. Navy SEAL; Sergeant Samuel Bowman, U.S. Army, Signal Corps; PFC Joseph Molinski, U.S. Army, Special Forces; and SFC Sean Morgan, U.S. Army Special Forces; PFC Patrick Blake, U.S. Army Special Forces.

Begin construction for the PRU Compound.

On May 2, 1968, Major Stanley Roland, Petty Officer First Class Billy Flynn, and Petty Officer First Class Jesse Roberts reported to Nate Shaw.

Nate took them to meet Lt. Col. Berry and Lt. Col. Minh. During the meeting, Lt. Col. Minh said his agents reported fifty to seventy-five Viet Cong were operating east of Kien Binh District and were recruiting boys to join the Viet Cong, posting propaganda, buying food and rice and carrying AK-47s, .30 caliber machine guns, RPG rockets and wearing black pajamas.

After the meeting, Nate told Stan Roland, Billy Flynn, and Jesse Roberts he was going to relay the Province Chief's intelligence to Major Lam.

Major Lam said, "I do not act on only one source of information."

Major Lam continued. "I'll send my own PRU scouts to collect the information, draw maps, or kidnap a wood cutter, farmer or VC to interrogate—they know the locations of the Viet Cong. We won't disclose any information, no spies and no tricks by the VC against my PRUs."

Nate told Major Lam, "With solid intelligence I can get Huey helicopters, Cobra gunships, and artillery fire to support the operation. If the enemy has strength of 200 to 300 Viet Cong, the Air Force at Ton Son Nhut will scramble F-102 and F-105 jets, and drop napalm and fire rockets on the enemy. I have my own intelligence agents and get some information from the PSB, the Chieu Hois, prisoners, or the Provincial Intelligence Center."

Major Lam said, "The VC have many tricks and put out information to trick U.S. soldiers or PRUs into an ambush or trap. My PRUs will capture VC, make them talk or kill one in front of their comrades so others talk soon. Mr. Nate, when do we get our new equipment and a compound? My men are very impatient and more unhappy and no like Rach Gia."

Nate told Major Lam, "Very soon, a week or two, I promise."

Nate received a shipment of Australian bush clothing that he had purchased which was more suited to jungle operations. He purchased five Australian field uniforms, two pairs of tough leather boots with a steel shank in the sole, a two-way radio with a 100-mile range, German field binoculars, and newer maps. He decided to carry a .9-millimeter Glock pistol with a nine-bullet magazine and two additional magazines in his field pocket. He also had a GAR-15 automatic rifle with a folding stock in his OSA office.

Lester Shockley told Nate he could go on field operations with Major Lam, but was never to fly on assault helicopters. His job was to collect intelligence, locate and identify enemy targets for the PRUs to attack. If he were captured he would be tortured and shot. He was given a tin with two cyanide capsules.

Nate had his operation nearly ready to go, and he was getting anxious for MACV personnel to arrive at Rach Gia.

The PRUs still wore assorted uniforms, and needed more equipment, weapons, and homes for their wives, children, and animals.

On May 15, 1968, Lt. Col. Berry called Nate to the Colonel's office, which was now located in a renovated villa in the center of Rach Gia.

The Colonel told Nate that Lt. Col Minh had given the PRUs land by the old French school for their base camp.

Nate told Major Lam who was pleased. Nate also told Major Lam he was going to Saigon to pick up the shipment for Major Lam. He needed to have thirty PRUs and five two and one-half-ton trucks at the airfield to unload the C-130 when it arrived. The shipment he ordered had been approved at Langley.

On June 17th, Nate Shaw and Stan Roland sat in an OSA van at the Rach Gia airstrip. They saw a silver Air America C-47 circle the airfield, descend and make a landing facing north on the runway. The pilot taxied the C-47 and stopped 200 feet from their van. The crew chief opened the cargo door, set a four-step metal ladder on the ground below the open cargo door, and motioned Nate to board the airplane. The pilot, Joe Anderson, left the airplane's engines running, which churned up dust, dirt, and sand, around the airplane.

Stan looked at Nate, "He wants you to board the airplane. The pilot wants to have a quick return take-off."

"You're right," answered Nate.

"Pull the van alongside the airplane. I don't want to get covered with that dirt and crap."

"Sure," said Stan. He started the engine, made a circle, and pulled the van on the left side of the aircraft in front of the open door. Wind and turbulence from the engines kicked up more dust and sand around the airplane.

Nate took a handkerchief, placed it over his face, got out of the van and hollered, "Call you tomorrow," and climbed up the metal ladder into the C-47. The crew chief said, "Welcome aboard, Mr. Shaw. I'm Dale Hawkins, crew chief; Joe Alexander is the pilot. Joe didn't want to shut the engines down in case we came under fire. Have a seat."

Dale Hawkins put a radio mike in front his mouth; he asked, "Ready to depart?"

Nate sat down in a jump seat, and buckled the seat belt and harness tightly over his chest.

The pilot pushed the throttle of the C-47 engines, which made a high-pitched roar, and the C-47 taxied down the runway and was airborne; Nate looked out a window and saw familiar jungle foliage and rice paddies pass below the aircraft as it gained altitude.

Dale Hawkins spoke to Nate, "Our flight to Saigon is one hour and forty-five, weather is clear; ETA at Ton Son Nhut is 1531."

"Fine," replied Nate.

Nate rested his head back on the interior nylon netting behind the seat and fell asleep. He awoke at 3:00 and heard Dale Hawkins say, "He is meeting someone at the terminal at 1600—that's all I know."

The C-47 landed at Ton Son Nhut and the pilot taxied the aircraft to a stop two hundred feet from a white metal-clad building. Beside the building were parked a Cessna 110, C-130, and four silver Huey helicopters with Air America on the fuselage.

Joe Alexander saw Nate, "Your C-130 is over yonder, number 4961. Your equipment arrived from Bangkok yesterday on the same C-130 with Alan Shepherd and Brian Post, the pilot and co-pilot. Alan Shepherd wants to see you inside the terminal at 1630 to make the final arrangements to deliver the equipment at Rach Gia."

"Good," said Nate.

"I've got to debrief, see you later."

Joe and Nate shook hands; Joe walked back to the C-47. Nate walked toward the Air America terminal, entered through a door, showed his I.D. tag to a security guard, and walked down a hallway to a room with a sign on the door, LOUNGE-AIR AMERICA PERSONNEL ONLY.

Nate walked into the lounge, and up to a man standing behind the counter and presented his AA I.D. card. He said, "I'm Nate Shaw here to meet Alan Shepherd at 1630."

The man said, "He's here, I just saw him." The lounge was cool from air conditioning. The man at the counter called and said, "I'll page Alan, have a seat."

Nate went to the soda machine, and bought a Coca-Cola and sat down at a table. He picked up a *Time Magazine* dated May 20, 1968, and began to look at it. *Time* had a featured report of ten pages of color pictures showing Vietnam. Nate leafed through the magazine and saw an article entitled "The Agony of Vietnam." Three pages showed pictures of U.S. Army soldiers with the First Infantry Division, the Twenty-fifth Infantry Division and 101st Airborne Division during combat operations. One picture showed a 155 artillery battery fire base for the Twenty-fifth Division; two pictures showed the huge explosion of B-52 bombing and napalm explosions in vivid red and orange over the jungle; one picture showed South Vietnamese refugees fleeing down Highway One. The last two pages showed wounded American soldiers lifted on Medivac helicopters and graphic pictures of wounds and blood on torn green jungle fatigues and an M-16 lying on the ground.

Nate put *Time* back on the rack, finished his Coke, and put the empty can into a trashcan.

A middle-aged man, with salt-and-pepper bushy hair entered the lounge; he was wearing a black Air America flight suit. He looked at Nate and said, "You must be *the* Nate Shaw from Rach Gia? I'm Alan Shepherd; you have the hottest damn air cargo shipment into Saigon I've seen in a long time!

"I arrived from Manila on Tuesday flying in a C-130 to Bangkok and was due for a four-day layover in Bangkok. I no sooner was debriefed in Bangkok when Tray Atkins, the director of AA flight operations, told me, 'There is a loaded C-130 with 18,000 pounds of cargo due at Ton Son Nhut on Thursday.'

"I said 'Tracy, what's the rush?'

"He said it was an urgent shipment from CONUS through Manila; the other pilot, Brian Pearson, deadheaded back to Honolulu.

"Tracy said, 'You and Tom Healey are laid on to fly the C-130 to Ton Son Nhut on June seventeenth and meet a Mr. Shaw at 1600 in the AA lounge.'"

Nate said, "I'm glad the shipment arrived so quickly, with all the cargo coming into Saigon."

Alan said, "I checked flight operations. They told me Rach Gia has a ten-thousand-foot-length air strip made from asphalt and concrete in 1952 by the French. It is visual approach only with encroaching jungle and there are no runway lights or markers, except some faded directional arrows on the runway. Does that sound right?" asked Alan Shepherd to Nate.

"Yes," said Nate, "No control tower and the runway is in fair condition with small potholes, and the surface is mostly rough and uneven."

"Okay. My co-pilot, Tom Healey, is a good pilot. The weather tomorrow is ninety degrees, humidity, intermittent rain and wind at forty-five knots off Rach Gia Bay. We'll have 18,000 pounds of packed cargo, bound in plywood containers with steel bands and nine containers each weighing two thousand pounds. I will arrive at 1230 and depart NLT 1630," said Alan.

"I don't want to wait one minute more than is necessary for a possible VC mortar attack. We'll have two, 2,500-pound forklifts with us. I want to leave in four hours; bring enough men with steel band cutters, crowbars, heavy sledgehammers to break open containers and two drivers to operate 2,500-pound forklifts. You will also need four two-and-a-half-ton trucks to load the equipment and transport it back to Rach Gia."

Alan handed Nate a manila envelope. "Here is the inventory of your equipment."

"The weight shows 18,000 pounds of nasty stuff for you and your CIA mercenary army of paid killers," said Alan and smiled.

"Only my opinion," added Alan. "Any questions?"

"None," Nate replied.

"Good, I'll meet you tomorrow at 1000 in the lounge. The pre-flight check will be done and Tom and I will chauffeur you and your shipment to lovely Rach Gia by the bay. Have a good night," said Alan.

"I will."

Alan and Nate shook hands. Alan left the lounge and went into the crew locker room. He reappeared in ten minutes wearing a yellow golf shirt, a gold-link chain necklace, dark gray slacks, and black Dingo boots. He departed through the back door of the terminal, and walked across the tarmac toward the main gate of Ton Son Nhut. A very attractive young woman with white blonde hair arrived, driving a black French Peugeot. She wore a lavender sundress and a matching lavender headband; she stopped on the road, met Alan, and gave him a hug and kiss. She then placed her tote bag into the car's trunk, and got into the front passenger's seat. Nate thought, *Alan has a Swedish companion in Saigon!*

Nate went back to the Air America terminal and called the U.S. Embassy. He requested transportation from the terminal back to the Blanchard BOQ. The U.S. Embassy dispatcher told Nate to meet the black Land Rover at Tran Duc Gate; Mr. Diem was the driver. Nate left the Air America terminal and walked along a massive building to an eight-foot-high wrought-iron gate on Tran Duc. The weather was warm and balmy. Nate saw the ever-present layer of blue-gray ozone smog over Saigon. The sounds of horns and traffic continued to honk along Tran Duc Boulevard. A South Vietnamese soldier came to the gate and unlocked it for him when Mr. Diem arrived in the Land Rover.

As Mr. Diem drove Nate to the U.S. Embassy he perused his four months in Vietnam. The OSA building renovation was finished. Mail was arriving from Janet and she now received his monthly pay allotments at the Bank of Tucson, and had the health insurance for the children. Nate had his Memorandum of Agreement from Langley specifying that he had operational control of the PRU; MACV Advisors were present for duty. He also felt much better since his bout with the bacterial infection had healed. He was ready to kick ass.

Nate had dinner. Mr. Diem gave him a package with a watch worn like the one worn by Captain Graham. Lester Shockley bought the watch for him at the PX. Mr. Diem took him to the Blanchard BOQ. Nate bought a *Stars and Stripes,* went to his room, took a shower, and turned on AFN radio. He fell asleep and was awakened at 0600 by a telephone call from Lester Shockley asking him to have breakfast at the U.S. Embassy dining room at 0730. Nate got up, got dressed and met Mr. Diem and arrived at the U.S. Embassy dining room at 0730. Lester was sitting at a table in the dining room with its white linen tablecloths on each table, freshly cut flowers, and a breakfast menu of eggs, pancakes, waffles, bacon, sausage, cereal, fresh fruit, toast, and coffee for $1.75.

Lester Shockley said, "Well, Mr. Shaw, I haven't seen you in eight days. Where have you been?" and laughed.

Lester ordered a waffle and sausage for breakfast; Nate ordered two scrambled eggs, bacon, toast, and coffee.

"Rusty Reed called me yesterday from AA air cargo," Lester told Nate. "He met Alan Shepherd and everything is in order for the flight to Rach Gia."

"Yes, I talked to Alan yesterday," replied Nate.

"Alan was concerned about the length and condition of the air strip at Rach Gia to support the weight; he checked with AA operations who said the airstrip is ten thousand feet and accommodates a C-130. Otherwise, we'd have to unload the C-130 and reload it onto a C-47 and make two flights, which would be a hell of a job.

"I checked the inventory and it included everything I requested," said Nate.

"Beginner's luck! They like you in Washington for the work you did in Europe; we want to see you succeed in the next two years," said Lester.

"President Johnson recently allocated thirty million more dollars for intelligence in Vietnam. The CIA receives twenty million for Phoenix.

"Chris Larson, the Deputy Director of Logistics at Langley said he never saw any field request get approval so quickly. Your request arrived at Washington on March twenty-eighth, went directly to Harold Taylor, Director of Logistics, who endorsed it over to our comptroller, Steve Carter. Steve looked up the GSA wholesale cost and delivery schedule. The request was approved. Everything you requisitioned was available from stocks at Fort Dix, Fort Hamilton Depot, New Cumberland Army Depot and Anniston Army Depot.

"The shipment arrived at Fort Dix on May first, was loaded on railroad cars and arrived at Oakland Army Base on May fourteenth. The shipment was boxed into containers at Oakland Army Base on May twentieth and arrived on June eleventh at Bangkok, where it was loaded onto a C-130 and flown to Saigon on June seventeenth. Amazing.

"The cost of your purchase, Mr. Shaw, is $301,000, Congratulations!"

Lester reached into his coat and handed Nate a sheet of paper. "These are my operational requirements:

"Get PRU strength to 175 troops.

"Your monthly PRU payroll is thirty thousand dollars, send me your payroll each month and unit strength.

"The base pay of a PRU recruit is one hundred fifty dollars, compared to an ARVN private who gets twenty-seven dollars, if he is paid at all."

Lester continued, "Your intelligence operations fund is

twenty-five thousand dollars a month, I'll break it out later. Your operation costs a cool one million dollars a year."

Mr. Mhi brought their breakfast.

"Have you heard from your family?" asked Lester.

"Yes, mail now comes to Rach Gia in the mail pouch," answered Nate. "I received seven letters—everyone is fine, thank you."

Nate and Lester finished breakfast at 8:30.

"Care for another cup of Joe?" asked Lester.

"No, thanks."

"Mind if I have one?"

"No, boss, take as many as you like."

"Good answer," said Lester.

He motioned to Mr. Mhi to bring him another cup of coffee.

"Yes, Sir, Mr. Lester, let me take plates and bring coffee," said Mhi.

"Mr. Shaw want cup of coffee?"

"No, thanks," replied Nate.

Mhi returned with Lester's cup of coffee in a china cup and saucer with a white linen napkin.

"I no longer light up a cigarette on my second cup like I did flying in the Army Air Corps in World War Two," added Lester.

"You were a pilot in the Army Air Corps in World War Two?" asked Nate, sounding surprised.

"I sure as hell was."

"Still water runs deep," said Lester.

Lester finished his coffee, gave Mhi ten dollars and told him, "Keep the change."

"Let's go to my office," said Lester.

They left the dining room, walking through a set of white double French doors, down a hallway with thick gray carpet into Lester's office.

"Have a seat, Nate. Let me use the little boy's room."

Nate sat down in a large burgundy leather chair, beside another matching leather chair in front of Lester's desk. Lester also had an executive leather chair, a desk with two telephones, and a sign on his desk which read: THE BUCK STOPS HERE—OTHERWISE, THE BUCK GETS FUCKED UP.

The air-conditioning made his office cool by 8:30. It was decorated with gray carpeting, blue drapes, a conference table in the back of the room with four chairs, sofa, and on one wall was a bookcase containing books with history, aviation, Oriental art, and the classics. On another was a walnut gun cabinet, holding two M-16 rifles and two UZI submachine guns with loaded magazines. A large Oriental fish tank set next to the gun case containing Japanese goldfish and a sign, USE WEAPONS WITH CARE—YOU MIGHT HURT SOMEONE, INCLUDING US.

Lester's office also had plants, bonsai trees, and some expensive Oriental art hung on the walls. An American flag stood behind Lester's desk.

A framed document hung on the wall behind Lester's desk from the Federal Aviation Agency, Washington, D.C. saying, "This is to certify that Lester Maurice Shockley logged 10,019 hours of commercial aviation from 1943 to 1966." On a wall to the right of Lester's desk pictures hung, with autographs of Lester and South Vietnam President Nguyen Van Thieu and Vice-President Nguyen Cao Ky. There were also pictures of Lester standing beside actor Jimmy Stewart; Ted Williams and a F-86 Saber Jet; Mickey Mantle, Whitey Ford and Billy Martin of the New York Yankees at the Yankee Spring Training, Tampa, Florida, April, 1956.

Lester returned to the office.

Nate said, "Those are great pictures of you with those celebrities."

"Thanks," said Lester.

Lester called the U.S. Embassy switchboard and said, "Miss Bach, hold my telephone calls until eight forty-five," and hung up the telephone.

"Nate, I called you here today to discuss the Phoenix Program, and tell you about my career and why I'm in the Phoenix Program. We'll conclude at eight forty-five; Diem will drive you to the terminal for your ten o'clock flight to beautiful Rach Gia. Any questions?"

"Yes," responded Nate. "How did you get your picture taken with those famous people?"

"What you mean to ask me is how did those famous people get their pictures taken with me?"

Lester smiled, "Just luck, being in the right place at the right time with my Nikon."

"Oh, come on," said Nate, "you're being modest."

Lester turned and looked at the pictures.

"I carry a Nikon in my attaché case to witness history—like President Kennedy's assassination, and Zapruder with his eight-millimeter movie camera in Dallas on November 22, 1963. Let's see," thought Lester, "the picture of President Thieu and Vice-President Ky was taken in South Vietnam's national press room the day President Thieu was selected to be President, October 21, 1967.

"CORD'S Staff were invited; I was leaving for a reception when a UPI photographer asked me to stand with them to demonstrate American-South Vietnamese friendship, and the reporter snapped my picture.

"Ted Williams was taken with other Air Force personnel in front of an F-86 at Kimpo AFB, Korea in 1950. Ted Williams was also a pilot in the Korean War; I saw him several times, but never met him. Jimmy Stewart was at Ton Son Nhut for a USO tour in December, 1967. I was lucky. I asked him for a picture, and a friend took the picture. The picture of Mickey Mantle, Whitey Ford and Billy Martin is a great story. In April, 1956, I was at Tampa and I went to see a Grapefruit League pre-season game between the Yankees and Detroit.

"I got to the ballpark at eleven thirty. Mickey Mantle was sitting on a bench near the Yankees' dugout; Whitey Ford and Billy Martin were playing catch.

"I walked down to the field and asked, 'Mr. Mantle, may I have my picture taken with you?' Mickey turned, looked at me like, 'Who the hell are you buddy?' and said, 'sure' and unlocked the gate; 'We're not supposed to do this, but if you came to the game at eleven thirty for a one o'clock game—you are a Yankee fan.'

"I said, 'I *am* a Yankee fan, and a fan of Mickey Mantle.'

"Mickey called Whitey Ford and Billy Martin and said, 'Here is a real Yankee fan, take our picture with him.'

"They came over, and a groundskeeper snapped the picture for me.

"In 1956, Mickey Mantle won the American League Batting Championship with a .353 average—it must have been that good deed he did taking that picture in spring training.

"Let's get down to business. You've been in country four months; what are your impressions of the war?"

"Well, Lester," Nate spoke. "The war is far from being won or brought to a negotiated settlement. The NVA and Viet Cong are both tough and determined in spite of their heavy casualties and fifty thousand killed in the Tet Offensive. If something very dramatic doesn't happen on the military front and in the GVN Pacification Program, we're going to lose the war. Americans are fed up with Vietnam, the casualties and the quagmire."

"Excellent," commented Lester.

Lester then said, "I would add that the U.S. missed a great opportunity to back the ARVN and invade North Vietnam after Tet. There would have been complete justification and neither China nor Russia would have come in the war after that rotten attack over the Tet ceasefire. The communist bastards have had a free ride in this war, attacking South Vietnam's homeland for twelve years; the U.S. air campaign is ineffective, and we are now on the defensive. North Vietnam has not been attacked and destroyed like South Vietnam, what bullshit! We are now fighting a defensive war trying to stop NVA infiltration and we won't win fighting a defensive war.

"Johnson's senior policy advisors say we don't want to threaten the Chinese or Russians' national security by widening the war. Well, I'll be Goddamned, so let our own American soldiers bleed to death in South Vietnam. Johnson should have bombed Hanoi and destroyed the fucking country, and told Peking to stay the hell out of this war, or the U.S. will drop an atomic bomb on Peking if you fuck with us in this Goddamn mess. The Chinese have never forgotten their horrendous casualties by their People's Army in the Korean War—250,000 dead in three years. Now those are real casualties!

"It pisses me off to no end. We get Congressional junkets coming to Vietnam, and receive a canned briefing, visit a pacified village two miles from Saigon and then believe that Pacification is making progress; they return to Washington thinking the Vietnam War is being won! It's fucked up to the max!! John Paul Vann told President Johnson the real facts about the war and Mr. Johnson didn't like what he heard and told Vann to get the hell out of his office."

"In December I was at a Vietnamese news conference held at the Ministry of Information. A *Reuter's* correspondent asked the South Vietnamese information puppet 'If the war is being waged successfully, and the GVN control the countryside, why don't the ARVN fight at night or drive a convoy from Saigon to Tay Ninh or An Loc without getting ambushed?'

"Do you know what that little South Vietnamese runt asshole said?"

"No," said Nate.

" 'It is contested between the communists and ARVN.'

"Contested my ass, the ARVN don't fight, that's the problem."

Lester removed a bottle of French Perrier water from refrigerator. "Care for some?"

"No, thanks," said Nate.

"Nate," said Lester, "I can't get you to accept anything, can I?"

"I'm not thirsty," replied Nate. "Sorry."

Nate sensed Lester's frustration over Vietnam, the increasing U.S. casualties, inept political leadership in Washington, and indications the war was going to be lost.

Lester opened a shirt button below his neck. "If you want to know what I really think, the GVN is playing the U.S., knowing this Goddamn war really won't be won, milking the U.S. for every last cent before we throw in the towel and then bail out and call this son-of-a-bitch lost, done, and history. I don't see it going any other way without major changes in the next year. Many high-ranking Vietnamese are buying gold and now have passports to France to leave on a moment's notice. Not good." Lester took a swallow of Perrier.

"Nate, now I want to talk privately. I chose you for the Phoenix Program among seven candidates submitted to me by

Langley. You have a solid educational background, are very intelligent, have had good Army training and extensive covert intelligence experience, and speak Vietnamese. You do have an impressive career and may be on a fast track into Senior Management. However you must be successful in this assignment.

"This is a different time, place, and war than during the time I came to Saigon with Air America in November, 1959. Shit was just starting to happen. Washington never grasped the depth of the communists' insurgency in South Vietnam. South Vietnam was just too small, remote, and far away, to worry about.

"I was told by an old OSS hand that if we ever were to prevail in South Vietnam, we had to bomb Hanoi, invade North Vietnam, and prohibit Laos and Cambodia being neutral. Make a mutual defense pact with Laos, Cambodia and South Vietnam, or cut off aid to Vietnam and let it fall to communism. If China is not a threat, why in the hell is Vietnam a threat to U.S. national security?"

"Those CIA men knew how to operate.

"Since 1959, we've had to prop up South Vietnam's house of cards; it gets worse every year; we now have over 500,000 U.S. military in South Vietnam. McNamara's policy of graduated response has eroded into military and political failures, by sending the wrong signals to Russia, China and North Vietnam about the U.S. commitment to the war. The Russians and Chinese Communists think we're political and military dilettantes—we don't know what the fuck we're doing in Vietnam. They think the U.S. government views Vietnam as a Boy Scout's adventure or a military lark. This is McNamara's War.

"South Vietnam's Generals, for the life of their corrupt asses, just don't grasp why the world's greatest military power fights a defensive war, and are afraid to bomb North Vietnam in case fucking China comes into the war. North Vietnam does not want Russian or Chinese military forces in their country for God's sake! They've been trying to expel foreigners from Vietnamese soil the past 100 years. The Vietnamese have hated the Chinese since 1200."

Lester drank more Perrier.

"Then we endure Johnson's Goddamn ceasefires every other

month, bombing halts, hoping North Vietnam will surrender when we resume bombing. NVA prisoners tell us North Vietnam doesn't give a shit about ceasefires, ignores them, and blames the U.S. for ceasefire violations. They use the time to improve their military positions on the battlefield to attack U.S. troops. This war is insanity! Who in the hell are the pencil-dick civilians advising President Johnson that ceasefires improve the U.S. position? Those Ivy League nincompoops smoking meerschaum pipes, wearing penny loafers, tweed coats, and their natty four-in-hand bow ties don't know shit from shinola about Vietnam. They have advanced degrees from Columbia and think they are now foreign policy experts—Lord help us.

"They don't know their ass from third base with one hand in their back pocket about Vietnam. I agree with the President, who calls Vietnam 'a bitch of a war.'

"I'll wager ninety-nine percent of Johnson's senior policy advisors have never served in the U.S. military or worn an American military uniform. It makes me sick to think about it and Johnson's reliance on his old-man council of 'wise men' that think the Vietnam War is World War Two over again. Just bomb the piss out of the commies below the twentieth parallel, and hope North Vietnam surrenders."

Nate said, "Excuse me, Lester, I need to use the men's room."

Nate got up from the chair and went to the lavatory across the hall. When he returned, Lester was not in the office. Nate sat down and thought about what Lester said about the war. *He is right,* thought Nate.

"Sorry, Nate, I get wound-up and emotional over this war being directed by uninformed assholes in Washington who obstruct the U.S. military from winning the war. The U.S. military is fighting in Vietnam with one hand tied behind the back; it is not fair to the American soldiers sent to fight in this stinking shithole."

Lester leaned back in his chair, "Here is the synopsis of my career."

Lester began to talk.

"I was born on April 15, 1923 in Missoula, Montana; I am

forty-five. Mother called me the income-tax-day baby. My father was a geologist for Diamond Mining Company in Helena. Mom, Dad, my brother and sister and I moved to Helena, Montana in 1928. Dad was overseas on explorations six months a year; my mother became an alcoholic.

"As a kid, I was an aviation enthusiast and then a nerd in high school. Other children wanted to play cowboys and Indians, while I built model airplanes. I read about Charles Lindbergh and Amelia Earhart. In high school my nickname was 'Divebomb' Shockley—with a derisive connotation.

"I spent three years at the University of Montana, left college and enlisted in the Army Air Corps in May of 1943. I passed the examination for flight training, and received my commission as a Second Lieutenant. I soloed on the AT-6 North American Texan fighter plane, Lackland AFB in Texas, and was selected for flight training for the B-24 Liberator. I flew B-24s from October, 1943 to September, 1945 in the Pacific, bombing Jap Navy convoys, airfields and targets flying out of Australia and Hickam.

"In September 1945 when the war in the Pacific ended, I had logged 3,400 hours and was promoted to First Lieutenant. I was then assigned to Hickam from 1945 to 1948 flying B-24s air cargo and later assigned to Clark AFB in the Philippines from 1948 to 1950. I was promoted to Captain, and planned to make the Air Force my career.

"During the Korean War, I flew C-47s. After the Korean War I went to aircraft maintenance school to be trained for a non-flying back-up job.

"I was assigned to Fairchild AFB in Spokane, Washington in May 1955 to the 649th Bomb Wing as Squadron Maintenance Officer. That is where the shit hit the fan. I was eligible for promotion to Major. In short, the 649th failed an operational readiness inspection (ORI) due to maintenance deficiencies; shit flows downhill. The Squadron Commander, Colonel Billy 'Chicken shit' Jones, made me his scapegoat. I was passed over for promotion to Major by the two OER's written by Colonel Chicken Shit about my attention to duty. That was enough of the Air Force for me. I had been a combat pilot in two wars, but the bean counters win in the bureaucracy. I resigned with fourteen years' service.

"In 1957 I went to the Philippines and got a job flying for Flying Tigers. In 1958, I applied to Air America with ten thousand hours in the cockpit. In June 1958 Air America hired me. I went to the agent basic and area studies for covert operations at Langley, and arrived in Saigon in June of 1959. I flew DC-3s and C-47s air cargo between Saigon, Bangkok, Manila, Honolulu, Phnom Penh and Vientiane from 1959–1963.

"In November of 1963 I was flying a C-47 into Vientiane, Laos during a heavy monsoon rainstorm; I got bad landing instructions from the tower and should have gone around another time to land with the wind; I was cleared to land by an idiot Laotian air controller and then ploughed into a hilltop. The co-pilot and I got out and I suffered a broken right leg and fractured wrist. The C-47 exploded five minutes after the crash, but we both got out alive. At age thirty-eight, that crash did it for me; I was through flying after eighteen years in the cockpit.

"I spent a year in physical therapy in Texas, and was assigned the job at logistics on Ton Son Nhut from 1963 to 1965; in 1965 I was assigned to field operations. I speak good Vietnamese."

Nate was in shock from what he heard from Lester. Who would have known?

"I worked in Dinh Tuong Province from 1965 to 1967, and in December 1967 was assigned here to the embassy to coordinate logistics and the Phoenix Program. I was assigned to the Phoenix Program as Deputy Director in January 1968, before Tet. That's it; here I am today.

"I'm pleased that your request for the PRU equipment was approved so quickly. That request would have taken the military six months and probably would have been denied due to the cost. Congress allocated one hundred million dollars to the Agency for worldwide intelligence operations in the next fiscal year."

Lester said, "I'm going to make sure the president gets his money's worth."

Nate checked his wristwatch, it was 0845, he had to leave at

0930 to clear the BOQ and get to Ton Son Nhut for his 10:00 flight to Rach Gia.

Lester said, "Let me get rid of this borrowed coffee, and I'll conclude. I have some 'helpful hints' to tell you."

Lester returned to his office, and the telephone rang.

"Shockley," he said.

"Okay, Sam, another aircraft . . . an Otter? Okay, I'll tell him . . . Leaving at eleven sharp . . . pilot has four stops in IV Corps. Okay, Sam, he'll be there.

"That was Sam Parks at Air America at Ton Son Nhut. You'll be flying back in an Air American aircraft called an Otter."

"An Otter," said Nate.

"Yes, a mighty good airplane, the C-130 is too crowded to hold passengers. I've flown the Otter—you take off and land on a runway the size of a basketball court—all engine, super-strong aluminum frame and fuselage. It is a two-seater—pilot in front and one passenger in back. You can take a small suitcase, and unless you have a strong stomach, don't eat before flying to Rach Gia—any weather will make it a bumpy ride and you will get airsick."

"Thanks," said Nate.

"Okay, where were we?" said Lester.

"We are in a protracted guerilla war with the Viet Cong. We know the Viet Cong have marked Vietnamese and Americans working in the Phoenix Program for assassination. I went to a meeting in Can Tho after Tet to get briefed on Viet Cong prisoner interrogations. The Viet Cong control South Vietnam through COSVN and NLF, who control the Viet Cong. The NLF is a pervasive grassroots organization. Tet may have been the prelude to larger attacks to cut South Vietnam in half across the central highlands and eventually attack Can Tho, Chau Duc or My Tho to show Americans at home the war cannot be won.

"Let me tell you about a successful Phoenix operation in Dinh Tuong Province last March.

"We had a Chieu Hoi rally after Tet from the 270th VC Battalion. They attacked My Tho and got mauled. The Chieu Hoi said, 'Eighty comrades were killed along the My Tho River when they were hit by air strikes and artillery fire.'

"His name was Nguyen Tran Long; he was the VC Company Commander. His battalion political officer blamed him for cowardice in the face of the enemy. The Chieu Hoi said an ARVN battalion moved into My Tho with artillery and three hundred troops, unknown to his battalion commander. When they attacked My Tho, ARVN were dug in and they got blocked, as his company tried to advance to reinforce another VC company. They were caught in a crossfire and got mauled. He was to be executed for cowardice as an example to other VC. He told us during his interrogation, 'I will not accept a mistake made by a political officer and be called a coward.' The Chieu Hoi escaped from a labor detail, and railed at My Tho.

"He went through hell with the South Vietnamese until Joe Buckman learned about him at the PIC. Joe talked to the Chieu Hoi with a trusted interpreter and was told on February tenth 20 important Viet Cong political cadre would meet at Chau Thanh, and he indicated their meeting location on the map. Joe sent a PRU scout platoon to scout the village. The Chieu Ho pointed out precisely those huts where the meeting would take place at the edge of the jungle, 1,000 meters south of Chau Thanh. Joe Buckman called me to discuss the situation and how to react with the PRUs.

"We decided to send in one PRU company of sixty men, with air support from three Cobra helicopter gunships and obliterate the huts when the meeting took place. We felt the VC could escape, but we were ready to nail the bastards in the vicinity of the village.

"The Chieu Hoi went with the PRU company as a scout. At 1000 on February tenth we blasted the shit out of four thatch huts. The plan worked. The Cobras destroyed the huts and blew the fucking place to smithereens. Thirty VC were security. A violent firefight ensued, between the VC and PRUs. The next day an ARVN company combed the area and they counted twenty-two dead VC. On two dead VC bodies were political diaries, plans, and instructions to attack My Tho and kill American soldiers. So, this crap about the Phoenix Program being an assassination program of 'civilians' is just that, crap! Some fucking politician's idea of what the war is all about over his two nightly martinis in Georgetown.

"As far as that VC, Choi Hoi, he was given $50,000 Thailand Baht and flown to Thailand with his Vietnamese girlfriend."

"Thanks, Lester," said Nate.

Nate thought as he rode to the Air American Terminal, that he was ready to begin the Phoenix Program. If Viet Cong political cadre and infrastructure organized combat operations to kill U.S. soldiers, he would reciprocate and kill Viet Cong political infrastructure from intelligence to locate them.

On June seventeenth, Nate arrived on the Otter at Rach Gia. Stan Roland, Ted Graham, and Billy Flynn met him at the airfield with thirty PRU soldiers, three 1-1/2-ton U.S. Army trucks and one 5-1/2-ton truck.

Nate Shaw had his first formal staff meeting on the twentieth of June with his Advisory Team, which included:

Nate Shaw, OSA Team Chief
Stan Roland, Assistant OSA Team Chief
Captain Ted Graham, Army Intelligence
Captain Jeff Madison, Special Forces
Chief Petty Officer, Billy Flynn, Navy SEAL
Chief Petty Officer Jesse Roberts, Navy SEAL
SFC Sean Morgan, U.S. Army Special Forces
SGT Sam Bowman, Radio/Commo, Army
PFC Jeremy Hunt, Radio/Commo, Army
PFC Donald Blake, U.S. Army Special Forces
PFC Joseph Molinski, U.S. Army Special Forces

Captain Graham, was designated to work in The Provincial Intelligence Operations Coordination Center (PIOCC). His mission was to:

- Brief visitors and keep up the Provincial S-2 map in the OSA compound.
- Coordinate logistics with all DIOCCS.
- Work with the Vietnamese S-2 on VCI Intel.

- Fly aerial observation/surveillance to call-in artillery fire or air strikes.
- Perform mobile riverine U.S. Navy swift boats and TANGO boats operations w/RF/PF Units.
- Go on search and destroy ops with RF/PF,

Captain Madison:

- PRU Operations Officer
- Assigned to PRU Bravo Company with SFC Morgan

CPO Roberts:

- PRU Operations

CPO Flynn:

- Assigned to PRU Charley Company for Ops with CPO Roberts and PFC Blake.

Sgt. Bowman:

- Chief, OSA Communications Center/Logistics Coordinator.

PFC Hunt:

- Assistant to Sgt. Bowman

PFC Molinski:

- Special Operations with CPO Roberts

Nate wanted all information verified within eight hours into intelligence before PRU operations were conducted. Helicopter, insertion and night ambushes would be done by CPO Roberts and PFC Molinski.

Support from IV Corps with twenty-four hours notification could release the following air support:

eight Huey helicopters
four Cobra attack helicopters
DC-3, Puff the Magic Dragon
F-102 and F-105 from Ton Son Nhut
B-52 to bomb large VC unit locations

The first major PRU operation would occur in twenty-one days.
MISSION: Destroy VCI in Kien Giang Province.
Nate said he talked to Major Lam daily and would be at the PIC, or conducting his own intelligence collection ops in the field.
Information was developed that 80–100 VC were infiltrating into eastern Kinh Binh District. MACV said POW revealed NVA regiments were moving south on the Ho Chi Minh Trail with 24,000 soldiers toward Cambodia!
The meeting concluded.
Nate Shaw received the following classified message from Lester Shockley.

TOP SECRET (TS)—EYES ONLY

TO: N. Shaw
FM: L. Shockley
Re: Scarecrow
Date: 25 August 68
F.Y.I.
    Scarecrow op 23 August 0300 vic Vung Tau resulted in killing TRI and 11 associates during a violent ten minute fire fight. Positive I.D. made of TRI.
Recovered from his Cambodian ocean barge:
    $2 million in white heroin in bags.
    $1 million in cocaine in bags.
    $1 million U.S. cash in suitcases.
    $200,000 in stolen U.S. aid/materials.
    Madam Tri shot to death inside TRI compound. Verified.
Recovered:

$100,000 U.S. cash
$100,000 in gold bullion, and $100,000 in uncut diamonds,
Total recovered: $4.5 million
A good night's work!
TOP SECRET (TS)
DESTROY IMMEDIATELY!

10

Sue Ellen Harris and her roommate Elizabeth Huntley stood inside the foyer of the Third Field Hospital in Saigon, waiting for a commuter bus to take them to Clara Barton Hall. Sue Ellen wiped fog off the window of the double metal door, "Look at that rain, this monsoon is awesome."

Loud thunder resonated outside with bolts of jagged white lightening in the distance. Traffic on Bien Duc Long Boulevard moved at a snail's pace. There was the constant sound of honking horns and beeps as if blowing a car horn would speed up Saigon's horrendous traffic. Elizabeth looked at her wristwatch, "It's 6:10—I hope the bus arrives so we don't miss dinner by 1900."

Two U.S. Army MPs entered the foyer; one MP said, "Ladies, I'm sorry to tell you, but the bus is thirty minutes late."

A moan rose from the nurses huddled behind the front door. The nurses were the blue team who had arrived at the hospital at 0630 that morning. They had been in the hospital twelve hours and were tired, hungry, and ready to go home, have dinner, and call it a day.

"Well, Susie Q, what do we do? Care to join me in the tropical bar?" asked Elizabeth.

Sue Ellen said, "I wish we had a cocktail bar at times like this. Let's go sit in the lobby. I hope we make it back to Clara Barton for dinner by 1900, or we'll have another night of tuna, chips and soda."

"Well, tomorrow morning we'll have bacon, eggs, toast and coffee," said Elizabeth.

Sue Ellen opened the front door and saw two MPs standing next to a sandbagged bunker.

Elizabeth said, "Want a Coke and some pretzels?"

"Sure."

"Let's sit in the lobby."

She brought Sue Ellen a Coke and pretzels.

Six nurses went into the lobby and sat waiting for the bus to arrive.

Sue Ellen and Elizabeth found two chairs and sat down.

"Age before beauty," Elizabeth motioned to Sue Ellen to sit down in a chair.

Several other nurses lit cigarettes and began to smoke.

Sue Ellen said, "Thank you, roomie, and remember age, like fine wine improves with time, but beauty fades."

Elizabeth responded, "Touché."

She whispered to Sue Ellen, "Look at those nurses smoking; I declare, what did they learn in nursing school? Emphysema, cancer, and smoking are deadly for pregnant women. I don't get it."

Sue Ellen replied, "They must not get it either."

A tremendous thunderclap and boom with lightning exploded outside the hospital and the lights in the hospital went out, making the area dark.

Sandra Wells screamed, "We're being attacked!"

A veteran nurse, Nancy Webster, said, "Stay calm, I'll find the electrical panel and turn on the emergency generators."

Nancy flicked a cigarette lighter and used the flame to see the electrical panel in the hallway next to the lobby. She shined the flame from the lighter on a panel box and suddenly the lights came back on inside the hospital.

"A-hah," said Nancy, "see what a good nurse does in times of trouble."

The air-conditioning began to hum and blew cool air from overhead vents into the hot muggy lobby.

Sue Ellen and Elizabeth finished their Cokes and pretzels.

Elizabeth said, "Can you believe tomorrow is Thanksgiving; we've been in country six months?"

Sue Ellen responded, "Thank God for tomorrow, we have three-and-a-half days off after 1500. I've got so much to do, I hope it doesn't rain until Monday."

"Me too," said Elizabeth.

She continued, "We each must have ten pounds of dirty laundry for Chin's Laundry."

"I know," said Sue Ellen, "Can you believe here in a war zone we found a great Chinese laundry that washes and folds two duffle bags of laundry for ten dollars and returns it within twenty-four hours?"

"I've got to rest Sunday," said Elizabeth. "We worked sixty hours, and we'll be off three-and-one-half days; and then we start that killer shift from 1500 to 2400. I can't sleep when we get off at 2400; I get to sleep; I wake up at six A.M. I'm not rested; I get up at noon, instead of breakfast, it's lunchtime—all I want is coffee, then I get hungry. We stand on our feet twelve hours—my feet kill me by the end of the shift."

"Poor baby," said Sue Ellen to Elizabeth. "Hang in there, roomie, we'll make it 'til June. Next June."

The rain outside lightened into a light drizzle.

Two medical doctors entered the lobby. One doctor said, "Ladies, I'm driving a van to Clara Barton Hall."

"Oh, Dr. Holmes, you're such a sweetheart," said Nancy Webster.

An MP came into the lobby and said, "Doctor, your van is waiting out front."

Two doctors and six nurses walked from the lobby, down the sidewalk, around the large puddle, and climbed into a fifteen-passenger hospital van.

Dr. Holmes got behind the steering wheel, announced, "Bon Voyage," and he pulled the van into traffic on Bien Duc Long. It was 6:25 P.M.

The van crept along as the rain stopped. The nurses were silent; Elizabeth slumped her head against a window and fell asleep.

Sue Ellen remained awake, and thought, *Elizabeth is right about duty hours at the Third Field Hospital.*

Sue Ellen had met Elizabeth Huntley at the Third Field Hospital in July, where Elizabeth was also an operating room nurse. Elizabeth was attractive, not a great beauty, but had a heart of gold. Elizabeth received her R.N. nursing degree at Vanderbilt University in June, 1958. Her father was a retired U.S. Naval Captain who also graduated from the U.S. Naval Academy in 1935. He spent his Navy career in the submarine service. Elizabeth received a U.S. Navy scholarship to Vanderbilt and decided to make the U.S. Navy her career. She was a Navy Lieutenant, the equivalent of a U.S. Army Captain and a skilled "O.R." nurse. She had served at the Naval Medical Center, San Diego, from 1958 to 1962; Pensacola Naval Hospital 1964 to 1967, and at Subic Bay Naval Base in the Philippines from 1967 to 1968 and arrived in Saigon in June 1968.

Elizabeth and Sue Ellen became friends when Sue Ellen's first roommate was reassigned to a MASH Unit, Sue Ellen asked Elizabeth to be her roommate. They were compatible and called themselves "Army-Navy belles."

The van arrived at Clara Barton Hall at 1755. Sue Ellen and Elizabeth had dinner and returned to their room. Elizabeth said she was exhausted, took a shower, turned on AFN radio, and fell asleep on her bed. She and Sue Ellen awoke at 0530 Thanksgiving Day, November 20, 1968. They arrived at work at 0700 and had breakfast in the hospital's cafeteria. Their shift ended at 1500 and they went for Thanksgiving dinner with all the trimmings and got off duty at 1500 until Monday. Sue Ellen had a "to do list" for the next three days.

1. Take laundry to Chin's.
2. Call parents.
3. Write Nathan Stewart.
4. Write Ted Graham.
5. Fill out paperwork for R & R to Sydney, Australia 15-22 February, 1969.
6. Get haircut, manicure, and pedicure at Le Femme France.
7. PX run.

Sue Ellen had held up after seeing and experiencing the horrors of the Vietnam War for six months in the Third Field Hospital O.R. The doctors and medical staff were magnificent. It took Sue Ellen a month to become steeled to seeing young American soldiers carried into the hospital from Huey helicopters, having ghastly body wounds, mangled arms and wounds from shrapnel. Nine soldiers died on a stretcher before reaching the hospital.

Many wounded soldiers were brought directly to "O.R." from the field in bloody jungle fatigues, and were given anesthesia for an emergency operation. Elizabeth called it "a bad Saturday night car wreck, ten times a shift."

The Third Field Hospital was built in 1965 with 125 beds, three operating theaters, three wards, morgue, and a cafeteria. The medical staff had ten board-certified surgeons, twenty medical doctors from all specialties, and thirty-six nurses. The medical staff was organized into three teams covering three shifts twenty-four hours. Medical personnel came from the Army, Navy, and Air Force. Sue Ellen and Elizabeth were assigned to the blue team under Colonel Harvey Keenan, M.D., U.S. Air Force heart and lung surgeon.

Dr. Keenan was pleasant, but did not tolerate incompetence in the operating room. He required precision in the procedures and proper instrument handling at the operating table. He asked for an instrument one time, which had to be passed to him chest high, placed into the palm of his left hand and removed from his right hand. He did not speak during operations, except to ask a nurse for his instruments, blood pressure, heart rate, pulse, and breathing, which had to be answered precisely. One nurse was removed from his team who got nervous, and handed the doctor a number six blade instead of a number nine blade; when the doctor said, "Nine, nurse," she handed him the same number six blade. He told her, "Take the day off, and relax." She was assigned to the recovery ward.

Sue Ellen's job was to observe all nurses in the O.R, and give assistance if necessary. Elizabeth said, "I do what the doctor says and hope for the best."

In spite of a full medical staff, fatigue and stress were ever present. The staff had two days off every ten days, and three days off every twenty-eight days. The average work week was sixty hours. Sue Ellen and Elizabeth were present in the operating room and saw American soldiers die on the operating table. Dr. Keenan was reassuring and said, "There is only so much the best surgeon can do, and the rest is in God's hands." Dr. Keenan said the team was credited with saving seventy-nine soldiers' lives, stabilizing two hundred and ten soldiers who later recovered. Sue Ellen and Elizabeth were looking forward to the end of their tour in June, 1969.

Friday morning, Sue Ellen and Elizabeth awoke at 10:00 A.M., dressed, and went to Clara Barton Hall cafeteria for juice, coffee, and French toast. They took the bus from Kelper Compound to Ton Sun Nhut, and dropped off their duffle bags of clothing at Chin's Laundry. Elizabeth went to the PX to go shopping. Sue Ellen went to Le Femme France, a salon owned by two French ex-patriot women who were married to South Vietnamese businessman importing/exporting between South Vietnam and France.

The women's names were Yvette-Maria Nguyen and Antoinette Duval Nguyen, both of their children attended private schools in France. They planned to leave South Vietnam in 1970, fearing the country would fall to communism. Yvette-Maria was taken with Sue Ellen and did not understand, as she frequently said, "Why does such a beautiful woman come to Vietnam as an American soldier?"

Yvette told Sue Ellen, and other women present in the shop while she cut Sue Ellen's thick dark brown hair, "Look at this beautiful child, you could be an American movie star like our Brigitte Bardot or Catherine Deneuve in France."

Sue Ellen said, "I am a U.S. Army medical nurse, and nurses are needed in Vietnam." Sue Ellen finished getting a manicure and pedicure and felt feminine for a few hours in Saigon's heat and humidity.

Sue Ellen met Elizabeth at the PX, where they both purchased personal items. They returned to Clara Barton Hall at 5:30 and had dinner, and then they returned to the room. Sue Ellen took a shower, washed her hair, put on pajamas, and began to read *The Quiet American* by Graham Greene. She fell asleep, awoke Saturday morning at 8:30 A.M., and went to breakfast. Elizabeth said she was going swimming at the Officer's Club at Ton Son Nhut and then to the MARS facility and call her parents in Florida. Ellen said she was going to write letters and meet her at 5:00 to go to dinner and see *Some Like it Hot* in the Clara Barton dayroom.

Sue Ellen was glad for several hours by herself. Elizabeth

said good-bye and left at 10:00 A.M. Sue Ellen took the sheets from their beds, found an empty washing machine in the basement, and washed their sheets, towels, and medical scrubs. She returned to the room, opened the blinds, and sat down in a chair to re-read letters from Nathan Stewart and Ted Graham.

Nathan Stewart wrote that he had finished his physical therapy at Walter Reed Hospital in June and then reported to the Infantry Officer's advance course at Ft. Benning, Georgia on July 7, 1968.

Sue Ellen looked at the date on Nathan's last letter, dated October 21, 1968, Columbus, Georgia. She had written to Nathan on August 10, 1968. Time flew by and the months went slowly. Nathan wrote and said he had gone to the U.S. Army Office of Personnel Operations in Washington in August, and had an interview with Lt. Col. Edward Bradford, his Infantry Branch Personnel Action's Officer. Lt. Col. Bradford reviewed his Field 201 file containing his ten Officer's efficiency reports (OERs) between 1963–1968.

Lt. Col. Bradford said his record based upon his OERs, student academic reports, and ten-month tour in Vietnam as an infantry platoon leader had placed him in the top 1 percent of Infantry Captains in the branch on the order of merit's list. He received a Silver Star for gallantry, a Bronze Star with "V" device for valor in battle, a Purple Heart, and Combat Infantryman's Badge. After he graduated from the Infantry Officer's advanced course, he had been requested by USAREUR and Seventh Army to be aide-de-camp to General James Larson, Commanding General USAREUR, and Seventh Army for eighteen months. After that assignment, he would be assigned to the Fourth Armor Division for eighteen months as Company Commander in a mechanized battalion to gain experience. He would be submitted for promotion to Major "below the Zone" in 1970, with seven years' service. Lt. Col. Bradford told him, "Captain Stewart, there are stars in your future."

Nathan's father, Bucyrus, had also suffered a second heart attack in July, and now used a respiratory bottle to breathe. Nathan ended his letter saying that if Bucyrus died, he would attend the funeral. Scarlett was at Southern Mississippi. His injury in Vietnam required the insertion of a metal rod into his right tibia, and his paratrooper days were over. He told Sue Ellen he loved her, "like he was eighteen" and wanted to visit in Memphis.

Ted Graham wrote two thoughtful letters to Sue Ellen, showing concern for her well-being. Ted said his assignment in Vietnam was classified, but that he did intelligence and combat operations with the South Vietnamese and had been on eleven combat operations. He was applying for R & R to Sydney in March 1969 and wanted to know if he could see Sue Ellen in Saigon.

Sue Ellen thought about how to respond to Ted. She liked him, but was in love with Nathan Bedford Stewart. She wrote to Ted and thanked him for the thoughtful things he said and told him she was marrying a man she had known since childhood. She told him she could not see him in Saigon and wished him the best of luck.

On Sunday, Sue Ellen and Elizabeth attended a non-denominational church service, had lunch, watched AFN TV, and wrote letters to their families.

Sue Ellen wondered about Elizabeth—she was normally back by 3:00 or 3:30. She went to the dayroom and dropped her letters into the U.S. postal box. At 5:00 Elizabeth returned and was "all a twitter," and told Sue Ellen she went to the Officer's Club, swam twenty laps and lay down on a lounge chair. An older man kept looking at her. Finally the man walked over to her and said, "Excuse me, aren't you Lieutenant Huntley?"

She said, "It was Doctor David Lowe from the hospital. He must have been lonely; he asked if he could buy me a cold drink. I said, 'Yes, Sir.'

"He said, 'Call me David, we're off duty.' I had rum and Coke and he had iced tea. He is an internist on active duty with the U.S. Navy Reserve and is a widower. He lost his wife to cancer in 1965, sold his medical practice in Seattle and went on active duty at Whidbey Island. He is forty-two and putting his life together. We talked about our careers. He asked if I would like to have dinner at the Officer's Club. Can you believe it Susie Q? I'm thirty-two, my biological clock is ticking, and I have not met my

Prince Charming. Today, I met a forty-two-year-old medical doctor, Yikes! It must have been the lightning on Wednesday."

"Ten years difference in age is nothing, go for it," said Sue Ellen. She continued, "I've made up my mind today, I'm going to marry a man I've known since first grade. Nathan is a West Point graduate, an Army Captain at Fort Benning; I'm going to see him in Memphis—just watch—you'll be invited to our December wedding! What a day! Let's go eat and see *Doctor Zhivago.*"

Nine months had passed since Nate Shaw came to Vietnam; the Phoenix Program was showing progress, but not as much success as he wanted. The problem remained, obtaining timely, accurate information to evaluate for intelligence to conduct PRU combat operations against VCI political infrastructure.

Lester Shockley was correct when he told Nate, "Everyone lies to save their ass, avoid detection or stay alive."

Nate had interrogated seventeen Viet Cong Chieu Hois with the help of his interpreter, Mr. Tot, whom he hired last July. His counterpart, Lt. Col Than at the Police Special Branch always required more time to investigate, and more money for information. The Province Chief, Lt. Col. Minh was livid. He was pissed off at the extravagant waste of American dollars spent on criminals and ex-Viet Cong PRUs who were paid more than his own RF/PF soldiers and were now armed with the best American military equipment. He was really only angry since he could not extort graft, money, or material for himself.

In July, three PRU operations were run with support of U.S. Army helicopters from IV Corps. The PRUs raided a village on July 9 and found the village empty with no VCI; the raid was based on information Nate thought was reliable from two VC prisoners he interrogated at the PIC. The next two PRU operations hit Viet Cong infiltration routes on the Cai Son Canal, Northeast of Rach Gia on July seventeenth at 0300. They hit the jackpot and caught ten Viet Cong boats moving south on Cai Son Canal and killed eleven Viet Cong, three were VCI officials with papers, found on the bodies.

The third PRU operation was a night ambush and Cobra helicopter air strike at Truong Thuan Village with information from a Viet Cong prisoner that Jesse Roberts captured during night operations two days before the raid. Jesse Roberts brought a young boy, about 17, hands tied and a razor-sharp Bowie knife blade under his throat; the boy told Jesse about thirty VC located at Troung Thuan, and VCI were collecting taxes, recruiting soldiers and doing communist propaganda indoctrination. The PRUs took up their positions at 0200, but no Viet Cong came into the village. Nathan wrote down who knew about the plan of attack: Major Lam, PRU Commander; Captain Dai, his X-O; Stan Roland; Jeff Madison; Mr. Tot. There was an informant in his organization. He would now vet that person with extreme prejudice.

In September 1968, Nate took his first home leave. He had a wonderful month with Janet, his three children and Tyler. On October fourth, he returned to Rach Gia. Stan Roland met him at the airstrip and told him the PRU compound had come under a VC mortar attack on September ninth at 0100—three PRUs were KIA along with nine of their family members. The other devastating news was that at 0300 on August fourteenth, VC fired a seventy-five caliber recoilless rifle rounds and had killed 13 U.S. inside the BEQ on the canal in Rach Gia. Several mortar rounds landed near the OSA compound, but none hit the OSA building. "The shit will hit the fan in Washington, D.C. over the stupidity of putting GI's along a canal and jungle."

Nate met with Lt. Col. Berry and the Province Chief to discuss the VC's attack. Lt. Col. Berry said it looks like VC are preparing to launch new attacks. Two nights later, the VC made another mortar attack on Rach Gia. The next morning at breakfast Nate learned that Miss Thu and her entire family of seven were all killed when a mortar shell made a direct hit on their home. On September fifth, Lt. Col. Minh made an urgent call to Nate to meet him at his headquarters.

Lt. Col. Minh told Nate, "I have intelligence: one hundred fifty to two hundred VC are camped near Kien Binh. We will attack them tomorrow."

Nate said, "Colonel Minh, what do you want me to do?"

Lt. Col. Minh told him, "Get U.S. Cobra helicopters; and we will strike the VC location at coordinate 421639 at Ngoc Hoa.

Send two PRU companies to Ngoc Hoa and I will send 200 RF/PF, we'll cordon them and call in air strikes."

Nate told no one on the OSA Advisory Team about the forthcoming operation except Stan Roland and Jeff Madison. On October seventh at 0300, three Cobra attack helicopters fired rockets near Ngoc Hoa at coordinate 421639, and received heavy return AK-47 fire. At 0400, 100 PRUs in U.S. Army Huey helicopters landed to set up a blocking position near Ngoc Hoa; at 0600, 200 RF/PF arrived in trucks and soon a full-scale battle ensued for five hours. At 1600, the PRUs and RF/PF moved through the area and counted fifty-one dead Viet Cong, collected forty AK-47s, three .82-mm mortars, papers, and maps. Nate concluded his leak was "one Vietnamese talking to another Vietnamese."

November began the six month monsoon season. Heavy monsoon rains limited mobility across the Mekong Delta. Nate would focus his intelligence collection on VC infiltration routes, river traffic, and VC base camps and hopefully identify the location of the Committee on South Vietnam (COSVN). In November, at the PIC, Nate recruited two new intelligence agents who told him the VC were going to attack Kien Binh. Nate's agent told him he had gone into Kien Binh to buy fish. A fisherman told him the VC have base camps along the Thanh Hoa Canal and were infiltrating soldiers to attack on American "Thanks Day." That was all the information Nate needed. He told his interpreter Tot a bogus story about another PRU operation and sent an agent to follow Tot when he went home at night.

At 0430 on November twenty-third, Tot rode his bicycle to a location one mile outside Thanh Hoa and met a man. The following night, two PRU companies were flown to Thanh Hoa. Nate requested Puff the Magic Dragon and three Cobra attack helicopters for the operation. Tot had bought Nate's bogus story. Tot told his contact the PRU attack would occur at 0600 at Soc Son; the VC had moved out of Soc Son into a tree line. On November twenty-fifth at 0100, the Puff-the-Magic-Dragon fired into the tree line where VC had moved and the PRUs attacked Thanh Hoa. The VC were caught in a crossfire.

The next day, the PRUs combed the tree line and found twenty-seven dead VC. Tot was his traitor! No PRUs were killed.

Tot came to work and was quickly arrested by the PSB. Tot protested, cursing Nate. "This is a big mistake." The PSB interrogated Tot, told him he was a traitor and shot him, and threw his body into a lime pit. The PSB subsequently identified Tot as an NVA Captain working undercover as an interpreter to spy on U.S. personnel. Nate thought, *Lester was right: Trust no one.*

On December eleventh, Ted Graham and Jeff Madison took a Jeep and drove for lunch at the MACV mess hall.

On the way through Rach Gia, Jeff asked Ted, "Did you hear from that Army nurse, Sue Ellen, what was her last name, girl from MISSISSIPPI?"

"Harris," replied Ted. "Yes, I received a letter from her two weeks ago."

"A letter, what does that mean, I hope it was not a Dear John letter," answered Jeff.

"Sort of. Bottom line, she said she has had a relationship with a man from her hometown named Nathan Stewart; he is a West Point graduate and served in III Corps with the Eighty-second Airborne for ten months, and was wounded in April, 1967. She is not looking for any relationship, she wished me good luck for Vietnam and Georgetown Law School."

Jeff said, "Well, at least she was civil and didn't keep you in reserve if Captain Stewart dumps her. Are you going to see her in Saigon on R & R?"

"No," said Ted. "Her desire was no contact and good thoughts."

"Good enough," said Jeff. "She is not the one for you, and there is someone waiting to meet you."

"I suppose. I really like her and fell in love last June; we do what we have to do," answered Ted.

Ted pulled into the gravel parking lot at the MACV mess hall. Stan Roland, Billy Flynn, and Jesse Roberts came out of the mess hall.

Stan said, "There are mercenaries if I ever saw any," and slapped Ted on his shoulder.

Ted and Jeff finished lunch.

Jeff said, "Let's check mail." They went to a bank of mailboxes at MACV Headquarters; Ted opened his mailbox and received a letter from his mother. Jeff opened his mailbox and found four Christmas cards and a piece of paper saying he had a parcel in the mailroom.

"What could this be?" asked Jeff.

"Let's find out."

They walked to the mailroom; Jeff gave the yellow paper to PFC Jones, the mail clerk. PFC Jones brought Jeff a five-foot-long, two-foot-wide box.

"Did someone send you a bazooka?" asked PFC Jones.

"Thanks," said Jeff and he picked up his box up off the mail counter.

"What is it?" asked Ted.

"Do you belong to an adult sex club and they mailed you a rubber six-foot blow-up doll whose mouth opens when you inflate her?" laughed Ted.

"Perhaps," said Jeff.

Jeff reached beneath his jungle fatigues, took out a steel U.S. Army combat knife from a sheath, cut the end of the box, and tore off the cardboard paper.

Inside the box was a synthetic Christmas tree, a stand, and boxes of red, green, blue and gold Christmas ornaments and silver garlands to decorate the tree. The box was mailed from Senator and Mrs. J.L. Madison, 2119 Kings Lane No. 14, Georgetown, Virginia.

"Well, I'll be damned, it's from Mom and Dad," said Jeff. Inside the box was a Christmas card and a handwritten letter to Jeff from the senator and his mother, Martha.

"Let's get back and decorate the tree."

"A good idea," said Ted. "I hope we have a white Christmas."

They returned to the OSA compound, cleared off the dining room table and decorated the tree, which expanded to five feet and was shaped just like a Christmas tree. They put on Christmas ornaments, and when Stan Roland saw the tree, he sang "Jingle Bells."

A week later, Ted Graham was assigned on an amphibious

operation with the Rach Gia RF/PR company of sixty soldiers by boat at 0200, to sail four hours and come ashore at 0600 at An Giang Village. SFC Jimmy Hughes, Infantry, was his radio operator, and on his second tour in Vietnam. It rained all night on the boat, Ted stayed topside with the RF/PF soldiers who squatted in the traditional Vietnamese position and ate cooked food from black pots. Ted was offered food, but declined. Ted had a flack jacket, steel helmet, two canteens of water and an M-16 rifle with him. At 0530 three boats put down anchor and they went ashore into An Giang village where women, children, and dogs greeted them at sunrise. The sun came up at 0630, and SFC Hughes said, "Our objective is three miles away, Sir, dump your flack jacket; don't load up on water."

Ted said he preferred to wear the flack jacket.

SFC Hughes said, "Sir, keep up."

Radio checks were made, and at 0700, the lead platoon of RF/PF began walking briskly down a narrow, rocky, dirt trail outside An Giang. The RF/PF troops moved at a quick pace and Ted began to fall behind. His uniform was soaked with sweat and his steel helmet gave him a headache.

SFC Hughes told the Company Commander to stop and rest, and allowed the Captain time to catch his breath.

The Vietnamese Company Commander, Captain Thu, came to SFC Hughes and said, "Two miles to objective—does Dai-uy need to stay?"

"Do you want to wait?" SFC Hughes asked Ted.

"No," said Ted. He took off the flack jacket and steel helmet and left them along the trail. He took out a jungle hat with a handkerchief tied around his forehead to soak up sweat and said, "Let's go."

The company resumed its march and in a few minutes, the sound of heavy automatic weapons fire was ahead on the trail. Ted stood and looked toward the direction of palm trees, jungle growth, and high elephant grass 2,000 meters from the position. The RF/PF platoon rushed past them carrying 60-millimeter mortars, Browning automatic rifles, M-79 grenade launches and M-16 rifles. SFC Hughes grabbed Ted's fatigue jacket and yanked him to the ground.

"Get down," he hollered. "You are one hell of a big target."

Automatic weapons fire grew louder.

SFC Hughes said, "Lock and load your weapon and fire into that treeline."

SFC Hughes fired his M-16 at the tree line. Ted squeezed the M-16 trigger, but lost his grip, and the M-16 fell to the ground.

"Hold your rifle steady, Captain," yelled SFC Hughes who fired another burst from his M-16. Ted activated the M-16 chamber release lever, cleared the weapon, and squeezed the trigger, firing a burst into the treeline. Weapons fire grew louder; the company commander crawled to Ted and SFC Hughes.

"Stay down, we might get mortar fire. First platoon says it is an ambush, ten or fifteen VC."

An RF/PF mortar round exploded into a treeline where the enemy was firing at the RF/PF's position. Ted saw brush, trees, and elephant grass blown apart and bursts of mud and debris fly in the air. The RF/PF mortar fire continued ten minutes with continuous automatic weapons fire from SFC Hughes, Ted, and the RF/PF platoon. Ted looked at his watch—the contact was twenty minutes. Captain Thu ordered the company, "Hold fire!"

Everyone waited.

Captain Thu told the first platoon to check the tree line for VC KIA's. Ted and SFC Hughes sat in the boiling sun forty-five minutes; Ted was nearly out of water. An RF/PF platoon returned down the trail, pulling a hollowed-out tree as a boat.

They reached Ted's position; inside the boat, Ted saw a dead old man and blood-soaked black pajamas.

Captain Thu came to Ted and SFC Hughes and said, "Important dead VC!"

The company moved back along the trail into An Giang village and arrived, hearing old women wailing, crying, moaning, and beating their breasts with their hands. The dead VC was placed in the village square, as dogs sniffed the corpse; flies began to crawl on the dead man's face. Two RF/PF soldiers stood over the body and counted seven bullet holes in the corpse in an almost perfect line.

"He caught a burst of Browning automatic weapons fire," said SFC Hughes, "it is a classic close pattern of the Browning."

"What do we do now?" Ted asked SFC Hughes.

The dead VC lay in the boiling sun with his eyes open staring at the sky; his bare feet were callous with cracked black toenails. His hands were brown with age lines, and his face had dark brown skin and deep age lines around his eyes and chin and gray hair.

Captain Thu came to Ted. "The women are shouting obscenities at you for killing the old man named Tran Tung Diem. He left this village in 1950 to fight the French and now the Americans. They call you Americans devils."

Captain Thu pointed to a wailing woman, "That old woman says she is his wife; he is sixty-seven."

Captain Thu talked to a Vietnamese official who told him there were forty to fifty VC near An Giang and they heard the approaching boats this morning.

Ted asked, "Why did they wait down a trail two miles, how did they know we would go that far?"

"They didn't," answered Captain Thu. "We got lucky."

Captain Thu came to SFC Hughes, "We leave now and come back in a month—VC still be here, maybe next time they meet us at the beach," and he laughed.

The return boat trip to Rach Gia took four hours. Ted told the OSA team about the combat operation and dead VC.

"Good for you, Ted, that's one less gook," said Stan Roland. "Let's drink a beer."

Nate Shaw returned and Stan Roland told Nate, "Ted Graham bagged a gook today—KIA with seven bullet holes to wear."

"Really," said Nate. "Where?"

"An Giang on the coast."

"Good man," said Nate. Ted, Jeff, Nate, Stan, Billy, and Jesse went up to the fourth floor to drink beer.

After three beers, Stan Roland and Sean Morgan left to visit their "girlfriends" at an old French hotel, Le Chateau.

11

December 1968, ended as the fourth year of the Vietnam War; heavy fighting continued on both sides; no progress had come out of the Paris Peace talks to end the war.

On January thirty-first, the communists launched their Tet Lunar New Year surprise offensive during a ceasefire.

On March thirty-first, President Johnson announced he would not seek re-election for another term. March thirty-first, President Johnson curbed bombing of North Vietnam for the eighth time in the war.

By March, 1968, there were 525,000 U.S. military in South Vietnam.

On May thirty-first, peace talks between North Vietnam and the U.S. began in Paris. North Vietnam demanded all U.S. forces be withdrawn from South Vietnam before any meaningful negotiations took place to end the war.

On June fifth, Senator Robert F. Kennedy (D-NY) was fatally shot in Los Angeles; he had campaigned to end the Vietnam War.

On October thirty-first, President Johnson halted all bombing over North Vietnam for the ninth time.

The strategic bombing over North Vietnam between 1964 to 1968, called "Rolling Thunder," was later determined to be ineffective air power; four years of bombing had not convinced North Vietnam to seek peace. Photoreconnaissance and bomb damage assessments showed the damage had been quickly repaired and did not discourage North Vietnam's population. 900 U.S. aircraft and 1,000 crews were lost during "Rolling Thunder."

The B-52 Arc Light bombing to stop communist troop infiltration and materials down the Ho Chi Minh Trail into South Vietnam was ineffective. Four hundred U.S. soldiers were being killed a week in the war.

Neither South Vietnam's Pacification Program nor Strategic Hamlet Program had been effective in "winning the hearts and minds" of the people in the countryside. Communist political control of the countryside was unbroken throughout South Vietnam. North Vietnam continued receiving huge amounts of modern Russian and Chinese Communist military aid bringing supplies into North Vietnam's port of Haiphong. No U.S. bombing was done over Haiphong for fear a bomb would hit a Russian ship as an act of war against Russia.

Ho Chi Minh and General Vo Nguyen Giap both continued to observe the Anti-Vietnam War protests in America; they felt time was on their side. General Giap's strategy was to maul ARVN units and "bleed" the Americans to death.

The communist two-pronged military strategy was designed to destroy the effectiveness of the ARVN and force more U.S. ground combat involvement in the war. This would cause higher U.S. casualties. By 1968, NVA began to fight in large, set formations against U.S. firepower and to make maximum pressure on U.S. soldiers and thereby greatly increase U.S. casualties. Meanwhile, U.S. combat units were forced to defend permanent base camps and could not pursue NVA or Viet Cong due to a lack of manpower. By 1968, the U.S. military posture had eroded into a defensive enclave with U.S. resources being greatly overextended. General Giap reinforced what Ho Chi Minh had warned the French, "You can kill ten of my men for every one I kill of yours, but even at those odds, you will lose and I will win." North Vietnam's leadership began to see a change in the war effort against the Americans.

A clear message was sent to Washington in early 1969, that unless the South Vietnamese assumed a greater burden in the war, the U.S. would have to send more soldiers, material, arms, and money to fight the war; this meant South Vietnam would rely more on its American ally. There was no indication the American military strategy of attrition was effective to defeat communist forces, or to convince North Vietnam they could not win the war. The only way to achieve a U.S. victory appeared to be by use of tactical nuclear weapons or to drop atomic bombs on North Vietnam.

On January 20, 1969, Richard M. Nixon was inaugurated the thirty-seventh President of the United States. President Nixon campaigned saying he had a secret plan to end the Vietnam War. The president's secret plan was "Vietnamization," a phrase coined by President Nixon's Secretary of Defense, Melvin R. Laird. Vietnamization was the plan to turn over fighting the war to South Vietnam and begin the gradual withdrawal of U.S. military forces from Vietnam. The U.S. would continue to provide financial, air, and military support with strategic bombing to South Vietnam. The U.S. troops' withdrawal began in June, 1969.

1969 did not bring dramatic changes for the OSA's Advisory Team at Rach Gia. In January and February 1969, there was a decline in Viet Cong activity across Kien Giang Province. Over two months, no major PRU combat operations were conducted against the Viet Cong, while the Viet Cong continued making isolated attacks on district towns, and villages, ambushing ARVN and harassing U.S. troops. The predicted communist mini-Tet Offensive did not occur. LTC Minh, Major Lam, PRU Commander, and Nate Shaw felt something significant was "blowing in the Delta wind." Major Lam sent PRU scouts into remote villages and learned the Viet Cong were actively collecting taxes from the beleaguered peasants, recruiting boys as young as age fourteen for their decimated Viet Cong military units, doing propaganda and indoctrination of the peasants.

On March fourth, Nate Shaw had been in Vietnam a year. On March eighth, he received two letters from Janet. One letter reported that she, the children, and Tyler were fine, and looking forward to his home leave in April. The other letter contained a newspaper article from a Phoenix newspaper, which Nate's father cut out and mailed to Janet. The article read: "CIA hires Phoenix Program mercenary soldiers to assassinate Viet Cong infrastructure (VCI) in the Vietnam War."

Nate took the mail pouch, went upstairs to his room, sat down at his desk and read the article. It began:

There are no beautiful blonds, or fast Italian Maserati coupes from James Bond's 007 movies to fit the CIA's Phoenix Program in Vietnam. The CIA created the Phoenix Program under its covert intelligence collection program cover name the Office of the Special Assistant (OSA) to fund and employ mercenary soldiers called the Provincial Reconnaissance Unit (PRU) to assassinate Viet Cong Infrastructure (VCI). The Phoenix Program is the brainchild of Mr. William Colby, who heads the CIA's covert collection program at CIA Headquarters, Langley, Virginia. In 1967 the Phoenix Program was implemented in Vietnam. The Phoenix is an Arabian mythical bird, which lives 500 years, burns itself to death, and rises renewed from its own ashes to live another 500 years.

The Phoenix Program uses intelligence collection programs in a Provincial Interrogation Center (PIC), South Vietnam's Police Special Branch (PSB), South Vietnam's FBI, to identify and arrest VCI suspects, a Chieu Hoi Program to encourage Viet Cong to rally to the Saigon government and Provincial and District Intelligence Operations Coordination's Centers. Once information is obtained on the location of VCI, depending upon the size of the VCI unit or organization, the CIA OSA Chief dispatches PRUs to conduct "combat operations to root out the VCI." If a VCI unit is identified, the OSA Chief may call in U.S. attack helicopters to destroy a village or location, or conduct PRU combat operations to kill the VCI. The CIA vehemently denies the Phoenix Program is an assassination program, but instead is a response to communist political control of the Viet Cong who kill U.S. and ARVN soldiers.

The VCI are communist political cadre who provide political propaganda and control of the National Liberation Front founded in the Mekong Delta in 1960. The VCI are tax collectors, planners, administrators, and recruit to fill Viet Cong military units. A VCI political officer has more power than a Viet Cong military commander to insure that proper political indoctrination remains strong among Viet Cong soldiers.

The NLF grassroots organizations are at the countryside. Each village has three-man VCI cells with as many as thirty to forty-five cell units in a district, controlling 100 Viet Cong soldiers. The district organization is subordinate to the Committee for South Vietnam, which directs the Viet Cong in the war. COSVN controls up to forty district VCI organizations, twenty provincial organizations and three hundred to ten thousand Viet Cong soldiers. COSVN has mobile headquarters near the Cambodian border in the Mekong Delta and in Tay Ninh Province northwest of Saigon. COSVN reports to North Vietnam's ruling Lao Dong Party, which is under the political leadership of President Ho Chi Minh and North Vietnam's National Liberation Committee.

U.S. MACV advisors are assigned to the Phoenix Program for intelligence collection and to advise PRU combat operations. The PRUs are autonomous and work for OSA by virtue of CIA money spent to arm the PRUs with modern U.S. Army Military equipment.

The PRUs are well paid, have their own compound, and wives receive a lump sum of money of $2,000 (14,000 piasters) if a PRU husband is killed. The communists maintain the PRUs are used to murder anyone suspected of being a "VCI" for no reason, to settle old grudges, or avoid making arrests. The CIA maintains the VCI/VC is "one and the same" and the enemy who is killing U.S. military or ARVN are soldiers. It is impossible to separate VCI/VC since both are combatants.

As of March, 1968 the Phoenix Program operates in twenty provinces. Some 100 MACV advisors have been assigned to the Phoenix Program. An estimated 5,000 PRU soldiers and 53,000 VCI have been killed by the Phoenix Program.

Nate folded the newspaper article.

Great, just great, he thought. As if Janet doesn't have enough to worry about. Now some left wing son-of-a-bitch writes this propaganda.

On March 10, 1969, Nate Shaw received a message from Lester Shockley. He would attend an important meeting in Lester's office at the U.S. Embassy on March 15. An Air-America D-3 would pick him up at the Rach Gia airstrip on March 14 at 1400. Nate was requested to re-schedule his April home leave in May or June. Mr. Diem would meet him at the AA terminal at 1530 and take him back to the Blanchard BOQ. Lester Shockley requested Nate to meet him for breakfast at the U.S. Embassy cafeteria at 0730. The meeting with personnel from Langley and Saigon would convene in his office at 0900. Lester said he read the "liberal trash" about Phoenix and to ignore it.

CORDS has the legal authority to collect VCI intelligence and PRUs are a privately funded paramilitary force the same as the French Foreign Legion. Anything to sell newspapers; if you are questioned by the media, maintain your cover as a CORDS police advisor and we will locate that reporter and verify his bonafides, and determine if the reporter works for a communist-front newspaper. Forget the crap!"

Nate met Lester Shockley for breakfast at the U.S. Embassy. Lester told Nate, "Something very important has occurred; we will discuss it in my office inside the Special Compartment Intelligence Facility (SCIF)."

They finished breakfast and went to Lester's office at 0830. Lester made telephone calls; Nate read the morning cable intelligence summaries, and fed Lester's Japanese goldfish, which had multiplied since he last saw them. Lester said, "Those fish are eating me out of house and home, time to think about a visit to the Saigon River—only kidding!"

At 0900 the meeting began with the following personnel present:

Jim Patterson, Deputy Director, Far East Operations, CIA, HQ, Langley, Virginia
Joe Miller, Director, CIA Field Operations, Southeast Asia, Bangkok
Dinh Chau Ching, North Vietnam Analyst, CIA, HQ
Frank Dowling, Director, Phoenix Program, Saigon
Lester Shockley, Deputy Director, Phoenix Program, Saigon
Nate Shaw, OSA, Rach Gia

Jim Patterson opened the meeting, extending cordial remarks to all in attendance and made reference to the Phoenix newspaper article. He said, "The Phoenix Program is controversial because it has been very effective in 'rooting out' the heart of the enemy who run the war for North Vietnam. We can't get to the bastards in North Vietnam or their sanctuaries in Laos and Cambodia, but we've certainly been able to nail the bastards all over South Vietnam and now the commies are crying foul to international amnesty agencies in Europe and leftwing commie sympathizers.

"These commie sons-of-bitches are now using fourteen-year-old boys as soldiers, they place landmines in roads along which innocent civilians drive cars, and get killed hitting a landmine, or blow up a bar in Saigon with impunity. No, the Phoenix Program is not an assassination program of innocent civilians—it is retribution against evil atheists.

"We've killed 53,000 VCI to even the Goddamn score in this fucked-up war. Excuse my language. I've been in South Vietnam five years since 1963. I was privy to the CIA and to read the report written in 1965, saying the war is now deadlocked and could not be won. Here, four years later, it's deadlocked, and beginning to look like we are on the short end of the stick this time. I called you all here today to brief you on a major military operation that will occur on April 1, 1969. Lester, let's adjourn into the SCIF."

They left Lester Shockley's office, walked down a hallway to the rear of the U.S. Embassy, and stopped in front of a steel door with a sign outside, saying SCIF—NO ADMITTANCE.

Lester Shockley punched six buttons into the keypad, then a buzzer sounded, and a red light went on above the door. They entered the cooler room, which was pleasantly cool, a CIA security employee brought out a manila envelope with a red border saying Top Secret. The CIA employee verified all their security clearances and then they went and sat down at a walnut table, with six leather-back chairs. The CIA employee handed a copy of a document to each person.

Jim Patterson said, "Have a seat, gentlemen, no smoking, we will be here for some time."

He gave each person a Document to read. The group began to read the Top Secret document.

TOP SECRET (TS)
SCI/NOFORN
DATE: 8 March 69
FM: CIA, HQ, Langley, Virginia
TO: Frank Dowling, Saigon
SUB: Reported North Vietnam (NVA) and Viet Cong Attacks on/about 1 Apr 69 in III and IV CORPS
SOURCE: Sensitive Collection—South Korea

Central Intelligence Agency (KCIA)

EVALUATION:	Highly reliable; highly accurate
MISINFORMATION:	NONE SUSPECTED
METHOD OF COLLECTION:	KCIA fishing trawler operating seventy miles East of Hai phong in int'l waters using intercept communications equipment captured the following radio transmission, 3 Mar 69 @ 0400 from Hanoi to Peking on UHF radio transmission and the code was broken by KCIA.

Text Reads

FROM:	HQ, High Command, Hanoi
TO:	Chinese Comrades, Peking

F.Y.I.

Rec'd the shipments of 25,000 AK-47s 500,000 rds ammo; 2,000 RPG rocket launchers w/10,000 rounds; 1,000 82 mm mortars w/10,000 rounds, 500 tactical radios, and 10,000 uniforms w/boots.

To victory over Imperialism!

Text continues:

Liberation attacks begin 1 Apr 69 at 0200; 8 NVA regiments, 2/sappers battalions and 40,000 new troops set to attack.

OBJ 1—Bien Hoa/Saigon 20,000 NVA and 10,000 VC, 1 Apr 69

OBJ 2—Ha Tien, Tri Ton 10,000 NVA, 1,000 VC

OBJ 3—Three Sisters Mts. To attack Kien Tan District 1 Apr 69 2,700 NVA/VC. Attacks to show U.S. Govt. U.S. cannot win war.

Comrade General Than Ngoc

Lin

TOP SECRET

END OF TEXT

They sat in silence and disbelief at what they read.

"Not another Tet, this is a major knock-out punch to end the war on their terms," said Lester Shockley.

Jim Patterson asked Dinh Chau Ching, "What is your evaluation?"

Dinh Chau Ching, defected from North Vietnam, in 1960, "North Vietnam is hurting for manpower. They have three million young men ages sixteen to nineteen to draft, but they will also soon need men as doctors, teachers, policemen, healthcare workers, farmers. They want one more spectacular attack to demoralize the ARVN and the GVN and to establish a stronger negotiation position at the Paris Peace talks. We have information NVA forces moved south of Phnom Penn, into the Iron Triangle and labor units digging tunnels at Three Sisters Mountains. Air photos show seven new large openings on Three Sisters Mountains.

"Kien Tan was not attacked during Tet, not to bring attention to this area while the laborers dug tunnels and built caves."

"Yes, Nate," said Jim Patterson.

"I've noticed a slow-down of VC activity throughout Kien Giang in January and February of this year. Now I know why. That KCIA information provides the answer about the lull and what's going on in the bushes with the VC."

"I'll be damned, not again," said Nate.

"Those bastards are uncanny," said Jim Patterson, "but you've got to admire their tenacity."

"Well, gentlemen, let me brief you on what will happen on April first," said Jim Patterson.

He reached into another folder and pulled out several Documents classified Top Secret, and handed them to his assistant, Jim Thompson.

"Here, gentlemen, is the VISE GRIP OPLAN to whip their ass," said Jim Thompson.

"On March twelfth, I met with the Vietnamese Joint Staff in Saigon and also with General Tran Van Loc, President Thieu's military advisor; I gave him a sanitized copy of the KCIA message for President Thieu. I briefed President Thieu, who said, 'General Loc will prepare a counter-attack OPLAN for Lt. Gen. Thanh, Commander, IV CORPS by March fourteenth.

"I picked up their plan at the JCS yesterday and talked to the Air Coordination Center at IV Corps and laid on U.S. Air support. All ARVN preparations have begun and will be completed

OPERATION VISE GRIP
Operations Plan No. 78-10-69

FM: HQ, Lt.Gen. Thanh CG IV Corps, Can Tho

TO: CO, 9th ID, Soc Trang
CO, 21st ID, Bac Lieu
CO, 410 RF/PF, Rach Gia, Kien Giang
CO, PRU, Rach Gia
DATE: 19 Mar. 69

SUB: Operation VISE GRIP

MISSION: Cordon and destroy NVA 29th, 66th and 327th Rgts **VIC WY 361 849**

by March thirty-first. 'No exceptions,' says General Loc. Take a look at the VISE GRIP OPLAN, I will explain it."

"On April first, we will cordon and secure Three Sisters and let air power destroy the enemy with B-52s. I learned from General Loc that General Thanh will deploy elements of the ARVN Ninth and Twenty-first ID with M-113 APCS and 4,105 howitzers to support the maneuver elements. Air Coordination Center in Can Tho has allocated 4 C-47 chinooks to ferry ARVN troops, and two C-130's to move supplies to Ap Phung Airfield, A battery, 405 Artillery from the Ninth ID.

"We'll have the enemy cordoned and their backs to Cai Son Canal if they try to escape. I know how they think," Jim Patterson continued. "A battery, 405 BN Arty Bn, with 4, 105 howitzers to fire direct support.

"The Operational Commander is Lieutenant General Tran Van Thanh, with tactical command under Major General Nguyen Van Tan, CO, Ninth ID, and Major General Mi Kiet, CO, Twenty-first ID. The GVN will release misinformation on March twentieth that the ARVN divisions in IV Corps are rotating among Can Tho, Rach Gia, Bac Lieu and Dong Tam. Viet Cong spies will pick up false information and report it to the VC by seeing ARVN convoys along Highway Four between Bac Lieu, Dong Tam and Long Xuyen. Helicopters will fly over Highway Four to simulate air protection for the convoys from ambush.

"On March twenty-fifth, the ARVN will announce giving sol-

Three Sisters Mts., Kien Tan District

MAP: WY 361 849

DATE OF VISE GRIP: 1 Apr. 69, 0500 hours

SUNRISE: 0605 hours-sunset 1907

WEATHER: Hot, overcast

TASK ORGANIZATIONS:	PERSONNEL	LOC.
CO		
1ST Bn, 19th Inf, 9th ID	310	Soc Trang
LTC Thuy (Assault)		
W/10,M-113 APC's		
W/402nd FA BN, 4,105 howitzers	22	Soc Trang
MAJ Trung		
(Direct Spt)		
2nd Bn, 11th Inf. Rgt., 21st ID	297	Bac Lieu LTC Minh
(Assault)		
3rd Bn, 12th Inf. Rgt., 21st ID	301	Bac Lieu LTC Quan
(Assault)		
410 RF/PF Bn, Rac Gia	175	Rach Gia LTC Sau
(Blocking Force)		
Rach Gia PRU	100	Rach Gia MAJ LAM
(Reserve)		
Total Personnel	1,205	

US AIR SUPPORT:

5-Cobra helicopter gun ships
3-F-105 fighter aircraft
B-52 bombers

INTELLIGENCE

Enemy: NVA 29th, 66th & 327 regiments w/Viet Cong

Strength: Est. 2,000

Artillery: None

Heavy Weapons: .50 caliber machine guns
                    .57 caliber recoilless rifles

Discipline: Excellent
          Mts. Have caves, tunnels and positions for heavy weapons

Rations: Food & Water. Est. 14 days

                    Signed
                    Lt. Gen. Thanh

PLAN OF MANEUVER
"Cordon & Destroy"

Advance Lines to Assault Postition

- Dinh My
- 405 RF/PF
- CO B
- 1/19
- AP Phung Airfield Rearming/Refueling
- Staging Area
- Three Sisters Mountains 341'
- CO A
- 2/11
- 4-105's
- C-47
- PRU Rach Gia
- 3/12
- Cai Son Canal
- Rach Gia
- C-47
- Thanh Hoa
- Kien Tan
- 10 Kilometers

diers false three-day passes to account for their units moving into new staging areas. Air surveillance will photograph Three Sisters looking for any communist reactions. ARVN Patrols will begin at 0100 on March thirty-first to observe Three Sisters and watch for communist sappers moving forward for the attack. President Thieu said he expects an ARVN victory with air support from the U.S. Army and Air Force.

"As you can see, gentlemen, the NVA/VC strength is unknown, but I estimate there are two thousand to three thousand enemy soldiers in those mountains."

"Lieutenant General Thanh stated, 'the enemy has put himself in a box and has no way to escape except across the Cai Son Canal.'"

Jim Patterson continued, "Air recon shows there are new holes in the mountains on the south sides; we don't have a complete view of the mountains due to the terrain. Again, Lieutenant General Thanh thinks they may be inviting us to attack, with their fortified positions and protection from air strikes, artillery or bombing. They can't hold out long with 2,000–3,000 men in this heat; the monsoon season over, we'll have dry rice paddies firm enough to support the M-113s and howitzers. Weather will not make a difference in this operation.

"The local district chief in Dinh My reports the ground is ninety percent dry and the rice paddy berms on which the farmers walk planting rice provides cover for troops on the ground. Here are my concerns," said Jim Patterson.

"The NVA/VC are formidable fighters, they are up to something. If they attack Bien Hoa and Saigon there could also be some simultaneous attacks against Ha Tien, Tri Ton, and Kien Tan. If they attack April first, according to the message, we will have a massive battle; the ARVN could bail out. Lieutenant General Thanh says our F-105's bombing and helicopter attacks will dislodge the NVA and bring them into the open to fight. They're not planning to remain in the mountains. We are going to use flags to confuse them about the size of our force.

"The NVA/VC can muster fire with recoilless rifles, heavy machine guns, RPGs, and also shoot down the COBRAS and destroy the M-113s. I don't envision an ARVN ground assault since

General Thanh does not want heavy ARVN casualties. The ARVN will hold the line, but if the NVA launch a human wave assault and destroy the M-113s, we must react quickly. We will have five sorties of F-105's with 100-pound napalm bombs; high-explosive 100-pound bombs, Cobra attack helicopters and 105 canister fire.

"Now, if the NVA won't quit, I'm going to make sure we finish the job." Langley called General Clark in the Pentagon. The Air Force is sending two B-52s with 500-pound daisy cutters to demolish the Goddamn mountains into mounds of dirt or anthills—tough shit, too bad. The B-52s come out of Takle, Thailand.

"We have unconfirmed intel reports there are three hundred VC near Dinh My hiding in graveyards, towns, or who knows where else, so be prepared for that contingency. The ARVN will contain any VC attack and we'll concentrate on the sons-of-bitches in those mountains. Here are my instructions.

Major General Tan, CO, Ninth ID, and Major General Kiet, CO, Twenty-first ARVN have a CP at Kien Tan. They will have radio contact with all maneuver battalions, RF/PF, and PRUs for coordination; they do not command the RF/PF and PRUs. Once the bombing is done, we'll wait to see how the NVA/VC react; they may counterattack and we'll begin artillery fire, and 1,200 troops will repel their assault. If the NVA/VC breaks our line a four-hundred-man battalion from the Ninth ID is at the staging area to counterattack. I cannot imagine them surviving the bombing. It could get dicey.

"The COBRA attack helicopters will strafe their lines as they move across the rice field. Nate Shaw, I want you to remain at the firebase with the artillery and coordinate air strikes with artillery fire. Your X-O, Roland, will remain with the PRUs. Now, if the shit hits the fan and a rout starts and the ARVN split, withdraw to the staging area where we will set up a defensive line. I'll put in an SOS to the B-52s to hit them immediately. I will be at the CP in Kien Tan; my frequency is 7811 VHF, and my call sign is Warrior. Any questions?"

Lester Shockley said, "Jim, it looks to me that if we want to bait those sons-of-bitches, why not bomb them to hell the first day with just B-52 bombing alone and forget the assault?"

"The answer is, President Thieu wants an ARVN victory and not another operation where the ARVN sit and watch and then claim a victory in the newspapers. This is a test of his new CORPS Commander and two Division Commanders. Any more questions? None? Okay. We'll see you April first at 0100, AP Phung Air Field. Good hunting."

The meeting ended. Nate Shaw returned to Rach Gia to brief Major Lam and the OSA Advisory Team on Operation VISE GRIP. SGT Bowman met him at the airfield on March seventeenth at 1300.

"Welcome back, Mr. Shaw," Bowman said as Nate climbed into an OSA Chevrolet suburban van.

"How was the trip?" asked Bowman.

"Good, fast, up and back, the way I like to visit Saigon. Anything happening at the Compound?" asked Nate.

"No, not that I know of," responded Bowman.

"Captain Graham went to a meeting at the Province S-2 shop at 1100 and Mr. Roland, Billy, and Jesse are at the PRU Compound."

"At the PRU Compound?" responded Nate.

"Yes, Sir, Stan Roland told Billy and Jesse he wanted to know the results of the PRU scout platoon recon out near Kien Tan. Stan said Major Lam received information there were Cambodian wood cutters working near three mountains which is unusual for this time of year; he claims the rice-growing season is over and there are not a lot of available trees to cut near Kien Tan. I guess something doesn't sound right to Major Lam," said Bowman.

"Did Stan say when Major Lam received the information?" asked Nate.

"No, Sir, I don't know."

"Anything else, Sam?" asked Nate.

"No, Sir," answered Bowman.

They drove into Rach Gia. Bowman parked the van and Nate Shaw went to his room and locked the OPLAN Vise Grip in his desk.

Captain Graham, Captain Madison, Stan Roland, Billy Flynn, and Jesse Roberts returned to the OSA Compound at 1500.

Nate told Stan Roland to locate everyone for a briefing in his office and to update the situation map by 1600.

"Anything up, boss?" asked Stan Roland.

"Yes, Stan, I'll brief you at 1600," said Nate.

At 1600 hours the entire OSA Advisory Team were seated in Nate's office in front of the updated situation map.

"Let me begin by saying, men, I'm very proud of you and the fine job you have done during the past ten months in the Phoenix Program. You have a very difficult and demanding mission, which has come under media scrutiny. Don't be alarmed by anything you read in the press or hear about the Phoenix Program; it is not, I repeat, not, an assassination program and you know that from doing PRU combat operations. We are in a war and the VCI want to defeat our country so we are doing the right thing to defeat them.

"Do not answer any questions about the Phoenix Program; refer anyone who tries to talk to you to me—get their name, office, and organization, and if they do not cooperate, tell me, we'll locate them. There are newspaper articles in the U.S. media claiming Phoenix is an assassination program. Your careers are not in trouble, I can assure you. All of you have earned 'Max' OER's so put that to rest."

Nate addressed Jim Bowman, "Jim, you will not be involved in the operation. Stand outside the door, hold all calls, and any visitors; I do not want to be disturbed!"

"Yes, Sir," said Jim; he left the room.

"I just returned from a meeting in Saigon and we have very creditable information that the NVA/VC are planning major attacks against on Bien Hoa, Saigon and in Fourth Corps on April first at 0200 and probably Kien Tan district. Three NVA regiments are camped in the Three Sisters Mountains with an estimated 3,000 troops."

A gasp went up in the room.

Nate Shaw walked to the situation map and pointed out the location of the Three Sisters. "The ARVN Fourth Corps Commander, Lieutenant General Thanh has prepared an OPLAN to cordon and destroy the NVA and VC with a cordon operation, air strikes, and B-52 bombing. The ARVN force will include elements of the ARVN Ninth ID, Twenty-first ID, 405 artillery battalion, 410 RF/PF battalion, and the PRU as a reserve or blocking force.

"This operation has very important military and political significance since there is a new Vietnamese Corps Commander and two new Division Commanders will be tested in combat. It could be one hell of a battle. Here is a copy of the OPLAN Vise Grip."

Stan gave a copy of the OPLAN to all present.

Nate put the OPLAN on the situation map for reference, showing the locations of all friendly forces, the task organization, and scheme of maneuver.

He explained the plan the way Jim Patterson explained it to him in Saigon.

"Now, here is our position on the Southwest corner across the Cai Son canal above Thanh Hoa. Our mission is to block any NVA escape on the Cai Son Canal. We will have one hundred PRUs with M-60 machine guns, two fifty-caliber machine guns, four 81-millimeter mortars, M-79 grenade launchers and forty to fifty RPG rockets to fire against a human wave assault against the PRU position. Now, let's go down the OPLAN step-by-step."

For the next forty-five minutes Nate discussed OPLAN Vise Grip.

"I'll brief Major Lam and we'll begin preparation tomorrow. Here are your assignments. I will be located at the fire-support center with A battery, 405th Arty.

"Captain Graham, you and PFC Bowman will be the coordination element at Ap Phung airfield for refueling, reloading and all communications with the CP. Lieutenant General Thanh will have his CP at Kien Tan District. Stan Roland will be with Major Lam at the PRU position.

"Captain Madison, Moe Molinski, and Pat Blake will be with PRU Alpha Company, on the left flank.

"Billy Flynn, Jesse Roberts and Sean Morgan will be with PRU Bravo Company, on the right flank. There are three thousand meters for a field of fire between all units. We will go by C-47s from Rach Gia to our position at 0400, April first, and take up our position by 0500.

"I will meet at the Corps CP, get briefed, and move into my position at 0500 with ARVN artillery. When the air strikes begin, there will be five kilometers between the target and friendly units. I will be in radio contact with Stan Roland, Captain Madison, Billy Flynn, and Jesse Roberts and the Command CP in Kien Tan. Our mission is to hold the line. If the NVA break out and begin to assault the position, I will direct artillery fire and Stan Roland will direct air strikes onto the NVA position. We have five to six kilometers of open paddies so the NVA will be exposed when they attack. If the NVA remain in the mountains, we will hold them there until 0100, when B-52 bombing begins.

"I will fire four red smoke rounds on the mountains for the B-52s to spot so when you see red smoke, get the hell out to AP Phung air strip, the B-52s will begin bombing twenty-one minutes later, which gives us enough time to move back five kilometers. We have fourteen days to get ready. The South Vietnamese have begun their preparations.

"Billy, I want ten PRUs on security duty around the compound twenty-four hours the next thirteen days in case word gets out about the operation and we get VC visitors."

"Yes, Sir," said Billy.

"Finally, this is what we've worked for, now it is payback time. Go about your business as usual; get your gear and yourself mentally, physically ready. That's all. Let's go to dinner."

For the next fourteen days the OSA team began their preparations. Nate Shaw briefed Major Lam and he agreed to the plan. The Alpha and Bravo PRU companies got prepared and Charley Company with fifty PRUs remained to guard the PRU and OSA Compounds.

On March 31 at 1700, Nate Shaw, the PRU Commanders, and OSA team had the final preparation briefing at the PRU compound. At 0400 the next morning four C-47 Chinook helicopters arrived at Rach Gia air strip, loaded the OSA team and 100 PRUs to a landing position on the Southwest corner of Kien Tan district at 0430.

Captain Madison said to Stan Roland, "There they are, the Three Sisters and 3,000 NVA!"

"Stay cool, buddy, it's all business today. Keep your head and ass down, don't be a hero, and listen to what I tell you."

The PRU took up their positions. Fifty South Vietnam flags began waving in the morning breeze.

The PRU soldiers were ready with clean, prepared equipment, and four PRU mortar crews set up to fire eight .81 mortars. The remaining PRUs were on line with their weapons ready.

Birds chirped as the sun began to appear on the Eastern horizon.

Nate Shaw took his position, with the four 105 howitzers; he checked his map and watched as four ARVN artillery men pushed 105 shells into the breach of each artillery piece.

The sun's rays of daylight advanced on the horizon when four tremendous explosions broke the morning stillness as gray clouds of smoke and tremendous explosions shook Three Sisters.

Nate Shaw hollered, "Bull's-eye, Dai-uy" to the ARVN battery commander.

The 105s were reloaded; Captain Trung hollered, "fire," and four more rounds struck the mountains with more explosions and dust, dirt, and rocks flew into the air and soon men wearing khaki uniforms appeared moving across the mountains. Another round of artillery fire made four more explosions on the Three Sisters.

Then, to the sounds of whistles, NVA troops began to mass in tan uniforms, pith hats with a red star, and a returned fire from their own weapons as bullets snapped and ripped into the trees above Nate's position. Nate jumped behind a higher paddy berm as four more ARVN 105 artillery rounds exploded on the mountains; North Vietnam flags appeared and hundreds of NVA soldiers were now in formation for an assault on the artillery's position.

Nate turned on his radio, and hollered, "Open fire!"

A bullet round whizzed over Nate's head and killed an ARVN soldier at a gun position ten feet from Nate.

My God, thought Nate, and he crouched lower behind the paddy berm.

Four more artillery rounds were fired, all exploded as the ARVN, RF/PF and PRUs opened up with heavy automatic weapons toward the mass of NVA soldiers. The gunfire was deafening.

Nate cupped his ears. He looked through his binoculars again at Three Sisters and saw hundreds of NVA on line. The artillery battery fired again and again with twelve more rounds from the 105 howitzers at Three Sisters. The sound of reverberating weapons fire across the battlefield was deafening. Enemy shells exploded, shaking the ground and dirt, grime and leaves blew in the air. Nate watched two ARVN soldiers drag four dead ARVN soldiers from an adjacent treeline to the right of his battery.

Nate turned to find Captain Trung who was slumped dead against a 105 howitzer with a bullet in his head.

My God, thought Nate, *he's dead.*

An ARVN ran to Nate's position in a trembling voice, "DiDi MOW" meaning "Go, go."

Nate said, "No, DiDi!"

He spoke in perfect Vietnamese to the soldier. "I'll tell you what to do now."

"Lower the elevation of each gun twenty-five degrees at 15,000 meters range." Nate looked through his binoculars at Three Sisters Mountains. He hollered, "Fire your canister rounds." The ARVN artillerymen fired canister rounds into the NVA, which staggered from the impact creating huge holes in the formation.

"We got the bastards!" Nate hollered; more NVA bullets whined and struck trees overhead; leaves, twigs and dirt fell onto Nate. He felt a sharp pain in his left shoulder as a tree limb fell on him. The NVA were again reforming into smaller groups and were moving forward. Four more rounds of canister were fired into the advancing NVA; they fell in place; human piles of shattered bodies lay across the dry rice paddies.

The battlefield was covered with gray smoke and blue haze. Suddenly, new NVA appeared and fired RPG rockets at the ARVN M-113s. Two APCs exploded, one caught fire. The APCs slowed as NVA rocket fire continued against the M-113s. Nate told the ARVN to reload and fire more canister rounds into the advancing NVA. Nate thought there must be 700–800 NVA within 1,000 meters.

The NVA tried to advance, but were driven back again by a hail of bullets from the PRUs and RF/PF and artillery fire; NVA took cover below rice paddy berms.

NVA mortar fire exploded near Nate's artillery position; dirt and debris hit Nate's arms and legs. He looked at his wristwatch at 0715. Automatic weapons fire from the ARVN/RF/PF and PRUs created a deadly crossfire. The NVA mounted two heavy machine guns and returned more fire. Now directed at the PRU line.

Stan Roland made a radio call to Nate, "Archer, Madison, Moe, and Blake have been hit."

"How bad?" asked Nate.

"All KIA," answered Stan.

Three F-105s appeared and dropped napalm bombs on the Three Sisters Mountain. It looked like hell with tremendous red and orange explosions. The NVA and VC fire subsided; the F-105s circled overhead, returned and dropped high explosive bombs again blowing huge clouds of gray smoke, dust and chunks of dirt in the air; the smell was acrid from gunpowder and burnt human flesh.

Ten minutes later, five more Cobra helicopters arrived firing deadly cannon fire into the exposed NVA positions. The rattling of the helicopter's cannon fire continued. Two Cobra gunships were hit by NVA fired RPG rockets, and crashed. No one was alive.

The Three Sisters Mountains remained burning, the mangled M-113 APCs sat motionless, and two helicopters lay mangled on the ground. NVA came out of the mountains and again returned more fire. Three F-105s returned and dropped one-hundred-pound bombs, which shook the ground, as earth and mud flew into the gray air.

The F-105s made another run and dropped eight more bombs.

Stan Roland called on the radio, "We're taking casualties, three U.S. KIA."

"Jesus, Lord in Heaven," hollered Nate. "This Goddamn war—I hate it!!"

Nate's radio squelched, "Archer, this is Buckshot. We have 11 PRUs KIA."

"Fuck me," said Nate.

Nate called on his radio to Jim Patterson at Kien Tan CP. "Warrior—this is Archer. Call in the B-52s, right now, no delay! Over."

"Archer, this is Warrior. Why now?"

"We need them NOW—OVER! We could get overrun, they're massing again. B-52s, NOW—They're not on the run. Over."

"Roger, Archer will comply to call B-52s."

It was 1200. Smoke, haze, and intermittent movement of fallen and wounded NVA dotted the Three Sisters Mountains battlefield along with the odor of death.

Nate heard a call on his radio.

"Commo check—report casualties."

"410 RF/PF how many KIA?"

"Reply—forty-one."

"1/19?"

"Reply—twenty-nine."

"2/11?"

"Reply—forty-nine."

"3/12?"

"Reply—thirty-one."

"PRU?"

"Reply—thirteen, and three Americans for sixteen."

"16, Roger and out."

Nate looked at the stillness of the landscape with binoculars and saw heaps and mounds of dead NVA soldiers, and VC clad in black pajamas. Loud explosions came from one mountain. Two Cobra helicopters lay burning in ruins. Seven ARVN M-113s were blown apart. Nate's radio chattered—"Clear the area immediately. B-52 strike will arrive in fourteen minutes on target. Clear the area."

Nate ran back through a coconut tree line as Stan Roland ran to meet him.

"Jesus Christ, Nate, of all good men to die, Jeff Madison, Moe and Pat Blake."

"What happened?" asked Nate.

"Major Lam told Alpha Company to move forward into better protection in a dry canal from the one they were in. Captain Madison couldn't get his footing; Moe and Blake hesitated when an AK-47 round slammed into the PRUs' positions, killing nine PRUs, Jeff, Moe and Pat. None of them suffered, they were all hit hard."

"Oh, Lord," said Nate. "Where are their bodies?"

"The PRUs dragged them into a clearing, and I had the PRUs put them on a truck to Ap Phung covered by blankets."

"Did you see them?" asked Nate.

"Yes, I did." Stan began to cry.

"A terrible sight, just terrible, you'll see."

"Okay," said Nate. "Let's get going."

They got into a Jeep and drove to Ap Phung where Nate saw the three dead men.

Four more 105 artillery shells exploded with deafening explosions and plumes of red smoke rose on Three Sisters.

At 1503, a B-52 bomber appeared, and dropped ten 500 pound Daisy cutter bombs on Three Sisters—the ground shook and reverberated like thunder and earthquakes. Then the battlefield fell silent as it began to get dark.

Nate slept on the ground with the PRU soldiers below a dry rice paddy berm.

The next morning the sun rose and birds chirped, greeting the sunrise. It was a scene of death and destruction. The smell of dead bodies permeated the air.

At 0700, one hundred ARVN slowly moved to Three Sisters; they found a holocaust of dead and burned NVA. The remainder of the day was spent stacking bodies on both sides. The ARVN counted 1,011 dead communist soldiers.

The Three Sister Mountains were pockmarked with bomb craters, and caves crumbled into dirt. Twenty-one NVA were taken prisoner, and told the South Vietnamese there were 2,700 soldiers at Three Mountains.

The report on Operation Vise Grip stated 2,700 NVA/VC killed and one hundred prisoners.

The ARVN, PRU and U.S. losses were 179 killed in action.

Nate Shaw took home leave. He escorted the bodies of Captain Jefferson Lee Madison, IV, Joseph Paul Molinski, and PFC Patrick Allen Blake to Dover AFB. He attended Captain Madison's funeral at Spring Hill Farm, Virginia, and met Captain Jefferson's parents, Senator and Martha Madison, Jeff's wife, and children. The next night he had dinner in Georgetown with Senator and Mrs. Madison and explained how Captain Madison died in Vietnam in the service of his country.

Nate took home leave in July, and then flew next to Langley. He requested reassignment back to Washington. August 10, 1969 he left Vietnam. He and his family moved to Arlington, Virginia where he was assigned as CIA, Director, Soviet Area Operations for four years. His next assignment was CIA Station Chief, Moscow, two years, and then he and his family transferred to Geneva where he was CIA Station Chief five years. The children learned to speak French and German.

In 1980, Nate returned to Langley, where he remained until he retired as Deputy Director of the CIA in 1992.

In June, 1992, he, Janet, and the children went to see the Vietnam Veteran's War Memorial. Arthur located the names of Jefferson Lee Madison, Joseph Molinski, and Patrick Blake, whose names were inscribed on the black polished granite panels. Arthur wept at seeing the names of those brave men, who had once been with the OSA Advisory Team in Rach Gia, South Vietnam, twenty-three years ago.

The Vietnam War was now a closed chapter in Arthur Edward Norris' life.

Epilogue

No suitable epitaph can be written to atone for the 58,214 Americans who died in vain in the Vietnam War; perhaps only "that they fought bravely and honorably" in a totally misdirected war compounded by political meddling and a failed military attrition strategy.

The prevailing reasons with explanations have been thoroughly detailed in this book.

General William C. Westmoreland, Commander of U.S. military forces in Vietnam from 1964 to 1968, "blamed the army of South Vietnam for the defeat in the war." General Bruce Palmer, Jr. called General Westmoreland's strategy "the first clear failure in American military history."

The Johnson administration's role in Vietnam shares a major portion for the blame in Vietnam. The Johnson administration did not approve military operations necessary to win the war. President Johnson allowed Secretary of Defense Robert S. McNamara and his Whiz Kids too much latitude in overruling the military with unqualified civilians making military decisions, hindering U.S. military operations in Vietnam.

The article on page 351 appeared in the August 5, 2005 edition of *Army Times.*

William J. Lederer wrote in *The Anguished American* in 1969, the following about Vietnam: "In naming the South Vietnamese as the third enemy, the author produces pages of facts and statistics drawn up from his own observations and those of many other correspondents of varying nationalities. They showed how large elements of the population devoted themselves to exploiting the war; plundering American material, speculating in currency, selling drugs, organizing vice dens, hoarding, cornering commodities, selling stolen American arms to Vietnam, and outrageously profiteering in every form of enterprise associated with the war."

According to Lederer, this corruption permeated every class of society from top to bottom.

William Shakespeare wrote:

"There is a tide in the affairs of men which, taken at the flood, leads on to fortune;

Omitted, all the voyage of their life is bound in the shallows and in miseries . . .

And we must take the current when it serves or lose our ventures."

September 8, 2006
Collierville, Tennessee   Colonel Thomas R. Glodek, USA (Ret.)

DUTY, HONOR, COUNTRY
A 5-MINUTE HISTORY LESSON

ARMY HISTORY

Westmoreland remembered for his role in Vietnam War

By Robert F. Dorr and Fred L. Borch
SPECIAL TO THE TIMES

Gen. William Childs Westmoreland, who died at a retirement home in Charleston, S.C., on July 18, was a hard-charging soldier who fought in World War II and Korea and is best-known as the commander of American forces in Vietnam from 1964 to 1968.

Born in Spartanburg, S.C., in 1914, "Westy" enrolled in the Citadel but transferred to West Point in 1932. He was "first captain" his final year and, after graduating in 1936, was commissioned a second lieutenant of field artillery.

He served in Hawaii, North Carolina and Oklahoma prior to the outbreak of World War II. In April 1942, then-Maj. Westmoreland participated in Operation Torch, the invasion of North Africa. He later served in Sicily and in Normandy, where he fought with the 9th Infantry Division. By July 1944 — at age 30 — he was a full colonel and a division chief of staff.

After the war, Westmoreland completed jump school at Fort Benning, Ga., served on the staff of the 82nd Airborne Division, and taught at Fort Leavenworth, Kan., and Carlisle Barracks, Pa. During the Korean War, Westmoreland commanded the 187th Airborne Regimental Combat Team, the only paratroop unit to fight on the Korean peninsula.

By 1958, Westmoreland was a major general and the commander of 101st Airborne Division. Though he came to airborne duty only in the postwar era, Lt. Gen. Westmoreland was one of the nation's premier para-

THE ASSOCIATED PRESS
Then-Lt. Gen. William C. Westmoreland, when he became commander of U.S. forces in Vietnam in 1964.

troopers by the time he took the reins of the XVIIIth Airborne Corps in 1963.

Westmoreland was viewed as an outstanding soldier when President Johnson picked him to go to Vietnam to head the U.S. Military Assistance Command in 1964. Prior to Westmoreland's arrival in Saigon, Viet Cong guerrillas in South Vietnam faced a mediocre South Vietnamese army assisted by 15,000 American advisers. Westmoreland, certain the enemy would win unless the United States intervened directly, persuaded President Johnson to send U.S. ground forces to South Vietnam.

By 1968, there were more than 500,000 soldiers, sailors, airmen and Marines in country — and all were engaged in a war of attrition characterized by "search and destroy" missions.

But, while American forces inflicted tremendous casualties on the Viet Cong and North Vietnamese, the enemy would not quit. On the contrary, the communists appeared willing to pay any price to win. In late 1967, when public support for the war was eroding,

Westmoreland returned to the U.S. to tell the country that his tactics were winning and that end was near.

But when the enemy forces launched their Tet Offensive in January 1968, resulting media coverage convinced Johnson and others the war could not be won. It was a turning point for Westmoreland, too; when he requested an additional 200,000 combat troops for South Vietnam, Johnson refused. In June 1968, Westmoreland left Vietnam to take up his new duties as Army chief of staff. He stayed in that job until retiring in 1972.

The communists defeated South Vietnam in 1975. The next year, in his book, "A Soldier Reports," Westmoreland insisted that America could have won the war in Vietnam if only Johnson and other politicians had gotten out of the way and let the military do its job. He insisted that the army of South Vietnam was to blame for defeat.

But many disagreed, including former colleagues. Gen. Bruce Palmer Jr., who had been Westmoreland's deputy and later served as Army vice chief of staff, called Westmoreland's strategy "the first clear failure" in American military history.

Until his death, Westmoreland defended his Vietnam service, which he called "a noble crusade." □

Robert F. Dorr, an Air Force veteran, lives in Oakton, Va. He is the author of several books, including "Chopper," a history of helicopter pilots. His e-mail address is robert.f.dorr@cox.net. Fred L. Borch retired from the Army after 25 years and works in the federal court system. His e-mail address is orchfj@aol.com.

What Happens to the Characters

Arthur Edward Norris remained with the CIA, became the Deputy Director and retired in 1992.

Nathan Bedford Stewart remained in the U.S. Army and became a Four-Star General.

Sue Ellen Harris married Nathan Bedford Stewart and they raised three children.

Ted Graham left the U.S. Army, became a lawyer, served twelve years in the U.S. Congress. He was elected to the U.S. Senate (D–PA) in 1990 and served three terms.

Jefferson Lee Madison V became a lawyer in Washington, D.C.

Major Stan Roland remained in the U.S. Army and became a Major General.

Elizabeth Huntley married David Lowe, M.D. and they returned to Seattle.

Charles Fenton's film company won twenty-one Academy Awards between 1965 and 1991. He and Brecken had four children.

Miss Whipple remained with the CIA and retired with forty years of service in 1990 and moved to Florida.

In 1998, J.D. Stewart moved to Magnolia Plantation after Bucyrus Stewart passed and continued to raise cotton.

In 1980, Lester Shockley retired from the CIA (which no one believed), moved to Bangkok, married a twenty-five-year-old Thai woman and opened his own bar called "The Hangar."

Selected Bibliography

The Army Times, Springfield, VA
Bunting, Josiah, *The Lionheads,* George Braziller; (1972)
Burdick, Eugene, Lederer, William J., *The Ugly American,* W. W. Norton & Company; (1958)
Fall, Bernard B., *Hell in a Very Small Place: The Siege of Dien Bien Phu,* Doubleday; (1967)
Franks, Tommy General; *American Soldier,* Regan Books; (2003)
The Green Book, Association of the United States Army (AUSA)
Greene, Graham, *The Quiet American,* Penguin USA; (1955)
Karnow, Stanley, *Vietnam: A History,* Penguin USA; (1997)
McNamara, Robert S., *In Retrospect: The Tragedy and Lessons of Vietnam,* Vintage; (1995)
Moore, Robin, *The Green Berets,* St. Martin's Press; (1965)
Park, Ken, *The World Almanac and Book of Facts 2003,* World Almanac; (2002)
Sheehan, Neil, *A Bright Shining Lie: John Paul Vann and America in Vietnam,* Vintage; (1988)
Summers, Harry G. (USA, Ret.), *On Strategy: A Critical Analysis of the Vietnam War,* Presidio Press; (1982)
Taylor, Maxwell D., *The Uncertain Trumpet,* Greenwood Publishing Group; (1959)
Tucker, Spencer C., *Encyclopedia of the Vietnam War: A Political, Social, and Military History,* Oxford University Press; (1998)
Ward, Geoffry C., Burns, Rick and Ken, *The Civil War and Illustrated History,* Alfred A. Knopf, New York; (1990)
Westmoreland, William C. General, *A Soldier Reports,* Dell Publishing Co.; (1976)
Zinn, Howard, *A People's History of the United States: 1492–Present,* Harper Perennial Library; (1980)

About the Author

Colonel Thomas R. Glodek, USA (Ret.) is a Vietnam War veteran. He served as a U.S. Army Captain, United States Military Assistance Command, Vietnam (MACV) IV Corps, over fourteen months from June, 1968 to July, 1969. During his tour, he was a MACV intelligence advisor in Chau Phu and Kien Giang Provinces, assigned to the CIA's Phoenix Program.

The author's first assignment was at Advisory Team 64, Chau Duc, Cau Phu Province. His next assignment was at Advisory Team 55, Rach Gia, Kien Giang Province. In these assignments, he was the Phoenix Provincial Coordinator and worked in the Provincial Intelligence Operations Coordination Center (PIOCC) with his South Vietnamese counterparts from the Provincial Intelligence Staff, Chieu Hoi Open Arms Program, and local police agencies. He supervised five District Intelligence Operations and Coordination Centers (DIOCC's) located in Ha Tien, Kien Luong, Kien Tan, Kien Binh and Kien An districts.

The author's last assignment was at Phu Quoc District where he was an advisor to a South Vietnamese infantry battalion. Upon the completion of his tour, the author received the Bronze Star, Air Medal, Vietnamese Service Medal, Republic of Vietnam Campaign Medal, Republic of Vietnam Gallantry Cross with Palm Unit Citation, and the Combat Infantryman's Badge.

He is a graduate of the U.S. Army War College and holds his doctorate in Education from the University of San Francisco, has a grown son, and lives in Collierville, Tennessee.